The Stuff of Dreams

Eileen Ramsay

The Stuff of Dreams

HODDER &
STOUGHTON

Copyright © 2005 by Eileen Ramsay

First published in Great Britain in 2005 by Hodder and Stoughton
A division of Hodder Headline

The right of Eileen Ramsay to be identified as the Author of
the Work has been asserted by her in accordance with the Copyright,
Designs and Patents Act 1988.

1 3 5 7 9 10 8 6 4 2

All characters in this publication are fictitious and any resemblance
to real persons, living or dead, is purely coincidental.

A CIP catalogue record for this title is available from the British Library

Hardback ISBN 0 340 83512 5
Trade Paperback ISBN 0 340 83513 3

Typeset in Plantin Light by
Phoenix Typesetting, Auldgirth, Dumfriesshire

Printed and bound in Great Britain by
Mackays of Chatham Ltd, Chatham, Kent

Hodder Headline's policy is to use papers that are natural, renewable and recyclable
products and made from wood grown in sustainable forests. The logging and
manufacturing processes are expected to conform to the environmental regulations of the
country of origin.

Hodder and Stoughton
A division of Hodder Headline
338 Euston Road
London NW1 3BH

For my Godchildren, Helen Healey,
Mitchell McNichol and Megan Corcoran

ACKNOWLEDGMENTS

As always many people have helped with researching and writing this story and I am very grateful to all of them.

Anita Walker shared her knowledge of the exquisite art of gold-work. Forbes Sime of Fly Chart Air Ltd., Dundee, was meticulous in researching airstrips, flight paths, distances, times and aeroplanes for the period in which I set my back story. My friend Lesley Cookman and her daughters helped me with the art of acting as did Irene McDougall of Dundee Repertory Theatre.

Anne Styles, Jean Currie, Rebecca Leith, June Gadsby, were founts of all knowledge about roses. Rosebie Morton of Morton Roses, Nicola Blake of David Austin Roses, and Harkness Roses were most kind and answered questions even though they were all busy with the Chelsea Flower Show. June Gadsby made the ointment. Thank you June. Nick Gillies was unfailingly helpful in matters of law as was Inspector Gordon of Tayside Police. If any of the 'law' details are wrong this can only be the author's error. Sue North and Lalita Carlton- Jones are, as always, magical sources of information re the performing arts and this time around - thanks, Lal, for all the books about the stage. Lalita and Myfanwy Williams provided the Welsh language phrases and were wonderful at teaching me what Welsh speakers do *not* say.

Noelia Sánchez Ortiz and her husband, Ignacio Alcantarilla Medina helped with details of Spain's language and culture – *muchissimas graçias, mis niños.*

Jeannie Henderson and Janice Cowper of Elgin library were just so unbelievably helpful.

I hope I have remembered everyone.

I have every reason to thank my agent, Teresa Chris, and I am grateful to my meticulous editor, Carolyn Caughey, to my fantastic copy editor, Morag Lyall, to Lucy Dixon, to Alice Wright and all the other really lovely people at Hodder who work so hard. Thank you all so much.

I

Kate Buchanan. It was a simple name, a name, as Gran said, that could take you anywhere. For a long time she did not use it, but it had always been there, legally. Even though 'Kate Buchanan' had not been rushed to the hospital and had not featured so graphically and lasciviously in all the papers, including the ones that purported to be above such things, it was Kate Buchanan who came out of one prison hospital and went, for long years, to a hospital of another kind, and then to the Riviera. Doesn't that sound grand? She went to the Riviera. Once she had gone to the south of France to live in beautiful villas and sail on luxurious yachts. Not this time though. This time it was to live in seclusion, in a house that Hugh had found. Hugh Forsythe, dear, dear Hugh, another of the people whose devotion she had taken so much for granted. But there was time, wasn't there, to make amends and that had to be done here, in this house on which she had spent a fortune, and a year she feared she could not afford, restoring. She felt well, but then she had been in the peak of condition when the fire had occurred and look what that had done to her. If the glass into which she very rarely looked was to be believed, she was no longer a young woman. She was not old, middle-aged probably, but age was relative, was it not, and, like beauty, was surely in the eye of the beholder.

The house, Abbots House, was almost as it had been – if she had remembered correctly – but she could not trust her memory because it was both her friend and her foe. It allowed her to forget some things. Had the toile de jouy been pink or blue? Blue surely: she was not a pink person, was she, and those lovely greens were not available all those years ago? Each day she would remember a little more, that's what the doctors said. They would have preferred that she do her remembering in a safe clinical hospital where they would be on hand but it had to be here; otherwise she would never come to terms with life or with death.

Originally it had been the names. Friars Carse and Abbots House. Who would not want to live in an abbot's house with its romantic connections with monks and friars, with Knights Templar and crusaders? Friars Carse, the picturesque village built on the carse or low-lying plain that had once belonged to an order of friars – Grey Friars, she vaguely remembered – was far away, too, from all the places that anyone who knew her, or who had seen her, frequented. Remote, unsophisticated, not in the least smart, a backwater, yes, that's what her London friends, the ones who were allowed to visit, called it. Hugh had advised her to sell it, get what she could, at least for the plot of land, and she had vowed never to go near it again, so much pain, such horror. But once upon a time she had been happy there, every single second.

Had Kate been happy here or was it her, the other one? No one remembered Katherine. She had died, hadn't she, so long ago?

The name won't do, darling. Kate Buchanan would be just another talent among talents; Kate has a rather universal sound. We want something different. Katherine, yes, like the divine Hepburn. Although she, of course, is Katharine, but you too will be unique. Katherine Buchanan, too many syllables, but I like Katherine, so ladylike. Katherine Buchan. That will look good on billboards.

That had been Maurice Taylor. He, her first and only agent, had been right about the name, as he had been right about so many things.

Now Kate Buchanan took her pie and her dignity back to her newly refurbished house and when she got there she lay down for an hour on the day bed in what would one day, when there was a garden and not just a heap of rubble, be a study cum garden room because the effort of going out in public had exhausted her more than she had dreamed possible.

The woman in that lovely little shop had been nice though, and had assured Kate that she would be happy to deliver. She would be strong and she would go there again; she would not give in. She would look in the window first to make sure that she was there because, for a while, it would be one day and one person at a time.

She had to let the villagers see her and get used to her presence among them. They would talk. It was human nature to talk. They would add up, put two and two together and make five, but if she lived quietly in her lovely home, if they saw she was no trouble, minding her own business, they would accept her, get used to her infrequent appearances among them. But would they? They had been so happy to see her among them once, waved to her as she passed their windows, never getting too close, friendly but never intrusive. No, they had admired Katherine, not Kate, and Katherine was said to have done something so terrible . . .

Kate stared at the ceiling of the room and tried to think. 'What was the woman's name? I will remember. Maggie, yes Maggie. I knew a Maggie once, didn't I, in my past life, a will-o'-the-wisp, someone I worked with, or someone I admired: something to do with the theatre perhaps? That Maggie was not sturdy and down to earth as this Maggie was. I am glad I plucked up courage to go into her delightful shop. Will I be brave enough to shop there in the season, when Friars Carse is busy? Yes. One day at a time, like a recovering alcoholic.

She was recovering too, was she not, even if not from alcoholism? Never mind, never mind. What was it Granny had said? *Water under the bridge, darlings, water under the bridge.* So much water, Granny. So much and not enough to kill the flames, the flames that had killed . . . who had they killed? Him, yes, him and her, but Kate was alive, Kate would survive, and Kate would cope. Cope? That was everybody's granny's word. Every decent woman coped.

She stopped looking for answers in the white ceiling and looked around. Her desk, a mahogany kneehole desk with its beautiful original swan neck handles, had been a gift from Hugh.

Look what I found in an antique shop in Grasse, Kate. It said Kate needs me now that she is well enough to write letters.

She had bought the mahogany bookcase in Edinburgh. Their colours did not quite match but the periods did. Her books were still in a packing case under the stairs, except for her favourites that stood on the table by her bed. The rugs on the polished wooden floor were new as the curtains would be. She had designed them herself, chosen the colours and the fabrics.

'Look Hugh, I've discovered a talent. Should I have been an interior decorator?'

'You were, my dear. You did all our houses and we paid you nothing. You even made curtains, but only for my flat. The others were so envious.'

'I'm glad I did something for you, dear old Hugh.'

There was the other talent too, the one she had uncovered in the convent, or, to be more truthful, that Sister Mary Magdalene had uncovered. What joy that was. She raised herself on one elbow. Perhaps she could do a little now before she ate. No, she would forget to eat if she started.

Propped up by her elbow she could see her reproduction mahogany Gainsborough chair, upholstered in the material that she had chosen for the curtains. She should have bought two chairs, for Hugh would visit. Hugh, never conscious of his dignity, would sit on the day bed. She liked the room the way it was; it was exactly right. Had there been too much work to do? There had been no real self-respecting, keeping-the-elements-out roof, and many of the stones from the walls had been carted away, disappearing a few at a time over the years. Should she have sold it and left the memories behind? But it was impossible, if one had a memory, to leave memories behind. They had travelled with her, kept her company, the good ones and the awful, terrifying, frightening ones, wherever she was. Were there nice memories? Yes, oh yes, she had never forgotten him, nor Granny, nor dear Hugh and his mother who had been her stepmother for such a short time.

Long ago, in another life, she had found this house and had loved it immediately. Such a bad habit, loving immediately and irrevocably. Abbots House. A mile or so down the coast there was a monastery to which all the surrounding land had belonged. An abbot had built the original house on this site. Had he lived there? Unlikely. Surely he would live in the monastery but perhaps he had built it for important guests. An abbot? She thought of Friar Tuck, round and jolly. She should know better than to take refuge in stereotypes. Perhaps this abbot had been tall and austere, and very holy. Would he too demand that visitors be happy in his lovely sandstone house with its magnificent views over Monkshaven

Beach? The monks had found a haven here and so had she too once long ago. She had been supremely happy here. It had been simple to be content in a house built by a man of God on a beach where other men of God had found peace and security.

Rose Lamont? Could Rose be happy anywhere?

'The face, no one lives there.' The director was talking.

'The voice. It is . . . how can I say . . . technique is not everything . . . there must be . . . there must be life and there is no life here.' He was acknowledged as one of the stage's most brilliant directors and the students had been thrilled to have a masterclass with him, but sometimes it was a struggle to listen to him, as much of a struggle as it seemed to be for him to marshal his thoughts and march them up and down before them. He pointed at Rose again. 'Too many times she has been told, my God, how you are pretty, the pretty hair, the pretty smile, the pretty face.'

Rose smiled at him and he turned away from her to the other students. 'Forget pretty. To act from the soul is not pretty. You run the marathon with the Greeks and you are run to win. You are exhaust, you are sweat like the . . . like the pig. He is pretty? Mister Pig? No. Shirley Temple is pretty. You know who is Shirley? No. How can I explain? Your mama and your papa say, how you are pretty and you say, "Papa, who cares for pretty? I am an actor." To act well is to suffer, is to work, is to have total joy. To be Juliet or Rosalind or Jeanne d'Arc, or Hedda Gabler is to forget everything but to be Juliet. *Capisce*, You understand?'

And Rose had adjusted her Jaeger suit bought at the sale and moistened her lips, Estée Lauder on offer, and she had said yes and the director had looked at her and thrown up his hands in dismay and turned away.

'Do you understand what he's saying, Katherine Buchan?' Maurice whispered in her ear as they watched the great director marshalling his thoughts.

'That to act sometimes the veins must stand out on my lily-white neck like old ropes and my jaws must tense like prehistoric man in deadly combat? Is that what you mean? To forget everyone and everything that has gone before this moment, to be reborn: to make that frightening journey from safe, calm womb to becoming Jocasta, Lady Macbeth, Cleopatra?'

'Keep your hair on, dear girl.' Maurice had offered to represent Kate after seeing her in a student production: he knew just how great she might, with proper training and experience, become. 'Who the hell do you think you are, Isadora twinned with Sybil Thorndike on a good day?'

'No. I'm me, just me, and one day, Maurice, *mon ami*, you'll tell people you knew me when.'

He laughed but he was disturbed by her intensity coupled with a matter-of-fact realisation of her own talent. 'Dear God, she's never set foot on a stage and she's preparing her obituary.' He had turned again to look at Rose, pretty, pretty Rose with her lovely blonde hair and her china-blue eyes. 'You're not quite so bad as Rose. She has better physical equipment but she'll never learn how to use it because she's so determined to stay bloody British middle class, and pretty. Her whole body language tells her story. Poor Rose, if she could relax, she could be . . . not great, never great but quite good, perhaps. She needs a good fuck. What everybody needs is a good fuck, you too, plain Katherine Buchan. And don't go eyeing up all those young actors, fairies all of them.'

Kate blushed because there was a boy in her class who was not at all as Maurice described, and there was an older one too and they had each asked Kate to lunch. The boy was a sandwich in the park but the older man, who had a small part in a paid production, had invited her to an expensive French restaurant and she had gone. Naturally she would never tell him that she had gone mainly because she longed sometimes to be reminded of Tante and Provence and the warm waters of the Riviera, and on her allowance French restaurants were definitely out.

She had bought a new blue suit for her lunch dates; she suited blue. Ten whole pounds for a straight skirt with a kick pleat and a button-to-the-neck boxy jacket. Very demure, very flattering.

'Where are we going?'

'Green Park. Isn't that the most intelligent name for a park you've ever heard?'

But she could think only of her hard-won ten pounds that had been spent on a suit that he had not said he liked and which was being taken on a picnic. It had not been an auspicious beginning.

Who would have believed that that first, not terribly successful, outing had led to this? But she would stop reliving the past, for she had a pie to bake in her lovely new oven.

Kate got up from the day bed and stood for a moment looking out of the window, over which she had hung a sheet. Soon her beautiful blue curtains would be ready and she would install louvred blinds for daytime so that she could see out but no passer-by could see in. Idly she picked up the delightfully carved little seabird she had bought in the shop, Maggie's Fine Foods. It seemed an odd thing to find there but he was so beautiful. He was trapped on his stand but looked as if, just maybe, he could break free and soar into the wide. Maggie had said that a monk from the monastery in the woods carved the birds. 'The monk who walks on the beach with the great grey dog,' was what Maggie had said. Religious were good at artistic things weren't they? After all, just look at Sister Mary Magdalene.

She put down the bird and allowed the sheet to fall across the window.

Between the house and the wall there would, one day, be a sheltered garden. The high stone wall that completely surrounded the house had one break, the wrought-iron gate at the front. The top of the wall was set with hundreds and hundreds of shells, an unseen work of art. Whose hands had laboured there for no one but the swooping gulls to appreciate? Perhaps some nineteenth-century fisherman who recognised a link between himself and the great medieval stonemasons who had insisted that the unseen back of their work be as glorious as the front. That wall stood on the foundation of a wall that itself stood on even older stones. Beyond the wall was a stretch of rough grassland named the Sea Green that had always been common land. Early inhabitants grazed their few cattle and sheep there; twentieth-century residents played football. Beyond the Sea Green lay the beach, miles and miles and miles of beach that stood completely under water twice a day and often for days at a time in inclement weather. The seabirds loved it. *He* had spotted an oystercatcher one morning and ringed and golden plovers. Kate recognised lapwings and pretended to be annoyed when he laughed and said, 'Who doesn't?'

Now she walked into her ultra-efficient kitchen and turned the knob to the figure the nice woman had suggested. They had tried to sell her gas appliances but she would take no risks with fire. Once bitten, twice shy. What an appalling cliché. She took down a sea-green plate from the shelf above the sink. It was a nice plate. She had bought it in Provence. She found the mug that matched it and decided to make coffee.

Come along; let's drink up all our milk like a good girl.

Damn, how patronising some nurses were.

Drink all the milk you want, nursey dear. I am having whisky.

She took the mug back to the desk and she giggled a little at the pretentious title of the room. The Study. What am I going to study? But it was a beautiful desk. She had bought one like it for *him* in Salzburg. Had Hugh remembered? Probably not. He would not want to remind her, dear old Hugh. Pull your mind away from Salzburg. What will you study? There is the tomb of a crusader in the Templehall Woods. Study the crusaders. You meant to learn all about Friars Carse and the Templehall Priory. You were looking forward to becoming part of the life of the area when you retired. And now you are retired, Kate, somewhat forcibly. If not the crusades then shells. There were shells of all shapes and colours and sizes on the beach. Shells. Hard outer casings enclosing . . . what? Seeds, fruits, animals. She had a shell but it was not hard.

The pie was ready, perhaps burned. She went to rescue it and on the way she saw a reflection of herself in the glass door and, for once, stopped and looked at it. *She* was not there and neither was Katherine. How ugly the face in the glass was. She had never been pretty like Rose but her face had had . . . character. Now it had an ugly disfiguring scar. She pulled her hair forward to hide it and saw her hands. Nothing to cover them except the sleeves. Who was it who had invented wide sleeves to hide disfigurement? Anne Boleyn. Poor Anne, her extra little finger was no match for these ugly, ugly hands. A judgement. Did God judge? Vengeance is mine, saith the Lord. This ugliness, this wrinkled scarred skin that she would carry with her to the grave, this was God's vengeance?

'I think not,' she told the face in the glass. 'Not God's.'

She was surprised at how much of the pie she ate. Could she face the rest later or tomorrow? Kate, there is no longer an unlimited expense account, and there are expenses. I'll feed the birds, but I'll learn to cook. That nice lady in the shop will help me.

Would she? People had always rushed to help Katherine but Kate, would they rush to help the ugly, spoiled woman who was Kate? Human kindness was underestimated. She remembered thinking that as she stood by her window looking out on dull February mornings that were bright with mimosa. Mimosa, so sunny, so yellow, like heaps of Granny's scrambled eggs. Granny was kind, and Tante. Hugh? Hugh is kind.

She got her cloak with the hood that hid her scarred face, picked up the remains of the pie, and went out into her walled garden. Funny that the walls of the garden should have survived while the walls of the house had slowly eroded. The monastery had been built in the thirteenth century and so a house had stood on the site for over six hundred years; not this house. This house replaced one built in the seventeenth century; it was that house that she had tried to recreate. Soon it would be quite whole again. She would ring the builder as soon as she got rid of the evidence of uneaten pie. She crumbled some crust into very small pieces and left them for the robin she had seen once or twice and then she wrapped the scarf of the hood tightly around her neck and, trembling slightly, went out again on to the road. No, no one would define this track as a road, this track that led to the beach.

It was September and it was not cold but a wind had sprung up. She would not look odd, all wrapped up so closely in a scarf She would worry about the summer, like Scarlett O'Hara, tomorrow. Being out in the world, in the wind, was exhilarating, exciting, almost like . . . no, nonsense, naughty Kate, it was nothing like that. The tide was out and she had to walk a long way to reach the sea, past the Sea Green where a flock of wild geese were resting, across the road that led to the town of North Berwick and the south, and on to the beach itself. She would love it here for she loved the sea. Madame Bovary loved the sea too, but only when it was rough.

What did that tell the reader about Flaubert's flawed creation? Kate loved it in its every mood: its soft murmurings, its roaring crescendos, just outside her windows, shells and seaweeds, and funny bits of . . . now which was flotsam and which jetsam? Something else to study, to fill up the time.

A stone invaded her shoe and she winced. Imagine flinching at the pain of a stone in a shoe. It was not a very serviceable shoe. She would need to go shopping but even thinking of it made her weaken. Who had bought her shoes when she was dead? Mail order, there must be mail order. How strange to be reduced to mail-order shoes for someone who had had her shoes made by hand for years. She could write *there* and specify *serviceable* but then they would know that she was alive and no one must know.

She could go no further and she stopped and threw the remains of the pie as far as she could. Ah, Kate, you have lost your cricketing skills too. She smiled as she watched the grateful gulls swoop to pick up the bits. She could just have dropped it at her feet but although she liked watching the gulls in flight, they were terrifying when they were too close. For a while she stood and watched the water tumbling head over heels on to the shore.

I'm going to hit your shoes, it teased, and raced madly up the sand towards her, and then, just before it reached her, it stopped and whispered its way back down the beach.

There's music in everything.

The sound of his voice in her head hurt her and instinctively she put her hand up to her ravaged cheek. She had not heard his voice when she was dead and she had been dead, it appeared, for years. Would she die again, another death, if she allowed it to invade her mind, her heart, her very being as it used to do? How she had welcomed it then. Don't think, don't think. Think of the new house, a new life, a new beginning. God did not want you to die. Did He want me to suffer longer for my sin, my great, great sin?

Vengeance is mine. Vengeance is mine.

She was sobbing now. The doctors had said that rebirth was painful. The first journey into the world was said to be the most traumatic and painful of all journeys, but to be reborn . . . why didn't I die? I begged them to let me. What reason is there for me to live, to exist? Everything is gone but my shell. But her home had been nothing but a shell for thirteen years and look at it now. Nothing that time and money could not fix. Would it be the same for Kate who had been the great Katherine Buchan and was now a shell too? She turned into the wind so that it would dry the tears on her face: she hated to touch her skin. She was alone on the beach. No one anywhere.

I will like it here. I will remember everything.

She walked briskly back up the beach to the track. There was a man on the track approaching her. He was tall and thin and he too was wearing a cloak. How incongruous. White tennis shoes peeked out from beneath the coarse brown material. Instinctively she lowered her head and turned away.

'Good afternoon,' he said. 'A fine day.'

'Yes,' she said and hurried past. She did not look back before she reached the safety of the house and so she did not see him look after her. She let herself into Abbots House and hurried to her garden room but no, she would not fall apart, she would sew; she would not lie down to recover from the effort of saying one word to a man whom, if she could help it, she would be sure never to see again.

'Maybe she's escaped from a loony bin.'

Maggie Thomson looked at her fourteen-year-old son with a feeling akin to disgust. Where did these young people get their ideas and their appalling lack of human kindness? 'I hear you saying anything like that in the village, Cameron, and I'll tell your father.'

Cameron grinned at her while he checked carefully that the spikes in his new haircut were still perfect. Then, relaxed and relieved, he returned his attention to a very large hamburger, made, naturally, from the finest beef his father could find – no preservatives here. 'Mum, there's something very strange about a woman who covers her face and only goes out at night. You know she's a murderer and nearly got hanged but she was criminally insane or pretended to be: she was an actress, after all.'

Maggie turned from the stove and clouted her only son. 'Don't you dare bring all these vile stories into my home, Cameron

Thomson. Miss Buchanan could sue if she wanted; wicked, wicked people with nothing to do but stir up trouble.'

Cameron stared in open-mouthed astonishment at his mother, but his sister sprang to his defence. 'That house was burned down, Mum, and they say there was a murder. You must admit it is quite a coincidence, a woman the right age, with terrible scars, coming back to the scene of the crime.'

'Murderers do that all the time,' put in Cameron as he watched his mother's right hand warily.

Maggie was too busy thinking to worry about her son. 'Something awful happened to her, a car accident or something. She has a very pale scar on her cheek and I think her hands are scarred or deformed because she tucks them up into her sleeves. Obviously she has had some plastic surgery and is shy, hesitant really, about being seen. So what? She has a lovely voice,' she finished.

'Mother.'

With what disdain a teenager could say that word. Cameron stopped shovelling food into his mouth and looked at his mother and sister. 'She has a nice voice so she can't be an escaped murderer? I bet loony bins are full of people with lovely voices.'

Maggie undid the top button on her cherry-red sweater and then the one below that; it was too hot in the kitchen. 'Enough, Miss Buchanan is a reserved person; she wants to keep herself to herself. All she asks is that we deliver her orders without intruding on her privacy. The money is always waiting for the delivery boy. I wish all our customers were as easy to deal with.'

'Do you think she managed to bake the pies, Mum?' To oblige her mother Stacie had cycled over to Abbots House with one of her father's famous beef pies and she had noticed that a simplified set of baking instructions had been taped to the packet.

'I do everything but put them in the oven for her, pet. I think she manages.'

Cameron could not conceive of a woman incapable of cooking. His entire life had been spent surrounded by wonderful, mouth-watering smells since both his parents were excellent cooks and, moreover, owned two shops, Maggie's Fine Foods and the best butcher's shop for miles, each a treasure-trove of taste and smell. 'Why can't she cook?'

Stacie stood up and posed by the table. She was being Eustacie Thomson, Oscar- winning actress – that ghastly name would come in useful yet. Pity about the plebeian Thomson, although it had not done the famous actress Emma Thompson any harm. 'Some women, darlink, are above such things. They know that there are greater things than cooking and . . .' Suddenly she realised what she was saying and blushed furiously. 'Sorry, Mum, but you know what I mean.'

'Yes, I do. Some women have been waited on hand and foot all their lives.' Maggie regained her equilibrium as quickly as she had lost it, and her round pretty face relaxed. She liked their mysterious new customer; she had no objections to doing just that little bit more. 'Miss Buchanan's different. It's no trouble to coax her along. Anyone that's gone through—'

'What has she gone through, Mum? You don't know a thing about her except that she's had plastic surgery. Maybe she had a face-lift that went wrong like some of those gaga old film stars; who knows, maybe she's wanted for a different murder and had her face done so the cops won't recognise her. All you know is that she's hopeless in the kitchen, has an ugly old mug, hides her hands, maybe because they did the dastardly deed, and must be rolling in it if she paid for the renovation of that house.'

'When we first came here, when Stacie was little, you could still see charred beams.' Some memory of old gossip stirred in her mind but she ignored it. 'The war, I should think.'

'The war? There wasn't any war damage to this village, was there, Mum?'

Maggie stood up and went to the professional stove where, for no good reason, she adjusted every perfectly adjusted pot. 'Don't know, love. I wasn't born, strange as that may seem, Cameron Thomson, but we are quite close to Edinburgh. Friars Carse could have got something meant for the Forth Rail Bridge.' Maggie turned back to her daughter who was setting up the ironing board. 'There was quite a bit of talk in the shop when the renovations started, Stacie, all sorts of improbable stories. There was even talk that it had been a secret home of some duchess or something. Her husband found it and burned it down with her and her . . .' She looked at her son but he was busily cutting another slice of chocolate cake and so she mouthed *lover* and then carried on normally. 'inside. And no it wasn't Miss Buchanan because, in that fire, everybody was killed. It was a long time ago, before we came to Friar's Carse. The make-up of the village is very different; families come, families go. No one really remembers, except maybe longtime residents and any of them who are still able to come into the shop tell the most scandalous stories. Where do they get the imagination, I should like to know? It's soap operas,' she answered herself.

'It's very romantic,' breathed Stacie. 'A ruined house fabulously renovated and a woman—'

'Also fabulously renovated,' interrupted Cameron. 'Don't be silly, Stace. If you were burned to a crisp with your . . . *lover*,' he mouthed at his mother, 'you'd hardly come back to the same place. No, I go with the bank robbery story myself. Jim's dad saw the furniture going in and said it was worth a fortune, antiques and stuff.'

'Mrs Robertson said it was a load of old junk,' contributed Stacie, 'and only a few of the rooms have curtains but the ones there are, the upstairs rooms, are really beautiful, Mum, lovely quality white cotton with lace. I think it was a shop in Edinburgh that hung them so I suppose they made them too. I saw them when I went over with the pie and just drooled. They'd look lovely in your bedroom, Mum.'

'Great. Maybe you'll get them cheap when she's arrested,' said Cameron and ran laughing from his mother's ire.

2

Kate did see the man from the beach again, a few days later. He passed the house just as she was going round the first floor, closing such curtains as there were. For a moment she watched him and so she saw what she had not seen the first time. His cloak was not a cloak but a habit of some religious order. Around his waist was a knotted rope and he held another in his hand. Conscious that he could not see her Kate stared until he was out of sight. What could he possibly want with a length of rope on the beach? She hesitated, reached for her cloak, and then sighed and went back to her chair in the study. There were miles of beach but she did not want to share her space with anyone, not even a monk.

She walked that night and he was not there, but the next night, when the wind had died down, she stood marvelling at the artistry of the sky and saw a dog. This dog was not small and ugly and belligerent like Maggie Thomson's Cromwell but was tall and slender and very hairy. He galloped towards her and she closed her eyes so that she would not see his huge teeth as they ripped into her. The dog stopped at a command from his master and Kate opened her eyes and tried to breathe normally. She was so unnerved that she forgot to hide her face.

'Sometimes he forgets his breeding and he can be rather unnerving.' It was the monk.

Kate gasped with relief in the darkness. The rope in the monk's hand was obviously for this giant. 'I confess to reliving a few pages from *The Hound of the Baskervilles*. What is he, the breed, I mean, and what's his name?' Instinctively she had turned away as she spoke; it could have looked as if she were trying to see the dog better.

'He's a deerhound and his name is Thane.'

At the sound of his name the dog left his investigation of a pile of flotsam and returned to his master. He pushed against him and then turned and pushed his head into Kate's stomach.

She steadied her feet in the sand and vainly tried to grab for her hood. 'Good heavens.' Had he seen her scars? Had he? No, it was too dark.

'He likes you,' said the monk and if he had seen her face or her hands his voice gave nothing away.

Kate turned away a little. 'What would he do if he did not?'

'Merely ignore you. They are gentle giants, these fellows, and he himself had a very unfortunate start in life; some horrid person starved him and abandoned him in our grounds. Perhaps that makes him even kinder than the norm. Hold your hand out to him.'

Kate looked at the dog that was standing between them, his great jaws open, his eyes alert as he looked from one to the other. She could see two rows of firm white teeth but the dog's face was not only beautiful but also kind. She hesitated, then edged her arm further up inside the sleeve and held her hand, well covered, out to the dog. He did not mind the scars and sniffed her gently. She could feel his breath on her puckered skin and then she winced more in surprise than in fear as the dog gently licked her hand. How unexpected. She put her scarred hand on his head. 'Hello, friend Thane,' she said.

The monk laughed. 'He'll move away if you fondle his ears for a moment. He wants to know if his affection is returned. Dogs are among the most wondrous of God's creations. In return for some food and affection he gives everything he has and once he loves, he never changes. He's not demanding; a little caress and he will go off about his own business.

Kate looked at the dog, happily rooting among the seaweed. 'How nice to be a dog.'

'But how sad too. He can look forward to no afterlife.'

Deliberately she avoided his eyes and kept watching the dog that was quivering with excitement at some scent he had found in a pile of seaweed. 'Can any of us? Surely one life is more than enough? Who wants a second chance at meeting all the people one has wronged, or hated?'

'Or loved.'

'Goodnight,' she said abruptly and turned away, and although she did not look back she sensed that his face would be sad. She shrugged. There would be many people who appreciated his platitudes; she would not feel sorry for him.

She had her worst dream again that night. In the dream she saw herself lying naked, asleep on a rug, in front of the fire. The fire had died down while she slept and when she woke she felt cold. She shivered and then she smiled, for she was warm again; she was in the bath. The bath was full of lovely scented bubbles and she lay there unable to wash the languid satisfied body that Bryn's hands had been caressing so recently. She would call him and he would come and she would give him her flannel. She squirmed in the water. Naughty, naughty Kate. She closed her eyes and lay back, ducking her head under the water. When she emerged like Venus from the waves she heard voices. Voices, but how could there be voices since no one knew that they were there? She felt fear. Why should she be afraid? The scene changed and she was standing in the hall wrapped in a towel. Once again she was very cold. Shouting. Who was it?

'*Control yourself.*'

'*There's an odd thing for an adulterer to say.*'

Kate hurried into the bedroom where she dropped the towel on the floor as she picked up her pink silk peignoir. Again, quite loudly, she heard the voices. Damn it, who was it? Bryn and who else? His voice was calm and placating but the other was strident, hysterical and angry. She knew that voice; if she could just get closer she would recognise it. She bundled herself into the robe and hurried down the stairs. Bryn was talking, shouting really. That glorious, magical voice. He was wearing only his under-shorts and she laughed; he looked so absurd, standing there yelling, and half naked. Where was his bathrobe? She turned and ran back to the bedroom; it would be in the wardrobe still. She got it and, laughing, ran back downstairs, the laughter dying in her mouth as she reached the dining room. It was completely dark and she could no longer see or hear Bryn. And then the flames. The toile de jouy

17

curtains were on fire. Flames licked at them, sprang voraciously across them. How very odd. They seemed to race up the masts of the ships that had sailed so gaily across the vast expanse of their cotton ocean, jumping from ship to ship and now, dear God, they attacked the wooden rails on which the heavy blue curtains hung.

She ran forward, her arms outstretched, and fell over something lying on the floor. She began to scream and her screams woke her up.

She woke late next morning and, as usual after a nightmare, her nightgown and the bedclothes were wet. Was it the heat from the flames that had made her sweat or the paralysing fear? She did not know but pulled all the covers from the bed and went into the bathroom to wash. Scalding-hot water obligingly filled the bathtub but she stood there shivering in her damp gown for some time, trying to summon up the courage to do something extremely simple. First part of the ritual: take off her watch. She went everywhere, except into water, wearing the watch. She had not been wearing it that night; the bracelet was too fine and had snapped when she caught it on something in the theatre. Hugh recovered it for her from the little jeweller's shop in Edinburgh some months after the fire. Next she reached into the tiny linen cupboard, took out a soft Irish linen guest towel, an old one, one of Granny's and therefore large, and tied it around her eyes before she hauled her gown over her head. She kneeled down carefully and tested the water and when it was not too hot she stepped into the bath and washed herself quickly with a soft cloth. At no time did her bare hand touch any part of her body.

Then she stepped out and dried herself and only when she had wrapped herself in her soft satin dressing-gown did she untie the towel. Silly Kate, she told herself. Vain Kate. She sighed. Now she had to keep a promise and she did not want to do it. If, however, she did not . . . who knew what might happen. Perhaps the nightmare would be worse the next time.

Coffee first. She was not delaying her phone call but she would feel better after coffee. He would ask and she was too weak to lie. She made a slice of toast and buttered it immediately. Sister Mary

Magdalene had told her that she loved to make a slice of toast at night and eat it, hard and cold, next morning. Bizarre. Kate laughed as she always did when she thought about the gentle French nun. How could such a perfect person like cold toast?

He was in his office; she had hoped that he might be out, on a ward, anywhere.

'Dr Whittaker.'

'Simon, it's Kate. I had a bad dream last night.'

'Yes?'

Damn him, why wouldn't he help? 'The same one, more or less. I think I'm mixing two different times. This time I started out on the rug, rather cold but then I was in the bath, very mixed up. I heard the voices and tried, I really tried to recognise the other one but I fell asleep or blacked out at exactly the same spot.'

'How do you feel now, Kate?'

'I'm fine,' she said and was delighted to find that this was true. 'Fine. I thought about Sister Mary Magdalene and her appalling taste in toast and that made me laugh. That's progress, Simon?'

He said nothing. How exasperating psychiatrists were.

'Simon, you have to agree. I got over the nightmare very easily. That's being back in my own lovely house, isn't it?'

'I don't know.' As usual his voice was neutral. She could never tell anything from his voice.

She picked up a small Chinese bowl and glared at the pot-pourri it held. She sniffed it, apple wood and what . . . musk rose? She would not get upset. He was waiting for her to react. 'I'm considering having guests to stay.'

'It's an excellent idea.'

'I know.'

'How do you plan to handle it?'

'I don't know. You sound unsure.'

He sighed. 'Kate dear, I'm a doctor but I'm not telepathic. You have been hiding for many years and now—'

She interrupted him. 'I don't think being locked away in a sanatorium is hiding exactly.'

He heard her laugh along the wires, more a chuckle really: such a pleasant sound.

'Be honest,' he said gently. 'Physically you could have left years ago, and mentally—'

'My dear Simon,' she interrupted him. 'You are the expert. Mentally, I'm still not sure that I'm ready.' She paused and he waited. She must speak first. He would not lead. She sighed. 'I didn't want to die in an institution even one as lovely as Le Prieuré.' She stopped talking for a second as a picture of the mellow old convent building invaded her mind, bringing with it the sounds and scents of Provence as well as of the religious life. 'You must come and see the house. It's almost as it was and it was lovely. Wouldn't Rae love a weekend at the beach?'

He did not hesitate; his professional side needed to observe her in the house. As a friend he would enjoy being with her. 'She'd love it; we both would. Tell me what you've done.'

'The actual structural work is complete. The walls and the roof were done first, of course, and the layout is, I believe, more or less what it was when I renovated it in the sixties. From the upstairs you can see the sea. In fact you can see everything, the Sea Green, the beach, the road to Templehall Woods. Downstairs there's a rather large hall with doors off to various other rooms and halfway along the hall is the staircase; at the back I have a kitchen, rather splendid and mainly unused; it's for Hugh really. Off that there's a tiny breakfast room. That leads into my rather formal sitting room, lots of large comfy armchairs and a sofa, all upholstered in white but with piles of cushions in blue and gold. The sitting room occupies almost the entire front of the ground floor. It has good light and I will do my sewing there. The dining room, which is also rather grand, is on the other side and has a view of the garden. Next a skinny room that looks out on to my side garden, such as it is. The garden is walled, although there are a few places that require work. It's warm and sunny and I think I shall enjoy becoming a gardener; I'm creating something, Simon. At the moment I spend all my time there - mainly tidying up - or in the garden room. I have books there and a day bed, a lovely chair, a bookcase and my desk and so it will be the study. I intend to improve my mind; shall I finish Proust?'

She was quiet. Proust? She had said she intended to finish Proust and so therefore she had once started him.

Only one hundred and three pages to go but life's too short, my darling, for finishing Proust.

He broke into her silence. 'Is there somewhere for us to sleep, or is it all jolly fun and sleeping bags on the sitting room floor?'

'I said it was a *grand* sitting room. No bodies on my floors. Murdo is attending to the guest bedrooms now but if you were to come before Christmas you would have to go to a hotel. It's called Greenhill Park, the nearest hotel, rather splendid, and with what psychiatrists are paid, you can certainly afford it.'

He ignored that remark: he was interested in the casual *Murdo*. 'Tell me about Murdo.'

'He's my builder and he's worth his weight, which is considerable, in gold. And yes, damn you, I summoned my courage and confronted him, face to face. Not unlike going on stage for the first time. My darling Hugh found him for me, of course, and he's quite wonderful. He said, "Hell, missus, you've had a hard time, have you no?" I like Murdo. Not that we see much of each other. We speak on the phone or I leave notes. I don't know what he has told his men, probably nothing. Sometimes when they're here, I walk on the beach. I walk for miles. Sometimes I stay in the garden or in the garden room. I have met two other people. Maggie Thomson has a shop, Maggie's Fine Foods, that would not be out of place in London; she's married to the village butcher; his shop is very old-fashioned, just like the one my grandmother favoured, spotlessly clean white tiles and lovely, lovely meats. I went into her shop; she was reaching into a glass counter for cold meats. I thought it was a funny picture, this rather large lady, her head almost following her hand as she bent over. She has the loveliest smile and her food is fabulous. And by the way, she has the most belligerent little Jack Russell, called Cromwell.'

'I don't believe poor old Cromwell was as nasty as history has made him out to be,' he said, and then asked her if she had revisited the shop.

'I phone Maggie and go and collect things when it's quiet, or she has them delivered; her children, I think. Then there's a monk who walks on the beach too. Maggie let me buy a little carving he made: ridiculous price. Should have been ten times what he asked. We said good evening, so politely and had an almost conversation. I suppose it was a conversation, and he had a rather splendid dog.'

'A St Bernard?'

'Very droll. No, but can you imagine me and a monk? I will go out and meet more people – but when I'm ready. Three new people in six months is quite good, I think.'

He remembered when he had first read about her, surrounded by, it seemed, hundreds of people: secretaries, dressmakers, managers, agents, coaches, hairdressers and assorted hangers-on; Rose, of course, and him. Not that *they* were there very often, being too busy following their own glittering paths; three brilliant comets with star-spangled tails. Maybe Rose wasn't a true comet; maybe she flew to success on his tail, or on Katherine Buchan's? He was not clever enough to know and all the tabloid writers had let the stories die long ago. He no longer cared: if he had ever. He cared about Kate, once his patient, now his friend.

'How long have we known each other, Kate?' he asked suddenly.

'Known? What does that mean, Simon? We met when I was . . . it was in 1972, so fourteen years or so. Mind you, Doctor dear, it depends on what *know* means. Biblically, we didn't know each other at all.'

'You are incorrigible, Kate Buchanan. I'll ring again in a few days. You ring any time.'

She hung up, quite pleased with herself and immediately the phone rang again. She stared at it. Who could it be? Who had her number? Simon. Hugh Forsythe, her stepbrother and lawyer. Would it be Hugh? It was Murdo. He wanted to finish the upstairs rooms.

'Gin we have a good week, missus . . .'

Oh, she would give them their good week. To have them, nice as they were, out of her house . . . the mind could not comprehend the joy of being, at last, alone in her own home. 'The weather can be so lovely, Murdo, and I shall take advantage and explore. Maggie Thomson from the village tells me . . . reminds me that there are lovely walks around here; those woods a mile or so down the coast.'

Murdo reminded her that he was not local. 'Maybe no a good idea to go wandering in woods by yourself, missus.'

Another friend; someone who cared. 'There's a monastery in the woods, and the tomb of a crusader. With all those holy people around, I should be quite safe.'

He was sceptical. 'Whatever turns you on, missus.'

Maggie was correct in saying that the monastery was set in beautiful woodland. It was a perfect place to eat one's lunch and, with luck, to see no one, not even a holy monk. Monks, surely, would be at prayer or work during the day. Kate found that she did not mind if she did meet her monk but Maggie had recommended the crusader, or his tomb rather, as a place for privacy: 'No one goes there; it's quite isolated and lonely. It has whatever it is that my Stacie calls atmosphere.'

It was quiet, a peaceful and serene stillness. It was a strange place for a tomb, so far from the abbey, but then maybe Sir Knight had also valued his privacy. Perhaps, since he had been hideously deformed in battle, he and she were soul mates. There was no way of knowing how he had died. It was assumed that he had been killed, poor man, and carried home to his beloved woods by his faithful servants. Kate sat down on a large stone and let the peace of the place settle around her. She was quite sure that she had never been in the woods before: no sluggish memory stirred as if trying to find the surface of her whimpering mind. She was not afraid. It was a holy place: she could feel it. The man who was buried here had been a good man.

You were faithful to your wife, weren't you, my friend? You ignored the lures from all the exotic maidens and remembered the mother of your sons here looking after your lands, your house and your children. You lie here in peace. Kate stood up abruptly as another thought invaded her mind. But, if you were so good and faithful, where is the tomb of your wife? You lie alone, Crusader.'

She went over to the great crumbling stone monument. The ivy that had clambered over the tomb had been firmly cut back, but the stone was disintegrating and it was easy to see that, if any bones had been laid to rest inside, they were no longer there. She laid her hand on the carved lid and the peace descended again. The stone was cold but it was not the chill of horror and decay. It was a friendly cold, the natural feeling of stone that is out of doors at the closing of the year. Kate sighed with relief. Maggie had said that she would like the place and she did. She sat down on a fallen stone beside the tomb and ate her lunch – two oatcakes, two small pieces of cheese, Scottish Cheddar and French Brie, a pleasant habit picked up and nourished in Provence. Well done, Kate. She looked at her apple, round and red, and she knew it would be crisp and juicy but suddenly she had a longing for a ripe fig. When had she last had a fig? They must be available in Scotland. She would ask Maggie. And just as quickly she decided that she would not ask. She would eat her firm red apple and would enjoy every mouthful.

There was a slight stirring around her and she looked up and, to her delight, watched delicate golden beech leaves flutter to the hard brown earth. How beautiful, how beautiful. She turned her scarred face up, hoping that a leaf would land on her and was reminded of childhood when she and, one winter, dear Hugh, had turned their cold faces up to catch snowflakes. She stood up joyously and held out her hands like a trusting child.

> Down, down, yellow and brown,
> The leaves are falling all over the town.

From which memory drawer had that childhood poem come?

A single yellow leaf drifted down through the air. She watched it as it seemed to hang in a current and then spiral down to join its brothers. Kate stepped on them for the joy of hearing that once favourite and particular autumn sound.

'I had a nightmare and I'm fine. I'm thinking of the taste of apples and the joy of the leaves. I'm fine.' She turned back to the ruined tomb. 'Thank you, Sir Knight. I shall come back to see you often.'

For now she had to return to her home. By five Murdo and his men would have left and she had a great deal to do. She felt no fear as she retraced her steps through the woods. She could hear her own footfalls in the leaves as she walked along the paths and sometimes she heard birds calling, not singing but calling as if to keep in touch with one another. As she stopped at a fork in the paths to decide which way to go she sensed rather than saw a sudden movement and was captivated by the sight of a small red squirrel. It clung to the trunk of a huge beech tree and she could have sworn it glared at her before scampering up the trunk and disappearing among the leaves.

Now, which is the native – the grey or the red?

Red ones, Kate. The greys are predators.

That was Hugh's voice. He knew everything about everything – so annoying sometimes, like Bryn.

She smiled. New things to interest her; new things to discover. Life was good. She would spend her free time either in the woods or on the beach. It would depend on the weather and the time of day. Soon it would be winter and she could not walk in the woods on winter evenings.

The house was quiet: the men had gone but there was evidence of their having been there. She could smell wood shavings and the smell enticed her upstairs to see the progress. Clever Murdo. He had suggested building in shelves and wardrobes in the smaller guest rooms so as to make better use of the space. 'Very elegant,' said Kate, 'very modern. Very clinical? Do I want clinical? No, but the staining will make a difference, and the bedcovers. They will be sumptuous. I'll sew them myself.'

She went back downstairs happily thinking of colours and fabrics. She would start today, tonight, immediately. No, one more telephone call. She stood for a moment thinking of the call and as she did she smoothed the soft brushed blue denim of her long skirt. She never wore short skirts now. Ugly, skinny legs.

'Skinny legs require feeding.'

The bright new kitchen cupboards were almost empty and they should be full of tins and jars. The freezer already housed lots of fascinating packages that she had bought from Maggie. But there were things that Maggie did not sell.

'There's a van comes round,' Maggie had said. 'Save you going out in bad weather.'

How kind Maggie was. Perhaps it was a cowardly way to shop but surely any woman would be glad to have the convenience of a van that came around the streets driven by a friendly man who left the order on the step and went off whistling. She looked at her watch and hastily dialled the number. Please be there.

'Maggie from the delicatessen tells me you deliver.'

'Yes, indeed.'

'I'd like to order by telephone and then I'll leave the money in an envelope for the delivery man.'

'Of course, madam. He'll give you a wee knock when he gets there, just in case you're out. We wouldn't want ice cream to melt.'

A frisson of panic, swiftly dampened down. One more face-to-face encounter. No, not yet. 'No need. I'm always at home but I'm working and prefer not to be disturbed.'

'If you're sure.'

She was sure and she made an order and waited patiently for him to calculate the cost.

'It'll be some time tomorrow morning. We load the van first thing.'

'Wonderful. My cheque will be in the basket at the door.'

Cowardy Custard. She shook her head and wrote the cheque. She looked at the cheque and at her signature. Would he recognise that name, Kate Buchanan? It was so similar, perhaps too similar. Katherine Buchan, Kate Buchanan. Should she have changed it yet again? No, she had spent her working life being someone else and now she wanted to be herself.

He had always been himself and *he* had stood out – everywhere. Even when he was silent his presence dominated the stage.

'Katherine Buchan. Sounds more like a pirate than an actor. Are you a wild buccaneer, Kate?'

'No, I take no risks, unless with the parts I play, not in my private life.'

'All life is risky . . . as is love, Kate.'

His eyes, his beautiful eyes, smiling at her, laughing with her, encouraging her. 'Katie, Katie, you bewitched me, you did. Ach, cariad, *there's no one can hold a candle to you.'*

Kate shook her head as if to detach that memory. She did not want to think, to wallow in grief. She had almost drowned in her grief.

Beans on toast. There is something so wonderfully satisfying about beans on toast. Sister Aquinas had brought Kate a tin of Heinz beans back from a visit to London once, and how slowly she had eaten them. She took her supper to the breakfast room window

26

– why did she persist in calling it a breakfast room when she ate all her meals there – set it down on the table and opened the blinds.

How beautiful, almost ethereal the light was in Scotland. The world outside her window was blue, pale blue, or was it lilac, but there was grey, and there was green surely, faint, faint green. Impossible to describe it, but enough to say that tonight it was beautiful. Look, over there, an artist was washing the horizon with a flash of red.

'Red sky at night, shepherd's delight.' Proverbs, sixteenth century. She could study literature.

But you have studied it.

Only a small part, and very little French or Russian. No, I almost finished Proust. How did I do it when there was only time for my work or him?

'There must be hundreds of books I have not read,' she told the beans balancing on the last little triangle of toast. 'Thousands even, and lots of them worth reading.'

How to get a book without going into a bookshop? Mail order. How cunning she was becoming, how devious. She had never been devious before. Perhaps that had been the trouble. For a moment she wished one of those annoying nurses would come bustling in with a pill or a thermometer but she had proved that she did not need them and now she was alone and she was in grave danger of beginning to think, and thinking, remembering, was so painful.

'Kate, you promised to think, to try to remember.'

She closed the blinds and turned on another lamp so that chinks of light would show to any interested observer. Kate put on her cape and, out of habit, pulled the hood up over her head. Then she slipped out, locking the door behind her. The night was quiet but she tuned her ears waiting for the sounds: the sea whispered softly but it could be heard by those trained to listen. In the quiet dark- ness sound travelled unerringly. There were birds and distant traffic, and even a shout of laughter that must come from the open fish and chip shop on the main street. Main Street; how far away was it? She thought it slightly more than one hundred yards but in the night it seemed closer. She heard giggles from the teenagers who stood under the streetlights; did they know that such light was unflattering and stripped them of any individuality? Perhaps, though, they preferred that, not to stand out, but all to be the same metallic grey. She tried to remember her teenage years. Had they been called teenagers in the fifties? She didn't think so but could not remember. Teddies. There. Now what were teddies? Underwear – or was that later? Nothing to do with bears though. Edwardians maybe: she could not remember. She did remember that there had never been time to stand on a corner under a street-light. Had she missed something? Of course. But that was life. Fleetingly she wondered if any of the giggling youngsters had ever heard of Goethe or Ibsen or Anouilh? Had they ever listened to the music of Beethoven? The house in Provence had been full of music: the singing of the nuns in the chapel, the glorious paeans from the organ, her records – gifts from Hugh and Simon.

You told me you loved Beethoven. That was Simon.

Remember this Bach cantata, Kate? That was Hugh.

Chacun à son goût. But you can't know your taste unless you are offered a sample.

'Good evening.'

The voice, the man coming suddenly out of the silence startled her.

'Forgive me for startling you. I do apologise. It's only me, Miss . . . ? He finished questioningly but she said nothing. 'I'm Father Benedict from the retreat centre.'

She stopped and, even though there was very little light, turned away instinctively. 'You startled me,' she said. 'Shouldn't priests or monks be in bed at this time or praying or whatever it is that monks are supposed to do?'

He did not take offence. 'Arthritis is a mean taskmaster. If I lie in bed accepting the pain he sends me, he might just reach my hands. Upright, I try to fight.'

'I'm told that the waters that lap the coasts of Hawaii do wonders with arthritic old bones,' she said and then cursed herself silently. How could a monk from a monastery in Scotland get to Hawaii?

'That's very interesting. Perhaps those Jacuzzi things work on the same principle. We have a brother who is a miracle worker with his hands but can you imagine his consternation were I to ask him to make me a Jacuzzi?'

He was laughing at her but she did not mind.

'Are you in pain too, my dear?' he asked quietly and she was able to answer truthfully that she was not.

'There are worse pains than the merely physical,' he said.

'I wouldn't know,' she lied. 'Where is Thane?'

'He elected to stay with someone whose need is greater than mine.'

She turned away from him towards the sanctuary of her home. 'Goodnight, Brother Benedict.' She could not address a man as Father and from his clothes he was a monk, was he not?

He would not be rebuffed. 'May I not know your name?'

'Kate.'

'Goodnight, friend Kate.'

She hurried. She wanted to get home; home to Abbots House, for it offered sanctuary today as it had done, in one guise or another, for hundreds of years. Sometimes she was conscious of others who had found rest there. Friend Kate, he had called her. Was he her friend? If he was, then he was joining a small select group. Many of the friends who had swarmed around her once had denied close friendship in an undignified and humiliating scramble to disassociate themselves from scandal. Except Hugh, of course, and now there was Simon. A lawyer and a doctor. Did their professions insist that they be faithful? No, circumstance more likely. She looked at the house and saw the welcoming friendly chinks of light. She stopped. Why am I rushing? He is Benedict, my friend, and I am safe. She stood for a moment looking back down towards the beach. The monk was standing where she had left him but he was looking out to sea. She looked past him and smiled. The sea was beautiful. She could see it swell; she could hear it murmur. She watched the play of light across the top of the water. Poor Father Benedict. She could not call a man Father. He had called her friend Kate; he would have to be friend Ben, if they were to be friends. So he fought a battle with arthritis and worried about his hands? How sad for an artist. Would the disease cripple his hands before he finished the work he wanted to do? She knew only that he carved small creatures from driftwood. What painstaking skill was needed to create these small masterpieces? Oh, yes, masterpieces. She recognised genius, for he was good as she had once been good.

'Will it be the end of your world if you don't carve, friend Ben?' she asked the solitary figure.

'There are worse pains than the merely physical.'

What a pleasant voice he had, but not like *his* voice. That voice had caused heads to turn, conversations to stop, and in a theatre . . . Oh, dear God, she could remember his power in the theatre, the power he knew he had, in which he revelled.

Of course I know what I'm doing, Kate. I work damn hard at it. All these stupid people who say it trips out: no, it doesn't. Every syllable, every gesture is the result of hours of study. And the tone, the music, that's Welsh water, my darling. I take no credit for the accident of quality, but only for what I achieve with the instrument. It's as much an instrument as a violin and must be played. Shall I play it, Kate, and watch the effect?

Like all men he could be a bastard sometimes.

3

The distance from the beach back to the house seemed longer somehow. Perhaps it was just that she had been anxious to put as much distance as possible between herself and the monk. Silly Kate. At last she was inside and she leaned back against the door in relief. The soft light from the lamps shone on the silks bundled on the sofa and she smiled at the sight.

Sister Mary Magdalene's voice came to her. *'You have a gift, Kate. We must foster it; gifts are evanescent and will fade if not respected.'*

'Evanescent, ma soeur? I had thought gifts ephemeral.'

'Semantics. A gift is not given for a week or a year; it is for ever. Therefore if you do not school your artistic gift it begins slowly to fade until it disappears altogether. Evanescent is a better word. The dew on that rose you are embroidering is ephemeral – the sun will dry it in an instant.'

'Well argued, ma soeur. And what of other gifts? Will they too disappear or fade to nothingness?'

'There are books in the library, Kate, plays too, and poetry. Shall I bring one, Anouilh's L'Alouette, for example?'

She did not want to remember the theatre. 'I prefer to learn a new stitch.'

She would work on her embroidery but first she would have to ring Hugh. She took off her cloak and dropped it on the sofa as she reached for the telephone. At this time of the evening where would he be? Snug in his beautiful book-lined flat, a comfortable cardigan with the obligatory leather elbow patches hauled on over his shirt; at the opera or the ballet; having dinner with friends or alone at his club? She stifled the longing to be with him there. This, now, was the place for Kate Buchanan.

'Hello, dear. I quite expected you to be out on the razzle-dazzle.'

He laughed. 'As you well know my razzling days are over.'

She interrupted. 'Hugh, don't be silly. You're not even fifty yet.'

'I am a highly respected lawyer, Kate, and we merely glow, not dazzle. I was just about to ring you. How are things?'

'Better. I'm cooking my own meals; well, that's not strictly accurate. The nice woman in the village shop sends over these divine little pies, complete with monosyllabic instructions, and I carry them out.'

'And are you eating them?'

'What an unusual question for a lawyer. Even Simon doesn't ask me that.'

'Perhaps doctors are more sensitive than lawyers. Are you eating them?'

She could almost see the worried look on his honest craggy face. Oh, what a treasure is a good friend. 'Can't you smell? My lovely kitchen is full of mere memories of chicken pie, and even of the more prosaic beans on toast. Shades of winter nights at Granny's.' She looked across the room to her scrupulously clean and bare dining table and crossed her fingers superstitiously against the little white lie. She had heard him laugh when she had reminded them of their shared childhood memories. Some memories are always a joy. 'You did a wonderful job, my dear, and I'm ready to receive people. When can you come? I rang Simon, Hugh, because I did have a little bad dream but I wanted him to see how easily I got over it.'

He sighed but his voice was encouraging. 'That's wonderful – the getting over it bit; the same dream, I suppose.'

'Yes, so tiresome, but I recovered quickly, no blue funks, no cowering in my bed. I did the right thing by coming back, Hugh. Just wait and see. The dreams will fade out completely.'

'Kate, you said you wanted to remember. You have to remember what happened that night.'

She said nothing.

'Kate.'

She picked up a skein of gold thread and held it briefly against her unmarked cheek. 'I'm here. I was merely wondering if the truth really makes any difference, not at this stage. It won't bring Bryn back or my career, or my face. I rang mainly to issue an invitation. Simon, by the way, is thrilled that I feel like entertaining. He thinks I don't know that he wants to observe me *in situ*. *I* am issuing invitations; but only to special people.'

'My dear Miss Buchanan, if you needed me I would be there now. You said you wanted a few months on your own.'

'I'm not lonely, Hugh. Funnily enough I miss the bells and the plainsong that sometimes drove me bonkers, but there are sounds here. You should hear the rooks gathering in the woods, what a clammering they make, and then suddenly they rise from where they have all been sitting gossiping and fly en masse, like a great black cloud, to another tree.'

'What woods?' And now he sounded nervous.

'Didn't I tell you about them?' asked Kate, affecting surprise. 'Just a little down the coast, Hugh, a mile or so, and I go in broad daylight. There's a monastery or retreat house or something of that sort. I shall make it my special place; no one goes there.'

'I shall drive up this weekend and take you for a spin.'

'You're worrying and I don't want you to worry. I love you dearly, Hugh, but I was thinking of visitors after Christmas. The guest rooms aren't ready.'

'After Christmas? That's nearly three months; too long.'

'No, we agreed, my dear. I need some time to get used to this way of life, no bells telling me what to do, no lovely nun demanding that I eat or walk in the garden, or take a nap. I have a whisky every night.'

'Such depravity.'

They laughed. Alcohol had never been a problem.

'Very well. I'll come for a few days after Christmas if you promise to ring me immediately if anything goes wrong before then. You are sure you want to be alone for Christmas?'

She could not bear *not* to be alone for Christmas. So many wonderful memories, and so many absolutely ghastly ones when she had wished she were dead. Much better to be alone to try to remember only happiness; at the very least, no one else would suffer in her company should misery conquer. 'I have my Christmas routines, Hugh,' she lied.

'New Year then? May I invite myself for the New Year, Happy Hogmanay and all that? Give me that little room at the back of the house; it will remind me of spending Christmas with your gran. Yes, a few days at the beach in peace and quiet.'

'And very probably torrential rain. That's all it seemed to do here initially, although it was lovely and cool and crisp today. I thought they would never get the reconstruction finished.'

The word *reconstruction* hung in the air between them. Not a happy choice of word. Reconstruction did take a long time.

'But it is finished,' he said. 'All the work is done, Kate, and we will go onward together.'

She laughed, that delicious sexy laugh that had always turned his bones to jelly. 'Stand in line, lawyer dear. I have two friends here, four if you count the dogs. There's Maggie from the shop and Benedict, a monk from Templehall Priory, the retreat house I mentioned that's hidden in the trees. The monk has a most magnificent deerhound. Maggie's dog is Cromwell, an ugly, belligerent little brute, rather pompous.'

'Sounds just like Cromwell.'

'So you'll be here for New Year's Eve? Come earlier, the twenty-ninth. She tried not to sound anxious. He must not know how much she wanted to see him. 'I think Simon and Rae might come too.'

He remembered the days when everyone begged for an invitation, any kind of invitation, just so that they could be in the same room with her and with *him* of course. 'It'll be like old times. I can't wait to see all the finishing touches. Have you had time to work?'

She looked across at the sofa with its heap of beautiful threads. 'Of course, it's like yoga, a little every day keeps me focused and structured.'

He thought quickly as lawyers do, adding and subtracting good and bad, benefits and disadvantages in his head before speaking. 'What about the commission? Given it any thought?'

'Not enough time.'

'You're right, of course.' If she hurried, there would be stress, and stress was not allowed. 'Never mind. A better one will come along.'

'After Christmas,' she said and she was talking about accepting commissions for her exquisite goldwork. 'When will you come?' she asked again, 'You did say the twenty-ninth?'

'Yes, but I will come at once if you ever need me. Tell me about your pet monk.'

'How irreligious of you. He's taller than you and thinner, handsome in an ascetic sort of way, refined, nice voice but quiet. Lucky for him I didn't know him in the old days. I would have swallowed him whole.'

'Is the poor lamb safe now?'

She laughed, a heart-warming throaty laugh. 'He has already fought and won all his battles. I wouldn't even be a distraction.' She winced and then smiled. 'Distraction? Do you remember, Hugh?'

'Of course, that nice American.' He assumed a very accurate mid-Atlantic accent. *I hear you have a distraction.* I wonder whatever happened to him.'

'He found a distraction of his own, I suppose, and married her.'

'Sensible fellow. I should have done the same. I'll ring tomorrow, around six, before I leave the office and we'll call you a business expense.'

'It was more fun being a distraction.'

'You still are. Now goodnight, my dear. We'll talk again tomorrow.'

She hung up, stood for a moment wondering what to do, and walked upstairs to her bedroom. There she went to the window, the window with the curtains so admired by Stacie Thomson, and looked out at the little lane outside. How dark it was. Almost winter. Dark by three, Granny used to say.

'I am looking at the weather,' she lied to herself. Not that the weather made much difference. After years and years of 'Mustn't get wet, dear,' 'Mustn't get cold, dear,' to struggle with the elements was an increasing joy. She exulted in being blown along the shore by the wind. She relished defying its temper and daring it to do its worst. They were worthy opponents, she and the weather.

'What a lot of porkies I have told today. I must eat something now and that will cancel out the fib I told Hugh.' She picked up a shawl that she had earlier thrown across the bed, wrapped it round her shoulders and returned to the sitting room. She did not sit down at her embroidery frame as part of her wanted to do but went into the kitchen.

Bread and cheese? No, that was the lazy way out. Scrambled eggs? Perfect. But how on earth does an egg get scrambled? Was I always so useless in a kitchen? Surely Granny or Tante taught me basics. I must ask Hugh. Kate stared at a box of six eggs for some time. Well, the answer isn't going to jump out at me if I stare long enough. I have to get them out of the shell and then mix them all up. Beating the eggs was accomplished without too much difficulty and she quite enjoyed trying to fish escaped pieces of shell out of the bowl. How they eluded her. She left the last few small pieces, deciding that her body had absorbed so much in one way or another over the past fourteen years that a few pieces of shell could not possibly hurt.

She licked her fingers and discovered that raw eggs are dull. Seasoning? Salt, pepper. What did Granny do? These are so pale; hers were yellow. She laboured on; she was capable of looking after herself. She was. She thought of Sister Aloysius, soft and fluffy as one of her own soufflés. Got it, butter.

The light supper was a triumph. The eggs had perhaps too much butter and not quite enough salt and a perfectionist might say that they were rather lumpy but to Kate Buchanan they were delicious.

Shall I ring Simon again and Hugh and gloat at my cleverness? She looked at her watch. It was after eleven. No, she could certainly not telephone anyone now. She washed her plate and left the pot, with its burned-on bits, to soak. She should go to bed, try to sleep, make an attempt at a regulated life.

She did not. She decided to escape for a time to her other world, the world of creation. The threads were still lying on the sofa and she sat down beside them and began carefully to sort them out. Japanese gold thread, very expensive and rather difficult to find. Imitation Japanese gold thread, a very good substitute that does not tarnish; excellent for ordinary commissions. Then the Admiralty gold threads which had only a percentage of real gold but which were, of course, not nearly so expensive as Japanese gold. She had been allowed to use only the imitations for nearly two years. Now she worked almost exclusively in Japanese gold. The people who bought her work or who asked her to repair their precious gold-work heirlooms were prepared to pay for only the best.

Carefully she freed her special embroidery scissors from the thread. This particular pair she used only for cutting gold; they could not be used for any other cutting because over time the gold blunts the blades. She also moved a funny little tool called a mellor which she used for handling the gold threads, turning them over for instance or disentangling them should they become entwined due to her own carelessness. Then she went back to her threads which, as well as being of different qualities were of different types: thick ones, thin ones, broad ones, narrow ones, all with their own names and their own purposes.

She had become interested in embroidery in Provence. She had been living in the convent Hugh had found for her for several months and had, at last, ventured out of the cool dark room where she had sat day after day staring at the wall, and gone into the garden. There was a stone fountain in a courtyard, some flowering shrubs, a white iron bench with rather past their best cushions, and a chair. In the chair was a nun.

Kate had made to turn around and retreat to the privacy of her room. It was a comfortable room and she liked it; there were no mirrors. But in the nun's lap was the most amazing river of liquid gold. Later she learned the threads were called purls and there were smooth purls and bright check purls, super pearl purls and Elizabethan twist purls, rococo and broad and passing and so many others and they were alive in the woman's skilled hands.

One long beautifully shaped hand gestured calmly to the bench. Kate hesitated for a moment and sat down and she stared at that beautiful smooth hand with its tapered fingers and neat business-like fingernails. She could see half moons of white at the base of each nail. Did nuns have manicures? Kate did not look at her own hands but tucked them even further up her sleeves.

The nun said nothing but went on sewing calmly and Kate sat and listened to the sound of the water and the soft cooing of doves. The air was full of fragrance, pear blossom, and lemon, and

jasmine. The nun worked slowly and patiently; there was no stabbing at the cloth stretched on the square frame. Each stitch was
placed with consummate care. And then a bell rang and at once
she gathered up her materials. She said nothing but nodded with a
smile to Kate and walked away and, although the garden was full
of light and colour and the nun had been dressed from head to foot
in black, it was as if the light had gone.

Next day Kate went out earlier. She did not actively hope that
the nun would be in the garden but she knew that she would not
avoid her if she were there. She was sitting in her seat and again she
had her embroidery with her.

'Bonjour,' said Kate.

'Good morning, Kate,' said the nun with a very faint French
accent and went on with her work.

As the day before, they sat quietly until the bell rang. The nun
left and Kate sat on for a few minutes and then rose and walked
around the garden.

The next morning Kate found herself speaking. 'That is beautiful, Sister. What is it?'

'An altar cloth for the feast of Christ the King.'

'May I look?'

'Mais bien sûr.' She anchored the needle and gestured for Kate
to approach the frame. 'It is goldwork, Kate, a very time-
consuming type of embroidery.' Again Kate noticed the hands – so
different from Sister Aloysius's blunt red fingers.

The nun stood aside from her work just a little longer as if in hope
that Kate might give in to temptation and touch the cloth but the
hands stayed firmly inside the sleeves.

'And very difficult,' said Kate as she marvelled at the tiny, sometimes, it seemed, invisible stitches that compelled the heavy gold
threads to form the pattern.

The nun neither agreed nor disagreed but simply smiled and
went on with her work.

That was the sum of their first conversation, but for the rest of
that year while the altar cloth took glorious shape before her eyes
Kate talked in the garden with the nun who was called Sister Mary
Magdalene. Later when the embroideries were being assembled

they sat in the convent parlour and that was when Kate was encouraged to participate.

'You would like to try, Kate?'

Try. No, she knew nothing about sewing.

'You are a patient woman, Kate, and the background of the angel's vestments needs patience; it needs someone who will not be bored by filling in large areas with a simple stitch in rather a dull colour.'

'My hands?'

'Are badly scarred I know but perhaps to sew would be a therapy, stretching the skin a little more every day. You must allow Sister Aloysius to give you some of her herb ointment. It keeps my hands soft for this work and yet I also work in the gardens.'

Kate had shaken her head at the mention of ointment. Did they not understand that she could not bear to touch her scarred skin, or to look at it more than was absolutely necessary?

'I would be happy to apply it for you, Kate.'

'No,' she said abruptly and too loudly and got up and walked away. That night a small jar of something that smelled like basil was on her supper tray. She did not touch it but it was there the next night and the next and at last she opened it. Sister Aloysius worked so hard and worried so much about Kate that she felt she owed her at least to smell it. But she could not apply it; she simply could not touch her burned and scarred skin.

While Kate was trying to screw the lid back on the door opened and Sister Mary Magdalene came in without apologising. As if it were the most natural thing in the world she took the jar from Kate's unresisting hands and sat down.

'Aloysius is convinced that had you been given her ointment in hospital your skin would be much more flexible.' She was holding one of Kate's hideously burned, and, now, trembling hands. 'Calmly, Kate,' she said quietly. 'See how good it feels and all from natural ingredients, basil, maybe lavender; I don't know. Somewhere dear Aloysius has written all her recipes.'

She finished one hand and gently took the other one and, talking quietly all the while, began to work the pale green ointment into the taut and puckered skin. Gradually the tenseness left Kate's

39

shoulders and she relaxed and the soft voice with its pleasant French accent went on and on.

'*Voilà,* much better I think; you need to use your hands more, Kate; the muscles are so out of practice. I will come tomorrow after Mass and you will think about convincing these fingers that they can be useful.'

Kate could say nothing but sat still for some time after the nun had left. As always a space seemed darker after she had left it. At last Kate sighed, stretched and stood up. She looked at her hands; there was no difference in their ugliness but they did feel better, softer, more flexible. 'Only for a moment,' she said into the stillness. 'They will still be ugly and deformed tomorrow.'

And they were, but once again the nun treated them, and in the evening too, and a few days later in the garden she gave Kate a small piece of fabric with 'Kate' drawn on it in blue ink. With it was a fairly large needle and thick thread. 'Did you do cross-stitch in school, Kate? Usually little girls are taught some embroidery stitches and this one – see, how very easy.'

She did not seem to mind that her patient could not talk, could not say thank you, could only sit there, perhaps in misery, perhaps in anger; it was difficult to tell because, as usual, her hair hid her face. She did take the material though, and after sitting in the sun while the nun sewed quietly beside her, she did attempt to pick up the needle. What effort was required. It hurt but she had decided that she would do it and so she persevered while her poor burned skin protested that it could not move itself in this or that direction and her fingers screamed silently. At last her thumb and forefinger held the needle and a shout of laughter disturbed the quiet of the garden. 'I've got it,' said Kate exultantly. 'Pity it's upside down.'

Sister Mary Magdalene took the needle and turned it the right way and she guided the hand to the beginning of the letter K.

Kate looked at the beautiful hand clasping hers. Not even Hugh had been allowed to touch her hands. 'My hands never were as finely shaped as yours, Sister. Is Aloysius's ointment capable of miracles, for we'll need one if I'm ever to set a stitch in your altar cloth?'

'The shape is nothing; for a ballet dancer maybe,' she added with a smile. 'You'll sew if you put your mind to it.'

Kate sighed and let the needle drop; the effort of holding it was just too much. 'I talked with my hands once, Sister.'

'They say you were a wonderful actress, and you can be again.'

Kate laughed. It was not a pretty sound as her joyous shout had been. 'Who would hire an actress who looks like me?'

'You have a few scars, no more.'

'Great dramatists haven't written too many parts for leading actresses who would frighten the horses,' Kate answered wryly. 'Even the wicked Lady Macbeth in the Scottish play has to ooze sex appeal or why would Macbeth do the terrible things he does? Besides, my ticket value nowadays would be, "Come and see Katherine Buchan, the woman who murdered her lover, the greatest actor of the twentieth century," or perhaps, "Come see Katherine Buchan, the actress who spent years in a secure psychiatric unit."'

The nun finished the stitch she was setting and snipped off the gold thread, very close to the cloth. She looked at Kate and smiled. 'You cannot possibly believe that you murdered anyone, my dear.' She stood up and held out the cloth. 'Look, see how I too talk with my hands.' She made no comment about the tears slipping down Kate's cheeks. 'This evening Sister Aloysius will massage your hands and soon you will hold that needle and you will help me. We will talk with our hands together.'

She turned and walked away just as the bell began to ring and Kate sat on, crying quietly. The nun did not believe her guilty of murder.

'She believes in me. Hugh believes. And what do I believe? I can't remember how I felt that night. The dream tells me I was deeply in love and deeply loved, but Bryn is dead. Someone struck him and set the house on fire and we were alone. Did I go mad?'

She shook her head as if to shake away the question. She did not want to ask it because she did not want it to be answered and she did not want to think. Oblivion; she wanted oblivion. The rough piece of material still sat in her lap with its single solitary stitch. Wincing with pain she forced her misshapen hands to pick up the needle but she could not insert the point into the cloth. She dropped it on to her lap and then steadied the hand that still held

41

the needle and guided it to the top of the letter K. In. 'I have made an X; I have begun to work cross-stitch.' But now the needle was through the material and on the other side. She gritted her teeth and turned over the material. 'Damn, double damn, how do I finish off the bloody thing?'

It was a beginning and it took weeks of toil and tears to coax her almost petrified hands into some small flexibility but she forced herself to try. The effort required made it impossible to think of anything but the task in hand, but eventually she finished her cross-stitch and tentatively tried to set some stitches in Sister Mary Magdalene's exquisite work.

'I can't; it's ghastly. Look, they're all over the place.'

'And so today I will remove the worst of them, Kate,' said the nun calmly, 'and each day, you will see, I will remove fewer and fewer, and *le bon Dieu* will love the cloth more because your pain is in it.'

She was right and Kate persevered even though the relief of thinking of nothing but stitches was paid for by the worsening night-mares. She was glad that her room was so far from the sisters' cells; she would not have wanted to disturb their rest.

She spent an hour every day of that year working on the cloth. Sister Mary Magdalene was the most restful person she had ever been with. They rarely spoke but they worked together in harmony, Kate eventually setting tiny almost perfectly matched stitches on the background and Sister Mary Magdalene creating exquisite flowers and stars. At Christmas Kate found a small soft packet on her breakfast tray between the plate with the croissant fresh from Sister Aloysius's oven and the jar of her *miel de lavande*.

Her first feeling was of embarrassment; the packet was obviously a gift and she had bought no gifts for anyone in the house. She picked up the tissue-wrapped packet and a card slipped out.

You are ready to try, ma chère Kate.

Inside was a small piece of fabric left over from the altar cloth and some lengths of embroidery threads wrapped around pieces of card; some were jewel bright, some were pale, and one was Japanese gold. Kate gasped. Never had she dreamed of working in gold. She had taken each day as it came, enjoying the work and the association with the nun, feeling better inside herself as the glorious cloth took shape. She was a part of it, a small but very necessary part, and it was good to have a share in such a creation, but that one day she might be good enough to do more than background had never occurred to her. She held the threads to her heart and a tear slipped slowly down her scarred cheek. She wept with happiness, for receiving the gift showed her, as the words of all the doctors did not, that she was recovering. She had no gift for the nun or for Sister Aloysius who tried so hard to tempt her appetite and, until the moment of opening the little packet and looking at the gift, she realized that she had thought of no one but herself for a very long time. Even Hugh, dear, kind Hugh who visited her as often as he could, had been taken completely for granted.

She left the table and her cooling coffee and went to the drawer where she had put the parcels that had been sent to her from Hugh and Simon. Childish behaviour, keeping gifts till Christmas morning but surely there would be something in one of them that would do.

Hugh had sent her a magnificent caftan in blue satin. Sister Mary Magdalene would enjoy seeing the lovely embroidery but Kate could not picture her wearing it. There was also a very generous packet of Scottish smoked salmon: Katherine Buchan had loved smoked salmon washed down with champagne but Kate Buchanan had simpler tastes. Would the sisters appreciate a little taste of Scotland with their Christmas lunch? She could give that to Sister Aloysius. Simon and Rae Whittaker had sent fragrant hand-milled soap, another luxury that Katherine had appreciated. Would Mary Magdalene be allowed to use something so frivolous? And what of Hugh? He would neither appreciate the soap nor the return of his caftan; the second parcel also contained a new novel called *The Human Factor,* but the title was intriguing and, selfishly, she wanted to read that herself.

Then she had a lovely idea and when the two gifts were wrapped and labelled for the nuns and her croissant with honey eaten, Kate sat down at her desk. She put the fabric and the threads into a drawer and took out a sheet of paper. Trying to remember every-thing that she had seen Sister Mary Magdalene do, she carefully and painfully drew the letter H. It was neither so generous nor so flamboyant as she had envisaged it, but it was a start.

Kate looked down at her hands; the threads were still tangled. She looked at her watch and frowned at the passage of time. She had been sitting for hours doing absolutely nothing. Was reliving memories nothing? At least they were happy memories; without Hugh she would not have met Sister Mary Magdalene and without the nun she would not have found this wonderful source of creativity.

'And, face it, Kate, source of income.'

For Sister Mary Magdalene had taught her well and for almost three years she had been greatly in demand as a restorer or a designer. But goldwork was time-consuming and expensive. Kate calculated her profits from her last two commissions: very good but not enough to live on. She frowned. How did I afford the renovation? And all those years living in La Prieuré? Did I save well when I was working? I seem to remember spending as quickly as earning. Hugh was always in charge of my money. I have never once asked if I can afford to live. Who paid for everything? Hugh? He will not tell me if I ask him. She remembered tentative questions about expenses brushed aside. *Don't worry, Kate. Your investments are healthy.* And she remembered thinking that it was nice that something was healthy. Rebirth is not only painful but frightening. For years Kate had behaved like an automaton. Only with Sister Mary Magdalene had she been herself, had she been interested in creating, in learning, two facets of her life which had been vitally important till . . . that night. She would not think any more, not tonight, perhaps tomorrow.

Bed. I should go to bed. But she was strangely awake. Too much reliving the past, perhaps. She put on her cloak, an impractical garment, since it allowed the wind to invade. 'I should tie a belt around it so that I don't take off like a balloon.' But she did not and she smiled wryly because she found it interesting that she was still aware or, at least, concerned about the hang of a garment. 'Somewhere I must have a warm coat,' she told herself as she shivered in the wind.

Would the monk be there? Surely not at this time. She had seen him in the distance several times, his white tennis shoes looking so odd under his gown. She would ask him. Me, Kate, initiate a conversation and with a monk? Why not? He must have made vows to keep secrets. No, only the confessional was sacred, but she would tell him nothing anyway. Perhaps he would not speak to her, apart from the civility of a polite greeting. He was a monk after all. Did they not take vows of silence? What vows had he taken? Chastity. Poor Benedict. Do you know what you have missed?

Her last remark made her ashamed of herself even though she had spoken only to herself. Flippant, Kate, you always were too flippant. Or was Katherine the flippant one? Stupid. I am Kate. I am Katherine.

She was so busy castigating herself for her impertinence that she almost bumped into the tall dark figure.

'Good evening, friend Kate, or should it be good morning?'

'Friend Benedict, and friend Thane.' She was surprised at how pleased she was to see him. Was it because he was no threat? Stop thinking, Kate.

'I was thinking about you,' she said. 'I mean, I was thinking about your shoes.'

Benedict laughed. 'Sandals are impractical for the beach,' he explained as he too looked down at his incongruous footwear. 'But if it makes you happier I admit to wearing sandals at home.'

They looked from his shoes to each other and this time Kate laughed too. 'We must both look ridiculous.'

'No, merely alike, Kate, two fairly tall, rather emaciated hooded figures.'

He frowned and Kate realised that she was looking directly into his face. He had seen her scar; he had seen her face, but he was a monk, a man of God so it did not matter, did it?

She turned abruptly and walked away calling, 'Goodbye, friend Benedict,' as she hurried away from the beach to the safety and seclusion of her house.

4

She dreamed of Provence. Perhaps it was because she had been thinking so much about Sister Mary Magdalene and her embroidery but, in her dream, she found herself, perfectly happy, running through a field of sunflowers and she realised that she was twelve years old because some of the sunflowers were bigger than she was. They were all bigger than Hugh who puffed along behind her slender flying figure like one of the dumpy little pleasure boats in the harbour that sometimes followed in the wake of the sleek yachts.

'Kate,' she could hear him calling and she knew she should stop but she loved this headlong rush. She was running for the joy of running, for the feel of the wind in her hair, the softness of the bright golden petals as she touched them in passing. She was going nowhere, reaching nothing. She was supremely content. But she could not stay happy if Hugh were miserable. Poor Hugh; perhaps he would shoot up like his uncles when he went off to school. She stopped and jogged back towards him.

'Darling old Hugh,' she said when she met him. 'You don't have to keep up with me, you know. I will always come back.' She threw her arms around him and he pushed her off indignantly and so she threw her arms out as if to embrace the world or at least the sunflower field. 'I'm sorry, Hugh. It's just that sometimes I have to run and run. Look, let's go back to the villa and we'll ask Tante to drive us into Fréjus and I shall treat everyone to an ice.'

He sighed in exasperation. 'Mummy never eats ice cream and besides she's playing bridge this afternoon.'

'I think I run here like a mad March hare because I'm so happy that Tante lets me visit.'

He wiped his red perspiring face and neck with a rather grubby handkerchief. Kate was not sweating and looked pale and cool. Her blouse, he noticed in some embarrassment, was slightly damp and therefore sticking to her. He turned away. 'You do love a good drama. Why shouldn't she let you visit? She likes you.'

'Isn't that nice? Not every ex-stepmother would want evidence of a dreadful mistake around and that's what I must be.'

'No, Kate, your father was the dreadful mistake and she's forgotten all about him.' He sighed. His mother forgot very quickly the men she loved and then abandoned – or who abandoned her.

'I shall be just like her when I grow up, except three months is hardly long enough to count as a marriage; much better to live in sin until you're sure.' If she had hoped to provoke him she failed. She shrugged. 'Come on, I'm starving and I can't remember where we left our bicycles. Everything looks the same from here; just huge plants everywhere.'

Hugh smiled. Something he could do better. Unerringly he led her back through the field to the road while she pretended that all the time she knew the way.

'Which do you love most, Hugh, the sunflowers, the lavender, or the mimosa, or the beach at St Raphaël or, no, the harbour at Fréjus?'

'The mountains,' he answered without hesitation. 'I wish we had a house among *les villages perchés*. Then I could climb up the hill and stand and look out over the Mediterranean.'

Kate looked off into the distance to where the mountains soared above the sea and thought of the villages that seemed to cling to their impossible sides. 'Yes, I like the mountains, but no, a field of giant sunflowers is my favourite . . . or no, perhaps mimosa. Yes, mimosa, I think, probably because I don't see it in bloom very often. Or,' and she was still arguing with herself when she woke up, but she was calm and rested.

She spent most of the day on her goldwork. She was repairing a hanging that had been sent to her from a stately home in Ireland. It would be good to get it finished because although she loved to see the life return to old hangings, to sit sewing while she thought of the woman or women who had created the masterpiece originally, she preferred to create her own designs. She liked to fashion small pieces of exquisite delicate beauty. She was paid handsomely for every stitch but she paid for them too in pain. Not that the pain was so intense now; partly she was used to it, but mainly it was because of the nightly nourishing with Sister Aloysius's herbal ointment.

She forgot to eat until pangs of a different kind reminded her. On the way to the kitchen she looked out of the windows towards the sea and saw that the afternoon was beautiful. An Indian summer afternoon: perfect for a visit to the crusader's tomb. She was quite excited as she assembled her simple but perfect picnic: bread, cheese and an apple; an English apple, so much tastier than a French one, and a small battle of water. Still no figs; she had forgotten to ask if they were available. Aware of a heartier appetite than usual, and absurdly grateful for it, she added two slices of sausage bought from Maggie's delicatessen counter. She put on her dark green cloak, but did not put up the hood. Carefully she arranged her hair so that it fell forward. For the first time she was conscious of the amount of grey among the brown and she remembered an image of her in hospital with no hair on that side at all.

'Count your blessings, Kate,' she scolded herself, 'and if you feel so badly, you can dye it.' That thought made her laugh, conjuring up, as it did, visions of startlingly coiffed ladies of indeterminate age pretending to be happy on the white beaches of the Mediterranean.

'You'll stay as God made you,' she began but that produced a memory of what fire had created and she hurried out, locking the door behind her. She looked towards the beach but no tall thin figure walked the beach and no great grey dog rooted among the shells. What do monks do during the day? Pray a lot, perhaps; carve little birds; work in herb gardens. They could not be so different from nuns, could they, and therefore some would be responsible for the messy, dirty jobs that made life easier for others – scrubbing floors, cleaning toilets.

'I clean toilets, and scrub floors, at least mop over, and I love it, love it. I must have done domestic things before.'

If your horde of admirers could see you now, my Kate.'

She was on her knees in the kitchen with a bucket of hot soapy water and a brush that she was wielding vigorously.

'They'd be proud of me.' *She laughed up into his wicked dancing eyes.* 'Dirt is no respecter of persons, you know.'

'Is that another of Granny's sayings?' he asked, kneeling down beside her.

Bryn, oh Bryn, I didn't kill you, did I?

She walked more quickly to outrun her thoughts and then, realising that for a middle-aged woman to be seen almost running along the street would surely lead to the kind of talk she wanted to avoid, she slowed down and calmed her breathing. Breathe.

The first term had been spent learning how to breathe. They had also tried to learn how to relax and how to mime.

Even then, so early in his career, Bryn Edgar's breath had seemed inexhaustible. Words had rolled or whispered out at will, his will. There was a rumour that he could swim underwater two lengths of an Olympic-sized pool without coming up for air. No wonder he never seemed to take breaths in the middle of speeches. But the others, even, in those early days, this newly hatched Katherine Buchan . . . She could see them, flat on their backs on the floor.

She could hear the tutor. 'The voice is not developed at seventeen. We need to ripen it and to do that we get your breathing equipment working properly. We will open the resonators – I assume you all know what a resonator is – to resonate, to reverberate, to prolong the sound. The resonators are in the throat and the chest. Let us begin. Close your eyes . . . start breathing on a vowel . . . build up . . . your limbs are limp. Totally limp. Bend your knees. Now, the neck, work your neck . . . along the spine down, down, gradually . . .'

More than once she had fallen asleep and been awakened by laughter, or, from Bryn Edgar, an unromantic kick, but the technique had come, slowly but eventually, before she lost all hope and gave up.

'Poor old Kate, you mustn't be embarrassed to make a fool of yourself and you must push yourself beyond your limit, every single time.'

That was in the early days before she had learned that she really would be good, might even be great, days before she had fallen completely under Bryn's spell. Mind you, they were all in thrall to him, the golden, the gifted one. Rose too. She had never really taken to Rose. She was too beautiful, too phenomenally elegant, too cold. She was the complete solipsist, but then they all were, her too, but to a lesser degree, and as for Bryn, he worshipped himself, or was it his talent?

If I hadn't been so fond of myself you wouldn't have died, Bryn.

But that was another thought that was too awful to contemplate. Think of the woods, of the beauty of trees in autumn, of the kindness of Maggie Thomson, of the unfailing goodness of Hugh. She tried to recall her dream: Hugh had been in it and Provence and sunflowers but now it had slipped away and all she could remember was Hugh, sunflowers and a feeling of happiness. She reached the broken five-barred gate that led into the monastery property, opened it and carefully closed it behind her. Rupert Brooke had written a poem about a broken gate once, or, no, he had likened love to a broken gate. Impossible to get back through a broken gate and impossible to get back to being the person you had been before you loved. So true, Mr Brooke.

She had no idea whether or not the monks kept cattle but Granny had taught them, all those years ago, to close gates and she did it without thinking. The path to the tomb was rocky and hard and the grass that grew between the stones was sparse. Plenty of rain so the soil must be poor – too many stones.

Does Benedict walk here in his cheap white tennis shoes? She recalled the expression on his face as he had looked at her the night before on the beach. There had been that look, had there not, a disturbing look as if he had recognised her, or was she so sensitive that she had imagined it? But if he had seen her all those years ago he could not possibly find that serene, elegant woman in the scarred, thin face that had looked back at him last night. She was perhaps twenty years older; her hair had grown back, lighter in colour than it had been and, for some strange biological reason, straight instead of curly, and now she was turning grey. And she was glad. She wanted no one from the past to console, to pry. Could he have seen her then? He was not born a monk, although he seemed as if he had sprung from the womb a brown-habited man of God, with no past. She chided herself for her arrogance, an old failing. Naturally he had a past. Perhaps he had seen her, that is, seen *her*, but *she* was dead. Kate found herself wondering if the young Benedict had liked Katherine Buchan. She hoped he had.

She had reached a clearing in a glade with a crumbling stone wall and three badly corroded stone steps up to a platform where what was left of the tomb stood. 'Arrogance again, Kate. Do you think you gave him something to remember? I hope if he saw me, he remembered, because I'm still vain, Crusader,' she answered herself. 'Benedict is a monk and supposedly above such things as prettiness in a woman.' This time her laugh was an ugly sound. 'I was never pretty like Rose but I loved being admired, looked at, courted. And now I hide the face I once wanted the world to see. Shall I show it to you? You won't mind how ugly I am.'

She pushed her hair back from the fine bones of her face and sat still, facing the tomb. Such winter sun as there was shone on both clear and puckered skin, and fine, almost undetectable, scars from many surgeries. 'That feels good, Crusader. I'm sure you saw worse, caused worse? They try to tell me I'm not ugly but I know better. It shouldn't matter to me now since *he* is dead but it does. I am vain and that is a weakness in a woman.'

Her hood still around her shoulders, Kate sat on. 'I was not vain of my looks before, Sir Knight, because, frankly my looks were nothing really to be vain about. I wasn't beautiful, not even really pretty. It was my skill, my talents, my ability that called out for acknowledgement. Rose was beautiful – on the outside anyway. She was a shell, like my home before Murdo and his men got to work on it. Sometimes, when she was on stage, I wanted to shout, "Hello, is there anyone there?" because there was no passion, no feeling, merely technique. She didn't even really love *him*. He loved her though, at first, or I thought he did and so did he, for he married her, didn't he? I said "No," and he went straight to her. What a quick temper he had. He wanted me to feel badly and I did, oh how I did. Bryn, my teacher, my friend, my love.'

She was quiet for a moment, looking back, remembering. 'They looked so fantastic together. He wasn't tall, about the same height as me although I'm rather tall for a woman, but he had the most beautiful eyes, slate-coloured, like a quarry in Cornwall; they could have been so cold but they never were, never when he looked at me. *Courage, mon ami, le diable est mort,* some phrase he had learned in a school book: it lurked in those compelling eyes. "Courage, friend, the devil is dead." But the devil was alive all the time. Rose Lamont? Rose could only be Rose, exquisite. These days one would think a computer had made her. Size? Tiny. Hair? Blonde, of course. Eyes? Blue as a summer sky but cold, cold. I saw them warm only once, warm with passion.' Rose? Rose and passion? *How could you, you slut?* She stopped but the hazy memory in her head would not clear. She could see Rose and Rose's face but it was swirling away into some fog and then it disappeared completely and she sighed.

'Don't struggle,' Simon Whittaker, the psychiatrist, had said. 'Let the memories come back in their own time.'

'I do want them to come back, Crusader, the bad as well as the good. I have to know. At least that is what I tell myself in daylight, in sunshine. It's rather different in the dark of the night.' She leaned her scarred cheek against the cold stone. 'Don't worry, I'm not looking for a miracle only for peace of mind. Rose. Beside her fragility I always felt ungainly, awkward, heavy, and I was never heavy. I had Granny's bones, like my father, I suppose, if I remember him properly, tall, thin. Tante was so fussy about diet. "Only thin women look good in absolutely anything, Kate." What a good stepmother she was. I'm so glad she never saw the trouble I got myself into. Now how did I remember that? Hugh must have told me.'

Suddenly she became aware of her voice in the stillness of the wood and she pulled the hood firmly up over her head. 'Is that why Maggie sent me here, because she knew you would make me talk? Are you a psychiatrist too, Crusader? They sit and let people talk but they charge at the end of the session. What is your price? There is always a price to pay.'

She had eaten the meat and she had been talking. Now she found herself thirsty. The water tasted good and the apple looked appealing. She smelled it. There is a world of experience in the smell of a cold crisp apple, and how satisfying was the crunch as she bit into it, feeling the juice spurt against her gums. Such a simple pleasure: a fresh apple, hunger and good teeth. 'I still have my teeth,' she said, but whether she was telling the crusader or reminding herself, she did not know. 'Damn you, Crusader,' she said aloud and threw the core of her apple as hard as she could into the wood behind his tomb.

She did not look back as she walked along the woodland path that led to the road and then she remembered that Benedict walked from the monastery to the sea and so there must be another road. She sniffed the air like a stag at bay and plunged off the road into the wood in what she hoped was the direction of the sea. Quite some time later she remembered that she had never been known for her sense of direction. Ahead of her she could see the great oak that grew near the tomb. She had walked round in a circle and was almost back where she had started.

> '"Look on thy country, look on fertile France,
> And see the cities and the towns defaced
> By wasting ruin of the cruel foe."'

Stacie Thomson ended on a gasp and started again. This time she took a deep breath, pushing out her diaphragm and trying to make sure that her shoulders stayed still. '"Look on thy country, look on fertile France, And see the cities and the towns defaced By wasting ruin of the cruel foe. As looks the mother on her lowly babe, When . . ." when what? Oh, shit, what comes next?'

'". . . death doth close his tender dying eyes, See, see the pining malady of France."' The answer, low and clear, came in a beautifully modulated voice from, no, surely not from the tomb.

Stacie turned, heart jumping, ready to take to her heels.

'Sorry. You did ask and since I knew it . . . I didn't mean to scare you.'

Someone had come out from behind the crusader's tomb and Stacie stood, anxious to run, but held by the voice. Her heart had stopped racing. After all, she knew the voice, didn't she? 'Who is it?'

'Kate. Kate Buchanan from the village. I didn't mean to intrude. This is one of my favourite places too.'

Stacie laughed weakly. 'For a moment I thought . . .' She was calm now but her heart was beginning to beat more quickly as she realised that she, Stacie Thomson, was speaking to the woman whom every single person in the village was gossiping about.

'That I was Sir Knight. And even if I had been a visitation, my dear, you can't seriously believe that he would hurt you, such a *Goodly Knight*.'

'After hundreds of years,' said Stacie, who was almost at ease, 'his personality could have changed.'

Personality changes in a lot less than a century, thought Kate, but she said nothing. She smiled in appreciation of the girl's attempt at appearing poised. She moved up from the wood and stood before the tomb. 'His bones are gone now. This is empty. It was your mother who told me. He was interred in the chapel many years ago. A shame, I think. I enjoy chatting with him. Silly, isn't it, but I feel he's listening.' Was that why the girl came here? Did she need someone to listen?

'Do you feel that way?' asked Stacie happily. 'I found him almost as soon as I was old enough to wander by myself.' She looked around. 'My dad will go spare if he finds out that I come here by myself.'

'I won't tell him; I rarely see him. You're the first person I've spoken to, face to face, for a few days. Perhaps you should bring Cromwell with you.'

Stacie shrugged. 'His name is the toughest thing about him.'

'At least he would have let you know I was there. I'll say goodbye.' And then, to her surprise, Kate heard herself offering to share the lonely walk back to the village.

They walked along the rough path that skirted the fields. Stacie looked curiously at her companion. 'You're not afraid of being alone.'

'I never think about it.' And she didn't. It was so long since she had been afraid of anything. 'I'm used to being alone, Stacie. I take it for granted that there is no one else in the wood.'

'Courting couples use it or so I've heard,' said Stacie and Kate was surprised to see the slight stain of a blush on the cheek she could see out of the corner of her eyes.

How old was the girl? Her poise and conversation was quite mature and so she was probably at least sixteen but the long straight hair made her look very young, as did the sexless jeans and sweater; face, quite plump, but good bones.

'But we scared one another when we were kids; headless knights wandering in the woods.'

'Oh, poor Sir Knight. Was he headless?'

'I don't know. I suppose if he got killed in the crusades he lost something, and if you want to terrify your horrible little brother, a headless ghost is as good as anything.'

They walked in companionable silence for a while and then Stacie asked one of the questions for which Kate had been psyching herself up. 'You were able to finish the lines. I suppose you learned it at school too or was it . . . ?' As soon as the words popped out Stacie blushed scarlet with embarrassment and stopped talking. What a dumb thing to say. Now the woman would know that she was the prime subject of conversation in the village.

Kate noted the embarrassment. Poor kid. Of course I know they're talking about me. She could tell the truth. It was easy. 'I really don't remember where I first learned it, Stacie. It's rather like "The quality of mercy" speech, comes almost it seems with mother's milk.'

'Not my mother's,' said Stacie and the tone was sad and angry at the same time.

Don't get involved, don't get involved. The warning calls were in her head as she heard herself asking, 'Maggie doesn't like Shakespeare?'

'I think she prefers Alan Ayckbourn, but it's not that,' began Stacie. 'She's been to the theatre, she watches plays on television but she won't help me. Dad says only loose women go on the stage and he wants me to be a teacher. I'll be the first person in my family ever to go to university, but I'm trying for the part of Joan in the school drama club's end of the year production, and I thought if I was marvellous, good that is, they might change their minds.'

Kate was still dealing with the news that only loose women go on the stage. 'How many actresses does your father know?'

'None. I keep telling him but it's the way he was raised, Miss Buchanan.'

'What does he think of your taking part in a school play?'

Stacie almost shrieked. 'He doesn't know. I haven't told him. You mustn't tell him, not yet. I'm not ready.'

Why in the name of God didn't I stick to the beach? Kate stopped and turned to face the girl. She was glad that the rapidly decreasing light meant that Stacie could not see her too clearly. *How could you, how could you, you're my best friend and he's my husband, my husband, you bitch, you slut.* The words from the past bludgeoned her. 'Stacie, you have to tell your parents. It's not exactly something you can hide from them.'

'If I get the part. My parents know I'm in the drama group; there isn't a major problem about that; my dad wants me to learn to speak nicely, sort of like you, maybe. It's not as if I had to learn the whole part. We're only doing scenes from some Shakespeare plays. This bit from *Henry VI, Part 1* between Joan and the Duke of Burgundy, something from *A Midsummer Night's Dream*, the balcony scene from *Romeo and Juliet*, maybe. Joan's speech is the best, the most dramatic, and Craig's going to audition for Burgundy.'

Did she know how her voice changed when she said Craig, how her face changed, losing its angry tenseness and becoming softer? Kate remembered a girl, older than this girl, who had spent hours practising saying Bryn.

'There will be extra work after Christmas, rehearsals and such and my exams are next term, and that's the difficulty. If my work, academic work, falls behind, then – kaput – it will all be over. You have no idea how hard it is to do everything, but I'll manage. I will.'

'It will be easier if they know, and being in a school production doesn't mean you have sold your soul to the devil. Tell them. Now, I must go.' She left the girl and, trying hard not to run, began to head for Sea Green and the haven of her home where she could hide from Stacie and her problems and from the voices that had been with her today. Or could she?

'Goodnight, Miss Buchanan.' The voice was small and cowed, the voice of a child.

Kate stopped but did not turn round. 'The wood isn't a sensible place to do your homework; it's much too late in the year, unless someone else, Craig perhaps, is with you. My walled garden has a gate. It's private there.'

She did not wait for an answer and did not see the joy that transfigured the girl's rather plain face. Already she was more than annoyed. Stupid, stupid, acting instead of thinking as always. What would it take to teach her? God in heaven, when did I last speak to a child, a young woman? A plumpish, rather sullen-looking child taking over her garden. She was different when she thought of Craig . . . rather a good voice. Abysmal breath control. She had taken breaths, hadn't yet learned that breath was a gift; it came, it did not have to be taken, but she was young, she could learn. An embryo Sarah Bernhardt? Not likely, but, you never knew, you never could tell what might be lurking under the covers if you didn't encourage, motivate.

How subtle she is . . . able to convey the deepest feeling with the minimal means of expression . . . and her body language, my dears, so cleverly controlled.

Another voice from another time.

'Oh, God, I should have stayed where it was safe, safe.'

Kate had reached Abbots House and let herself in quickly. Stacie watched her and tried to get her rapidly beating heart to slow down. It was her; it was. All the rumours were true. Mum's new customer had to be the woman who had murdered her lover and tried to commit suicide and that woman had been an actress, a real actress. It was the most fabulous, exciting . . . Miss Buchanan had not just spoken the words; she had acted them. Damn, the library had closed because of council cutbacks but perhaps it wouldn't have had old newspapers or microfiche anyway. Maybe she could take a bus into Edinburgh. The newspapers would be there with all the details. If Miss Buchanan was the murderess then she had probably played St Joan. There would be reviews and possibly pictures.

Stacie hugged herself hard to keep herself from dancing for joy. Miss Buchanan was a nice woman; her reaction to Stacie's silly question about learning lines showed that. She stopped abruptly, the most wonderful, amazing thought having flown unheralded into her head. What if Miss Buchanan would coach her? Oh, she could hardly hold her excitement. With expert coaching she would surely get the part and she and Craig would have to spend a lot of time together. Dad could hardly go on with his 'It's not suitable.' If only Craig's house was not quite so far out of the village: she could go there now and tell him the news. He would be thrilled at the prospect of meeting a real actress. Stacie sighed and walked more rapidly towards her home. She was going to have enough trouble explaining where she had been tonight.

Her parents were both in the living room and both were pretending to be engrossed in a television programme. Jim switched it off and Maggie stood up and faced her daughter. 'We didn't wait tea for you, young lady, and Cameron did your turn at the dishes.'

'I'll do them for him tomorrow night.' She leaned over and kissed the top of her father's head. 'Sorry, I'm late, Dad, but some of us stayed late at school and then went to the café for a cup of tea.'

'Your mother has tea, biscuits, scones even.'

'Oh, Daddy, I know we're always welcome here but sometimes it's nice to be on our own.'

Maggie leaned over and took the television control from her husband. 'Makes you feel all grown up, sitting in a café. We did it too, James Thomson.' She switched the set back on. 'Go and get your tea, Stacie, and then get to your homework.'

Stacie looked at her parents already turned away from her and seemingly engrossed in the picture in front of them. She read the body language. She was in disgrace, not serious, just enough. She went out into the kitchen where she ate everything that her mother had left keeping warm in the Aga. She had gone to the café with her friend Rachel and some others and so she had not exactly lied to her parents but she had not stayed to eat and so she was very hungry. When she was finished she washed her dishes and put them away instead of merely rinsing them and putting them into the dish-washer. Then she left the kitchen and walked up the staircase with its high wall lined with safe reproductions – Monet's *Water Lilies*, Gainsborough's *Blue Boy*, Constable's *Haywain* – and went into her bedroom. She dumped her briefcase on to her desk and sat down on the bed.

'"Look on thy country, look on fertile France . . ."'

Stacie could hardly wait for school tomorrow. She had met the mystery woman and she would tell everyone. No, she could not possibly tell anyone anything. Craig; she could tell Craig. She would telephone him now. She ran downstairs. 'Mum, I want to phone a friend. Okay?'

'Since you've just spent hours with your friends,' began Maggie but Stacie was already dialling.

'You'll never guess,' she said when Craig Sinclair eventually came to the phone. 'I was in the wood near the tomb and I met that woman, you know, the odd one who's rebuilt the old house.'

'What was she doing there?'

'Out walking, I suppose, but Craig, she helped me with my lines. I got stuck on the big speech and all of a sudden this voice came from behind the tomb. Spooky.'

'I can imagine.' There was humour in his young voice. 'Stacie, you haven't told your parents.'

Stacie pulled open the door of the cupboard under the stairs and tried to ease herself and the telephone inside. 'It's easy for you,' she hissed. 'Your parents are sophisticated. Mine think a night at the pictures is a big deal.'

'Have you asked them if you can come to the Christmas party?'

Stacie hesitated for a moment. 'I'm coming.'

He sighed. They had gone over this so many times before. 'Stacie, your medieval father has got to be pulled into the twentieth century, for his own good. You're not descending into a life of crime if you attend a party at my house.'

'Your parents are customers,' said Stacie defensively.

'And your father pulls the proverbial forelock with all his customers, does he?'

'Don't be silly. Oh, Craig, it's just that he's . . . old-fashioned.'

'He's got rather a nasty mind, if you ask me.'

The earliest loyalty surfaced and Stacie slammed down the receiver. She extricated herself from the cupboard just in time to avoid her brother who erupted into the hall in his usual attention-gathering way. She stumbled past him and hurried upstairs to her room. What had she done? Meeting him and making friends had been like finding a missing piece. Should she ring him back and apologise? No, he had been rude about her father.

Stacie opened her desk drawer, lifted up the lining paper and there he was, Craig Sinclair, her ideal man, all of six foot two inches, nice broad shoulders, fair hair that flopped over his eyes in the most endearing fashion, the leading light of the school drama group, head boy, a sure thing to enter Oxford or Cambridge if he decided he would honour them with his presence, captain of the rugby team: the list went on and on. With all his advantages, Craig was nice, and he liked her, Stacie Thomson, and had invited her to a party at his parents' posh house just outside the village.

'You know that laddie is only at Priory School because his mother thinks the snobs' school he was at hadn't handled his asthma right.' Her father had tried to dampen her enthusiasm for her new friend. 'They're not like us, Stacie, and he'll drop you as soon as he goes back among his own kind.'

'Craig's not like that and, anyway, he's not going back to his old school.'

'Keep him at arm's length. The Sinclairs are good customers. I've got all the county people since they started buying from me.'

'You've got all the custom because you're the best butcher in the area, Jim,' Maggie had argued with her husband.

Stacie looked again at the photograph and, sighing, slipped it back into its hiding place. She would try to recover in the morning.

5

Maggie's shop was always busy but she was surprised to see so many customers on such a rainy day. It was, as Mrs Dixon had just said, raining stair rods, whatever that meant – very heavily, she supposed, but what had that to do with stair rods! While two people were being served those waiting stood gossiping or looking at her displays. Today, Maggie noticed, once the customer had been served she did not, as she usually did, leave the shop but rejoined the queue. She strained her ears to hear the conversation, keeping one ear on the person with whom she was dealing and the other on the waiting women. Only snatches came to her and that was extremely frustrating. She managed to stop herself becoming annoyed with one of her most frequent and loyal customers who was having difficulty making up her mind.

'No, no problem putting these slices back, Jean. Save me cutting for someone else later on.'

'It's just that Mrs Hargreaves said she's tried the garlic-flavoured and it was delicious.'

'It is,' said Maggie modestly, hand hovering over the roast ham in question, while she tried to hear what Mrs Simpson was saying. She was sure she'd heard the name Abbots House.

'Mind you, Stanley isn't too keen on garlic; he never eats Italian food, you know.'

'It's a very delicate flavour and garlic is so good for the digestion. Would you like a sample?' Yes, they were talking about Miss Buchanan.

'. . . in prison for years . . .'

'No! And now living here?'

'Beggars belief. I heard she was criminally insane. Maybe that's why they didn't hang her. Were they still hanging murderers in the seventies?'

'I would like a sample, Maggie, if it's not too much of a bother,' said a very put-upon voice.

Maggie hurried to cut the ham with its garlic-flavoured coating. 'There you are, Jean, you know it's never a bother.' She watched her customer chew. 'What do you think of that?'

Jean made a very uncomplimentary face. 'Sorry, Maggie, you've made a mistake with that one whatever Mrs Hargreaves says. I'll have the usual.'

Maggie smiled grimly and retrieved the already cut slices of plain boiled ham. 'Can I get you anything else?'

Jean veered between the quiche with roasted vegetables and her usual quiche Lorraine, and perhaps in order to make up for disliking the garlic ham, decided to forgo the Lorraine and essay out on to the dark uncharted waters of roasted vegetables.

'Wonder how long it takes Jean to dress in the morning,' said Ciss, who finished serving at the same time. 'Morning, Jen. How's Pen? What can we do for you this beautiful morning?'

'Very funny. It's pissing it down out there. Pen fancies some of those eggy things we had in the summer; the ones that are pies without pastry.' Jen, one of two single sisters who had lived in the village as long as the Thomsons had, turned to Maggie. 'What do you think about this murderer running loose in the village, Maggie? Pen says she saw her in here buying last time she was in the village.'

The old lady managed to make the word buying sound sinister and Maggie took a deep breath. 'I don't know about any murderer, Jen. Think we should all be careful about muck-raking.'

'No, Maggie,' put in one of the other women. 'The woman that did up Abbots House is the same one who lived there in the sixties.' She lowered her voice. 'Angus's father was in the police then and he says she went to prison for murdering her lover and trying to kill herself. She was in one of those psychiatric prison places.'

'If,' said Maggie, 'and I mean if Miss Buchanan is the woman you're talking about and we have no evidence to show she is, then obviously she has been released. That means she's been punished for what she did if she did anything. Now, Clarice, what can I get

62

you this morning? Ham with garlic-flavoured coating is particularly tasty, and I have some new olives. I thought of your Angus when we were tasting these; he likes a nice juicy olive, doesn't he?'

'Goodness, you are a marvel remembering what everyone likes. I'll take a quarter of the olives then, Maggie, and a small jar of your own mayonnaise.'

Maggie's rebuke had quietened the other customers and she noticed sadly that one of them left without buying anything. 'I'll have to watch my mouth, Ciss,' she said to her assistant when they were alone. 'Can't afford to alienate customers.'

'What a crowd this morning. Let's have a quick cuppa, Maggie.' Ciss went into the back shop and a few minutes later came out with two steaming mugs. 'You go and sit down, take the weight off your legs. I'll have this here in case anyone else comes.'

Maggie tried to peer out of the rain-streaked windows. 'I didn't know Miss Buchanan wandered around. Did you hear that? "She goes walking around at all hours of the day and night." Sad, if it's true.'

Ciss popped one of Maggie's new olives in her mouth. 'Oh, these are good. I'll take some home myself. I wouldn't believe a word either Pen or Jen say, Maggie. Nothing to do all day but look out of their windows.'

Maggie put her mug down and wiped the top of the glass counter almost violently: she always found cleaning a refuge. 'Look at those finger marks.' She almost tutted. 'I didn't know old Mr McNicol had been a policeman.'

'Made sergeant.'

'So someone did die in that beautiful house.'

'No one died in that house, Maggie. It's been rebuilt.' Ciss moved away with her mug just as the door opened and another customer was almost blown in and Maggie did not have time to point out that if the Misses Jen and Pen spent all day looking out of their windows then perhaps they had seen Miss Buchanan 'wandering'.

Stacie had not had the best night's sleep of her life after hanging up on Craig. She had been so excited to meet Miss Buchanan and instead of sharing the excitement with him she had fallen out with him. What if he never spoke to her again? What if he changed his mind about his party and invited Morag. Morag ogled him every minute of every day. Oh, Craig, please forgive me, please. I'll never fall out with you again. Don't be such a wimp, Stacie Thomson; he said nasty things about your father. She argued with herself for some time about women's rights and female emancipation before falling asleep.

She examined herself very closely in the mirror next morning. Were there great dark shadows under her eyes? Were her eyes dull? She dressed as carefully as she could in a regulation school uniform and, heart beating uncomfortably and a slight feeling of nausea in the pit of her stomach, set off for school. To speak to Craig she had to wait for the first break. Because it was raining she waited for him in the common room and had almost given up hope of seeing him when he arrived. His smile when he saw her made the frustrating wait worth while. Elegant; that was the word for Craig. He looked great in school uniform; his blazer seemed to sit on his shoulders so easily, as if it had been made for him. It probably had. Her stomach seemed to be doing little flip-flops as she watched him walk across the floor, stopping to say a word to one friend, to listen to a remark by another while all the time his eyes were on her. He was not angry; they were still friends.

'Sorry,' he said. 'Everyone has problems this morning.'

She smiled. Craig was the honey in a honey pot and everyone wanted a taste.

'Let's have some coffee?' He walked over to the coffee machine and she went with him.

'I'm sorry I . . .'

'I shouldn't have said . . .'

They spoke together and laughed with relief. Everything was fine.

'You first,' said Stacie.

'I was only going to say that I had no business criticising your father. I'm sorry.'

'And I was going to say that I'm sorry that I was so rude. You're quite right about Dad. He is antediluvian but I'm educating him slowly. I will ask his permission to come to your party. I've already seen a dress I like: it's quite short, sort of silver lurex with thin, thin straps.'

His eyes gleamed wickedly at her from over his coffee mug. 'Can't wait. Now tell me more about Miss Buchanan. I asked my father about the murder/suicide thing, but he was in Hong Kong at the time. He says my grandfather did write to him about one of the old listed buildings burning down but he can't remember what Granddad said. My mother isn't too thrilled, wasn't thrilled, at the idea of someone who's been in jail living in the village but Dad says that, if there is any truth to these rumours, she's paid for anything she did, if she did anything, and that she should be left alone. She's fairly reclusive, isn't she, and keeps herself to herself? Needless to say they won't be inviting her to their party.'

Stacie nodded. 'I made an awful *faux pas* but she pretended not to notice. I asked her where she learned the play; the words just slipped out and I felt awful.'

The bell rang and all the seniors gathered up their books and their blazers and, like lemmings, headed for the door, Stacie and Craig with them.

'And where did she learn them?'

'No idea. French next, but Craig . . .'

Other friends joined them at that point and so it was impossible for Stacie to tell Craig that she hoped to persuade Miss Buchanan to coach her.

How she was going to do this she had absolutely no idea, but she went through the rest of the day in a mood of utter bliss, augmented by Morag's snide comment about 'starry eyes'.

That night Father Benedict and Stacie Thomson each stayed awake thinking of Kate Buchanan.

Stacie was excited. Everything was great between her and Craig and if the odd Miss Buchanan would really allow her to rehearse in her garden it would mean that she could save valuable time and be safer and more relaxed than if she went all the way to Templehall Woods. She went over and over every word they had spoken from that first almost magical moment when the beautiful voice had seemed to issue from the tomb. 'But she was so peculiar, almost running from me, one minute so sophisticated and the next running like a . . .'

The word *loony* hovered on her lips. Cameron had called her that and that wasn't fair but she was different, not at all like Mum or any of the other women apart from, perhaps, Craig's mother. Stacie lay back against the floral Laura Ashley pillows. She had broached the question of attending the Sinclairs' party at tea and it was as she had thought. Her mother was excited and perfectly happy for her to attend and she was even prepared to go on Saturday to look at the silver party dress. Stacie could see herself in that dress. It would hang well and would cling in all the right places; it would be low enough to titillate without being vulgar; grown-up but not tarty. Stacie thought of the look that would be in Craig's eyes when he saw her in it. Then she remembered her father's reaction. He had, as usual, been filled with doom and gloom at the way the order of things was changing. He was, as Craig had suggested, in a rut.

Jim had very soft hands; he said it was because of the sausage skins. He stood in the kitchen and emphasised the points he was making by stabbing the air with his hands and Stacie watched his hands and thought how lucky he was to have such soft skin. Shall I tell him, she thought, or would that really put the tin lid on it?

'No good comes of mixing outside your class, Stacie. What good would being at a posh party – where I'll be supplying the meat, by the way – do you then?'

'It's just a party, Dad, not an audition for anything.'

'Have a party here. You have to focus yourself this year, love. You're going to be the first person ever in this family, both sides, to get a university degree; that'll move you out of the working class, Stacie. If you run after this lad and fail your exams, where will you be then?'

'I won't fail; I could do lots of extra things and still do well.' She turned imploringly to her mother. 'Besides, we're as good as the Sinclairs, aren't we, Mum? Your gran was from a posh Russian family; we'd have been rich if there hadn't been a revolution.' Stacie had been named for her great-grandmother, Eustacia Temirkanof, who had arrived in Scotland with nothing but a change of clothes, a picture in a small enamelled frame, and an encyclopaedic knowledge of Russian literature and music. 'Isn't that right, Mum? I wish she'd taught you Russian, then you could have taught me. Imagine being able to speak Russian in Friars Carse.'

'Too busy keeping her man alive after the war, love. Jim, there's no good reason for Stacie not to go to the Sinclairs' party; it'll be fun for her and maybe she'll meet other nice young people.'

Jim sat down but he was still muttering about class divisions when Stacie went to ring Craig.

'It's okay,' she said when he came to the telephone. 'I can come to the party, and I'm getting that dress; at least my mum's going to look at it.'

'Great, but I was going to ask you tomorrow, Stace, to drive into Edinburgh with me on Saturday, after rugby. We could have a burger somewhere, look up newspaper reports to see if we can find out anything about the house and the fire and Miss Buchanan, of course, and you might see a dress you like better.'

A date. This was a real date. Life, thought Stacie, could not possibly get much better. 'That would be fab, Craig. I'll ask my mum to look at the silver dress tomorrow. She can pop out of the shop; when you're the boss there isn't a problem.' No harm in reminding him that the Thomsons owned two up-market shops. Not that Craig cared but it didn't hurt, just the same.

She went back into the kitchen to be a perfect daughter. She would study all evening, making sure her father saw her. Later, when she was finally forced to go to bed, she was sure that she would fall asleep at once but she thought about the party and driving in Craig's little car to Edinburgh, and sleep evaded her. And again she went over her meeting with Miss Buchanan. I'll ask her outright. I'll just say, 'Miss Buchanan, will you hear my lines? Will you help me?' She rolled over on to her stomach and punched the pillow. I can't just ask her. She'll know that I know who she is or was or whatever, and I don't. I'm just assuming. I have to keep my mouth shut until after the trip to Edinburgh. I'll tell her I won't tell a soul, not even my parents. No one in the village will know. Her secret will be safe with me.

death doth close his tender dying eyes.
See, see the pining malady of France.

She heard again the beautiful voice; the way Miss Buchanan had said that last line was so sad that it had hurt. Stacie rolled on to her back and tried to say the lines just as she heard them in her head. Would she ever make anyone weep with her delivery? That was too depressing an exercise. Miss Buchanan is the famous Katherine Buchan; it is too obvious, and she has to help me, she has to. I bet she'll love coaching; I'll be her amanuensis – or is that too grand? But I'll bring her out of retirement and maybe she'll act again and it will be wonderful.

Father Benedict lay in his narrow bed and found himself reliving incidents from his past that he had not thought about for many years. It was the woman on the beach; her voice had struck a chord.
  'Kate.'
  One small word. Kate. Kate, Katherine, but it could not be because Katherine had died, had she not, in a fire with her lover, Bryn Edgar?
  But Kate's voice was so like the voice that used to torment his dreams; it had the same qualities, the accent, the modulation, the tone, but there was little self-assurance in it and much anger. Could he imagine it as Juliet, or Jocasta, or Electra? And she did not look like Katherine. The hair was fine and greying where Katherine's had been brown and thick and had – what did women call them? – waves. Father Ben smiled. He knew little of the artifice by which some women kept themselves looking young, but he knew he should not expect the passage of time not to have made a differ-ence. There were the scars too that Kate tried to hide. Some unimaginable horror had happened and he had seen the scars in the moonlight when Thane had frightened her and, without thinking, she had moved her head. She must feel disfigured but they were small in comparison with disfigurement that he had seen. He tried to remember her eyes but she had not looked directly at him. He was used to not being looked at directly; only the innocent looked in his eyes.

Katherine Buchan had looked directly into his eyes once when he had stood, awestruck by her vitality, in the snow, and happy to freeze while he watched her. And she had looked directly at the actors in the plays he had seen, always totally aware of the other person. How wonderful she had been, always believable. 'She became the part,' he decided. 'She was Juliet, or Viola, or Rosalind. I had come to my senses long before she did the heavies like Lady Macbeth. What a silly young ass I was.'

Since he had met Kate Buchanan on the beach, the buried memories of those people, those days, had pushed themselves to the surface and flaunted themselves again before his eyes, those eyes that had once looked with love, with longing, with admiration. Hero-worship, they called it nowadays. His father had called him 'a star-struck young fool' and he supposed now that he had been.

First came the dark stocky figure of Bryn Edgar with that un-believable voice that could charm birds from trees. The young Ben had not considered Bryn's physical beauty, had noted only that it made Hamlet, he supposed, more believable to those swooning women in the audiences, although Bryn was no blond Dane but a dark Welshman and proud of it.

Then there was Katherine, Katherine Buchan.

The director of the Edinburgh Festival had written in the papers about 'her deceptive frailness, her indomitable spirit, her obsessive sense of responsibility for the success of everything she was in, her professionalism, her intelligence; her lyrical voice'.

Miss Buchanan's voice when she spoke calmly, had, indeed lyricism and he believed he'd found echoes and shadows of the voice that had stirred his imagination? Had he loved her or had he just been one of the many flies caught in her web? Surely you cannot really love someone whom you have never actually met. He had been a stage door Johnny or perhaps he was not even as grand as that; they sent flowers and champagne, did they not? He had hung around outside theatres waiting for them to appear, just to look at her and him, and even, once in a great while, to have his cheek patted or his hand shaken. How she had smiled and sparkled and laughed at her poor trapped insects, without ever really seeing them, accepting their devotion either as her due or as something she could not control. Katherine Buchan, whose talent, he had once told his exasperated father grandly, was the yardstick by which all other actors would be judged, Katherine Buchan, who had burned to death, with her lover, in a fire.

How long ago was that? The seventies, a lifetime ago, but that was not the beginning.

The winter of 1962, that was it, the year he went up to study in London. What a time to leave the comforts of home. It was the coldest winter on record and he went home for Christmas and came back from playing with his young cousins in snowdrifts, fifteen, even twenty feet deep, to find the Thames freezing over in places. January was the coldest since 1814 and he had huddled in his digs trying to make sense of first-year physics. How long ago physics was. He racked his memory bank, and out they came, determinants and matrices, integrating by parts, and differential equations – or had that come later? No matter, it was all as nothing now. He remembered that he had got up, wrapped the university scarf of which he was so inordinately proud several times around his neck, and gone out to warm up by walking. He had trudged all the way into the West End and he'd seen them, three of them, three glorious creatures from another planet, going into a restaurant. The women wore floor-length fur coats and their hands sparkled with diamonds as they lifted their skirts out of the snow and slush. The man walked between them, shepherding them across the pavement and they laughed at him and at each other, and it was then that he had recognised them, Bryn Edgar and Katherine Buchan, the glorious new stars of the theatre, and Rose Lamont, Hollywood's new darling.

Miss Buchan had seen him gazing, had lifted her bejewelled right hand and blown him a kiss and then she had turned back, moving herself even closer to Bryn and they had all disappeared into the restaurant, laughing, already forgetting him. No doubt she had erased the memory completely from her mind; it meant nothing to her but, for a long time, it had meant everything to him.

Father Benjamin smiled wryly at the memory of his young self. He had haunted the theatre where they were playing; waiting outside in dreadful conditions just in the hope that he would see them. He had saved every penny to buy seats in the gods, becoming an authority on Ibsen and Shakespeare and even Oscar Wilde when his parents hoped he was becoming an authority on nuclear physics. He read every review he could find, every interview.

Edgar [said one famous critic] is to look and wonder at. There is technique, yes, unsurpassed, but it's the warmth he projects that is communicated to the audience. And listen to the voice. It's got to be something in Welsh water or the honey their bees produce; that voice can lull babies to sleep or slice through steel, make virgins pray to be allowed to surrender, and thank God he has decided not to prostitute himself by going to Hollywood. He is an actor; nothing matters to him but the play.

Obvious that life outside the theatre mattered though, for he had married Rose who had been lured away by Hollywood and he had died in a fire with Katherine Buchan. He was unsure of the exact date. After his own Saul on the road to Damascus conversion there had been the years in the seminary in Paris, then his beloved Ireland, a mission in the Philippines, and after the Philippines, Palencia in Spain. Where had he read about Katherine's death? He could not remember. But she was here now and her spirit was troubled. She had not recognised him. Why should she? He would help her if he could.

Father Benedict prayed for the repose of the soul of Bryn Edgar and he prayed for the woman who called herself Kate Buchanan. At last he rose, tired and stiff, and slipped back into bed to sleep like a log for the few hours that remained of the night.

6

Miss Galbraith was talking.

'I want you all to take these next few weeks very seriously. You're in training like athletes readying themselves for the big race. Some of you have already chosen your favourite part, but it's not going to be enough for you to study that part. Romeo, for instance. Perhaps all the boys will want to play that young man.'

There was a snort of laughter from a group of boys in a corner of the room and Miss Galbraith rounded on them. 'Right, you lot. Let's get one thing straight right now. Take this seriously or get out. If you feel you can't make a stab at Romeo—'

That got another laugh that interrupted her but she had the grace to laugh at herself: 'A wee Freudian slip there, but I mean it, boys, if you feel you can't attempt to act Romeo, then you're in the wrong after-school club. And girls, we can't all be the beautiful heroine; someone has to be the nurse, and I don't want tantrums. Some of the greatest actresses of all times have been cast as Juliet's nurse; it's a good part. Bottom, as I'm sure you all know, is a biggie, even though whoever plays him will have a mask on most of the evening and his mum won't see his face. Craig, are you looking at Bottom?'

Another snort and Craig coloured. 'I haven't started reading *A Midsummer Night's Dream* yet, Miss Galbraith.'

'Get to it. Now, exercise. Let's do our warm-ups. We'll do bobbing and circling this evening, and no clobbering anyone with the swings. Charlie, you hit anyone and you're out'

The class, chastened, stood in lines and went through two of the exercises recommended by their teacher.

Daft, thought Stacie as she stood legs apart, trunk and arms hanging down from the waist and bobbing gently trying to reach the floor. Out of the corner of her eye she saw Peggy touching the floor with the palm of her hand and hoped Craig had not noticed how supple the blonde girl was. *I think we should be working on voice, not exercise; I'll bet Miss Buchanan never had to do silly exercises as if it was a gym class.*

She had little time to do any other thinking as the class progressed. They were to read all three plays and familiarise themselves with the selected pieces; auditions would be held at the first class after the Christmas holidays.

'For now,' explained the drama teacher, 'we are all going to read through everything and we'll start next Tuesday with *A Midsummer Night's Dream*.'

'Dad's picking me up on the main road, Stacie. I'll walk down a bit with you.'

Oh, the joy of being chosen in front of everyone. They walked slowly out of the school, across the car park and on to the road that led down to the village.

'Still on for Saturday, Stacie?'

'Yes.'

'Great.' He smiled and her heart turned over. *So clichéd*, she decided, *but it did, it had. It felt wonderful.*

'Rugby is off so we could go up first thing in the morning and do you mind if we take the bus? Parking can be a nightmare in Edinburgh.'

No need to tell him she was prepared to walk. 'The bus will be fun.'

'Great.' He smiled. 'Let's meet at the bus stop at the top of the road. Then we can have coffee somewhere and go to the main library. I think it's on George IV Bridge; I know where it is but not sure about the name of the street. There are lots of fab little delis and we can have lunch and then maybe you'd like to see a film or go to an art gallery or something like that.'

'Sounds great.'

He took her hand and pulled her to a standstill. Around them a streetlight threw a yellow glow. 'I think you're great, Stacie. I like girls who are clever and sporty and feminine all at the same time.'

'Thank you.' *She was not good at sports but if he thought she was she would certainly try.* 'I think you're great too.' *Oh, God, did girls say things like that?*

She moved forward quickly, out of the misty but unflattering light.

'Stace.'

She stopped and turned and they stood face to face. Stacie was looking down as if admiring the shine on Craig's rather nice black brogues and he laughed a little and, putting one hand firmly under her chin, lifted her face up – and kissed her. It was so soft, so light, so quick that she was unsure that it had ever happened. 'I wanted to do that when your poor little face fell when she asked me to read Bottom. Your face is so expressive, Stacie. You'll make a great actress.'

'Perhaps I'd be better if my face didn't show everything.'

'Then I might not have plucked up the courage to kiss you.' He bent down and kissed her again and this time there was no doubt. His lips were soft and cool on hers. 'See you tomorrow. I'd better go; I think that's Dad.'

He started to jog along the road that led out of the village and Stacie stood for a moment. 'See you tomorrow,' she whispered and drifted like a leaf trapped by a playful breeze down the hill towards her home. To her parents' amusement and some annoyance she drifted through the next two days in the same fashion. She had not told them that she had been kissed but Maggie knew that something momentous had happened and tried to protect her daydreaming daughter from her brother's teasing.

On Saturday morning Stacie dressed extremely carefully. She wore her imitation leather trousers and a voluminous red sweater hand-knitted by Maggie. Over that she pulled her dark blue cagoule. To Maggie's chagrin she was unable to eat any breakfast but allowed herself to drink a cup of tea.

'I'm having coffee as soon as we get to Edinburgh, Mum.'

Stacie tried to avoid her brother but he insisted on walking up the road to the bus stop with her. 'I have to see what his intentions are,' he insisted.

'I'll kill you if you embarrass me and Dad'll kill you when I get home and tell him.'

'Can't kill me twice.'

Stacie said no more and managed not to hurry; she could not get away from him and would have to try to pretend that she cared little whether he was there or not. In the end it made no difference. The bus came and went but Craig never appeared.

Cameron hooted with laughter. 'You've been stood up, Stacie.'

Stacie stood at the bus stop and tried to look nonchalant. So, they had missed the first bus. Craig had slept in. There would be another bus. Cameron waited with her but after twenty minutes or so his teasing turned to anger. 'Posh bastard has dumped you, Stacie. He's not coming. Please, Stace, come on home. You're too special to wait for any boy; all the guys in my classes think you're great.'

It was meant to cheer and Stacie knew that it had been hard for her younger brother to make himself say nice things about her; he much preferred to tease. But she refused to move. Craig would never be so cruel. He liked her. He had kissed her twice, and she had kissed him back the second time. They had held hands between classes for the past two days. Her friends were envious. It had all been wonderful. 'I've got the wrong bus stop. It's got to be the one closer to his house. I bet he thought Dad would drop me off on the way to the shop. God, Cameron, how silly can you get?' She walked, almost ran out of the village along the road towards the open country. Her stomach felt full of fire and ice and her heart seemed suddenly to be so heavy. He would not; she just knew. He was incapable of such deliberate cruelty. Somehow she, Stacie, had made a mistake.

He was not at the bus stop and another bus, headed for Edinburgh, came and left without them. Stacie stood and the misery inside her grew and grew until it threatened to choke her. He was not coming.

'Of course, something's happened and he's phoned the house. What an idiot. There will be a message.'

But there was no message.

Stacie crept upstairs and locked herself in her room. She refused to come out when Maggie, summoned by Cameron, left her shop on the busiest day of the week and hurried home to see her daughter.

'Stacie, love, open the door.'

Stacie said nothing.

'Did you phone his house, pet? Maybe something's happened.' Maggie stood, her face against the closed door, and listened to the sound of her daughter breathing. 'Do you want me to ring them, pet?'

'No. Yes. No.' Stacie burst into tears again.

'Stacie. I am going downstairs to telephone Mrs Sinclair.'

Stacie shot from the bed and ran to the door. 'No, you can't do that. I'm not a child.'

'Then stop acting like one and ring his house. Either they're dorks and you're better off without him or something has happened.'

Stacie rubbed her lovely red sleeve across her face and walked downstairs to the telephone. 'I'd prefer you didn't listen,' she said in as dignified a way as she could.

'I've no intention of listening,' said Maggie while she stood as close to the top of the stairs as she could without being seen. She heard her daughter dialling.

'May I speak to Craig, please?' Silence. 'Then may I speak to Mrs Sinclair?' Another silence. 'Mr Sinclair is unavailable too, I suppose.' Stacie, her voice hampered by fresh tears, put the receiver down and ran back upstairs where she locked herself in her room and no matter what Maggie said she would not open the door.

It had rained at the end of October and it had rained at the beginning of November and it was still raining in the middle of the month.

'Where, oh where is the season of mist and mellow fruitfulness?' Kate muttered as she looked out of her windows at grey skies and her rain-soaked garden. Even the trees seemed to feel rather sorry for themselves when being battered by high winds and icy rain. When she walked later she would have to take care; fallen leaves would be wet and therefore slippery. At least she had had no excuse not to work on her sewing. She judged everything she created with Sister Mary Magdalene's criteria and found her own work lacking, but this panel she was creating was quite lovely. She had turned down a valuable commission from one of her wealthy regular clients and now she realised that, since this work would be finished in a few days, there would have been time to repair the tapestry.

'Never mind,' she told herself. 'I can let Monsieur Le Duc know that I will be available before Christmas. Perhaps he hasn't sent it elsewhere.'

Conserving historical tapestries was a job that was usually only entrusted to qualified conservators and Kate, completely unqualified, was very lucky to have been a student of Sister Mary Magdalene. It was the recommendation of that once most famous of conservators that had earned Kate her first commission to this same elderly aristocrat. She did not turn him down lightly, for his sake and for her friend's.

She fastened her needle in the material and pushed it aside for a moment. There was a difference in sound outside; perhaps the wind had died down. She listened carefully and then stood up and went to the window. The rain had stopped and the wind had indeed abated in the time that she had been sitting sewing quietly but that was not the difference in sound that had alerted her. A boy was in her walled garden and he was spraying paint on the wall.

Murdress go home, in large red letters.

Kate was calm. He could not even spell. Should she open the window and tell him he had missed out the second vowel?

As that thought entered her head she felt her stomach begin to churn and hurried to the bathroom where she was quickly, violently, and neatly, sick. She held on to the lavatory seat until her legs stopped trembling and then walked slowly to the kitchen where she drank a large glass of cold water. She went back to the window. The boy was gone but his message remained.

Murdress go home.

Kate sat down beside her sewing, put her head down in her scarred hands and began quietly to cry.

Her bout of tears lasted only a few minutes: she would not be beaten by the unkindness of a boy. She refused to listen to the words in her head that whispered that the boy had merely been reacting to what he heard – in his home perhaps, in school, for he had appeared to be quite young, fifteen or sixteen perhaps. 'Old enough to know better,' Granny would have said.

Kate stood up and breathed deeply, calming her nerves, preparing herself. She found her cloak and put it on and, in order to examine the graffiti closely, she reached for the torch that sat on a little shelf beside the door, lifted her head proudly as if she were about to walk on stage in a demanding role, and went out into her walled garden. How she loved to be in it, imagining the flowers and shrubs she had planted with her own hands flourishing in their containers. Occasionally on sunny days she had sat here beside the stone statue of the little girl and read or worked on her sewing. Now it was spoiled: her sanctuary had been breached, but it was only paint and paint could be cleaned off.

Murdress go home.

She reached out and touched the bold M; it was tacky and coloured the tip of her finger.

She returned to the house, got a bucket of hot soapy water and a brush, and hurried back out to the garden where, by the light spilling from the open door, she began to scrub at the graffiti.

'Well, you have made a right royal mess,' she told herself after fifteen minutes of hard scrubbing, which seemed only to have elongated the letters and spread them over the wall which had been wet as a result of recent rain. He had not chosen the best of days to leave messages.

Whom to ask? Hugh? He would know or be able to find out how to remove spray paint but he would be upset. Simon? Least he knew about her idyllic home life the better. Where was the vast crowd that had followed every move of Katherine Buchan? All gone like the leaves from her trees here.

The monk. She could tell him, ask him: he was a monk. They kept secrets, did they not?

But he was not on the beach and although she walked for miles she did not see him, and, exhausted, she almost stumbled back to Abbots House where, after removing her cloak, she poured herself a whisky.

Let's drink up our nice warm milk.

Drink up anything you like, nursey darling. At least no one had patronised her at La Prieuré and, if she was honest, and in these days of new birth she was trying to be honest, there had only been that sole exasperating nurse who was probably loved devotedly by all her patients.

She was physically but not mentally tired and she knew from experience that if she went to bed now she would be likely to wake, sweating, from the grip of a nightmare. Tonight she did not have the strength to fight. She would sew. She lifted her embroidery frame into the light and the threads seemed alive in her hands, the colours glowing in the light from the lamps. But she could not concentrate. Fine. She would not be upset; she would write to Mary Magdalene. At least that dear friend was bound to be sound asleep in her convent bed.

   Chère Marie Mag,
   It seems to have rained for days. Perhaps the next flood is coming.

What to say next? You'll never guess – some one has spray-painted my garden wall. No, she could not tell her although nothing ever surprised Mary Magdalene. How did these women accept all human frailty so patiently? Surely in their ivory towers, surrounded by walls and bells and strong faith in and love of God, little bits of unpleasantness should shock them, but their calm eyes seemed to say, we have seen everything and we accept. We will pray.

Kate could not pray, had never been able to do so. What was prayer? Mary Magdalene said that it was 'the opening up of the heart and mind to God'. Is my heart open? My mind is but no, it's not. If it were open then I would know exactly what happened that night.

Think of something else, something nice. Bryn. Always Bryn and yet, he was not nice, was he? Neither was he perfect but then what human being is.

It was 1957. She had been a student at the Royal Academy of Dramatic Art. She had had to audition for a place. There had been set pieces but all she could remember now was that she had sight-read a ghastly piece from the Bible and had been sure that she was quite dreadful but she had passed. 'I'm sure it's how you put yourself over, Kate,' Granny had said. 'The pieces are important but they're not crucial: more important to make the right impression.' How had Granny known that or had she made it up, as she was always doing, to make her orphaned and virtually abandoned granddaughter feel better? It did not matter for she had been successful. Oh, the heady excitement of winning. Next, the audition for a scholarship: Granny could not possibly keep her for another three years and she would not ask Tante, not again. She won the scholarship and trembled as she cowered in a chair reading the letter. I must be good; I must have something. I have a scholarship. Never before or since had her spirits fluctuated so much between delight and despair. No, that was not true but she would not think of that, not now.

For now she would remember the young Kate in her new navy blue, full-skirted shirtwaister dress with its tiny white piqué Peter Pan collar; she was wearing gloves. Ladies always wear gloves, Granny had said. The building had excited and terrified her. Perhaps it was the uniformed doormen at the grandiose main entrance that led to the main staircase and the lifts, absolutely forbidden to students. How long was it before she stopped noticing the Epstein bust of Shaw, or the painting of Sarah Bernhardt, two of her idols? How long before she took it completely for granted that Kate Buchanan should run in there every morning and check in with her precious little ivorine card?

Years later in interviews Bryn used to say grandly that he had chosen RADA because he believed, with its founder, Sir Herbert Beerbohm Tree, that acting could not be taught.

'Bryn, you ponce, we all learned to act there.'

'No, Katie. It merely drew out what was already there.'

She had been aware of him from the very first class although she felt that she should have been able to think only of actually being there. Kate Buchanan at RADA, Kate Buchanan winning one of the thirty places that had been fought over by more than one thousand multi-talented, multi-national hopefuls, but he had been sitting on a desk, his chin on his hand, very like one of old Mrs Jackson-from-the-village's garden gnomes, and he had looked up when she entered the room and smiled at her. She had not smiled back, had merely looked at him while she tried to make sense of the knowledge that something fundamental had just happened. She had not fallen in love, don't be silly, she was going to be the greatest thing since Sarah Siddons and so had no time for any of that nonsense, but in her gut she knew that nothing would ever be the same. She accepted it as part and parcel of the great scheme, the script that had already been written for her.

Act 1. Persuade Granny to allow her to go on the stage.
Act 2. Get into drama school and learn EVERYTHING
Act 3. Emulate Ellen Terry, Sarah Bernhardt, Edith Evans, Margaret Rutherford and BE THE BEST.

She sat down and he came over and sat beside her. 'Hello,' he had said, 'I'm Bryn Edgar and you are . . .'

But he did not listen to her answer, for the door had opened and an elfin creature with a cap of sun-gold hair and impossibly blue eyes in a heart-shaped face had entered.

'Kate Buchanan,' she had said to his rapidly retreating back.

Rose, for it was Rose, looked around the room measuringly and then walked over and perched herself beside Kate. She had learned very early that she shone even more brightly against a plainer foil and since Rose came he came too and the three of them became inseparable, and cruelly and deliberately they allowed no one else to breach the circle of their charmed triumvirate. It was obvious from the first that they were the gilded ones: Rose with her elfin charm and great personal beauty; Kate, who was too insecure to believe that her teachers were writing notes that said, *utterly absorbed in the role, artistically discriminating, sensitive;* and Bryn, to whose baptism all the good fairies had brought priceless gifts.

From that very first meeting Kate was emotionally affected by him but she denied it, consciously deciding that he was not her type. For a start he was about the same height, usually described as average, and Kate liked men to be taller. He was untidy; his hair was a tangled, uncombed mop and his clothes were scruffy, a perfect stereotypical image of a Celtic gypsy. The men Kate knew, and there were not many, were fastidious. Mind you, she argued with herself, they had money and, as became obvious in the next few days, weeks, months, years, Bryn had not. What he did have, apart from a beautiful speaking voice and very fine slate-blue eyes, was the talent that made them all gasp, students and lecturers alike.

From his first entrance everyone knew that here was the golden one, he whom the gods loved.

His dark Celtic masculinity was a perfect foil for Rose's delicate fairness and she attached herself to him. He did not seem to mind although, if they were together in a room, he always seemed to look round, almost anxiously, seeking Kate, and he would smile when he saw her, a smile of such sweetness that it changed his entire face and made, for some unfathomable reason, her heart beat faster. She dismissed his smile and its effect on her. What she could not dismiss was the effect of his voice. She wrote to Granny and Tante.

> He has the most incredible voice. I can't describe it. It's soft and then hard, loud and then a mere hush – but all voices are like that, are they not. But this voice is . . . mellifluous, yes, that's it, even when he's just chatting, and I want just to close my eyes and listen. Of course, it's probably because I'm unfamiliar with soft Welsh accents. If all Welshmen spoke like him, there would be a hysterical invasion of mad English women. He has absolutely no finesse and kicked me in class today when I fell asleep during relaxation exercises. Wasn't hard, not really, but I can't think why I didn't take offence.

Perhaps she already understood the message in those expressive eyes.

Exercise class, mime class, history class, ballet, fencing, everything, it seemed, but actual acting. 'Breathing lessons? God in heaven, when do we eat?'

'You were saying something, Mr Edgar?'

'No, sir.'

He had a healthy appetite and not only for food.

Rose and Kate were, at first, pleased to find that they were staying in the same area, near Euston Station. It was not too far from Gower Street and so they could walk almost everywhere they needed to go. Bryn lived with an uncle in Hampstead; within a few weeks of meeting all three of them had learned the tube and bus timetables off by heart.

'Well, we might as well learn something since no one seems interested in teaching us how to act.'

'Yes, isn't it strange that all we do is breathe and relax.'

'And mime: the end of term exam is mime,' moaned Kate, who was quite sure she would fail.

But she did not, and winter passed into spring and the seasons and the years went round and they learned the history of the theatre and they learned of Greek drama and eventually they were even allowed to act and then one day they found that they were graduates.

Kate did not know when she fell asleep but she woke up hours later, stiff and sore. A bath, and then bed; she would sleep in her lovely bed with its startlingly white lace covers and its crisp linen sheets with their beautiful embroidered tops; they were Granny's sheets. She was so grateful that two pairs had been in the London flat. The others had all burned.

Don't think, Kate. Baths had once been such joyous indulgence but now she endured them and got in and out as quickly as she could. She reached for a towel to wrap around her eyes and then dropped it beside the bath. She was going to accept herself and everything that had happened.

'You need to soak,' she told herself and obediently lay back in the scented water. Her belly gleamed up at her and she shuddered at the sight of the scars. The face, she supposed, was bearable, but the body and the legs taunted her every day with their ugliness, their refusal to allow her to forget. She closed her eyes. She counted slowly to one hundred and then another thirty and could no longer bear her nakedness. No, no, she would not think of those days when she had delighted in firm young flesh.

How luscious you are, like a ripe peach. I will eat you up.

She jumped up from the water and grabbed a towel.

'No, no, no. Go away, my darling. I do not want you here.'

He would not be driven away.

Where could she go to escape from him? If she went to bed he would be there, not that he had ever slept in this bed. This was new, a virgin bed.

'How girlie, Katie. Who needs all these pillows?'

'An actress who likes to sit up in bed learning her lines.'

'Even Rose doesn't have so many pillows.'

'But then, she's not an actress, is she?'

'Oh, catty, catty. Katie the cat has claws.'

Should I have married him when he first asked me? I thought marriage would ruin my career. Well, I certainly ruined it by having an affair. 'No, Kate, that's not true. Your career was over when Bryn was . . .' She could not say the words and tried again. 'When the accident . . .' She stopped, accident, accident. 'No,' she said loudly, 'it wasn't an accident. Bryn was murdered. That is an unassailable fact and I was the only other person in the house.'

But that thought was too frightening. She pushed it away, tried to pretend that she had not thought it. She began to dry herself furiously with the towel, rub, rub, rub out those thoughts. She did not want such thoughts; they brought pain and nightmare. She wrapped herself in a long, rather masculine, blue wool dressing-gown and realised, for the first time, that she had let herself get cold. The central heating system had switched itself off long ago. Something sensible and positive to do. Walk downstairs and press the little button that would override the system.

Bryn walked at her heels.

'I should not have mentioned Rose.'

'You're damn right; at least, not in my bed you shouldn't.'

'It's your fault, Kate. It's you I love. Why didn't you stop me marrying her? She's a leech, Kate; she's sucking my blood and I can't get rid of her.'

'Well, lucky Bryn, this way you have the best of both worlds: an adoring wife and an adoring mistress; with the adoring public you should be one happy man.'

'She doesn't adore me, Kate; she likes being Mrs Bryn Edgar. The name opens doors.'

How many doors did it open after he died?

It was such a long time since she had thought of Rose, her one-time friend, her roommate for the last year in college. She had been angry when Bryn and Rose had married, but with Bryn; had she been angry with Rose? Damn it. Did it matter now?

Kate reached for the whisky bottle; she would have her one-a-night-before-bed drink. She looked up and pulled the little beaded cord that controlled the dark blue Venetian blind on the small kitchen window. What a cost such a small blind had been.

The world outside was pearly grey and a ghostly mist was floating up from the sea. It was early morning; she had slept the night away, like a drunk, on the sofa. She put the whisky bottle away and made coffee.

'Go away, loved and hated ghosts. Today I will seek refuge in my work.'

She hurried upstairs and dressed in a long grey woollen dress with a generous polo neck. Over it she put a brown floor-length cardigan which revealed her hands, but who would see them today? She would sew; she would listen to music; it would be a productive day. Hugh had bought a television set which she never turned on and a radio that he had probably set to a classical music station. Memories of the convent, sitting in the sun, listening to music floating out of windows. Or were those memories from earlier days in her beloved Provence with Tante and with Hugh? She would listen as she sewed and she would try to place her memories; there were no unhappy memories set to music. But first she would eat. Food was such a nuisance but it was a necessary nuisance and she had enjoyed it once; she remembered a café in a *village perché*, a carafe of rosé and a sandwich. *Croque monsieur?* Probably. *Bouillabaisse* in a restaurant that was no more than a beach hut and 'Chansons d'Auvergne' playing on the radio and everyone enjoying it or accepting it and not demanding that it be turned off. That was with Bryn. Of course he had had to see her favourite place, see the lavender fields stretching for miles in every direction, now that the horrors of the war were well and truly over and *la belle France* was truly beautiful and productive once more.

'I don't want to remember.' She hurried into the kitchen and switched on the radio. Something classical was playing; it was familiar but Kate was no expert and did not recognise it and, better still, it held no memories. She boiled two eggs that came out of their shells like bullets. Still, last time they were raw; she would get it right next time. She mashed one of the eggs with butter and ate it on an oatcake. The second one she dropped, with an apology to the hen who had laid it, into the bin. Then she returned to the living room and summoning up all her reserves of strength she banished everything but the panel from her mind and began to work.

Kate heard the gate and winced. It was her own fault. Perhaps the girl, if it was the girl and not the cretin who had splashed paint on the walls, would find the dark garden unwelcome and would go. Her hand went to the light switch and then withdrew. She had made the offer. Graciously she would accept the consequences.

She sat down again with her sewing. The Venetian blinds meant that no one could see into the room. She was safe. If the child in the garden peered through one of the chinks of light all that would be revealed would be light, splashes of colour, a shape in a chair. As always her face was turned from the window.

In the garden Stacie looked around and shivered in the cold. The light from the window showed her a wrought-iron chair and a table, a really beautiful statue of a little girl, and a few seemingly barren flowerbeds. She went to the window, turned her back and said, 'Miss Buchanan, if you're there, it's only me, Stacie. If you really mean it, I'll practise here, sometimes.'

Kate said nothing. She returned to her sewing but it no longer had the power to hold her. She was too aware of the girl in the garden. She went to the window and leaned against the frame. All she could hear was a low murmuring.

She went back to her chair and addressed herself to her embroidery frame. She picked up her work. How well it had gone today; soon it would be finished and would leave her. She put it down again. For a foolish moment she wished that she had a fire so that she could stand and nonchalantly throw a log into it and watch it burn. But there could not be a fireplace. She stood up. She sat down.

Damn it, damn it, damn it.

She went to the door and opened it.

Stacie was in the garden, huddled on a seat, a place where the sun would be trapped in the summer.

'You'll freeze to death, child. Not even the theatre is worth that.'

Mutely, Stacie followed her into the cottage.

'Take off your coat and I'll make some cocoa. Then you can recite your lines at me. Better, isn't it?'

Stacie, with chattering teeth, merely nodded.

Kate made cocoa, acutely aware that it was the first time in this lifetime that she had acted hostess; she was serving someone else. It felt good. It felt natural.

'Blue doesn't suit you,' she told the girl, 'not in clothes, and certainly not in face. You must learn what suits, child. Warm tones for you, I think.'

Stacie smiled and drank her cocoa. How old-fashioned but how perfect. Miss Buchanan had settled back into her chair and obviously was quite at ease. She was not prepared to play hostess any more than she had already done but yet Stacie felt that she was welcome.

'I've finished the cocoa, Miss Buchanan, and feel lots warmer. I don't want to disturb you. Will I go back outside or maybe into the kitchen?'

'No, stay for a moment and tell me about your group.'

What on earth did she want to know? 'Well, it's an after-school group and Miss Galbraith, one of the English teachers, takes it; she did drama at university and acted in some plays. She's awfully good,' added Stacie and her voice was full of hero-worship. 'She makes us do exercises to keep fit and we're all going to read the three plays she's chosen even though we're only doing bits. We are allowed to try out for the part we really, really want but we may have to be something else. I think I told you that I'd like to be Joan and Craig' – as always her heart seemed to stop beating when she thought of Craig, but she went on – 'Craig wants to be Burgundy.'

'Craig's your boyfriend?'

'Sort of. We should have had a date, a real date last Saturday but he had an asthma attack and I didn't know and it was just awful. The maid won't tell anyone anything; she just kept saying, "Mrs Sinclair is not at home." It was ghastly, waiting and wondering and thinking. It was nearly a week before I knew what had happened.'

'It'll be different when they get to know you better,' said Kate and wondered again at what she was doing. She had no idea what

Craig's parents were like; they might possibly be unspeakably rude people and here was she trying to cheer up this poor child with the unbelievably expressive face. She straightened up in her chair and turned to look at the girl aware that, in the good light from the lamp, Stacie could see the faint scars of the plastic surgery. She said nothing for a moment but gestured, forgetting for a moment that her sleeve did not conceal her hand.

Stacie obeyed the gesture and, standing up, moved away from the circle of lamplight but said nothing and Kate chivvied her. 'Well, girl, don't you want me to hear your lines?'

'Oh, Miss Buchanan,' Stacie began.

'The speech, child,' said the quiet voice.

Stacie felt herself tremble. She had wanted this and now it had come and to do well was important. Don't blow it, Stacie. Breathe. Relax. Pretend she's Mum. 'Look on thy country, look on fertile France . . .' She went through the entire speech and the listener said nothing, leaving the girl wondering. Should she say something else? Should she wait? She looked helplessly at her hostess.

Kate looked up at the girl and sighed. 'I remember a girl, not much older than you, who was overwhelmed to find herself asked to play Juliet in a cast that included Burton and Scofield. Magical, magical names. I don't know if anyone has surpassed Paul as the consummate actor, not even John . . .' She leaned forward. 'You are familiar with his work?'

'Paul Scofield? Not on the stage, Miss Buchanan, but Thomas More in the Robert Bolt play; at least, we saw the film. I saw it three times.'

'They tell me that's available on this video thing. I'd like to see that. But I digress. At the first rehearsal the girl was quite dreadful, the Juliet. The director was kind. Many of them are, Stacie. Don't fear them, respect them. He took her aside. "Passion is conveyed from the heart, not the head," he said. You must be Juliet: you must be in love. You are a young girl, not a woman. Behave like a girl." Do you understand, Stacie?'

'You're saying Joan of Arc is a young girl.'

Kate smiled. The girl was quick; that characteristic would help her. 'Frighteningly young and unsophisticated; an unlettered child pitted against the wit and wisdom of the courts of both France and England.' (Not unlike yourself, she added to herself.) 'And she faces Burgundy. The Duke of Burgundy.'

A voice came from the woman in the chair and Stacie felt a current of something like electricity run up her spine across her neck and on up into her hair. '"O, turn thy edged sword another way; Strike those that hurt, and hurt not those that help."'

'How much do you know of him, of Burgundy?' Miss Buchanan asked in her usual tones and Stacie dropped her head in shame, for she had learned only the words of her speech.

She looked up to meet her hostess's candid gaze. 'Go home, Stacie, read the whole play, read this Saint Joan, and Shaw's, and Jean Anouilh's *The Lark*. You do know who the lark was?'

Stacie nodded although she did not and was convinced that Miss Buchanan knew that she was lying, but it had to be another name for Joan of Arc.

'Study the background of the story, and when you come back we will recreate Jeanne d'Arc, Joan of Arc, the Lark, La Pucelle.'

'La Pucelle? Goodness, I do French. Is that the word for lark? No, it's not.'

'It's French for maid, young girl. The Maid of Orleans.'

Stacie stood up. She felt mortified, destroyed. Then she looked again at her hostess who was smiling gently.

'We will recreate her. You will. Trust me.' It was a lovely smile.

Stacie felt her stomach fill with butterflies, or bubbles. She felt she could float away. 'Thank you, Miss Buchanan. Goodnight, Miss Buchanan.' But the woman in the chair was no longer looking at her, no longer, she felt, interested. She found her coat and went to the door but before she opened it she stopped. She had to tell her, warn her. She could not bear for this woman to be hurt any more. 'Miss Buchanan, there's some nasty stuff written on your wall.'

'I know.'

Stacie stayed looking at the door. 'It's on the outside too, I'm afraid. I didn't know whether you'd been out today.'

Miss Buchanan said nothing and Stacie turned round. She seemed to have crumpled into a heap in her chair, her head was down, her hair falling across the scar she usually tried to hide. Stacie went to her. Tentatively she put out her hand as if to touch the bowed shoulders but instinct stopped her. This was not Maggie for whom a warm hug cured everything. 'I could get some friends to clean it off for you. Do you want to call the police? It's just silly vandalism; it's happening everywhere these days.'

'You're a kind girl, Stacie. Thank you but I'll manage.' She looked up for a moment and Stacie thought she saw the sparkle of tears. 'Your parents will be looking for you. Goodnight.'

'Goodnight, Miss Buchanan,' Stacie whispered and almost ran from the house. She was furiously angry. If she could just find out which nerd, which species of low life had painted that ghastly message she would . . . well, she didn't know what she would do but she'd do something. She almost ran home. The Thomsons' solid stone-built house was one of four on a small side street at the top of the village. Because there was another street of even taller houses between them and the sea they had no sea view but if one should come on the market it was snapped up immediately. They were attractive houses with large back gardens that ran down the hill parallel to the road, and Jim, in an unaccustomed fit of humour, had called their house No Sea View, a name that still made him laugh and which had actually caused several potential buyers to offer bids on the house; it was not for sale. The Thomsons liked the comfortable house with its four spacious bedrooms. They had put two new bathrooms in over the years and an ultra-modern kitchen and the house, like Maggie and Jim, was solid and respectable. Stacie liked it; she could not remember having lived anywhere else.

She came to the front of the house by walking uphill from Abbots House and she saw the lights on in the living room, the hall, Cameron's bedroom, and the kitchen. The front of the house was immaculately pointed and there was certainly no nasty graffiti anywhere; it would not have been tolerated in this street. 'And poor Miss Buchanan shouldn't have to tolerate it either,' she said as she opened the black wrought-iron gate. But how could she tell her father about the graffiti without telling him that she had been in the house and, what was possibly even worse, that she was studying a speech from a play. He would flip.

'You're a bit later than you said, Stacie,' was her mother's greeting. 'The nights are really drawing in; your dad and I don't like you wandering around in the dark by yourself. Were you with Craig?'

'Mother.' Said disparagingly enough that one word was usually enough for Maggie but not tonight.

'Friars Carse may be a lovely village but things happen in lovely villages. You just have to tell us if you're having a coffee or whatever with a friend.'

'Well, I wasn't. He's still a bit wobbly and goes straight home these days, Mum,' said Stacie, throwing her school blazer over the lower banister. 'But you're right about nasty things happening.' Stacie crossed her fingers while mentally she thanked her mother for giving her an opening. 'I was walking near Abbots House and someone has spray-painted poor Miss Buchanan's walls.'

'Oh no.' Maggie led the way into the living room where, as usual, Jim was seemingly completely involved watching television and reading the newspaper. He watched the screen until he lost interest, then he read the newspaper until he lost interest in that, when he returned to the television. 'Jim, you'll never guess what Stacie's just said. Tell your dad.'

Stacie did.

'What did it say?'

'Murderer, go home or something like that.'

'Poor thing,' said Maggie, angrily shaking a cushion. 'She should tell the police, Jim.'

'Not much point, love. I don't suppose he signed it. Mind you, they could keep an eye out, but it was only a matter of time, you know. She's the talk of the village.'

'Surely not. They've stopped talking about her at school, yesterday's news. She's so quiet, keeps herself to herself. Mum must be about the only person ever to speak to her.'

Maggie said nothing. She was not so sure that gossip had died down.

'No,' said Jim. 'She's been into my shop for a chop and she deals with Stan Morrison, and you see her quite a bit, don't you, Maggie?'

'Once a week maybe, for fresh things. Usually we deliver.'

'Well, it's none of our business.' He turned to his daughter. 'You're late out, miss. School nights you don't go anywhere after school from now on.'

Stacie protested.

'It's too dark, even in a nice wee village like this for a girl to be wandering around late at night.'

'It's not even nine o'clock.'

'Is your homework done? Up you go. You need to apply yourself more to chemistry. Mr Carlton was in the shop today and told me.'

Stacie glared at her father and managed not to stamp her foot. 'I loathe chemistry and I loathe smarmy Mr Carlton, the silly old woman and besides, I'm passing his tests.'

'Not well enough. My daughter is going to do well.'

'In chemistry. Wake up, Dad. I hate it and I'm dropping it A.S.A.P.'

'Still no reason not to do your best while you're there.'

Stacie walked up two steps, stopped and turned round again, walked back down and hesitated and then thought better of her impulse. This was obviously not the right time to discuss being coached by Miss Buchanan.

Cameron came galloping downstairs followed by a tide of loud and discordant music. 'Hello, all. How about some supper, Mum? I've done everything I have to do.'

'Turn off that music,' said his parents together but Stacie said nothing. She was looking at the left leg of her brother's favourite old jeans that were stained by some red paint.

He saw her looking and turned to run back up to his room but not before Stacie had seen the tell-tale flush of embarrassed colour flood his face.

Cameron had vandalised Miss Buchanan's wall.

7

What a change in a night. The world outside her window was white and frozen, except for the sky.

'Red sky in the morning, shepherd's warning.'

The contrast between the sky and the frozen earth was phenomenal and breathtakingly beautiful. Kate stood for some time in awe. Great horizontal bands of red crossed the heavens. They started on the horizon just where the solid grey sea seemed to touch the sky and then they stretched upwards, sometimes pale, sometimes angry, always magnificent, as if they tried to reach the sun itself. In contrast to the living fire, the earth looked dead. The sea seemed frozen in place and the usually grassy stretches along the beach were white with frost; they looked hard and unwelcoming. There was absolute silence; no seabird stepped gingerly across the stricken earth, no great flocks of wintering geese flashed across the fiery sky. It was both glorious and uncompromising, and most assuredly unwelcoming. Kate shivered in her centrally heated home and reached for her warm dressing-gown, which she wrapped around herself tying it tightly and clasping her arms across her front as if to keep in as much warmth as possible. And then the sun triumphed over the painted clouds and appeared, a majestic ball of red flame. It touched the frost that began to sparkle; it caressed the remaining leaves frozen on the trees; it blazed through Kate's window. She relaxed.

The world is beautiful.

The graffiti, however, looked worse after another long night. Perhaps the heavy frost had burned the letters more firmly into the stone walls. It laughed at her, showed her that her fragile shell was nothing more than that; it was delicate and could shatter easily.

Someone did not want her here in this place where she had hoped to find some answers and some peace. She had to get rid of it. But how? It was much too early to telephone anyone. Better to prepare for the day.

At ten o'clock she telephoned Maggie and placed an order and then, as if she had just remembered and it was of no real consequence, she asked if Maggie knew of anything that was guaranteed to remove paint.

'Turpentine's what Jim uses, Miss Buchanan. We don't stock that here. Morrisons'll have it, I should imagine.' She stopped and then began again. 'I've just had a thought. Can you wait a wee bit because I could ask Jim for you; he's good with his hands, always painting this or papering that?'

Kate thought quickly. Maggie had not asked about the paint. Perhaps she knew. Stacie could have told her, but in that case Maggie would know that Stacie had been in Abbots House. 'I'll ring Mr Morrison, Maggie; I don't want to be a nuisance.'

'No, please, Miss Buchanan, it'll take a second to ring Jim at the shop.'

Eventually Kate agreed. She would sew for a while. The light was good and she could, if she was lucky, lose herself in her work.

Maggie hung up and called Ciss in from the back shop where she had been putting pastry tops on game pies. 'Ciss, watch the front for half an hour or so. I need to run home.'

She picked up her coat and fastened it as she hurried along the street. The buttons were difficult and she had to stop to fasten them. By breathing in she managed and puffed off down the road, vowing for the umpteenth time that she would not be such a whole-hearted appreciator of her own baking. 'This coat's new last Christmas sales, Maggie Thomson, and you're bursting out of it.' She turned down towards the sea and then let herself in the back gate of their home. She was so distressed that she failed to notice that the heavy frost had finally killed her late blooming white roses. That would be another unhappiness later on in the day. For now she was focussed on getting to her son's bedroom. Had she seen red paint on his jeans last night? He had been there on the stairs for a fraction of a second before whisking around and returning to his bedroom. She had seen his sister look at him. Maggie's heart was heavy as she recognised that there had been unspoken messages between her children last night and she had been too anxious to return to the temporary enjoyment of a television programme to follow up her instincts. Stacie and Cameron were both up to something.

The jeans were not in the bedroom. She looked in all the usual places: under the bed, behind the bed, in a chair. As a last resort she even looked in his wardrobe where he occasionally hung something but they were not there. Neither were they in the bathroom nor the laundry basket. Maggie sat on the toilet seat and worried. Her round pretty face was rosy with effort and distress. Cameron would not do such a thing. Would he? What was she to do? She had to ring Miss Buchanan but what could she say? I think my son did it. Jim? Her heart plummeted into her stomach. What would Jim say? It did not bear thinking about. Maggie pulled a long strip of toilet paper and blew her nose; a second sheet wiped her eyes. Oh, please. Don't let Cameron have done it.

The shop was busy when she got back. In dealing with customers she was able to calm down a little. When the shop was empty again Ciss went back to finishing off the pies and Maggie made tea. Ciss liked all that daft flowery stuff but a plain old Earl Grey was good enough for Maggie. Fortified, she rang Miss Buchanan and was delighted when, after eleven rings – which was as many as Jim said should be allowed to ring before it could be deduced that there was no one at home – it was not answered. Miss Buchanan had, no doubt, gone for a walk. Quite lovely it was now that the frost was burning off and a winter sun was trying to warm the air.

Her conscience was clear; she had tried to help and now, for the rest of the morning at least, she could try to forget that her only son might be a vandal at the beginning of a life of crime, and she could get on with her work. November was a busy month. People were beginning to plan their holiday meals. She finished her tea and went back to designing the Christmas meals display cabinet.

Father Benedict had seen the graffiti when he had walked past Abbots House on his way to the beach with Thane. As an ordained

Franciscan priest, Ben had said Mass for the community of monks a few hours before, and now, strengthened by the spiritual joy the celebration of the sacraments had given him, he was exercising the great dog that clung like a shadow to the skirts of his habit.

Murdress go home.

Not written by a university graduate, he decided and, from the height of the letters above the ground, put there by someone who was not very tall and therefore not very old. He lifted his own arm as if he were spraying and the message would have been at least a foot further up the wall. So a child, a disaffected youth, had played a nasty trick on Miss Buchanan. He wondered how she was dealing with it. The first thing to do would be to get rid of the horrid message before too many people saw it.

Father Benedict finished his walk and, once back at the monastery and in the refectory for breakfast, he looked around the table of middle-aged and elderly monks and wondered who might have the knowledge he needed. His gaze fell on Brother Anselm, seventy-three years old and over fifty of those years spent away from the world. If anyone knew how to get paint off a wall it would be Anselm.

Brother Anselm was delighted to be consulted but he shook his bald shining head in despair. 'Thirty years ago, Father, twenty, I would have been able to help you but there are so many new paints these days. They have these tins which spray paint, you know, and I very much fear that nothing I can concoct will be a match for them.'

'Let's give it a try, Brother. The lady has lived away from the world for many years and her health is delicate, I would suppose. The quicker we can clean her wall the better.'

That was Kate's feeling too. The quicker the better. She had waited for a message from Maggie and when none had come she had gone to walk her worries away, striding more and more quickly along the carse as if she could outdistance the nasty message on her wall.

Murdress, go home.

She looked up at the village as she paced. How beautiful it was as it strung itself out along the beach. Lovely homes for lovely people, but at least one person in one of those substantial homes wanted her to leave.

But I am not a murderess. Am I? I loved Bryn; never was I angry with him, never. I accepted him as he was. I am guilty of nothing.

How could you, you slut?

Oh, God, I am guilty of adultery. But no, not even of that. Bryn was the adulterer and was that my fault? Yes, for I gave in to him. I fought it, I did. I fought for years but I gave in because I could no longer – damn it all, be honest, you wanted him. But I didn't kill him. We were here, here for a few days. I had been in Friars Carse for a week, a week in my favourite place, my lovely house on the beach, my Abbots House with its gentle ghosts. No, Kate, honesty, there were no ghosts. No, but it was a warm house. It felt as if the men who had lived there, made travellers welcome there, welcomed me, for I too was a traveller. All my life I had wanted a real home. My mother dead when I was a baby. My father away on his business for months, years at a time, and so I went to Granny, dear Granny. And then there was Tante, Hugh's mother, who married my father. Why, darling Tante? In a moment of weakness like the one in which I gave in to my desire, my overwhelming need of Bryn? The marriage did not last but your love for a skinny nervous child remained. Did you love me, Tante, or did you and Hugh merely feel responsible in some way? Hugh still does. He worries about me. Please don't let me have ruined his life. I love him; have always loved him. He does know that. You're avoiding the issue, Kate. Go back to that time with Bryn. You had been in Russia. It was a fabulous tour. Everyone loved you but you were exhausted and so, before starting all over again, you took a break, two weeks in Abbots House. No visitors, not even darling old Hugh. And then, one night Bryn came. Where had he been? Oh, the West End. It was chilly and you had lit a fire. Remember how lovely it was to sit by the fire and read. You read, Kate, novels, poetry, and you listened to music, symphonies, Brahms, wasn't it? Someone told you that Brahms' Fourth Symphony would be played in heaven and you worried that you might never hear it there so you played it over and over. Pom, pom, pom parom pom, pomparompom, pomparom. Glorious, wonderful. And then one night you heard the gate and it was Bryn. Glorious, wonderful.

97

'You're in London.'

'I'm here and I will never leave again.'

Dear God, he actually said those words as I opened the door.

'I will never leave again.'

No, he did not intend to kill himself; he meant, he told me, that he was going to leave Rose, make a complete break. She could keep his name if she wanted but he was going to live with me if I wanted him. If I wanted him? I wanted to marry him but, by that stage, I was prepared to take whatever I could get. If Rose refused to divorce him I was prepared to 'live in sin'. After all what is the difference between living together clandestinely whenever an opportunity presented itself or letting the world know and taking the consequences? We decided that we would continue to be discreet.

Discretion is the better part of valour.

What a child I am for quotations.

We walked along this beach. We looked up at those houses. That one had a blue door then and that one was rather run down but now it's got a nice new face. Someone loves it now. We loved. That was all. We walked, we ate, we sat by the fire reading, listening to music, and we loved. It was what being together was going to be like, peaceful, calm, accepting, taking the other's dear presence for granted. He is there studying a script. She is there with her sewing. Good heavens, I did sew. Sister Magdalena said I learned too quickly for someone who had never done such work before. Curtains, Hugh said, not embroidery.

Kate, discipline. What happened next? Who came?

No one. We saw no one. We had supper. Bacon and eggs. I was never a good cook.

Thank God for London restaurants.

We laughed. But we had some wine. A rosé; Hugh had brought it from Provence. We sat by the fire and we drank rosé and we made love. How beautiful it was. Was music playing or was that only in my head?

'My grandmother would be furious with me, Bryn. Imagine, Kate Buchanan having an affair with a married man.'

'I love you, caru. *I have loved you since the moment I saw you sitting*

98

there in the classroom, so correct, so middle class, so bloody scared.' He had held her face in his hands for a moment. *'So bloody beautiful. You're beautiful, cariad, inside and out. You're good, not like me or Rose, out for what we can get. I've made so many mistakes, Kate: not convincing you to marry me is the worst one but we'll work it out. When Rose realises just how much I love you she'll give me a divorce and then we can marry.'*

But Rose would not agree. She kept his name; she kept his house although he was never in it. He had his flat and then we had Abbots House, my perfect house where we played at make-believe, where there was never tension or anger, no raised voices. But there were voices. I can hear them if I try hard.

He was angry. At first I thought he was rehearsing but the words were strange. What did he say? What was he saying, Kate? You can hear him. You know you can.

'I can't. I won't.'

She looked round. Without realising she had left the beach and headed up towards the woods. The crusader's tomb. She would go and ask her friend the crusader for courage.

The woods were full of weak winter sunshine. The ground under her feet was covered with frozen frosted leaves. The sun's pale warmth made no impression here but in the clearing by the tomb the earth was not so hard. The trees seemed more welcoming and the stone walls no colder than they ever were. Kate's heart eased and her ragged breath calmed as she stood for a moment leaning against the trunk of a great beech tree. She caught a glimpse of some bright red berries deeper in the wood.

Holly. I'll ask Benedict if I may have some or perhaps I can buy it from Maggie. Maggie didn't ring. I would have trusted her to ring. I wonder what happened? Do you know, Crusader, and do you know who hates me enough to daub messages on my walls?

Murderer, go home. Did people shout messages like that at you and your fellow knights, Crusader? Did you care? I thought I was home, you see. How stupid and naïve of me to think the past could be left behind. But where will I go if I leave here? I burned my boats, Sir Knight. So much burning in my life.

Kate straightened up. She would ring Mr Morrison and ask him about removing paint and she would talk to Simon, not to Hugh because he would be upset for her and was quite likely to come charging to her rescue in his beautiful car. Hugh, my own knight in shining armour. What a dreadful human being I must have been; I was so involved with loving Bryn that I never realised I was taking you far too much for granted. One does that with family. Forgive me, Hugh.

The walk back to the house exhausted her and she decided to lie down in the garden room to rest and she had just drifted off to sleep when the telephone rang. For a moment she thought of ignoring it, but thinking it might be Hugh, she went into the sitting room and answered it.

'Miss Buchanan, it's Maggie Thomson.' The voice was tearful and quite unlike Maggie's usual cheerful tones. 'Jim and me, Jim and *I* wondered if we could come down and see you for a moment. It's about the paint on your wall.'

They did know. By this time the whole of Friars Carse probably knew. 'It's all right, Maggie. I'm going to ring Mr Morrison or a painter; I never thought of ringing a painter.'

'No, please, you don't understand, Miss Buchanan. It was our Cameron. We're so ashamed and angry but his dad says he has to apologise and clean it up and if' – her voice broke completely for a moment but then she began again – 'and if you want to call the police, then that's what you should do.'

Cameron. Maggie's son. Stacie's brother. Kate did not know whether to feel sorrow or relief but she responded to the anxiety in Maggie's voice. Poor Maggie, her first friend in the village. 'Maggie, it's all right. Thank you for telling me. As long as I can get it cleaned off I'll be perfectly happy.'

She heard Maggie blowing her nose loudly. 'You're too good, Miss Buchanan, and thank you very much. But we do want to come down. Cameron has to apologise to you in person and his dad says he has to get it cleaned off.'

What Jim had actually said was, 'You'll damn well scrub every drop off or you'll rue the day you were born.'

'Isn't he still in school?'

'Jim fetched him. Told the headmaster there was an emergency and never a truer word was spoken. Can we come now and they'll get started? Better to do it while there's still light.'

Still light. Kate looked at her watch and, as always, just seeing it calmed her. Almost three o'clock. No wonder she was tired; she had had no lunch. She sighed. She wanted the wall cleaned but she was exhausted and a hysterical mother, a furious father and an embarrassed and possibly frightened boy were three people she would really rather not see, but she agreed and a few minutes later all three were at the door, Maggie tearful, Jim embarrassed and angry, and Cameron surly and ashamed.

He had obviously rehearsed his speech several times and she was pleased that, after the initial embarrassed mumbling, he did attempt to look directly at her, and he managed to meet her eyes when he actually apologised. 'It was some chums talking at school; I didn't think and I'm sorry. It was a stupid thing to do and I don't mean it anyway.'

He hung his head now, relieved that his confession was over, and Kate was about to speak, ready to forgive him, but Jim forestalled her. 'I've got some industrial cleaner here, Miss Buchanan, and we'll get it cleaned and I give you my word that nothing like this will happen again. Silly empty-headed kids larking around when they should be studying. This one won't have time for larking for some time.'

'The rest of my life,' muttered Cameron and got another furious look from his father.

That remark would be commented on when the family were back in the privacy of their own home. Kate did not envy young Cameron. 'I'm sure he's sorry, Mr Thomson, and thank you for finding out how to clean it. I shall leave you to it then.' She was beginning to feel very shaky and knew her legs would not support her much longer. When had she last spoken to three people together? They had all looked at her face and looked away again and then forced themselves to look and she had managed not to put her hand up to hide the scars on her cheek or to check that her hair really was covering the worst of them. She nodded and stepped backwards into her house and closed the door, shutting out the world and the Thomsons and then she began to shake all over and could only blindly grope her way forward until she found a chair into which she collapsed.

When she was calm she telephoned Simon. 'I couldn't handle it; I was doing so well. I had forced myself to go over and over what happened that weekend that Bryn surprised me here at the house. I saw everything so clearly and then I just could not force myself to go on. I was so close, Simon, so close to discovering what really happened and then . . . I let go. And now this ghastly business. I knew people were talking but I didn't really take it in. People have always talked about me. I thought I could cope but this is suddenly so real. People, young boys, huddling together laughing at me and talking about me. They think I'm a murderer. The law said it could not prove it, Simon, isn't that so? Scottish law. What was it they said? The case will be held in abeyance *pro loco et tempore* until evidence is found and until I was mentally fit. But nothing concrete ever was found and so, in Scottish law it would have been not proven and I was eventually released. Now I'm being tried all over again and found guilty. And Jim Thomson. I could see it in his eyes. He's furious that his son is a vandal. He didn't bring up the boy to paint crude messages on walls and he's angry but his real anger is against me. I came into his lovely little town and my past followed. I caused his son to misbehave. How stupid can I be, Simon? You warned me. Hugh warned me, but I thought it was such a long time ago – such a long long time and I pined for Friars Carse and for my house and I should have known better. I'll close the house and go back to Le Prieuré.' She stopped talking and quietly began to weep. The convent no longer took paying guests. What in the name of God was she going to do?

Outside in the dusk the Thomsons had been joined by Father Benedict.

'How kind you are, Jim, Maggie.' He had seen Cameron trying to flatten himself against the wall as he scrubbed and suddenly understood. 'I had asked one of our order, Brother Anselm, about a paint remover; he's one of those seemingly not really of this world types whereas he's extremely practical. I came to tell Miss Buchanan that he's working on something.'

'Tell him not to bother, Reverend. These days it's actually

quicker to phone the council. They're used to vandals,' said Jim gruffly as he shot a glance at his only son.

'Let me help. Shall I do the outside? Anyone passing will think nothing of a monk cleaning a wall.'

Jim turned away. 'The lad did it and he can live with the consequences.'

'Jim?'

Benedict touched her arm gently and smiled at her and Maggie tried to smile back. 'Please allow me to help, Jim. Four pairs of arms are better than three.' He stopped and looked up at the sky. 'It's getting dark quickly; you won't be able to see the words at all soon.'

Jim's round, usually cheery face was glowering at them in the growing darkness. He was embarrassed, angry, disappointed and he was floundering. His son, his Cameron, to do such a thing. He knew that if he were not so physically strong he would hit the boy; he wanted to strike him and was alarmed by his own violence, and now to have this toffee-nosed man he could not understand sticking his well-bred nose into his business was almost unbearable.

Benedict could see the emotions chasing one another over Jim's face. 'Jim, a favour, please. In return for Maggie's kindness in selling my little birds for me.'

Jim capitulated. He could see the sense in having another willing pair of hands but Cameron would still not get off too lightly. If anyone in the village saw them cleaning and realised the name of the culprit then they would just have to live with the shame. Shame? It was already there. Somehow he had failed as a father. 'Only if the boy works with you, Reverend. Maggie and me'll do the inside here.'

Cameron was not too thrilled at being put to work with the monk. He was not a Catholic and had no experience of cloistered men. But Benedict said nothing except, 'Hello,' and they worked quietly and well together. When their side of the wall was clean the monk put down his scrubbing brush and Cameron tensed himself for a lecture on sin but none came. 'Say goodnight to your parents for me, Cameron,' said Benedict and he turned and walked away towards the sea. He had had other business with Kate but he would leave it till later.

Kate had stayed talking to Simon for some time. At least, this time, after she had broken down, it was Simon who talked, calmly, quietly, soothingly. Everything he said was sensible: the vandalism was the silly act of a young boy whose parents had shown that they did not condone it. With luck, no one else in the village would have seen it; her house was a long way from the main street of the town. On dank, muggy afternoons few people walked on the beach. She was to relax. In a few hours at the very latest, the horrid message would be gone.

She had interrupted there. 'It could happen again.'

'Possibly. Now tell me what you are going to do, Kate.'

She took a deep breath . . . *no shoulder movement . . . breathe from the diaphragm* . . . 'I'm going to have a sandwich.'

She made a sandwich and ate some of it but she tasted none of it. Another bite, Kate. Come on. 'Damn it, Kate, you sound like that nurse.'

She went to the window and peeked furtively through the slats of her Venetian blind. Two sturdy figures in dark jackets and trousers were at the wall. Maggie and Jim? Poor dear Maggie. Where was the boy? Released from penal servitude? Thank God, Kate, you are relaxing if you can make a joke, albeit a weak one. He'll be doing the outside, poor lad, no doubt so that as many of his chums as possible can see him scrubbing. He'll either be perfect after this or loathe me. She turned and looked into the room. I have no photographs. Why is that? Were they all burned? Surely I would have snaps of Bryn or would that have been too obvious? And there must surely have been pictures of Granny and Tante and Hugh. I should have one of Mary Mag but she is in my mind and heart, like Bryn, like Bryn.

She would work; she could lose herself in it. There it was in its frame standing to attention beside her favourite chair. She checked the tension. Goldwork becomes so heavy that if it is not properly supported it will sag and distort. Perfect; she took up her needle, pulled the frame over towards her and began to work, and eventually emotional and physical exhaustion took over and she napped in her chair, the needle forgotten in her lap. When she woke it was quite dark outside and Maggie and Jim were gone. She turned out the lamp, put on her cloak and went out into a cold beginning of winter evening. The sky was a black carpet sprinkled with stars. Seeing stars clearly had been one of the many joys of living in Abbots House; Kate had almost forgotten that.

The wall was clean, in fact cleaner than it had been, for all the little mosses that had grown on the surface had been scrubbed away. She opened the gate and stood for a moment listening for footsteps. Nothing. The wall was clean on this side too. She turned as if to return to the house and then decided against that course. She would walk by the sea on this starlit night. As if to spoil her pleasure in the night sky a flake of snow fell, and then another and soon a light drizzle was falling.

She walked quickly towards the sea and then changed her mind and, turning, walked back towards the town. She looked up to the top of the hill where the road wound around and through the village. In the glow of a streetlamp she could see a tall thin figure, a great grey dog loping by his side. She was absurdly pleased. 'Rather silly, coming out in weather like this, Benedict. There must be miles of cloister for you to exercise in,' said Kate as she stroked Thane's beautiful head.

'It has only just started to snow, friend Kate,' he said gently, and immediately she felt both chastened and angry, 'and besides, I came to see you.'

'You surely didn't expect to see me on the beach in weather like this,' she said and heard him laugh.

'I had hoped that you were sitting by the fire.'

She turned away. 'No, I don't sit by the fire.' She turned back. 'I'm all mod cons, my friend.' He had been coming to see her? A monk, even with a large dog, calling on her so late in the evening? 'What did you want?' she asked and then, conscious of how ungracious she sounded, she smiled at him. 'I'm sorry. You walked all this way to be met by a harridan. Won't you come back with me and have some cocoa? I suppose monks don't drink whisky and never with strange women.'

'There is nothing strange about you, Kate,' said Benedict, but he ignored her remarks. 'I was coming merely to slip this through the letterbox. Rather early, I know, but it has details of the Christmas services at the abbey. Perhaps you might like to come. We have mulled wine and mince pies after Midnight Mass.'

'Such dissipation,' she said but she took the leaflet. 'I'm not a churchgoer, friend Ben.'

'Come for the music. "Some to church repair, not for the doctrine, but the music there." Lots of people do. Goodnight, friend Kate.'

'Goodnight,' she said and watched him as he walked past her down towards the sea.

Christmas. Season of love and joy and peace. There is always something to look forward to, Kate.

8

Stacie was absolutely furious when she realised that her suspicions were correct and that Cameron had indeed painted the ghastly demand on Miss Buchanan's walls. Luckily for Cameron, he lived in the twentieth century. Any earlier and his sister would have had him boiled in oil, hanged, drawn and quartered – even in a fury, Stacie was conscious of correct grammar – and she envisaged herself beating her ghastly brother to a pulp. What would Miss Buchanan, the great Katherine Buchan, think of her, the sister of a vandal? She would never coach her, never; her life was in ruins; this pall of gloom under which she was living would never be lifted.

Even her parents had noted that their usually sunny daughter seemed to be somewhat dispirited; she was certainly off her food. Maggie had even considered making an appointment with the local doctor but it was Jim who dissuaded her. 'She's mooning over that lad, Craig. Ever since he had that asthma attack and couldn't take her to Edinburgh she's behaved as if the world was coming to an end. I told her: they're different. They're not our sort. I mean what kind of lad would leave a young lass standing for hours at a bus stop?'

'He was ill.'

'His parents weren't. If it had been the other way round we would have phoned, warned them.'

Maggie tried to calm him down. 'Yes, but, Jim, they might not have known. These young ones are growing up; they don't tell their parents everything. Half the time we haven't a clue what our two are up to. Tell you what, I'll slip out tomorrow and buy her that frock in La Moda; if there's a yard of material in that dress, Jim, I'll eat a pie pan but the thought of being all dolled up for a posh party will cheer her.'

Jim settled himself comfortably in the worn old chair as he waited for the evening meal to appear; Maggie had several casseroles and trays in the Aga. 'I haven't seen much of her the past few weeks. What do they do after school? She's never home before seven and school's out just before four, isn't it?'

'They have these clubs and things: Young Mathematicians, French Club, their drama club; she loves that. Craig's in it too.'

'Girly stuff; you won't get my Cameron in that club.'

Maggie ignored that remark and took off her all-covering apron, thus revealing herself in her second best dress, the dark blue wool with the crossover bodice and Jim groaned. 'What is it tonight? Rural or Young Wives Club?'

'The Women's Rural, thank goodness. I'm not talking just attending.' Maggie was very busy folding up her apron and putting it in a drawer of the old pine dresser. 'Actually, Jim,' she said without turning round, 'I think Stacie's still a bit upset about Cameron. She's got a bit of a crush on Miss Buchanan, you know.'

Jim almost choked on his pleasantly dry sherry; a bit of a poncy drink he had thought until he had won a bottle in the bowling club Christmas raffle.

'Perfectly normal.' Maggie smiled as she reached over carefully to take a tray of shortbread fingers from the oven. 'I had a crush on Rita Hayworth, all that fabulous red hair – and her figure! Don't these smell heavenly, Jim. There's a funny adjective, heavenly; you'd think something that smelled heavenly would smell of incense, candles, that kind of thing. Just thought of that but it's a great adjective for this time of the year. I love Christmas: cards, presents, carols.'

'Hours and hours of extra work.'

'You love it too, you old Scrooge.'

Cameron, dressed completely in an outfit that could easily have been borrowed by any soldier in desert combat conditions, erupted into the room as he always did but Stacie had to be called several times. She was in time to hear her father complaining about her brother's dress sense finishing with, 'I wouldn't mind if that lot didn't cost twice as much as your school uniform.'

'I hate uniforms,' answered Cameron.

'You're wearing a uniform,' thundered Jim.

To deflect Jim from Cameron, who had been in quite enough hot water lately, Maggie rounded on Stacie. 'I don't know what you're up to these days, my girl,' she complained, forgetting all she had said about normality earlier. 'Locking yourself in your room night after night.'

Stacie sat down at the table. 'You're exaggerating, Mum; it's not locked and I'm studying; you go on and on about keeping all my marks up, especially Dad's favourite.'

Her father looked blankly at her.

'Chemistry, Dad, had you forgotten?' She held out her glass to her brother. 'Pour me some water, General.'

'That was really helpful, my girl, and why aren't you having milk?'

'She's watching her figure so that her knight in shining armour will watch it too.' Cameron got his own back.

'Enough. Your poor father is so busy he won't even be able to come home for lunch from now till New Year.' She ignored the fact that Jim was sitting there glaring at his children and went on. 'We'll need help in the shops every Saturday in the lead-up to Christmas, Stacie, and you too, Cameron; there's deliveries.'

The weeks before the holidays were always fraught with one crisis after another.

'Has Miss Buchanan ordered something, Mum?' Stacie tried to make her voice sound normal and disinterested. Since the paint-spraying incident she had kept well away from Miss Buchanan. That is, she had walked up and down beside the garden wall night after night but had been unable to summon up the courage to go in.

Maggie handed her a plate. 'Help yourself to salad,' she said, and then answered Stacie's question. 'She has actually. I had wondered if she even realised it was almost Christmas but she phoned with a big order and she's phoned your dad too. She has friends coming just after for a few days, to bring in the New Year. That'll be nice for her. I'm glad she's got some friends. There are a few parcels come from arty-crafty shops but there aren't many letters come, mostly legal-looking ones, and no cards so far, if what Heather in the post office says is true. We'll send her one, as she's become such a good customer.'

Stacie let her mother chatter on while she thought again of those wonderful few minutes spent in Miss Buchanan's beautiful house. She had been taken seriously, not just dismissed politely. Miss Buchanan had told Stacie to study other playwrights and the history of that time, and she had, evening after evening, and she prayed her depth of knowledge and insights into the character would help her get the part, but now that Cameron had ruined everything she could not possibly go back for more help. It would be just too embarrassing. What if Miss Buchanan refused to speak to her? To her parents' surprise Stacie burst into tears and ran from the room.

She locked herself in the bathroom for a while and wept, sitting on the toilet seat and blowing her nose with toilet paper. At last she could cry no more. Her mother had come up once and Stacie had yelled, 'Go away,' and had heard Maggie retreat and then the front door open. 'Typical,' sobbed Stacie. 'My life is in tatters but off my mother goes to enjoy herself.' She blew her nose again, flushed away all the damp toilet paper and then stood up and looked at herself in the mirror. The obvious fact that she had lost weight cheered her even though her nose and her eyes were red but those were hollows under her cheekbones. 'Alluring,' she said to herself. 'I'm alluring.'

'And too damn conceited,' she said mournfully as she sat back down on the toilet seat.

She got up again, went to the sink and threw cold water on her flushed cheeks and eyes. She would wait no longer. She would go to see Miss Buchanan and throw herself on her mercy. She would apologise for her brother's abhorrent behaviour; she would do and say whatever it took to have Miss Buchanan admit her to the house again.

In fact she had to do nothing. Kate opened the door, said, 'Hello, Stacie, I wondered when you would come back. Did you study the Shaw and the Anouilh?' and led the way into the sitting room where she sat down in her usual chair. The embroidery on its frame was beside her, richer and deeper than it had been. She was wearing a long skirt in the softest brown suede imaginable and a beautifully knit brown sweater sprinkled with hand-crocheted blue flowers. Stacie sighed. It was hard for her to imagine women who sat by themselves in beautiful clothes like that. Who was to admire them? She had not yet learned that some women dress for themselves.

'Yes, Miss Buchanan,' she said in a low voice, the voice of a student who thinks the headmistress is justifiably annoyed. 'Miss Buchanan, I wanted . . .' She stopped on a loud sob.

'What do you think is the fundamental difference between Shakespeare's approach and Anouilh's?' asked Kate, ignoring the sob.

Stacie had not even considered the question.

'Shaw's and Shakespeare's?'

Stacie hung her head.

'Let us consult the texts. You did bring them?'

Stacie had not. 'I did get them from the school library and I studied them but tonight I . . . I . . . was . . .'

'Upset. About school . . . about Craig . . . about me?'

'I was sure you would be angry.'

'And never want to see you again?' Suddenly Kate smiled. 'Stacie, Cameron is a very young boy. What he wrote on my wall hurt me, frightened me. When I discovered that it was Cameron I was not so frightened as I had been originally.' She looked directly at Stacie and the light shone full on the side of her face with its pale scars. 'Your parents do not know that you are here?'

Stacie shook her head.

Kate stood up. 'Then you may not stay, my dear.'

'But I know you didn't murder anyone.' Stacie stopped, aghast. What had she said?

Kate ignored her expression of stunned horror. 'Then you are one of an elite few. I do not know for sure; I simply cannot, or will not, remember.' She wanted the girl to think well of her; she wanted to tell her what the judges had said but the girl was young, impressionable. Kate would say no more on the subject. 'Stacie, I was Katherine Buchan; I don't know if I can help you – I have never coached anyone – but I would like to try. I cannot agree to do so without the full co-operation and consent of your parents.'

'I'm sure it'll be all right. I'll talk to them soon; I've tried but there never seems to be a right time and after what Cameron . . .' She could not continue.

'That does not affect you. How is your friend? Is he working hard too?'

Stacie smiled and, for a moment, she was beautiful. 'He's back at school but he's not taking any of the after-school clubs for a while. He was so sorry about our date, not being well enough to ask his mum to let me know, that sort of thing. We talk every day and sometimes he phones. I told him to read all the plays too, the Shaw and the Anouilh. Gosh, was that all right?'

Kate got up and laid her embroidery frame, which she had just picked up, aside. Of course the girl had told her boyfriend that she had met the scarlet woman in Abbots House. 'Stacie, I would prefer not to be gossiped over.'

Stacie blushed a fiery red. 'I'm sorry,' she babbled. 'It wasn't gossip, just giving him some hints too.'

For a few moments Kate said nothing. Then she spoke. 'If your parents agree, I will coach you, but only if they agree.'

'They will; they have to. I want to go to RADA or the Royal Scottish Academy; I'll really need help to get in there. Please, Miss Buchanan.'

Granny sending away for the forms. *We won't worry too much about the pieces. They know you're inexperienced.* 'Not without your parents' consent.' Her voice was quite firm and Stacie knew she could not be coerced.

'Mum said you've ordered for Christmas.' Aware that that remark again demonstrated to Kate that she was discussed, Stacie blushed again.

'New Year, dear,' said Kate gently. 'Some old friends are coming.'

'Will you be alone for Christmas?'

Alone? What did that mean? That she would be the only living person in Abbots House. Yes, then she would be alone. But *he* was always there and memories of Granny and Tante and cousin David. Kate smiled as streams of old and dear friends jostled to be seen.

'You're a nice girl, Stacie. I'll be fine.'

She showed the girl to the door and stood watching her as she hurried up the path to the gate in the wall. 'Goodnight, Stacie. Tell your parents.'

The girl turned, her face again tearful. 'Goodnight, Miss Buchanan. I do hope you'll have a happy Christmas.'

'Happy Christmas.'

The words hung in the air. Christmas. She remembered Christmas. Once it had meant so much when she had waited, white with impatience, to see if there was indeed a plaster baby in the little manger that Granny had placed under the tree. A spruce, always a real tree, none of that shop-bought nonsense. She could hear her old voice still. Kate sighed. Gone: Granny and Christmas and the little manger with the plaster baby. It should be somewhere. Hugh would know.

She climbed the stairs to the attic storeroom and rummaged for a while among the trunks and boxes. Some of the boxes she could not bear to open, not yet, although she might have to beard them and find some old friends, Shakespeare, Ibsen, Wilde. At last, there it was, a rectangular box, someone's shoes or slippers probably, and inside some sheep, looking very much the worse for wear, one king – where had the others gone? – Joseph, standing patiently as he had stood for years and would continue to stand, and Mary, gentle Mary in her impossible blue gown. Yes, the tiny manger was there and deep down in this rather grubby cotton wool, the baby.

But what was this?

The voice, young and impassioned echoed across the years: 'There has to be a baby. I can't wait for Christmas. No one else waits for Christmas.'

Her cousin, David, all of seven. He had hated Granny's old customs and had made his own baby, which he had laid in the manger and which, for some sentimental reason, she had kept. It was no more than a piece of cardboard on which he had drawn features but when Kate picked it up, all the memories of all the Christmases came flooding back. She kissed the plaster baby and returned him to his cotton bed and then she took everything, the manger, the king, the sheep, the cardboard baby and his patient parents down to her sitting room and looked for somewhere to place them.

They had always been under the tree, *sans* baby, of course, until midnight. Who had come first, the baby Jesus or Father Christmas? She had never been alert enough to find out. 'You'll have to make do with this table,' she told her nativity set and with hands that had, for some absurd reason, begun to shake, she positioned them.

In the light from the lamp they looked pathetically vulnerable.

'You're looking your age, my dear,' she told the Virgin Mary, who ignored her blasphemy or levity and remained gazing in adoration at her cardboard baby.

'Constancy,' said Kate. 'Such an over-rated virtue.' She reached for her cloak and went out to seek answers to questions she had not asked. She walked for miles along the beach, into the woods where she avoided the crusader's tomb but walked up to the very walls of the old priory and then turned hurriedly away. Thane might be abroad and she did not want to speak to Father Benedict.

How stupid to go out in the dark. The sky was overcast and there were no streetlights. Still, for some reason, she did not feel afraid in these grounds. Her intellect told her that she was silly to put her trust in the goodness of living men who were hidden away behind high stone walls and long dead men, but she slipped quickly through the trees and did not think once on who or what might be hiding there.

The telephone was ringing when she let herself in to Abbots House and she hurried across the room to answer it. 'Oh, Hugh, I couldn't have asked for a nicer surprise.' She spoke without thinking, forgetting that he, more than anyone else, could read every subtle message in her voice.

'What's happened, Kate? Have you had another nightmare?'

She managed to laugh, the light airy laugh for which she had once been famous. Would he know that it was a Katherine Buchan stock-in-trade? 'Gosh, no, the exact opposite. I've been wallowing in lovely memories. Things are getting clearer and clearer.' Had Simon spoken to him? No, he would never tell Hugh what she had said but they had been friends since she had become a patient. Perhaps he might tell Hugh that she had rung; Hugh would know that was unusual.

'Tell me.'

'I'm actually beginning to believe that I didn't kill Bryn.'

'I never thought you had: never once, Kate. We, the family, always assumed, given that there was no real evidence of any kind, that it was a terrible accident.'

'Yes,' she said dryly. 'Bryn hit himself on the back of the head and fell into the fire.' She stopped. '. . . fell into the fire.' Bryn fell into the fire. How did she know? 'Hugh. Where was Bryn when we were found?'

'Kate, the house was razed. I think Bryn was found in what would have been your dining room, and, yes, close to the fireplace.' He thought hard, trying to remember. 'At least he was closer to the fireplace than to the door.'

'Hold on.' She put the receiver down on the table and hurried into the dining room, looked at the curtains and at the walls. Then she hurried back to the sitting room.

'It's almost exactly as it was, except that there are no fireplaces.'

'Good.' He tried to sound cheerful. 'How are the preparations for the holidays?'

'Wonderful, and yours?'

'I'm popping over to Grasse. Come with me, Kate?' he suggested wistfully. 'We could look up Mary Mag and old Aloysius.'

'No,' she said abruptly and then hurried to soften her tones. 'Hugh, I'm fine. I was upset and I rang Simon but it's all over; it won't happen again.' Enough said. She would change the subject. 'I decorated the sitting room today.' That was not really a lie. Surely putting out the rather sad nativity set was decorating. 'Nativity sets can't be sad, can they, Hugh?'

'If the donkeys have droopy ears?'

'No donkeys.'

'Then it's not sad.' He waited for a moment. 'What voice, Kate?' He knew her well; she was trying to fool him and he would not allow it, not now that she had started. 'If it's becoming clearer, what voice did you hear? Man or woman?'

But the questioning panicked her again and Hugh stopped. Simon had told him often that this healing could not be hurried, that it could reverse the process if handled badly. It was all so bloody futile anyway. Who hated either Kate or Bryn enough to murder them? No one; they were popular with everyone. Except with *her*, of course, but she had not even been in the country.

'Let's not worry about it then, Katie; it'll come when you're ready. Tell you what, why don't you make me a list of all the goodies you want me to bring you from Provence? I know, *un – miel de lavande, deux – miel de lavande, trois—*'

'No, no,' laughingly she interrupted him. *'Numéro deux c'est confiture de figues.'*

'Fig jam, how ghastly,' he teased her, glad to sense her relax. 'While I'm there I should pop over to St Raphaël and take some boxes to the convent.'

They chatted on for a few minutes on innocuous and un-controversial subjects and then when she had promised to send him some handwritten notes to go with the boxes he would take to Le Prieuré they hung up, but Hugh was still ill at ease.

His copious notes on her arrest and imprisonment, together with newspaper clippings, doctor and police reports, were all locked in his office; he would read them all again first thing in the morning. Without rereading them to refresh his memory, he still knew that each and every psychiatrist had said that Kate simply could not remember; they wrote gobbledegook sentences in which the words post-traumatic amnesia and severe emotional trauma featured heavily. After all, she had been unconscious for five days in the immediate aftermath of the accident. When she regained consciousness she spoke intelligently to doctors and nurses but, as one said at the trial, 'She was there and yet not there.' They spoke of cognitive impairment and intellectual dysfunction until Hugh, who loved her, wanted to scream, 'Wouldn't you have difficulty recognising anything if you'd been as badly burned as my poor Kate has been?'

For some time after the fire she had even been unable to access her own name. Her entire life seemed to have been completely wiped from her memory.

At one point it seemed that she would not recover from the damage caused by the fire but she pulled through and spent years undergoing painful plastic surgery. Her burns were labelled third-degree thermal burns and had affected, not only the obvious skin, but muscles, bones, nerves and blood vessels, and her respiratory system. Added to the physical damage, the young and eager psychiatrist, Simon Whittaker, told Hugh that the patient was suffering emotionally and psychologically. He hoped that her memory would return in full but warned that it would take time, and slowly, slowly, her memory had returned – or selective memories. She had been told her name, her history, but the words meant nothing. Hugh was humbly grateful that she had always appeared to know him although for some time she had not used his name, but she had always been happy to see him and was often distressed when he had to leave.

He had taken in photographs but she had recognised none of them, not even those of herself. Simon, who had become her psychiatrist after she had been assigned to the psychiatric ward of a prison hospital, had suggested that Hugh show her some favourite possessions from her London flat and he had carried in her favourite sea-green mug and bowl.

'Oh, how very pretty,' was her reaction.

Medicine cures the body – but the mind. Face it, Mr Forsythe, she may never recover. She may not want to remember; perhaps it is too horrifying.

Eventually he had been bold enough to show her a photograph of her beloved Bryn. As an experiment it had been a disaster. Her distress had been pitiful to witness. Had her nightmares started then or had she suffered from the moment of the accident? He did not know. All he knew was that something forgotten or deliberately repressed was causing her suffering. Tomorrow he would read those papers again and see if there was anything, anything at all that he had not done to help her.

9

Kate was surprised to find the abbey chapel so full.

Unafraid of the dark, she had walked alone through the woods to the monastery. Naturally she had stopped to wish the crusader a Happy Christmas but he, unlike the woods around him, had maintained a dignified silence. She heard an owl and saw him swoop silently, stealthily to a tree just beside her. He had, of course, seen something tasty, for he plummeted down; there was a tiny squeak and all was still.

Poor mouse, but it was quick, my friend.

Kate had slipped, like a phantom herself, through the darkness, and then had come out into a scene of almost medieval splendour, which was only right since the abbey had been founded in the thirteenth century and although the largest part of the buildings was much later, part of the original structure still stood. The driveway, or should it be called a carriage sweep, was busy with cars of all types; stately elderly almost vintage models; bright young things; the obligatory number of four-wheel-drive off-road vehicles; and something that to Kate's uneducated eye fitted somewhere between car and bus. Light shone from every window of the abbey and music followed it or wafted out on its beams. The light picked up the colours of the stained-glass windows and turned the gravel outside red or blue or gold. What would the subjects of the windows be? She longed to see them in their glory.

She circumnavigated the driveway so that she remained in the friendly darkness and attempted to slip into the chapel unobserved. A monk was there, not Benedict, but a Christmas card monk, round and jolly and tonsured, and he welcomed her.

Her footsteps echoed as she walked alone along a stone corridor to the chapel where the streaming lights were so bright that her inexperienced eyes closed against them for a moment. She opened them as the particular sights and sounds and smells of Advent assailed her. How many candles were burning? She could not tell but the smell of the smoke reminded her of Provence and the nuns. Someone was playing the great organ very well indeed and the voices of the worshippers sang out joyously and were lifted and made good by the resounding music: Angels we have heard on High. She remembered that carol immediately: *Les anges dans nos campagnes.* Kate smiled. She looked up automatically at the window above the main altar. It was a riot of jewel colours and its subject was the archangels. She recognised Gabriel, a Gabriel with golden wings and white lilies. Was he man or woman? Did angels have a sex? Naughty, Kate, enjoy the colours. Michael, definitely all male, in crimson and gold and silver, his sword held upright in his hand. A good man to have on one's side. Who were the other two? If she had ever known she did not remember. She would try to remember to ask Benedict. The great window was dedicated to the memory of a local family, not the one that had gifted the lands all those hundreds of years ago but a nineteenth-century family who had been, according to the flowery script on the panels, 'true lovers of their fellow man'. The chapel itself, unlike the splendid window, was old, which she liked, and the carved pews held untold stories as well as the warmly clad bodies of many of Friar Carse's residents. Where had they all come from?

Some use the church for christening, marrying, or burying.

Et tu, Brute, she chastised herself and lost herself in the smell of incense and heat, and the beauty of huge bowls of holly and ivy. She found a pew at the back that still had some space, squeezed herself into a corner and closed her eyes. What peace.

For some minutes she just sat quietly, receiving and absorbing emotions, but eventually she opened her eyes, fearful that someone might think her asleep or drunk. Which would be more unforgivable? The chapel was full and she looked around surreptitiously. The altar was a mass of flowers – mainly arrangements of holly branches, ivy and white Christmas roses – but there were brass bowls full of poinsettias, and tall while candles.

At the east of the main altar was a side altar which looked as if it was dedicated to the Virgin and in front of this altar a creche or manger had been erected. The Father Abbot, like her grandmother, had left out the baby Jesus. No, not Father Abbot: these Grey Friars were Franciscans and St Francis, although an aristocrat, had preferred the more democratic term Guardian. Kate smiled, almost squirmed with suppressed excitement, as the child Kate had squirmed, on her hard bench, and waited and at last the Christmas carol music was replaced by an even more glorious vaunting, flaunting sound and the procession began.

First, in quiet twos came the grey-habited monks, their sandals making whispering sounds on the stone floors, then a small girl she had once seen running around the High Street like a holy terror and now almost unrecognisable in her blissful solemnity – and her new red velvet frock. She was carrying a plaster statue of the babe, and she looked as if she would cheerfully kill anyone who tried to harm him, and behind her, the Guardian.

Many, many years ago, a college had put on *Murder in the Cathedral*, and a gangly, nervous student had played the saintly Becket.

Stop thinking about yourself Terry old fruit. Stop being miserable, frightened Terrence and BE Becket. That was Bryn.

You'll be wonderful, Terry. Why, you even look like Becket. And then, there's your goodness. Type-casting. Kate was delighted to remember that she had said something encouraging.

If you can't stop whingeing, Terry, Bryn will do it. He's a much better actor, after all. Rose being her usual, supportive self.

Better not to remember how Bryn had reacted to that. But she remembered Rose and her sobbing apologies – *it is better for him, Bryn darling, really it is* – and Bryn's softening.

Now Kate Buchanan looked at the Guardian as he made his way to the manger. It could not be but it was her friend, Benedict. How modest; he had never once said. Perhaps he assumed that she knew. More likely it did not matter to him. Closely she watched the monk, who was also Guardian and an ordained priest, all the way through the service. She saw his face as he elevated the host. He believed. His goodness radiated from him.

Kate had never experienced a religious service that had moved her more: the combination of the beauty of the church, built by men to the greater glory of God, the flowers, the music and, above all, the sanctity of the celebrant; how happy she felt. The Mass ended on a triumphal surge of music and Kate followed the other worshippers outside into the damp chill air.

'Should have been snowing, after that,' came one voice.

'Frost at least,' laughed another as they kissed and wished each other Happy Christmas.

Kate was moved along on the tide of humanity on its way to mulled wine and mince pies. Her grandmother had made mince pies and the best mulled wine in the whole county. She stood still and let the waves part round her. Not yet, not yet.

She turned and saw young Stacie with a boy, a handsome boy in an expensive coat.

'Come on,' she heard the boy say. 'Meet my people. They're not ogres and then we'll drop you. Come on, you'll be meeting them at the party.'

The girl shook her head. 'I'm too nervous, Craig. I want them to see me at my best, not with my nose all red and the rest of me bundled up like a polar bear.'

He hugged her quickly. 'You look cool and your little Christmas nose is perfect. Stacie, believe me, the parents feel absolutely ghastly about the mix-up that day; Mum goes into over-protective-mother mode and just won't speak to anyone till I'm on the mend.' He hesitate. 'And Stacie, I should have told you before but I hadn't told them I was taking you.'

She did not wait for him to finish. He had not told them. He was ashamed of her. Stacie jerked away from him and began to hurry down the driveway.

'I meant I hadn't told them I was taking a girl, Stacie,' he called after her. 'Any girl . . .' His voice trailed off.

Damn, thought Kate. Serves you right for eavesdropping. Quickly, quickly, get away. She turned and tried to hurry in a dignified fashion that would not draw any unwanted attention and then she heard Stacie running after her.

'Miss Buchanan, may I come with you?'

She stopped and waited. 'No mulled wine and mince pies?' she asked as the girl fell into step beside her.

Stacie's eyes were bright with unshed tears and she was not yet in complete control of her voice. 'I'm not Catholic,' began the girl and then stopped.

'I didn't see a notice that said, "Catholics only".'

The girl laughed, a sad little laugh. 'I know. I meant my parents, my father wouldn't be too happy. I only went . . .'

To meet a boy, thought Kate but she said, 'Like me, for the music.'

'Yes, yes, that's it, and it was lovely, like a play really.'

It was not a long walk to the village through the dark wood but Kate wondered what the girl would have done had she not been there. It was odd to think of her presence giving comfort. What use would I possibly be should some madman come stalking us through the woods? But she said none of this.

'There's something really special about Christmas morning, isn't there, Miss Buchanan, even if you're not a believer, I mean.'

'I've always liked Christmas,' said Kate untruthfully. There had been Christmases when she had been in so much agony, not physical – always so much easier to handle than mental – that she had hoped to die.

'I never expected, well, to see you at the abbey, I mean.'

'I never expected to see myself there either. The Guardian invited me to the service and I went . . . for the music.'

She had intrigued Stacie who seemed to brighten a little. 'What's a guardian?'

'Franciscans don't have abbots; St Francis wanted his followers to be very democratic and so Franciscans elect a guardian or warden to be their head, as it were, just for a few years at a time; someone, after all, has to have a deliberative vote, just in case there's a tie. He does not have to be an ordained priest like Benedict.'

'He's nice, isn't he? Really holy and a good artist too.'

'Yes, he is.' She was agreeing to all three.

'My dad thinks monks are a bit strange, not natural.'

Benedict? Strange? Unnatural? 'And you, what do you think?'

They had reached the road that ran along beside the sea. The moon shone on the water, which was so calm, gently lapping the shore and so one could hardly believe that the same sea could and would cause devastation. Kate breathed in the sea air. *Fill your lungs, Kate,* Granny had urged when they were by the sea. *Sea air is good for you.* She never said why but Kate believed and still breathed deeply.

The world at the dawning of this Christmas morning was lovely. If Granny was right, from somewhere they should be able to hear heavenly choirs heralding the birth of the Prince of Peace. Kate strained as always to hear, anxious as ever to see if Granny was right. How lovely to be good enough to hear heavenly music. All she heard was a car gunning through the village, happy voices from behind them, and some silly laughter from outside the hotel. The light was all on the water and where they walked it was so black that she could barely make out Stacie's features. And she cannot see mine either, she thought exultantly.

'I never thought much about them,' said Stacie who had been thinking, 'but I have a friend who's Catholic and he's quite normal. I've told you about him. Anyway, I was thinking that Christmas might be a good time to talk to my dad or maybe I should wait till school starts in January.'

Not a good idea, thought Kate but said nothing and the girl went on. 'He wants to go to the Royal Academy, you know, to study, and his parents will allow him.'

'It's a good school, I've heard,' said Kate simply. 'He won't go to a university first? Perhaps you will.' Kate was tiring of her youthful companion. She didn't want to protect her from bogey-men in the wood. Still less did she want to hear all her sad stories of unrequited or even requited love or the perverseness of parents. Stacie was spoiling the lovely feelings the Mass had given her and she wanted rid of her. With relief she saw the lights from the Abbots House.

'Goodnight, Stacie,' she said abruptly. 'Have a Happy Christmas.'

'Goodnight,' said the girl sadly and turned away towards the centre of the village.

'Miss Buchanan.' Kate heard the voice again as she put the key in the lock. 'I hope you're not alone for Christmas?'

What would she say if I confessed to being alone, to preferring it that way? Will she ask me to dinner? Poor Jim; I can imagine his face were I to turn up on his doorstep. 'No, dear, of course not. Goodnight. Thank you.'

She heard Stacie hurrying off as she opened the door and felt annoyed with herself for being so Scrooge-like. How kind and thoughtful the child was, even when the boy had so obviously upset her. She was a brave wee thing. Something was going wrong with her first love affair and so she would work harder on her plans for a career. Kate, who had done the same thing herself, saluted her.

The girl would be all right even if her parents had no idea where she had been. At least I was always able to tell Granny and Tante everything. Kate stood with her back against the door while she pictured Stacie hurrying through the dark streets. How melo-dramatic. They weren't dark. There were streetlights and Christmas lights and light spilling from houses as doors were opened to admit family and friends. She was alone in her sanctuary and she relaxed and let its warmth welcome her. She was not alone. *He* was with her.

She walked over to the table and looked down at the manger scene. In the moonlight it was ethereally lovely; even the card-board baby became more than he was. Or was that an impious thing to say about a representation of the Christ Child?

Kate smiled as again she heard her cousin's angry defiant little voice. 'Nobody else waits for Christmas.' David was in Australia now, had been for years. But he was with her here in Abbots House as he had been with her in Granny's beautiful home all those years ago. He had inherited the house, of course, and sold it when he left the country to get away from the scandal surrounding his cousin. How he had boasted once of being Katherine Buchan's cousin. She had not heard from him for years.

She had not lied to the girl, not exactly. The people she had loved were always with her. Impossible to explain that to a young girl who lived in the present, who was so patently in love with that boy. Nice-looking, and a nice voice. If he could use the voice, play it properly and his body too, he should be all right. And Stacie? Still too early to tell but she was coming along. Oh, Kate, be generous on Christmas morning. Yes, the girl could be good.

'I hope you don't come back until after the holidays,' she said into the darkness.

Who else was with her? Granny, Tante, two women who had disliked each other heartily but who had cared for the daughter of the man they had both loved. Hugh, her ever-faithful stepbrother, friend, lawyer, confidant. She felt a shiver of regret. She took Hugh's kindness for granted, always had done. For a moment she wondered if he had ever wanted more than a sister, a client, a friend, but she dismissed the thought; it would have been almost incestuous. Dear old Hugh.

And then there was Bryn Edgar. It was Christmas when she first admitted that she loved him: Christmas when he first said that he loved her. They were in New York; such a heady city. They had never been before and they revelled in every moment, every sight, every experience. They walked the streets, astonished by the cold, gawping at the decorations, so exquisitely beautiful in the city centre and becoming more and more tawdry the further they walked from the gaudiness of Broadway. They loved everything: the coffee shops where Bryn ate eggs, bacon, sausages, pancakes – 'with syrup?' You bet with syrup – toast and coffee for $2.95 maximum and Kate breakfasted on coffee and a bagel for less than a dollar; the shops on Fifth Avenue which were full of the most beautiful clothes and jewellery and where window dressing was in the hands of masters. They were in *A Woman of No Importance*, by Oscar Wilde, which had transferred, with its original cast, from London. Bryn was Lord Illingworth, a role for which he was far too young but for which he was admirably suited and he woke every morning to yet more hysterical notices. Kate was the young American, Hester Worsley, and she too was lionised, for her looks, her acting, even her clothes, which had nothing at all to do with her but were the fruits of the labours of the costume designer who bore her neglect gracefully. They were interviewed for newspapers from, it seemed, everywhere, and were on radio and on television which Kate hated but Bryn loved.

'In the theatre people see the character, Bryn, and I like that anonymity. On this television thing, they see me and I'm no one's business.'

'Silly cow,' said Bryn, but he was smiling and Kate had long ago learned that he only ever referred to women he liked as 'silly cow'. After their performances fans besieged them. Again Bryn loved every minute except when it went on interminably and his empty stomach reminded him of how long it was since he had eaten, but, as always, Kate hated it. Some nights they ate with the rest of the cast or were guests at lavish dinner parties given by amazingly friendly and generous Americans, but on other nights they walked along the streets, arm in arm, wrapped up in everything they owned because neither had ever experienced such temperatures, and they gawped like children at the displays of flying reindeer, animated Santas, skaters in Austrian clothes, dancers in eighteenth-century costume – the eye was dazzled wherever one looked.

'Katie, Katie, have you ever seen such examples of conspicuous consumption? I love it. I shall buy a flat here.'

'An apartment.'

'Aren't we prissy? Sometimes, I think you should have been a schoolteacher, Katie, like Miss Moffatt in *The Corn is Green*; she didn't stand for nonsense either. Will you visit me in my Noo Yawk apartment?'

'Of course, whenever I'm in New York I'll come for coffee and a blueberry bagel.'

He stopped and, since he was holding her arm, she was forced to stop too. He turned her round to face him. 'Is that all you would want from me, Kate?' he asked and he kissed her.

Kate was surprised but she realised that this was what she had been waiting for all along. This was the unfinished part of their relationship. They were friends, colleagues, soul mates. They understood each and every nuance of the other's voice, body language, thoughts, even, and why? They stood in the middle of Broadway while other pedestrians slapped them on the back, ignored them, or wished them well, and they kissed each other as if they might be torn apart at any moment, as if each could not get enough of the other. At last they broke apart and stood smiling for a moment and then Bryn hailed a taxi and when the yellow door closed behind them he said the name of his hotel and kissed her again.

It was right; it was perfect. Soon they were in his room and Kate leaned against him while he kissed her and undressed her at the same time and then she could not wait and began to help him, and they fell on the huge bed and upon each other and it was right. Every inch of Kate tingled with mingled pleasure and frustrated desire and just as she thought she would die of frustration he claimed her and she climaxed at once and Bryn followed her and collapsed on top of her. Someone had shouted. Who? Kate? Bryn? Kate neither knew nor cared.

At last he pushed himself up on to one elbow and looked down at her and his hand traced her face and down her long neck and across her shoulder blades. 'Katie, Katie, I adore you.'

'Silly fool,' she whispered as she responded to his kissing. 'If I'd known it was like that I'd have done it long ago.'

'Loose woman. With me, though, Katie, only with me. You would have waited for me?'

She would not respond to his vanity, although she had never ever experienced desire like that, a fire that, out of control, could consume her, burn her up so that she would shrivel and disappear.

'Katie. Tell me, you adore me too?' What a child he was.

'Adore? No, Granny always said only God should be adored but I love you, Bryn Edgar and I always will.'

'I'll make you adore me; I'll start here and then I'll go here and then here,' and soon she was once more moaning with pleasure in his arms.

At last, unable to bear more, they fell asleep. Kate woke first and remembered everything. 'I love you, Bryn Edgar, till death us do part,' she whispered as she looked at his sleeping face. He looked like a little boy when he was asleep, his long lashes lying on his cheek-bones, his curls damp with sweat.

He opened his eyes and smiled up at her and she felt herself melt with pleasure into his embrace. Oh, dear God, how beautiful love is.

'Marry me, Katie. We'll be bigger than the Oliviers, bigger than Burton and Taylor; we're equals, don't you see? Your talent is as great as mine.'

Was it? She prayed that it was so. But marriage would get in her way. Sex was wonderful; they could be lovers but she would go back to her own little flat and she would make her own decisions about her career. Bryn was too forceful. He would swallow her whole if she married him and she was not ready, not yet. 'Marriage, Bryn, I never thought of marriage, not yet, not when I'm just beginning. I'll marry you but not yet. Let's establish ourselves first.'

'Look at us, look at what the critics say. We've made it, Katie; we're there.'

But she would not agree to an early marriage. Why did he have to spoil this wonderful thing? She loved him. How could he be in any doubt about that? But this was the time to consolidate their place in theatrical history and she just knew she would have no place at all if they married.

'I'm not ready, Bryn. We can be lovers and we can be friends. Life is just too exciting and exacting now. There are roles I want to play. Failures I have to make. Try to understand.'

'You try to understand, Kate. We can succeed and fail together. Marry me now.'

'No,' she decided and only knew what she had sacrificed when he married someone else.

Christmas for Stacie should have been wonderful. She tried to forget that she was angry with Craig, that perhaps she had ruined whatever it was that might be between them. It was so great to have Dad home and with nothing to do for even two days. Although he had refused to close the butcher shop on Boxing Day, at least he had promised not to go in but merely to check his staff by telephone.

They said nothing controversial when she came home from Midnight Mass, assuming correctly, if somewhat misleadingly, that she had been out with friends. Mum had even given her a glass of eggnog, which had infuriated Cameron who had had to make do with a soft drink. They slept late and then spent a wonderful morning in the sitting room, opening presents and eating breakfast on their laps. It was Maggie's one day of dropping her standards, for on Christmas Day she warmed quiches that she had baked a few weeks before Christmas; that way she could stay with her family and watch rather than be in the kitchen fussing over pans.

But the ideal moment for Stacie to discuss her plans to study with the controversial Miss Buchanan never quite seemed to get there. She brought her name up. 'This quiche is so fabulous, Mum. Do you think Miss Buchanan is having something hot for breakfast?'

Maggie stopped with her own fork halfway to her mouth. 'I don't know, dear. She doesn't strike me as being much of a breakfast person. I'm sure she's fine.'

Cameron, who looked as if he had been about to say something, hurriedly crammed his mouth with a combination of eggs, cheese, cream and roasted assorted peppers in a rich pastry case.

'Don't stuff,' said Maggie automatically and reached down for another gift on her pile, Miss Buchanan and her breakfast completely forgotten.

They listened to the Queen, a part of Christmas that they shared with Miss Buchanan, ate an enormous and excellent meal and then went for a walk. Kate would not have recognised their saunter as a walk because they walked up the hill into the village, along the main street where they saw various friends and customers, and then retraced their steps, but since one of the encounters had been with a teacher, Stacie felt the time was right to mention school. Dad, after all, had had a sherry and two – or was it three? – glasses of wine. He should be in a mellow mood.

'Miss Gabraith should begin rehearsing the school programme as soon as we get back. What fun it's going to be.'

Jim stopped and so Maggie stopped and all four stood in the middle of the pavement. 'Silly waste of time.'

He had changed his mind. Stacie was appalled; she would start howling right here almost outside the manse. 'Dad,' she wailed. 'How can you say that? We're going home to watch at least one film, maybe two. How can acting be a waste of time?'

'It is for them that can do better, like you, my girl. Now calm yourself, I said you could be in the play, take the elocution lessons or whatever they are – that's good for a girl – and you can. But if your real work falls behind then you're out. Now come on, let's not spoil Christmas.'

Maggie smiled at her daughter reassuringly and obediently Stacie walked beside them. But what a quandary. She had a chance to be coached by a great actress but her father would see that not as a fabulous opportunity but as more extra fluff taking time away from what she should be doing.

But this is what I should be doing, thought Stacie as she faked smiling cheerily. I can't be anything but an actress. I just know that it's what's right for me and I'll be great, I know I will and Craig . . . Why had she balked at meeting his parents on Christmas Eve? Cameron was right. Sometimes she was a stupid cow. It had been the magic of Christmas; she had wanted to share it only with Craig. What if his parents had disliked her and took back their invitation to their party: Stupid Stacie, adults don't behave like that. But I would have seen it in their faces. Why didn't he tell them about me? What did he say, something about any girl? They would dislike any girl? Is that it? I'm not going to think about it. I won't. The new dress, bought with shoes, and bag, and even new underwear, was hanging in her wardrobe, so beautiful that she felt a frisson of excitement every time she looked at it or fingered the material. A grown-up party dress; it was a woman's dress, not a dress for a little girl and Craig would see her in it, unless she had now well and truly blown it. Why had she not gone to meet his parents? He will ring about the party. I will still go, won't I? Oh, I can't bear this. I want him to see me in my lovely dress and in my fabulous new jacket. Oh, Dad, dear Dad, what a beautiful beautiful jacket. Every girl in my class will hate me when they see it. I wish they could see the dress too.

Stacie sat beside her father for the rest of the evening, made him a sandwich because he was too lazy to go to the kitchen, and watched the telephone, willing it to ring. A sob escaped her.

Maggie was there. 'Stacie, love, what is it? You've not been yourself all day. Who's hurt you? Is it that boy?' Her round rosy face was creased with concern and the beginnings of righteous anger.

Stacie fought to control herself as Cameron snorted, 'She's in love,' and turned the volume up on the television set.

'I'm fine. Sorry, don't mind me.'

Jim took the control from his son and turned the television set off. 'Go on in the kitchen, Cameron, there's a good lad. Stacie, what's that laddie done? You were fine yesterday.'

Go for it, Stacie. Pull out all the stops. This is as good a time as any. 'Oh, everything's a mess. Craig said his parents didn't let me know because he hadn't told them he was going to Edinburgh with me.'

'Why not?'

'His mum is worse than you, if that's possible, Mum. She doesn't want him going out with me, with any girl really,' she amended quickly, 'and I'm scared he won't want me at the party now and Miss Buchanan says . . .' She stopped.

Maggie looked at her husband and then at her daughter and then she looked around her comfortably furnished sitting room with its tall Christmas tree festooned with lights and every Christmas decoration her children had ever made. She saw the family photographs in solid silver frames, her Lladro figures. There was a new one now, a Christmas present from Jim. She thought of the feel of it as she had taken it, with shaking fingers, from its box, smooth, cool, beautiful as Christmas and now Stacie was in tears. 'All right, let's sit down quietly and you tell your dad and me everything, and I mean everything.'

And Stacie did. 'Sometimes I just wanted to be on my own, to be private and still, and so I used to go to the crusader's tomb in Templehall Woods.'

His face contorted with fear and anger, Jim turned away.

'Nobody goes there,' Stacie pleaded to his back. 'Not even the monks. It's peaceful and I could really go over all the bits from drama class without being heard or looking stupid.' She looked at her mother, desperately hoping that she would understand. 'I could be as awful or as great as I could be and only the trees could hear and—'

'Christ.' Jim interrupted with what for him was a one-word prayer, and as his daughter flushed and looked ready to cry again he sat up and waved at her, turning his right arm round and round in the air as if he were winding up a barrel organ. 'I'm sorry, Stacie, love, I'm just a butcher from a wee village. I'm trying, pet, just tell me.'

Stacie blew her nose and gulped a few times and looked at her rather teary father and her surprisingly calm mother and went on. 'One night a few weeks – no it was October, I was practising this really important speech, really important and I got stuck.' She stopped and appealed to her parents in turn. 'Mum, Dad, it was just fabulous, the most beautiful voice spoke, filled in the lines. I nearly had a heart attack; it came from the tomb but it was a woman's voice, low and passionate and like nothing I've ever heard except in my head sometimes when I read Shakespeare and it was Kate. She told me who she was, I mean she said she was Kate Buchanan and she lived in the village and we walked back together and she said I could rehearse in her little enclosed garden. Dad, doesn't that show you what a decent person she is; she knew I was out alone and she knew I'd be safer in her garden?'

'It never occurred to her to tell you to go home.'

Stacie ignored him. 'I went a few times and never saw her; she walks a lot on the beach but it was getting cold and dark and one afternoon she let me come in.'

'And all that time we thought you were safe at the library.'

'I was there mostly, Dad, but it's not open much these days and I was perfectly safe at Miss Buchanan's house. It's so gorgeous, Mum. I'd love to live there.'

'Welcome to slum clearance.'

'Oh, Daddy, you're picking up everything I say all wrong. I was so worried that she might be angry with the whole family after Cameron's artwork, but she doesn't hold a grudge, even said she wasn't so frightened when she found out her vandal was our Cameron.'

'Frightened,' said Maggie, who had got to her feet again and was looking around as if desperate to find something to clean or polish. 'I never really thought of her being frightened but she must have been petrified that some louts were after her.'

'Sit down, love; just as well the lout was your son. I don't want you going there again, Stacie.'

'I'm going; I'm going as often as I can. You don't understand,

132

Dad, you've never understood and what's worse you don't try. You're always so sure that you're right. Everything is going wrong for me. I've fallen out with Craig, and the only thing that will stop me from having a life of total misery is to get a part in the school play and I have a chance to be coached by a great actress—'

'A woman who's been in jail for murder,' said Jim. Conveniently, for the moment, he ignored that school play. 'My daughter sitting alone in the house of a woman who's been in a mental hospital. My God, Stacie, is there anything else you haven't told us?' He began to pace the floor, most of which was still covered in the detritus left by a comfortable family Christmas. 'Damn it, Maggie, did we have to open two different boxes of chocolates?'

'Yes,' said Maggie calmly. 'Cameron doesn't like soft centres. Come and sit back down, Jim. It's not that bad. Miss Buchanan is a lovely human being. I have no objection to my daughter being coached by her.'

'Dammit, Maggie, the woman's—'

'Yes, been in jail, been in hospital. She's out, Jim. She's cured or punished or whatever.'

'And she encourages a young girl to meet her without her parents' knowledge. Some lovely human being.'

Maggie and Stacie both rounded on him then.

'She didn't; she thought you knew. She won't help me without your permission.'

'Well, you don't have it.'

Stacie fled from the room.

'Now look what you've done, James Thomson. This is Christmas Day, love and peace and thinking well of your fellow man. Miss Buchanan never murdered anyone and if you'd calm down you'd know that too. I'm quite chuffed she wants to coach our Stacie.'

'Dammit, Maggie, she's not going on the stage.'

'Besides, we owe her something for the appalling way our son behaved. This would show her and the village that we trust her. Poor soul, sitting there all by herself, maybe thinking that folk are talking about her and that maybe someone else will vandalise her walls.'

'What on earth did she come back here for?' Jim was sitting on the settee, his hands between his knees and his head bowed.

Maggie sat down and put her arms round him. 'Doesn't matter, love. She is here and she was famous and she thinks your little girl is worth coaching. Think about it.'

Jim had no chance to think about anything as Cameron came in at that point. 'Are you all deaf? Lover boy's on the phone. Where's Stace?'

Kate got her Christmas wish. Stacie did not come. She had seen the expensive car parked outside on the little road and had been glad that, at least for the New Year, Miss Buchanan was not alone.

Hugh Forsythe had driven up to Scotland planning to arrive at Abbots House on the twenty-ninth. He had telephoned Simon before he left for France and had spoken to Rae.

'Doctors don't stop being doctors just because the rest of the world is on holiday, Hugh. Christmas is usually a very busy time for Simon, all that misery.'

That was an interesting, and very different, way of looking at the season of peace and goodwill. 'I hope he'll make it up to Scotland.'

'Yes, but we're staying at Greenhill Park. I'm sorry, Hugh, but staying with Kate would terrify me. To me she's one of Simon's patients.'

'She was a patient and she's perfectly sane,' he said stiffly.

'Really, Hugh. I meant only that I don't know her the way you do. She's not part of my youth. I only met her once nearly eight years ago now when Simon looked in on her in that convent on the Riviera. It's different for you; you were always in love with her.'

In love with her. If Rae knew then everyone did and he thought he had kept it hidden so well. 'Kate is my step-sister,' he said coldly and then relented. 'Don't worry, Rae, everything will be fine. Kate's a rotten cook so you'll be better off at the hotel. I'm carrying lots of goodies from Fortnum and Mason and I'll do New Year's Eve. The local butcher will deliver venison and a brace or two of pheasants. I managed not to gasp when he quoted prices at me.'

'Expensive?'

'No, he's giving it away but I didn't tell him and if it's good I shall bring some home with me. Give Simon my best. Having Christmas with your family, I suppose. Me too, old cousins, all that are left, but then, duty done, I shall fly up to Scotland.'

'Fly?'

God, he had forgotten how literally she took everything. 'As in go really quickly. Merry Merry,' and he had rung off.

Chacun à son goût. Sometimes he wondered what Simon saw in Rae; she was so different from Kate. But then Simon had never known the vital, alive, incredible talent that was Katherine Buchan. In those heady days so long ago it was the done thing to be madly in love with Kate, or with Bryn. They all said they were, vowed undying love, and had affairs with anyone who would stay still long enough. Was he himself still in love with Kate? He was like an old dog and had got into the habit of being in love. No, he loved her, was not, he assured himself, in love. Thank God, such a distressing and tiring emotion.

He vegetated with his elderly relatives and then flew back to London where he picked up his car at the airport and drove straight to Scotland. No point in stopping; everything was already in the car or would be delivered. He reached Friars Carse in the early evening on the twenty-ninth and parked outside the house, Abbots House. Lights streamed from every window. The house looked warm and welcoming, as it must have looked in its various guises through the centuries.

He sat in his car, his beautiful Bentley, and found that his legs would not work. And then Kate came to the door and smiled at him and he got out. He looked at her shrewdly: she was thin but then she had always been thin – Buchanan bones – and the blue wool suit she was wearing accentuated her frailty. 'Hello, Kate old girl,' he said and enfolded her in his arms. 'Too old for all that driving. Stiff as a board.'

'Come in, Hugh, you old faker,' she said and kissed him lightly on the cheek. She looked into his eyes. 'There are no ghosts, you know.'

The house had been lovely when he left it in the summer; now, since Kate had been living there, it was more vibrant, more alive. Lights shone softly on well-polished tables, on her ever-present embroidery; the house was warm and smelled very gently of lavender, one of the flowers that she had loved so much in Provence.

'Give me your coat, your things and we'll have some tea. I just want to look at you and realise that you are really here. Can we go back thirty years, Hugh? Will we pretend?'

'Firstly, Madame Hostess, I've been drinking tea at motorway stops all day and I want a drink, and secondly, no, my dear, let's not pretend. I like us the way we are.'

Kate looked at him, at his receding hairline, his ever so slight paunch, and, as always for the country, his immaculately cut but rather old and much worn tweeds, and her heart filled with pleasure. Hugh loved her, had always loved her, the real Kate Buchanan, almost all her life. She had never before really appreciated what it is to have at least one person who knows everything and who still loves unconditionally. She said so and he laughed.

'Blimey, Kate, you make me sound like the nicest sort of old springer spaniel. Come on, where's the whisky?' He was already moving towards the kitchen and yes, it was in the same part of the kitchen as it had been all those years ago. He poured generous measures and returned to the sitting room where Kate was already sitting in her favourite chair, her embroidery frame with her glorious creation nearby.

He sank down into the sofa and sipped. 'Lovely. I was exhausted but am feeling better already.'

'Hungry?'

'Not enough to want to go out,' he said warily, automatically reverting to an answer of their early twenties.

'Flatterer. I haven't been "out" as you say for years and I'm not cooking . . .'

'Thank God for that.'

She laughed; it was a lovely sound. 'You'd be surprised. I am mastering a few things but they're mostly eggie so we'll keep them for breakfast. No, the Maggie of Maggie's Fine Foods has made a casserole and it just needs to be popped in the oven.'

They chatted easily and Hugh refilled his glass and when that was finished he decided to unpack.

'You fetch your things from the motor and I'll work terribly hard and switch on the oven.'

Hugh went to the door and looked out at his pride and joy. 'Motor. You're the only person I know who says motor these days and doesn't sound affected. I was at this country house hotel in Devon or somewhere. Fellow was washing his Rolls. I said, "Beautiful machine," and he said, "Pleasant little motor." Pretentious git. Pardon my French.'

She smiled up at him. 'Perhaps it's because my mind stopped functioning in the seventies. We all said motor before then, didn't we?'

'I always said car.'

'So you did.' Am I remembering or is it just that Hugh has reminded me? 'Hurry up, Hugh, you're warming the garden beautifully.'

Their relationship was as it always had been, he thought as he closed the door behind him to keep the heat in.

While the casserole was cooking, Kate showed off her house to her admiring guest, and then he made a salad and prepared coffee. They talked easily, naturally, through a simple but delicious meal; she told him about her visits to the crusader's tomb in Templehall Woods and she told him that she had been to church, to Midnight Mass. He did not make the mistake of showing concern but seemed to take it for granted that she would attend a midnight service; she always had, had she not? He asked her about the music and, more importantly, about the monk who had befriended her.

'I feel utterly at ease with him; he's seen my face and my ghastly hands. Do you remember how much I loved manicures, and rings, Hugh, remember how I liked rings? Anyway he doesn't react. Most people show some pity in their eyes; I can see pity and a little horror in young Stacie's eyes as if she can feel the pain of burning, but Benedict accepts and that is so relaxing. I have allowed myself to be natural with him.' She laughed at him over her coffee cup. 'Are you jealous, darling Hugh?'

'Madly,' he said easily and refilled her coffee cup.

It was quite late when they went upstairs. 'Sleep as late as you like, Hugh.' She kissed him lightly on the lips, went into her room and closed the door.

He stood for a moment looking at her closed door. I am alone

137

in a house with Kate for the first time in years and I haven't tried to make love to her, don't want to make love to her. God, getting old is a bitch. He laughed and went into his own room but, although he was tired from the long drive, sleep evaded him.

Kate's appearance had not shocked him. Like Simon he was one of the few people who had seen her constantly. She looked better than she had looked when he had gone that last time to Le Prieuré to discuss her plans and to try to talk her out of them. So, as usual, she was right and he was wrong. He had thought that rebuilding the house was madness and she had laughed at his easy use of the word.

'I was happy there, Hugh. Simon thinks I'm crazy too,' and she had laughed, that delicious infectious bubbling laugh that was once so much a part of her.

He lay propped up by quite masculine pillows in the bed and looked up at the stars. A bedroom made for romance, moonlight spilling over the covers. It had looked much like this when it had first been rebuilt, all those years ago when Bryn Edgar and Katherine Buchan had set the world alight with their brilliance. More of Kate's memories were surfacing than she perhaps realised. She had found the rather rundown old house when she had been at the Edinburgh Festival and, as always, since he was her lawyer as well as her closest friend, she had told him about it. 'Come and see it, Hugh. I can make it so beautiful and it will be my bolthole, my little hiding place. Who would ever think to find me here?'

Hamlet at the Edinburgh Festival: 1965. Bryn Edgar as Hamlet, Prince of Denmark, and Katherine Buchan as Ophelia. The reviews were glowing. A *tour de force*.

They rehearsed for six days straight at the lovely Assembly Rooms on George Street almost directly across the street from Bryn's hotel, had Sunday off, and then played three nights, Monday, Thursday, and Saturday; with matinees on Tuesday and Friday for three weeks. The entire cast was exhausted. On the first Sunday most of them slept late and spent what was left of the day washing clothes, writing letters, and wandering along Princes

Street, George Street and the Royal Mile. On the second Sunday they arranged to meet at the bandstand in Princes Street Gardens: by eleven, only Kate, Simpson Delacourt, a venerable old actor who was playing the ghost of Hamlet's father, and some of the understudies had turned up.

'Let's wait,' begged Moira Oliver, Queen Gertrude's understudy. 'Bryn promised to be here to show us the town.'

Kate looked at the girl, long legs, long blonde hair pulled back with a blue Alice band, and wondered just what part of the town either of them had in mind. Not her fault and not his either; he can't help himself and too soon she'll find that his flirting means absolutely nothing. She felt tired, tired and drained. 'I've had enough of towns,' she said. 'I'm going to take a bus somewhere.'

'A bus? What a fabulosso idea, darling.' That was Simpson. 'Where to?'

'No idea. Out.' All Kate knew was that she did not want to be here in the gardens when Bryn arrived to show them the town. He had never been to Edinburgh before and knew no more about it than she did and that was merely the taxi route from their hotels to the theatre or, in Bryn's case, the mad dash across the busy but always beautiful George Street.

She and Simpson headed up to George Street and along to St Andrew Square and found that a bus was leaving in three minutes for Haddington.

'Where's that?'

'Not far, down the coast a bit, I think.'

'Perfect.'

The bus took them out of Edinburgh and into the country. Fields and farms spread themselves out on either side but in a very short period the sea appeared on their left-hand side. Like children starved of beaches they stuck their noses to the window and gazed.

'I adore the sea.'

Kate sniffed loudly like a hunting dog, her little nose in the air. She laughed at the expression on Simpson's face. 'Me too. Any old weather. The sea, the sea, the ever free . . .'

The rest of the way they tried capping one another with knowledge of sea shanties. The bus stopped and they got out and so did one other passenger. They were in a small main street; there were two or three magnificent houses on the sea side and a few shops on the other.

'I expected something bigger,' said Kate. 'Haddington sounds larger than this.'

'So it is,' said the other passenger who seemed to be waiting to be picked up. 'This is Friars Carse. Haddington's a few miles down the road.'

Since the bus was already pulling away, leaving them stranded, whether or not to look around Friars Carse was a decision taken away from them. They laughed. 'More of an adventure than we'd expected, Kate dear.'

What an attitude. Kate was delighted. She had been anxious to get away from Bryn and his begging, cajoling, and to have been marooned with a moaning minny would have spoiled her day. 'I shall buy you a fabulous lunch, Simpson – if we find a restaurant. Which way?'

'Oh, towards the sea, my dear, always towards the sea.'

They wandered along the very pretty street, boldly and rudely looking in all the gardens and any windows that were not too far from the road. The houses were substantial, each one different from its neighbours, each with a large and well-cared-for garden. 'Have you ever seen such roses?' asked Kate as she tried to breathe in the scent of a flamboyant peach-coloured bloom which hung, tantalizingly, just out of reach.

'Fabulosso,' said Simpson who, being much taller, obligingly pulled it down for her and Kate decided she would forgive him for using such a schoolboy word since he was such a nice human being; besides, he was a superb actor, and she had learned a great deal from watching him.

They came to a fork in the road. Straight ahead were more houses and more shops, all closed on a Sunday, but there was a fish and chip shop that promised to open at 4 p.m. Kate noted its name, Demarco's; how interesting, an Italian cooking typically English fish and chips.

'Look, Simpson, do you think Signor Demarco puts the fish suppers on a bed of spaghetti?' asked Kate facetiously.

'Don't be silly. All fish and chip shops in Scotland are owned by Italians and they're fabulosso. We have a treat in store.'

They turned together to the left. They were at the top of a hill and they stopped and looked out towards the open sea. Neither said anything; some things are so lovely that silent appreciation is the correct response. The road plunged down as if anxious to throw itself into the sea but, luckily, the sea had retreated and the precipitate road was forced to wander into a large flat area of beach or shingle. It would not always be so. When the tide was in the road would achieve its ambition; it would indeed disappear.

'No fun in stormy weather,' said Simpson at last. 'Reminds me a bit of Norfolk: absolutely spectacular but a real bitch in a storm.'

'I love it. Let's go down before I get so hungry that all I can think about is food.'

They walked down admiring the names of little side roads on the way: Canon's Close, Monks' Walk, Cockleshell Lane. 'That street isn't so old as the others around here,' said Simpson. 'There must have been some great monastery or priory here in the Middle Ages. I would imagine fishermen moved into the houses down here when the priests or whatever moved out.'

But Kate did not answer. She was standing in front of a ruin. It was set back a little from the road, further back than the two houses nearest to it, and was bordered by the remains of a high sandstone wall. 'How sad,' she said when Simpson joined her. 'It looks so unhappy and no wonder. Look at its name – Abbots House – is that medieval punctuation, do you think, no apostrophe. Poor house; it's ashamed of itself, Simpson. It was built to give shelter and sanctuary and it's just been allowed to fall down.' She peered at the house from all angles. 'Can you see any evidence of bomb damage or fire?'

'Looks more like vandalism; perhaps it was too big for any fisherman to buy. Lovely setting. Pity it's so far from civilisation.'

Kate said nothing, but when she returned to London at the end of their run she rang Hugh. 'Hugh, I've found a house; it needs a little work but it will be a fabulous investment. Aren't you pleased that I'm taking your strict warnings about my spending habits seriously? It's called Abbots House and if I could give up the theatre I would be happy to spend the rest of my life there.'

He had been against the purchase even though the estate that owned it was asking a relatively low price for it, as it stood sadly there in its tumbledown garden. 'You are out of your pretty little mind,' he had said when he had made the journey to see it. 'It's a dump; the roof needs work. God knows how much it will cost to repair the damage done by rising damp. Because it's historic, you'll be tied up in all manner of legal clauses usually beginning Thou shalt not, and restoring it to any glory it ever had will take every penny you have.'

He had had a spaniel once with the enthusiasm for life that she exhibited. That spaniel had never been able to take no for an answer either and slowly, slowly, and very expensively, the phoenix had begun to rise from the ashes of decay. For months, when he had visited her backstage she had been sewing, curtains, bedcovers, some pretty things she said were table treatments, whatever that meant. She was clever, he had always known that, and it was amazing what she seemed to be able to do with a few yards of material.

'The furniture is costing nothing, sad old Hugh. I'm picking bits and pieces up all over the place; some paint, some varnish, and voilà. Next Christmas I shall have a huge party, with roaring fires, and holly and great green boughs everywhere, and pineapples and shiny red apples, and mistletoe. Shall I kiss you under the mistletoe, darling old Hugh?'

'How naughtily incestuous,' he had said, but he loved it when she did. She had run around like a rather tall sprite kissing everyone and the flames from fire and candles had lit up her hair and her gold dress. She could wear anything, his friend Kate, his sister Kate.

Hugh fell asleep and when he woke a weak winter sun was trying to melt the frost on his windows. He could smell coffee. Things had changed. He hurried to shower and shave and galloped downstairs, not unlike the progress of young Cameron, in time to answer a rather urgent ring at the doorbell.

'Hello.' A girl with a huge box at her feet stood on the mat outside.

'Hello,' the girl answered, smiling at him in a rather shy but attractive way. 'Delivery from Thomson, the butcher.'

'Wonderful. Golly, you didn't carry this, did you?' asked Hugh, bending down to pick up the box. He turned round. 'Kate, the venison's here. I'm bringing it in.'

Kate, an apron over her casual sweater and trousers, came into the hall. 'Stacie, how lovely. Come in for a minute and I'll get my chequebook. Hugh, this is Stacie. I did tell you all about Stacie? How was the party, Stacie? Did you have a lovely new dress?'

While Hugh and Stacie were trying to explain that the delivery was prepaid, Kate led them both into the kitchen, and then while Hugh unpacked the box with many small cries of pleasure at its contents, Stacie talked to Kate.

'It was wonderful, Miss Buchanan, and I did get a new dress but I remembered what you said about warm colours and bought it in gold. Craig liked it,' she finished with a blush.

'Lovely, you must come in a few days when Hugh has gone and tell me all about it.'

Hugh looked up from his box of delights. 'Perhaps I'd like to hear about a nice party dress too.'

'Stacie and I have work to do; bring the plays, Stacie, any evening you see the light on. You have asked your father?'

'Of course. Thank you.'

Hugh escorted her to the door and, unaware that Stacie had just decided that he was even more exciting than Craig's father, returned to pour himself a cup of surprisingly good coffee. 'She's lying, you know, about her father or, at least, she's ill at ease. Nice little thing, though. Now make me one of your eggie dishes while I put together a marinade for this venison. Wonderful cut of meat. I shall take some back to town with me.'

Stacie hurried to find the van from her father's shop but it had already driven back into the village. Because she had been in the shop when the assistants had packed the van she had a fairly good idea of where it should be. Cameron would be furious if he was left to do all the delivering. Only the super car outside Miss Buchanan's had persuaded him to carry the heavy box to the door for her. Then he had fled back to gaze longingly at the car and make mental notes that could be discussed later, with some authority, among his friends. He lived in hope that the other toffs supposed to be visiting Abbots House would also have perfect taste in cars. Stacie found him swearing like a trooper on Cockleshell Lane.

'Some help you are,' he said when he saw his sister.

'Could I help it if I was invited in to get the cheque?'

Cameron looked at his sister. She was wearing skintight jeans which might have showed something as flimsy as a cheque but the capacious pockets of her new ski jacket could hide anything. He knew she was lying but was determined not to pick a fight. She could, after all, tell her father the choice words he had been using. 'Nice of you to give me a hand, Your Majesty.'

Stacie grinned in triumph, ruffled his hair, which annoyed him even more, and went to consult the driver about the next delivery. He handed her several cheques and envelopes containing cash. 'Sit in the van, love, and put them cheques in the book. Mrs Bridges has paid her whole December bill in cash so count it up and enter that too.'

Willingly, Stacie went to sit in the warm front of the van and picked up the payment book.

'Hi.'

Her heart skipped a beat. 'Craig.' She felt her face light up with the unexpected pleasure of seeing him and so she allowed herself to forget that he had not answered her calls. She moved to get out of the van, forgetting the envelope of cash that she had been given. It fell to the floor and coins of all denominations went everywhere. 'Damn.'

Craig opened the door as she tried to retrieve some of them. He was laughing. 'Come out and I'll help. Look, there's a penny over there under the brake pedal. Have you been busking?'

'Very funny. It's an old lady—'

Craig did not allow her to finish. 'Someone around here has to save pennies to pay their bills? How awful.'

Stacie winkled out an escaping ten pence coin and straightened up. 'Not this old miser, Craig; rich as Croesus, my mum's always saying, but getting her to part with it is another matter. She's always writing to my dad. "You ought to be ashamed of the price you're asking for butcher meat. I remember when, etcetera, etcetera."'

'My grandfather's like that. Wrote a stinker of a letter resigning from the golf club when the subscription went up to twenty quid a year. "Extortion", he called it and that was before I was born.'

They were both standing very straight looking at each other. 'I love your new jacket, Stacie, cuddly and sexy at the same time.'

Stacie blushed. Sexy. She looked sexy. What bliss. 'Why are you in the village?'

He gestured to his clothes. 'I'm going shooting. We stopped for cigarettes for some old codgers, friends of my dad. Our house stinks to high heavens. They're having a quick puff now since Dad won't let them smoke in his car and I saw you coming up the hill.' He bent over quickly and kissed her very chastely on her lips. 'Did you enjoy the party?'

'You know I did; it was the most marvellous evening of my whole life. I sent your parents a note to say so.'

'But what about me?'

What could she say? Could she explain how unsure of him she was? She lowered her eyes and did not look at him directly. 'I tried phoning, Craig, yesterday, twice; you were out.'

He looked puzzled and waved his arm quickly towards the top of the hill where Stacie could see his father standing. 'I was only out with the dogs yesterday. No one gave me a message; I'm sorry.' He looked embarrassed and slightly angry. 'It's the Christmas hols, Stacie; my house is a madhouse. Look, I must go but I'll ring you tonight. Will you be at home?'

Not one word about how he had promised to ring. Challenge him.

She nodded.

'Elevenish; I won't be able to ring before then.'

He did not kiss her goodbye but looked into her eyes for a moment and smiled and Stacie's heart raced. Then he was running up the hill to where his father was rather angrily sounding his car horn. Stacie stood, leaning against the van watching him until the dark green Land Rover had disappeared along the main road. She forgave him for not ringing her. His life was so busy, so different from hers.

He kissed me. That was the third time, the first time was in the street outside school, and then at the party; she giggled, he had kissed her more than once near the school and at the party. Stacie closed her eyes again and allowed her mind to remember. Her father had insisted on driving her to Craig's family home just outside the village. How absolutely mortifying. It was a nice car but nothing like some of the other cars grandly sweeping their way up the well-lit driveway. She had begged him to drop her at the open gates: 'Look at the fabulous lampposts,' she had said but he had paid no attention. Cars were going in constantly, but no, he drove her to the very door and she knew he had watched her as she walked up the great stone steps and gave her name to the butler. A butler; she had never in her life met a butler, had never known anyone who employed such an august being. Already Stacie was enchanted. She left her coat – thankfully – in a dressing room set aside for women. It was her best coat but it was still a girl's coat, and certainly not the lovely green velvet cape she had tried to persuade her mother to buy for her. But her dress was lovely, soft and shimmery and she had brushed highlights on her hair and her cheekbones and even her lips. Through excitement and personal discipline – no second helpings of anything at any time for any reason whatsoever – she had been losing weight for weeks now and the dress floated round her hips more easily even than it had done when Mum had bought it two weeks before. Stacie had checked one last time that her dress was not caught in her knickers and that her tights had not run on the fifteen-minute journey, had picked up the little gold bag that dear, dear Mum had bought for her too – 'not a word to your father' – and had gone out and Craig was there.

The thrill of seeing him standing there had been almost over-whelming. He was wearing a dinner jacket over tartan evening trousers and his fair hair shone in the candlelight, for there were candles, masses of them, everywhere. He looked at least twenty, much older than seventeen.

'You look fabulous, Stacie,' he said and, taking her hand in his, he had kissed her gently on the cheek. 'Come and meet the parents, get it over with, and then we can have fun.'

She had said nothing at all but had allowed him to lead her down the great oak staircase and back into the hall where his parents stood beside a Christmas tree that rose from floor to ceiling. Breathe, relax, breathe, relax. Later she remembered a very soft handshake and a rather firm one and she thought Mr Sinclair might have said, 'Lovely to have you with us, Stacie,' but she could not be sure. She did know that Craig's mother had said, 'How do you do,' and nothing else. Her voice was almost as lovely as Miss Buchanan's but not quite. Miss Buchanan's voice was the loveliest in the world.

'Are you allowed champagne?' Craig was taking her into a dining room where the largest table she had ever seen in her life was covered in a landscape of crystal and silver on a startlingly white linen cloth, and everywhere else that was not covered by flowers and greenery and great silver candlesticks had huge platters of the most beautifully arranged food.

'Yes, but not much.'

He laughed and picked up a crystal glass into which a waiter poured some frothy bubbles. 'Don't worry,' he whispered into her ear. 'I won't allow you to get squiffy.' He took a glass for himself and side by side they walked out through some huge folding doors to a drawing room with yet another Christmas tree. There he stopped. 'To us, Stacie,' and raised his glass.

'To us,' she whispered and lifted her glass. Bubbles went up her nose and she sneezed but Craig laughed and rescued the glass that she was in danger of dropping. 'I should have warned you about the bubbles. Come on, I'll introduce you to some people. Don't worry,' he said, 'Nice people, my grandmother for one; I've told her all about you. Gosh, Stacie, I've just thought. Granny lives in London and loves the theatre. I just bet she knows all about Miss Buchanan.'

Craig's grandmother did not look old enough to be anyone's grandmother. She was tall and very elegant. For a grandmother she had remarkably smooth skin, her eyes were clear and unlined, and her hair was black with only a sparkling of silver, not grey, over her ears. She was wearing a blue velvet evening suit that looked so simple that Stacie knew it had to have cost a fortune and diamonds sparkled in her ears and on her hands and she was, rather dashingly, Stacie thought, smoking a cigarette. 'Hello, Stacie, my dear, how nice to meet you. Craig tells me you're a wonderful actress.'

After a welcome like that it was easy.

Stacie's delicious reverie was crudely interrupted. 'Oh, Craig darling, kiss me, kiss me like you kissed me last night.'

Damn it; she had had her eyes closed. 'Shut up, Cameron.'

'Why? So you can skive off here dreaming of lover boy while I work my socks off?'

'I'm doing the payment book.'

'That's clever. You leave the books in the van and you stand out here mooning over Lord Craig and the figures get entered into the book. Not word processing, thought processing.'

He had a point and he was indeed working very hard. 'Sorry Cameron, I just came out to say hello to a friend. Okay, keep your hair on. I'll take the next delivery and I'll enter the payments.' Quickly she got back into the van, took up the payment books and, conscious of Cameron's heavy breathing on the window, she started to work. Miss Buchanan's bill had been paid in advance from London by Mr Forsythe. Who, she wondered, was Mr Forsythe exactly and what was his relationship to Miss Buchanan? They had looked like an old married couple in the kitchen that morning and he was certainly the toff who had overseen the work in the spring and summer. Craig's grandmother had not mentioned him but then she had known little of Katherine Buchan; Craig had forgotten that his paternal grandparents had spent a long time in Hong Kong. Bryn Edgar had been dead for some years when the Sinclairs had returned to Britain and the stage was peopled by new if less exciting stars.

IO

Simon Whittaker and his wife flew to Edinburgh, caught a train to North Berwick and from there took a taxi to the hotel that had been recommended to them. Rae was not at all happy. Why on earth anyone would want to bury themselves in a village miles from anywhere that had no working airport within seventy miles was beyond her, and why her husband would choose to forgo the delights of several lovely parties to celebrate the coming of the New Year with a patient was just something she could not and, in fact, did not want to understand. How many patients had he dealt with over the years? She had no idea. How many had he spent holidays with? None – until now. She could, of course, have refused to accompany him and Simon would have stayed at home and at this very moment they could be driving down to Bunny's at Guildford or resting before joining the crowd at Alice and Charlie Howard-Smyth's annual party. But he would not have been happy and therefore neither would Rae. She was not exactly ecstatic now but, like many a good wife, was adept at hiding her own feelings or at least disguising them and Lord knows she would try to be cheerful. But Kate Buchanan had been a patient, introduced by a policeman. As Rae's mother had said many times in the early years of their marriage, 'Dear Simon is so clever. Why on earth didn't he become a brain surgeon?' Simon's answer to that, delivered in the privacy of their own bedroom, was short and to the point.

The hotel was graceful and the room warm and welcoming. A fire burned in the grate and there was a small carafe of really excellent sherry on a bedside table. Room service delivered some rather tasty smoked salmon sandwiches. Rae admitted that so far the hotel was as good as any she had visited. She would rest for an hour or so to prepare herself for the rigours of the evening ahead. At seven o'clock, bolstered by a comfortable nap and a luxuriously hot deep bath, Rae was ready for the evening. Simon, a man who preferred the speed of a shower, had paced as he listened to his wife splashing in her bath. If she took one more minute he would tell her to take a taxi when she was ready. He could wait no longer to see Kate, Kate who had been a patient and still was, but who was also a friend, someone he cared about very deeply. Remembering this, he sat down on the end of their bed and waited patiently.

How many times had he thanked God that Rae, his wife, the mother of his children, was not at all like Kate? Rae would insist on ringing the children at midnight – why he did not know. They were at the age where they would either be out and already tipsy or at home with friends and exceedingly tipsy, but Rae was obliged to go through all these 'mother' motions.

At last she made her entrance. 'That is a lovely dress,' he said. She always needed to have her courage propped up. This was another conundrum. How good a psychiatrist am I?

Rae smiled and twirled. 'Do you think so? Felicity thought it too young for me.'

'Jealous of her mother, dear. Ready to go?'

The last-minute adjustments to hair, to tights, to lipstick. Bag checked to make sure she had whatever it was that women checked to make sure they had. He was getting impatient again but if he showed it, she would slow down.

'Have you ordered a taxi for the morning?'

'Hugh will bring us back. A taxi would be impossible on New Year's morning.'

She was troubled. He could tell by the tense set of her shoulders. 'Don't worry, dear: we won't be coerced into staying and Hugh is such a good fellow, he will be perfectly happy to come out with us; it won't inconvenience him at all.' He smiled as he closed the door behind them. Surely she had not expected Kate and Hugh to be sharing a room, not after all these years, and all Kate had been through. As far as he knew Kate had never shared a bed with Hugh or anyone except Bryn Edgar but Rae still saw her as a predatory creature. Kate would adore knowing that but loyalty to his wife would prevent him telling her.

'I hate it when you smile like that,' said Rae huffily as they got into the taxi.

'I was just thinking about why I love you,' he said, which was a perfect remark. He was, after all, a psychiatrist.

The house was as beautiful as he had known it would be. Christmas decorations consisted of a few red or gold candles and a very unhappy-looking nativity set on a table. The manger contained two babies, one plaster and one made of cardboard. Kate looked quite frail but her skin had a healthy glow as if she spent time in the fresh air. Her lovely eyes smiled steadily at him.

'What a glorious caftan,' he said as he kissed her.

'Hugh sent it to me for my first Christmas in Le Prieuré,' she said as she turned to greet Rae, unaware that, without intending to do so, she had just destroyed Rae's faith in her own pretty dress.

'Can you all get out of the kitchen,' complained Hugh a few minutes later after all the initial greeting was over. The kitchen was barely big enough for one person. Four was definitely overcrowding. 'Simon, open some champagne, old boy. We thought and decided to go with it all the way through the evening although Kate does have some lovely claret which would be wonderful with the venison.'

The claret had been Simon's gift and so he knew how good it was.

'I'll have champagne,' decided Kate, 'and stick with it. I'll get squiffy if I mix. You and Simon have some claret with dinner. Rae, dear, tell me what you think of these curtains. Have I made a mistake? Too many patterns?' The women went off chattering about curtains and colours and exquisite taste. Kate had always been able to handle people; it was one of her abundant gifts.

Simon, tall, grey-headed, elegant, leaned against a dresser, with severe risk to some fine porcelain plates, as he watched the rosy-faced Hugh manhandle a large casserole. 'How is she?'

'Put that smoked duck on the tray, thanks. She seems well, better than I had hoped.'

Simon began to open the claret. He and Hugh worked quietly and efficiently together. It was as if they had been opening bottles and cooking meals together for years, while in fact they had met only when Simon had been assigned to Kate's case. 'I have to tell you I was particularly worried about Christmas.'

Hugh pushed his casserole back into the oven. 'Me too, although she tells me she went to Midnight Mass.'

'How extraordinary, but how nice. Memories of Provence or was it because of her monk, do you suppose?'

Hugh had his back turned to Simon but he nodded in reply. 'He'd made a point of walking down here to tell her about the service. She says the music was sublime. How well is she, Simon? I think she's even thinner than when I last saw her. You know she insisted on paying someone to drive her here and so I didn't settle her in and she wouldn't have me here until now? I saw her more frequently when she was in France.'

It was Simon's turn to nod. 'She's well, Hugh. She could have left Le Prieuré years ago; perhaps she stayed for that nun, the one who used to be something famous in the art world. I don't know. I thought renovating the house was a bad idea but, so far, it seems to be working.' He picked up the tray. 'We'd better join them.'

'Not if I have to listen to waffle about curtains. Has she told you about Stacie?'

Simon put the heavy tray down again. 'Who's Stacie?'

They could hear the women calling, wondering where their champagne was.

'I'd better rescue Rae.'

Hugh laughed. 'I was going to say exactly the same about Kate.'

'I had thought about decorations,' said Kate as much later they sat waiting for the BBC to tell them that it would soon be another year, 'but I saw some on display and I thought, how ghastly, and decided to do without.'

Hugh, who had seen her wonderful Christmas arrangements over the years, laughed. He had been wondering if Kate was remembering the decorations she had put in the cottage for that wonderful first Christmas.

'Can a Christmas decoration be distasteful?' Simon asked and Hugh enlightened them with ridiculous stories of tasteless arrangements he had witnessed, most of them in Florida.

Rae, who tried hard every year to make sure that her decorations were tasteful, felt left out. Her hostess and Hugh Forsythe seemed to know what the other was thinking or was about to say, just like a long-married and affectionate couple, and Simon too, her own husband, appeared to have a very special relationship with this woman. There was an intimacy there, but it was not a closeness that Rae recognised and so it worried her.

'You're such a storyteller, dear old Hugh,' said Kate, 'and you almost made us miss the New Year.'

She went to her front door and opened it so that they could hear the bells ringing in the local church. 'That's nice, isn't it,' she said when they had all finished kissing one another. 'I was unaware of that church's bells; never heard them before.'

'Probably a new vicar,' said Simon.

'I'm not brooding, Simon,' she said quietly and squeezed his hand. 'I do remember *Christmas past,* but with love and thanks, my dear.'

'Come in before you catch cold, Kate; that would be a lovely beginning to the New Year.'

Hugh was shepherding them back inside but Kate resisted. 'It should start to snow now, and then everything would be absolutely perfect.' She looked at them gathered together for warmth as well as conviviality in the hall behind her. 'It is perfect,' she said.

It was next afternoon before Simon remembered that he had not found out about Stacie.

Kate had been persuaded to join the Whittakers in their hotel for dinner. Occasionally, over the years, Hugh had driven her to quiet little hotels in Provence where it was unlikely that anyone would recognise the lady with the scar. Here though, in Friars Carse, she knew she was discussed. Women gossiped about her in the shops: on the few occasions that she had actually gone shopping, people had stared in a mixture of curiosity and hostility and others turned away. She had had first-hand proof that the schoolchildren talked about her and had no reason to suppose that the men of the village did not. Apart from that dreadful incident with Cameron, no one had been openly censorious, and at Midnight Mass everyone had been too involved with their own family and friends to concern themselves with her. She hoped the hotel dining room on New Year's night would be the same and so she agreed for Hugh's sake.

He liked his food; the hotel was lauded and he would not go without her.

Tasteful decorations were abounded. The old dining room was incredibly lovely with green boughs and pine cones everywhere. The table in a sheltered alcove was dressed in silver and they laughed, saying that Kate in pale grey pants and the palest of blue sweaters was in collusion with the decorator. Hugh looked tired, like someone who had had too much of a good night. Poor old Hugh, feeling his age.

What Simon and Rae would never know was that Hugh – and Kate – had had a terrible night.

Driving people home after a party was never a problem for Hugh, good old Hugh, who never drank too much. Kate had been in bed when he had let himself into the silent house. She had blown out all the candles but, since it was New Year's Day, he lit the gold ones that were on the dining room table and poured himself a nightcap, a glass of that really princely claret. They had been playing music as they talked after the bells and he had put the Missa Solemnis on again, such superb music to bring in a new year by, and he had sat and enjoyed the music – and the wine – until he had heard the soft moaning.

Hugh hesitated. A bad dream probably. Nothing to worry about. More solid food than usual and several glasses of champagne. He turned off the music and sat in the candlelight. Now there were sobs in the moaning and he moved halfway up the stairs and listened. She was muttering, sobbing; he could hear her moving on the bed and still he hesitated. Never since they were children had he gone into her bedroom. Those awful months in hospital didn't count. A woman swathed in bandages, lying in a narrow hospital bed, was not an object of carnal desire, was she?

The muttering grew louder, more feverish, more distressed and he started to run – as fast as sad old Hugh could manage – up the rest of the stairs. He reached her door and opened it just as she started screaming. Dear God in heaven. He had prayed never to hear those screams again. This time there was no friendly nurse with a nice little hypodermic. What in the name of God was he to do?

'Kate, darling Kate, it's all right, I'm here, Hugh, it's me.'

She was half on half off the bed as she tried to get away from God knows what terror or to reach some worse terror that was out of reach. She strained towards it and the veins on her neck and her carefully put together face stood out.

'Bryn,' she screamed. 'No, no, Bryn,' and he pulled her into his arms and held her as she fought and struggled to get away from him.

He had never dealt with a difficult client, never been physically attacked. He was Hugh, dear old Hugh, sad old Hugh, with his seats at the opera, a box at the ballet, tickets for every show that anyone with any taste would want to see, and he sat on that moon-splashed bed and fought with his love as she fought with her demons. And at last, he won. She relaxed, weeping, against his chest, and he held her and wrapped her silly feminine lace cover round her and hoped it was warm enough. 'It's all right, my darling,' he whispered. 'Hugh is here, and everything is all right.'

For hours she lay in his arms and he was stiff and sore and in more discomfort than he had ever been in his well-ordered life and never had he been happier or sadder because he had defied her ghosts.

'Was it a bad idea, my lovely house?' she whispered as the first dawn of the New Year began to light the sky.

'No,' he said. 'It was a good idea.'

'A party was a bad idea,' she whispered again after two minutes, two hours, he did not know or care.

'No,' he said firmly. 'It was a good idea.'

'Hugh, dear old Hugh . . . slayer of ghosts.'

She fell asleep and he lay with his love in his arms and held her while she slept.

'Slayer of ghosts,' he agreed with her and then he too fell asleep and when he woke she was gone and the silly lace covers – very pretty, he was sure – had been replaced by the magnificent quilt from his own bed, and by the smell of frying bacon.

The plumbing was excellent and he went downstairs after a hot bath to find that it was two o'clock in the afternoon.

Kate, in jeans and an old sweater, was in the kitchen. She smiled at him and handed him an orange juice. 'I gave you a bad time, my dearest of friends.'

'It was interesting.' He had thought while he shaved, continued to think in the bathtub and while he had dressed and he had to ask. 'Kate, were you afraid of Bryn or afraid for him?'

'I was screaming his name, was I? The doctors asked me that. Afraid for him, of course. He was too heavy to pull, you see, although I did try, and then I went up like a bonfire on November fifth.' She stopped talking and went back to the stove. 'Hugh, did you hear what I just said?'

'Yes. A returned memory, Kate. You tried to pull him. He was heavy and then whatever you were wearing caught fire. Can you see anything else?'

With her back to him she shook her head. 'Let's turn our attention to breakfast. This is the first bacon I have ever cooked.' She looked at him enquiringly. 'One egg or two?' And he knew that, at least for the moment, she would say no more. But she had divulged more than she had previously revealed to him. Possibly or probably she had told Simon more. Doctors and priests are usually told more than lawyers. There was just something about that prefix *law* that worried the most upstanding of citizens.

It rained all afternoon and so they sat quietly reading and listening to music; they never had had to chat to be at ease with each other. 'Would you mind if I repeated the fabulous Lydia and Sextus bits?'

Please do, I love Handel's music; Lydia's aria reminds me of the Largo, don't you think?'

That was the gist of their conversation. Then it was time to change for dinner and Kate was tense again. 'This is a stupid idea, Hugh. I've forgotten how to act in a restaurant.'

'No, you haven't. It's the perfect time, my dear. Everyone will be too involved in their own parties; no one will even notice us.'

'But I'm exhausted.' She could not bear to be looked at, gossiped over, not tonight of all nights. She had never really enjoyed public exposure; it was Bryn who relished it. 'You go and explain.'

'And have Simon up here with his little black bag. Kate, you could have stayed in the convent if you were determined to avoid the world. Come on, two middle-aged couples out celebrating a quiet New Year? It's a perfect first. It will be too busy for people to be aware of other parties,' Hugh had consoled her. 'Who ever sees

156

anyone else?' Unless they're famous or infamous and then they are seen, gazed at, wondered about.

Kate went to dress. Before, the *little black* had been the answer to every occasion. Now what? The caftan, glorious as it was, was out. She found a well-cut pair of woollen trousers and a pale blue cowl-necked cashmere jumper.

Cashmere is always right, darling.

Whose voice was that? Her own probably – in the days when the right thing to wear was important. Now she wanted merely not to outshine Rae again and to show as little of herself as possible without wearing her hood.

Simon and Rae were waiting for them and the hotel was lovely, all Christmas warmth and charm. The tree was so dazzling that, for a moment, she closed her eyes against its brilliance, and there was a huge fire blazing in an enormous fireplace. She looked away. 'Darlings,' she managed in the long ago voice, kissing air, as Bryn had called it, not really connecting, but no one seemed to notice.

Simon notices, she told herself with a smile as she sat down in a deep chair near enough to the fireplace to pretend that she was not scared stiff inside. At least he'd better or I shall find myself another shrink. But he was no longer her psychiatrist; he was now her friend.

It was an exhausting evening. Hugh, having been awake most of the night, was feeling his age, as he put it. Rae was ill at ease, as she always was near Kate, and tried too hard not to mention anything she feared might be controversial, which left her with very little to talk about. Simon worried about his wife and his friend. Only Kate seemed to be at ease and she was praying for the evening to be over. Her face ached with the effort of smiling and talking, and she used all her old methods to hold back the tidal wave of panic that was threatening to drown her. Those people were talking about her; she just knew it. Look at the way the woman examined her over her wine glass. Now she had told the fat woman in the ghastly wine-coloured silk sheath. What a ridiculous dress for such generous proportions. She's not afraid to be seen. 'Look at me', that dress shouts, and is that what my poor scarred hands shout? She tried to hide herself inside the generous collar of her lovely sweater. She made herself talk about Stacie and the play. 'You have a daughter,

Rae. You would want to know if some infamous woman was coaching your daughter in her home, wouldn't you?' But Rae was too flustered to answer.

'They'll be thrilled to have you help her, Kate. She's jolly lucky. Has she any idea who you were?'

She smiled at Hugh. 'Silly, of course she knows. She and her rather lovely beau have no doubt looked me up in old newspapers.'

'I meant *who* you were, Kate, the most famous actress of your generation.'

It was Simon who brought the evening to a close.

'We're leaving first thing in the morning, Kate. I'll ring you when we reach home.'

'Lovely evening,' she said too brightly. 'Lovely visit. Thank you so much for coming.' Act 1 Scene 1. Perfect hostess says adieu to dinner guests. Except that she was not the hostess.

Good old Hugh. Dear old Hugh. Sad old Hugh. She relaxed into her seat in his lovely comfortable car and said nothing.

'Get into your nightie and I'll bring some cocoa,' he said when they reached the house.

Cocoa? Did real people still drink cocoa? Someone had bought cocoa for the house; she had made some for the girl, for Stacie. Must have been Hugh. She waited for cocoa. But Hugh had known her a long time. He brought her a whisky and sat on the edge of her bed while she drank it.

'Now you're absolutely exhausted, dear old girl. Was it all too sudden?' he asked. 'You should have asked just Simon, or just sad old me.'

'Dear old you,' she said with an exhausted attempt at a smile. 'I was showing off, Hugh. I wanted Simon to see what a good job I was doing.'

'One event at a time, Kate. One friend. I'll leave in the morning.'

She reached out and grabbed his hand. 'No, don't. I don't have to pretend with you. Tomorrow, when I feel better, I'll remember all the nice things about this little attempt at joining the human race. But you're right. One old friend would have been enough.' She smiled at him. 'Just think, Hugh. What if I'd invited everybody and they'd come to see the Resurrection.'

He took the glass and, leaning over, kissed her gently on her scarred face. 'You're a very naughty girl. I'll stay until you're ready for me to go.'

At the door he stood watching her. Was she already asleep? She lay so quietly under the lace covers and he was happy to notice that the moonlight was kind to her.

'God damn it, what a bloody waste,' he said to himself angrily as he climbed into his own bed.

And then he remembered that she had screamed out in fear for Bryn, not fear of Bryn. The papers had said that she killed Bryn and then set fire to the house. Had she changed her mind at the last minute and found that it was all too late?

What was known? Kate had been rescued from her burning home and taken to the casualty department at the Western General Infirmary in Edinburgh. She was badly burned over her entire body and had a skull fracture caused, it was assumed, by a fall; she had been, said the fireman who had pulled her from the ruins of her home, lying face down half in and half out of her front door. She must, therefore, have been trying to escape. Bryn Edgar had been pronounced dead at the scene. The fire had caused his death but although he too was found face down there was a gaping wound on the back of his head. He appeared to have been struck with a heavy object from behind. That was the finding of the forensic scientist. Moreover he could not have struck himself and the wound had not been caused by contact with the floor. There was no evidence whatsoever as to the presence of anyone else in or even near the house. Eventually Kate had been arrested but since it was proved that she could not remember any of the events leading up to the fire she was placed in the psychiatric wing of a prison hospital. No murder weapon had been found; if the implement with which Bryn Edgar had been struck was wooden then it had been destroyed in the fire. There was no forensic evidence in the ashes and no fingerprints were discovered other than Kate's, Bryn's, and those of the cleaning lady with the odd name. Was it worth trying to trace her, all these years later? No, she had been thoroughly cross-examined and had been nowhere near Abbots House that fatal week.

'Sometimes she just wanted to be quite alone. I went in and left things. She wasn't a big eater, you see. Bread and cheese when she was on her own. I used to get quite angry and she'd laugh. "You'd have me as fat as a flawn," she'd say, though I never did ask what a flawn was. I cleaned up after she'd gone; no work at all when she was on her own, hardly touched the surface of the house but it was different with guests. Well, it is, isn't it?'

He had been through quite a bit with this step-sister of his. When she had first been charged with murder he had been shocked and angry and appalled that anyone could make such a stupid mistake. Kate murder Bryn? Not Kate. She loved Bryn. Hugh was sure that he was the only person in the world who knew how hard she had fought against her love for him.

'I can't help myself, Hugh,' she had cried on more than one occasion. 'Why didn't I marry him when he asked me? I should have and then there wouldn't be this ghastly sneaking around. I try to live without him but I don't eat, don't sleep, and it ruins my work. My work? I thought it meant everything, that it would be enough but I'm greedy, Hugh, I want it all, and bloody awful for all of us, I've only ever been in love with another woman's husband.'

'Damn Bryn,' Hugh said and, debating the pros and cons of getting up to pour himself another whisky, fell asleep.

11

Hugh drove back to London on January 3rd. He had purchased several haunches of fine Scottish venison and even a brace or two of pheasants; yes, pheasant was available in London – everything was available in London – but this venison and these pheasants, they were undoubtedly special. Hugh's mind, though, was not on his purchases. He wanted to get back to his office, but not to work. Never in a million years would he tell Kate, but in order to care for her and her complicated health and legal problems, he had been semi-retired for some time. These days he merely advised a few clients, mostly old friends, but he still spent a considerable amount of time in his chambers. There was always someone to meet for lunch, was there not, and he did like to keep abreast of everything that was happening.

With a passion, Hugh loathed and detested roadside restaurants and so he drove off the motorway to refuel and to have a bite to eat. He knew he was tired and had seen the aftermath of too many accidents caused by clients, perfect in every other way, who had assumed that they were superhuman and did not need to rest or eat. Therefore he had a list of a select group of little restaurants where he could have a decent meal, often combined with a pleasant view. 'Something with a horse in it,' he would have said had he been asked, 'preferably white.' He was never tempted to have a glass of something 'encouraging'. 'Bloody irresponsible,' would have been Hugh's comment on drivers who did, had he been asked.

On January 3rd, which was a cold day, he had found a charming inn in the Lake District where there was a drawing room with a huge roaring log fire at either end and a chef who knew his shallots from his onions. The chef had been, for a moment only, disappointed that his new client would not sample his extensive wine list but he proffered his card, which was accepted, and went away gleefully to prepare a sea bass that had been rushed up that morning from the nearest port. It would be expensive but delicious and his client by chance would become a client by choice.

Hugh sat in the drawing room part way between the two fires and, while he drank a cup of excellent coffee – he had assured his host that his appetite would not be blunted – perused some of the latest magazines that were displayed on tables. One had an article on luxury holiday homes in the south of Spain. Near Málaga there was a town called Nerja which seemed to have a *parador*, or government-run hotel, overlooking the ocean, and Hugh, who had spent several winters in the south of France, was definitely interested in a town with a lovely hotel in an area where the sun shone in December and January.

'Somewhere to take Kate,' he decided as he finished the article. He could not remember whether or not Kate had ever visited Spain; they had spoken of it several times but had she ever gone? No, work, her career, had interfered each time and besides, she had always loved the Riviera and Provence.

He closed the magazine and then opened it again. Something had caught his eye. In one of the pictures there were one or two women in quite skimpy bathing dresses, no, swimsuits, they called them nowadays, and one was Rose. He was sure of it. Blonde hair, styled within an inch of its life, fingernails and toenails painted scarlet, and very little material covering up rather nice bodily structures. He looked again, closely. No, how stupid; it was not Rose. The women in the pictures were young but oh, how like Rose Lamont or Rose Edgar that blonde one was.

He was called to the dining room and for some time forgot both the magazine and Rose, but after a truly excellent meal he returned to enjoy after-lunch coffee in the drawing room. He sat looking at the fire and the flames and red-hot cinders, sipped his coffee and nibbled a little chocolate mint; one mint could not do too much damage, could it, and he would be wiser when he returned to London and was back in his routine. The magazine with its enticing cover showing brilliantly white villas festooned with deep red bougainvillaea against a blue sky and bluer sea lay on the sofa beside him and he picked it up again. Yes, that young woman looked just as Rose had looked all those years ago. He put down his cup and saucer and looked hard at the picture and he saw not the girl in the picture but Bryn's wife. Where was she now? Was she still making films? Surely not. She would be what – almost fifty; that was too old for the sex goddess parts she used to play, was it not? Mind you, some women were still absolutely stunning even into their sixties. Off hand he could not conjure up faces or names but he was sure chaps in the club talked about them admiringly. He was not much into film himself; he preferred a live concert and sometimes a play, if it was not one that made him weep for what should have been and was not. Some great actresses in the theatre were, what would one say diplomatically – mature. Maggie Smith was still a stunner and Judi Dench, both of whom had graduated just as Kate was starting, and he had seen Joan Plowright in some-thing recently; she was hardly a young woman. Therefore Rose, who had been lovely, if one liked that simpering English blonde look, could still be in the business. He had not heard or read her name in years but that meant nothing. Besides, had she not re-married several times? He had certainly seen pictures of a teary Rose outside a divorce court weeping for her one and only love, Bryn Edgar.

'Silly to try to replace the irreplaceable. He was my first and only real love.'

She had said that at least twice if his memory served him well. Might just be interesting to find out where she was now and what she was doing; was she still living as Rose Lamont, her screen persona, or was she Rose Edgar, grieving widow of 'the most perfect Romeo I have ever seen'? No, he had not known Rose well but he could not see her giving up the blinding light that had been Bryn Edgar.

Snow began to fall the night before school started. Cameron was ecstatic; with any luck it would be so thick that the roads would be impassable and that meant that the school would be closed. Even one more day of Christmas holiday would be wonderful.

Stacie watched the snow drift past the living room windows with mixed emotions. If there was just the right amount then she could turn up at school with her gorgeous new red jacket on over her ghastly uniform. Not only would all her friends be envious of the jacket but Craig would see her in it again; he, being a sophisticated man of the world, like Miss Buchanan's Mr Forsythe, had shown that he appreciated what chic red and black did for her complexion and for her eyes. 'Cuddly and sexy.' If, however, as the forecasters were saying, this rather lovely Christmas card snow were to develop into a real blizzard then there would be no way that cars and buses could get anywhere near the school gates. She could walk but what would be the point of that? Craig's house would be cut off. The glory of Eustacia Thomson in her down-filled *berghaus* was not to be wasted on Form 5. Decisions, decisions. To wear or not to wear, that was the question.

There was another question but Stacie was almost sure she already knew the answer, Once again Craig had not telephoned her as he had promised and when she had rung his home on New Year's Eve, the housekeeper had said that the family had gone skiing. Why had he not telephoned and why had he not told her that he was going away when they had met in the street? No matter what he said his parents did not approve of her; it was as simple and as hurtful as that. Stacie looked at the snow falling and prayed that there would not be a blizzard They had to go to school tomorrow; Craig would explain and everything would be all right She made excuse after excuse. The Sinclairs were not like the Thomsons; they had different priorities, did things impulsively. She just had to remember that Craig had said that he loved her.

It was snowing but she paid no heed to the snow. Rather she welcomed it, cold and clean and white. She stopped running and held up her face. Flakes fell on her tongue and dissolved. She laughed. The world was an incredibly beautiful place. He kissed me. He kissed me. She started to skip like a child. It was the happiest moment of her entire life. She had thought that getting the part, when she heard the life changing words, that was the best moment but it was not. The kiss . . . She remembered his eyes gazing into hers as he lowered his head. She remembered how startled she had been. It had simply never occurred to her but oh, how she had welcomed it.

The snow was wet on her face. She woke up and it was not snow: it was tears. There had not been snow during that first tour, not a kiss, only steadily growing feelings that she tried to fight. It was too early; there was time for nothing but work. She lay for a moment in the warm darkness knowing that eventually the tears would dry. She could not wipe them off; that involved touching her skin. The only light in the rain came from the streetlamp outside and it was losing the battle against the thickness of the mist and fog. But it was steadfast, refusing to give up. The light was there – if she could find it.

An eleven-week tour. They were ecstatic, eleven whole weeks of work, a weekly wage, and cheap, possibly dirty theatrical digs. It sounded glorious. They embraced the prospect with as much fervour as later they were to embrace each another.

Already the critics were talking about him, about Bryn Edgar, this shepherd's son from Wales's majestic mountains.

. . . *beautiful voice* . . .

. . . *magnetic personality* . . .

. . . *utterly at one with himself, certain of his powers and sure of his sexual self* . . .

He was that all right but he was dead and it was her fault, was it not, his glorious voice silenced at the very pinnacle of its powers because she had stolen another woman's husband? That's what Granny would have said, Granny who had no time for Tante who had married her son and discarded him almost before the ink was dry on the marriage certificate. *What God has joined together, let no man put asunder,* was Granny's code and even her beloved granddaughter would have been faced with her wrath. Had Kate not given in to her own desires and to his persuasions . . .

Kate sat up quickly, throwing the covers off. I'm afraid, I'm so afraid. But why? What do I fear? That I killed him, that the police were right and they just could not prove it? But she knew that was not true.

I did not kill Bryn Edgar. I know that. Sister Mary Magdalene knows that and she was not there. Hugh knows it. What does Simon think or is he only interested in the tortured mind? I will remember everything. I will force myself to remember.

Kate got out of the bed with its lovely lace covers, its comfortable pillows, and she walked across the floor to her cheval glass. Over its revealing mirror she had thrown a lace shawl. Now she deliberately removed the lace and looked at herself; she opened the buttons on her long enveloping nightdress and let it slip from her shoulders on to the floor and then she stepped out of it and kicked it aside. Her eyes were closed but she forced herself to open them and then she looked at her body in the glass. For the first time in years she examined her whole body, from the toes of her feet to the hairs of her head. Dear God, how scrawny she was. She had always been thin, but thin can be beautiful if the proportions are right. Where had her breasts gone? She had been proud of them once and Bryn had loved them.

Where did such a slip of a girl get such irresistible breasts?

He would not find them irresistible now. And her flat stomach, her smooth white skin? It was flat enough; it was almost concave but the skin was red and puckered. Horrible horrible scarred skin. Her legs, those long well-shaped legs with their amazingly slender ankles – oh, how ugly they were now. She had covered them up for years, even envying Sister Mary Magdalene her habit. What pride you took in your lovely legs, Kate. Look at them now. Would Bryn slip his hands from ankle up up up? No, he would recoil in distaste as you do yourself. Touch them, Kate; accept them. She sobbed in momentary distress and then stopped.

Damn it, did I deserve this? Who did it to me? Who was there? She forced herself to remember the beginning of the nightmare and stood still, looking at herself in the glass that had reflected her in silks and satins, in tweeds and velvets, in furs, and proudly naked. Behind her in the shadows she seemed to see a memory of Bryn.

Oh, my Kate, my beautiful Kate, why didn't you marry me when you had the chance?

Who knew about them? Very few. They were amazingly discreet. Hugh, of course. Her dresser and that woman who used to clean here. Mrs? Mrs some funny name. No, not funny, just different, Mrs Balakirev. *Bally-kirev,* Bryn used to say, *you're no Russian, you're an Irish colleen, aren't you,* cariad? And Mrs Balakirev would scold and simper and love him devotedly like all the others. Where was she now? No matter, she was not there that weekend and she would never have hurt him anyway. Rose knew. Reluctantly Kate said the name. Rose knew, but Rose loved him and would never have hurt him and besides, she was filming in Spain. She was perfect for celluloid; she had learned that very early. When Bryn and Kate were swearing oaths of fealty to the stage, Rose was wooing this new and powerful and immensely rich lover, the motion picture industry, and she was a natural. She photographed beautifully and her small voice was just right for the intimacy of the camera. She made love to a camera as passionately as Kate made love to Bryn. Were the rewards greater? Financially they were. She tried to coerce Bryn into making films but he hated it, hated every-thing about it.

'It's so unreal; that bloody thing stuck in my face, spying on me. And there's no projection; we spent years, Rose, years, learning to project and now they would have me whispering like an old man with no teeth.'

'You're exaggerating as usual and you're being bloody childish. Tell him, Kate. He could be famous – immediately – all over the world with just one performance.'

'Tell me what, Katie, that film is as real as the theatre? It's not. One actor followed around by hundreds of little people with clipboards? How can I make myself believe I'm Hamlet, never mind the poor sod in the gods, with those bloody machines everywhere?'

He was exaggerating, of course; he always was. There were no poor sods in the gods in the cinema; the action could be heard as well in the one and nines as in the five shilling seats. And what was real? Kate had wondered. Is the stage any more real? We are the stuff that dreams are made on . . .

And, she believed, she had no right to tell Bryn anything.

The house was chilly since she had programmed the heat to go off at midnight and not go on again until six in the morning but still she stood looking at herself. 'Kate, you have said time and again that you are going to force your mind to tell you everything that happened that night yet every time you begin to see a way through the fog you retreat. What are you afraid of – apart from ending sentences with prepositions,' she added wryly and was pleased that she still had some humour. 'Someone hit Bryn and wanted you to die too. Are you afraid of a double hurt; are you afraid that it was someone you love who did this to you? Whom do you love, Kate? Hugh, only Hugh, and he didn't do it.'

The relief, the calm after the storm. Oh, there were other people that she cared about; there were others that she had loved, especially Tante and Granny, but in those days there had only been Hugh and Bryn. 'What a shallow selfish life I must have led, allowing no one else in.'

Her head full of new resolution, Kate dressed and went downstairs. The house felt different; Hugh had filled it with his energy, his warmth, his affection and now it was empty. Any house, any hotel room, any theatre had felt like that after Bryn left it. Would Hugh be pleased with the comparison? Indeed no. He had never liked Bryn; admired him, respected his talent, but liked him? No.

The house felt empty and cold.

Of course it's cold; it's early morning and the heat isn't on. Kate pressed the reset button on the dial of her brand-new boiler and then, gripped by new resolution, decided to start the day properly, even if a tad early. She made coffee and while the pot was purring happily she went to the window and looked out. Her breath caught in her throat and for a moment she was a child again, a child whose life was full of wonder. It was snowing. She remembered holidays at Granny's house. The house had always felt quiet and still when it was snowing. It was as if the magic and joy of snow needed silence in order to be fully appreciated. She leaned her head against the cold glass and looked out. Her dream returned to cheer her. What a happy dream. He had kissed her first in the snow. Perfect, perfect. His kiss had been as gentle as the kiss of the snowflakes. What term was that, because it had been at term time had it not? In the holidays she always returned to Granny or to Tante – oh, Tante, did I ever thank you for all those wonderful holidays or did I take everything for granted? No, I will not submit to self-loathing. I probably never actually said, Tante, I appreciate you, but she knew, didn't she? She knew I was young and thoughtless. All young are thoughtless. Bryn had to work; he was a waiter, a busboy, he delivered the post at Christmas; and me, what did I do? I swarmed off to my rich former stepmother in the Riviera. God, no wonder Rose hated me.

That was such a startling realisation that Kate left the window and returned to watch the coffee pot gurgle its way to her attempt at perfection. She ate a banana; bananas are so good. If you eat one before you make a recording your tummy does not growl, or at least so the delightful man at the BBC had always assured her. Actors and opera singers love bananas. It is impossible to work on a full stomach; the stomach, the body, uses all its resources breaking down the food eaten when it should be helping with projection and delivery and thought and and and!

How ghastly it must be now, thought Kate as she enjoyed her second cup of coffee with two sugars – no cream. Remember that nice boy at the Beeb. 'No clunky jewellery, Miss Buchan, no earbobs, and no slidey materials' – she knew what he meant – 'and for goodness sake, forget your figure and have some breakfast because I'll know all about your insides by line two.'

Today's recording machines, she assumed, would be so much more professional. No, that wasn't the word, for they had been absolutely professional; refined, that was it, machines must be more refined.

When had she stopped worrying about her shape? She had never worried; she had inherited her father's bones and little else, but they were good bones and her metabolism was fantastic – nothing stuck. Bryn was not so lucky: he drove his dressers wild. A decadent weekend could change his shape. *I get fat passing a bakery,* he groaned, *and you, Katie, you eat for England and look at you.*

I walk everywhere, Kate said. Bryn never walked anywhere if he could help it and when he became famous he crossed the street by taxi.

The kiss? The kiss in the snow? When? Miranda. Was it that part? No, for we were still at RADA when I got that.

It was the end of the last term. They were excited and afraid and they knew they had to part, of course. The girls had rented a ramshackle old house with three other girls. Since neither Rose's parents nor Kate's grandmother would have taken kindly to having a man as a house mate, Bryn planned to remain a little longer with his uncle while he tested the waters.

Every agent in the audience at their end-of-year matinee of scenes from plays fought to represent Bryn, Rose landed a television commercial, and Kate got a terrifyingly exciting phone call.

They want to see you at the Old Vic. Be prepared to do Miranda's "Alas, now, pray you work not so hard," from *The Tempest*.'

Why did they want her? What was the part? Perhaps it wasn't a part.

'For pity's sake, Katie, you're being auditioned for your first professional role, and it's the Old Vic.' His voice ended on an excited squeak. 'They don't ask cleaning ladies to recite Shakespeare, or have you applied for a job on the side? Get the play out and we'll go through it. Remember we need to look at the entire act, not just the few words they'll ask you to do. You need to know everything about the scene. Who is in it? What happened just before? What happens after your sweet little speech?'

She did not notice Rose curled up on a sofa looking sullen. 'I don't remember you offering to go over my lines.'

'Christ's sake, Rose. You don't have to be Ellen Terry to sell soap powder. Now, one more time, Kate, you've just discovered that your father, Prospero, is actually the Duke of Milan, and poor old Ferdinand's dad is his mortal enemy since he helped your uncle steal your old man's throne. You understand all that?'

Kate nodded. Of course she knew the story.

'You've got the hots for Ferdinand—'

'Don't be so vulgar, Bryn.'

'Shut up, Rose. Kate, it's a young girl's first love. She's in thrall to this handsome young prince and he for her, but you, that's Miranda, the innocent lamb, doesn't know it yet, but there's some little frisson, feel it. See the poor little bugger soil his lily whites humping logs of wood around. He's trying to impress you and your poor little virgin heart bleeds for him and you try to help. "Alas, now, pray you, work not so hard . . ."'

How did he do it? How did a stocky Welshman in old slacks and a sweater that had seen better days become a sweet young woman? Genius, she answered herself, but she had it too and she was Miranda watching Ferdinand. '"Alas, now, pray you, work not so hard . . ."'

'You're a marvel, Katie,' he said after they had spent the entire afternoon working on the lines. 'You're almost good enough to be Welsh.'

What should she wear? Miranda was young, virginal. Fine, a skirt and a white blouse would be good, buttoned, of course, right up to the neck. Shoes? Well polished, no heels.

Would the glorious day of the first audition ever come?

It did and it was not what she had expected.

'How tall are you?'

'Can you sing?'

'Let your hair down.'

'Walk across the room.'

Then there was quiet. The auditorium seemed empty but they had to be out there unless she had been so frightful that they had gone and just left her standing there. Surely not. She hadn't even given the speech yet. Damn it, her hair was wrong. She should have tied it back. Too late now. Was it the blouse borrowed from Rose? Too tarty for me? Shut up, Kate, a nun could wear it. She strained to hear something, anything, even breathing or the creaking of a chair. She stood in the middle of the stage and waited. If the doorman came to tell her she was about to be locked in she had to be able to look as if she knew what she was doing up here.

Then the disembodied voice: 'When you're ready, Miss Buchan.'

She was ready to assume the mantle of the girl, Miranda. Katherine Buchan knew everything that she had been able to learn about the play, and had even studied the history of the city of Milan, but Miranda knows nothing. Miranda does not appreciate that Ferdinand is delighted to be struggling to do something physical that he has never done before, or that he is trying to impress her.

Think, Kate, think. The scene is outside Prospero's cell and in comes beautiful, lovely Ferdinand who is carrying a big heavy log. You come in and behind you, but you don't know it, is Prospero, your father, who has ordered the poor lamb to move the woodpile. What are you feeling, Miranda? You want to help him, take some of the burden from him. Start, Kate.

> Alas, now, pray you,
> Work not so hard: I would the lightning had
> Burnt up those logs that you are enjoin'd to pile!

He was waiting outside, of course, and so was Rose and they went to the Lyons Corner House. All students ate there where they were allowed to eat as much salad as they liked for one reasonable price.

'I'd rather have gone to the Spaghetti House off Tottenham Court Road.'

'Oh la-di-da. Beggars can't be choosers, Kate. Time enough to blow your allowance if you get the part.'

She did, of course, and he was not thrilled that she played the Old Vic before he did. He did not kiss her then. Oh, Bryn, my flawed love, but had you been perfect you would not have been you.

No, he didn't kiss me then. I remember only that it was snowing and that he kissed me and I had been like Miranda and not realised that I was falling in love.

She went back to the window; it was much lighter and the snow had stopped falling. It lay on the ground, white and perfect and pure and again she felt that childhood delight. She would be the first to walk in the snow. She opened the door, looked out and shivered.

Deliberately she closed the door and stepped forward. So silent, so beautiful. She would walk quickly once she got to the carse and then she would not be cold.

'Kate, look at me, I'm an angel.'

In her head she could hear her cousin David's voice, and she could picture him, as broad as he was long from all the sweaters and scarves that Granny had forced him to wear. He was lying on his back in the snow, swinging his arms and legs, his cheeks as rosy as the red scarf wound twice round his neck. She laughed at the memory, for she had loved David. Did she still love him even though he had shown how ashamed of her he was? She pushed the memory away. Today she wanted only to enjoy the first snowfall and to remember her dream and her first kiss.

Had it been her first? Kate began to walk quickly towards the carse and was delighted to see that there was no one else in sight: no postmen, no milkmen, no delivery boys with newspapers. The streetlamps were on and, if anything, they made the snow appear even more ethereal. The sea fussed menacingly at her side and she stopped and looked out to where some white horses rode proudly, racing each other on to the sand and shingle. When the storms came the white horses would be larger, taller, threatening and she would love them as much or more than she loved these pretenders. Kate shook salt spray from her hair. She would go to the crusader's tomb and see how the snow changed it. Perhaps she would meet Benedict. She had not seen him since Christmas Eve.

The woods were grey and white and there had not been enough snow to cover the dark earth completely but the tomb was more open to the sky and here a blanket of snow disguised rough edges and decay; it was enchanting. There were no footprints except Kate's own and she stood for some time in the quiet calm. Nothing stirred: no bird moved. Smoke stood straight up in the air beyond the trees and at this further evidence of how cold it was, Kate shivered again.

You are a fool, Kate, to come out without a coat, and now you are miles from home and tired, and you must walk back and pray that you meet no one from the village. They'll think you mad. Goodbye, Crusader. What do they think of me already? I dare not add to my peculiarities. She turned quickly and her shoe caught on a loose stone or a surface root and she stumbled and fell heavily.

Years ago she had been taught to fall but she had forgotten so many of her lessons. She threw out her poor scarred hands to protect herself and felt a jar from wrist to shoulder and then she felt nothing.

Father Benedict went to a retreat house a few days after the New Year. He needed time to pray, but also to think. Benedict kneeled on the floor until he was in danger of falling over and a million sensations chased themselves around and around in his head. He did not want to think of her but his brain would not be mastered and he remembered Kate Buchanan at Midnight Mass. How exhausted she had looked and how alone. He grieved for her suffering of mind and body. But he rejoiced in her ability to come back to this place where she had known so much pain and to stand up with her head held high. She had killed no one. He knew that as surely as he knew his own name.

What was she seeking in Friars Carse? He wished she would confide in him but she was too proud or too private, probably the latter. She certainly was not the type to flaunt disgrace. He remembered the look in her eyes when Cameron had vandalised her wall. That had been the only incident but there had been talk in the village and, he was sure, cold shoulder treatment. There had to be a really good reason for laying herself open to unpleasantness, but what?

After his return, circumstances, pressure of duties, obligations, and even the weather kept him from the beach, and from the woods. But at last he was free to call the great grey hound and take his usual walk. He hoped to meet her; he prayed she might confide in him, and chided himself for his presumption in thinking a mere monk could help her answer questions.

She did not come.

For two nights she did not appear.

He would check to see that all was well. No harm in that. He was a man of God and she had been very ill.

A light was on downstairs.

He knocked on the door and a voice he barely recognised murmured, 'Yes.'

'It's Father Benedict from the priory. I wanted to check that you are well.'

She did not open the door and he thought he heard laboured breathing on the other side.

'Kate?'

'I am well, friend Ben,' she whispered after an eternity. 'Goodnight.'

He turned immediately and walked away, while inside the cottage

Kate leaned against the door in exhaustion and chastised herself for her stupidity. What harm to open the door and ask for help? But he was a monk. She did not want a churchman to see her like this. If she did not feel better in the morning she would ring Hugh, no, Simon, no. She would ring . . . Who would she ring? Who would help her? Maggie. Maggie would help.

Kate's knees gave way and she slid, unconscious, down the door and lay still on the cold floor of the hall.

Jim had given in. 'There is,' he told his wife, 'just so much pressure a working man can take.'

'She'll be thrilled, Jim, and who knows, maybe teaching Stacie will integrate Miss Buchanan a wee bit. We are thought well of in Friars Carse; wouldn't it be nice if others followed us, maybe invited her to join the Guild or something.'

'Heaven's sake, Maggie.' Jim helped himself to another piece, quite small, of Maggie's chocolate chip shortbread. The purists thought it shocking but chocolate, butter and sugar go well together. He licked his fingers when he had finished, looked longingly at the plate, sighed and sat back in his old chair. 'I suppose I'm not allowed to offer to pay her.'

'I think that would be wrong, Jim, but, who knows, maybe she's thinking of starting wee classes. You know, take one pupil, the pupil does well, gets a part in a school play and then her friends want to be coached too. Tell you what, I'll ring her and tell her we'd like her to do it, if she's willing, that is; we only know what Stacie tells us.'

'Which is sweet Fanny Adams since she's been involved with that boy.'

'Reading between the lines I'd say his mother thinks our Stacie's not good enough for him or' – she restrained her husband who had gone quite pink and was about to stand up, the better to shout – 'it's just that she worries so much about his health, she likes him where she can see him. And remember, Jim, poor Craig is right in the middle of all this, a girl he likes on one side and his mother on the other whisking him away for a nice treat every time it looks as if he might just want to ask the girl out. His dad was very pleasant to Stacie at the party.'

'Got better manners, is all.'

Maggie proffered the shortbread plate. 'I think we should just leave this to take its course. Stacie won't even be seventeen till March and he'll be gone in July. It'll all fall into place naturally. I'll ring Miss Buchanan and see if I can slip in a few feelers about whether payment would be appreciated but I'll have to be really careful there, Jim, sometimes poor people can be very tetchy about money.'

'We don't know she's poor; lives very well for someone poor.'

'The truth is, Jim, and we should remember it, we don't really know anything about her at all.'

But Maggie let the telephone ring several times and, since there was no answer, she hung up.

12

Several hours later Kate regained consciousness, dismayed to find herself on the floor beside the front door; she had a headache so fierce that she felt the top of her head might come right off. Her right arm and shoulder hurt too but by gritting her teeth, holding her head together with one hand and pushing up from the floor with the other she managed to get to her feet. She was cold and she was shaking and she stood for a moment leaning against the door trying to take command of her body and her brain.

Warmth, she thought, and brandy.

There had to be brandy somewhere, for she had bought a bottle in preparation for Hugh's visit. Gingerly Kate hobbled forward and into the dining room. Yes, the brandy, barely touched, was on the sideboard.

She managed a slight smile; Hugh had enjoyed Simon's claret. She poured herself a measure and was pleased to see that some of the golden liquid actually went into the glass and she put it to her lips. She heard her teeth knocking against the crystal as she swallowed the brandy and felt its warmth flow through her. Bed, she had to get to bed. She put the glass down on the table but misjudged its position and the glass felt onto the carpet and she did not hear it fall. Then she turned and made her way, slowly, to the stairs and, hanging on to the banister as if she were very old and frail, she managed to get to her bedroom. More than anything she wanted just to fall on to the covers but she knew she had to get warm and it would be hours before the heat came back on again. Undressing was completely impossible and after struggling for some minutes she gave up, pulled the covers aside with her last bit of strength and managed to get herself into the bed. She lost consciousness immediately.

When she came to hours later, the room was warm. She lay for a moment assessing the situation. Her bottom half was warm and comfortable although her feet, still in her little suede boots, were far too hot. Her head and shoulders were cold but she felt strong enough to grope around for the covers and pull them up. That accomplished, she thought about her head. I fell; that's it. I slipped at the crusader's tomb. How bloody stupid. I must have banged my head. She closed her eyes again and when she woke later she was ravenously hungry and thirsty.

Automatically she looked at her wrist. She did not remember taking off her watch but, since it was not on her wrist, she must have done. Carefully she got out of bed and looked at the tabletop. The watch was not there. Oh, damn, damn, double damn. Breathe, breathe. She knew that it was imperative that she not panic, that she wash, dress warmly and find something to eat; but the watch, Bryn's watch: she had to find the watch. Calmly, Kate, calmly. You hurt your head; you have put the watch somewhere. She searched but it was not in the house.

Kate was weeping now; her watch, the only concrete object that she had left that had been given to her by Bryn, was gone. She sat down, still in the clothes she had been wearing the day before and in which she had slept, and tried to think. I always wear it; therefore I was wearing it yesterday and I am not wearing it now. It is not in the house and so I must have lost it. I walked to . . . where did I go? The beach. I walked along the beach; I remember thinking about white horses. What time is it? Automatically she looked at her wrist and a sob escaped. Calmly, Kate. You have lost your watch on the beach. Then she remembered her fall. How stupid to slip there but perhaps when I threw out my hands – for I do remember thinking, this is not the way to fall, Kate – perhaps then my watch slipped off. I will go back and I will find it.

'Saint Anthony find it.'

Sister Aloysius had believed implicitly in the ability of Anthony of Padua to find anything that was lost. Kate was not so sure but, just in case, she too invoked the saint. She was still thirsty and was now even more aware of hunger pangs but above all a feeling of light-headedness. I think I've caught a chill. Silly Kate, why did you not wear your cloak?

She pushed herself to her feet and walked into the kitchen. For many years Kate had been learning how to deal with a body that had been terribly abused and although she wanted desperately to rush out to find her watch she knew that in her present condition she would be lucky to reach the front door let alone Templehall Woods. Slowly and methodically she made tea in a cup, swallowed three aspirins, and tried to eat a banana, but her throat seemed to have closed; even the aspirin, already dissolving in the hot sweet tea, seemed to have to force their way down. She told herself that she was feeling much better, went to the hall, found her cloak and, after struggling to fasten it securely, let herself out.

The snow had turned to sleet and although it was early afternoon, she knew that it would soon be dusk. There was a remarkable difference in the hours of daylight immediately after the midwinter solstice. On New Year's Eve it had still been light at four, whereas on Christmas Day she remembered going out to feed the birds not long after the Queen's speech at three and it had already been growing dark. In an attempt to clear her head she breathed in deeply. Even from the pathway beside the house she could smell the sea. Would it be angry on an afternoon like this?

She tried to retrace her steps but how can you know exactly where you walked on a windswept beach? She walked back and forth and then walked as close to the approaching waves as she could without getting too wet; the salt spray on her face and head was refreshing and not too cold. Nothing. There was no sign of her watch – could it have been washed away? – and she knew she had to hurry to get into the woods before dark. She bit back a sob and gave up searching the beach. She had forgotten all her concerns about appearing odd or peculiar in the eyes of any passing villager. She no longer cared: her watch, Bryn's gift, had to be found. She could not bear it if there was nothing concrete of him for her to caress.

I have the Salzburg desk. Losing the watch is not the end of the world.

I cannot hold a desk in the palm of my hand.

She reached the gate to Templehall Woods and went in. It was already darker under the trees and she went as quickly as she could towards the crusader's tomb and all the time she murmured, 'Please let it be there, please let it be there.' She kept her head bowed, eyes focused on the ground before her but there was no glint of lost gold and at last she reached the tomb. Even in her distress, its peace enfolded her and she put her scarred hands on the rough stone. Please, Sir Knight, please. Nothing; she had not lost it here. Now which way had she gone? Where had she fallen?

That was easy. She could see clear indications that something or someone had disturbed the ground, and there, was that not a dried bloodstain? She put her hand to her forehead; it was damp but it was sweat not blood. How strange to sweat out in a cold dark wood. 'I must have slipped here on this stone. There was snow or frost, wasn't there, or perhaps some ice.' She looked at the trampled earth on the pathway at the foot of the steps. Thank goodness there were only two wide steps; it had not been too bad a fall, just enough to knock her out but that was because she had landed badly, all lessons on how to fall obviously forgotten. But there was no watch.

The sun was setting. It would soon be too dark to see anything. Her headache was defying the aspirin and her temples were pounding. She lifted her hand again. Did I raise my arms as I fell? She got down on her hands and knees and began to inch forward away from the area in which she had fallen. Perhaps the watch had slipped from her wrist as she fell. Perhaps it had been thrown a distance, not far; it could not possibly have gone far. Forward, or should it be to the side? Which way? I should have brought a torch.

And at the very moment she decided to give up for the night Kate saw a glint, a tiny spark as if the dying rays of the sun had caught something that lay a foot at most from where she had fallen. She crawled towards it on her hands and knees, whispering, 'Please, please.'

The watch lay face down, its bracelet broken but otherwise unharmed. She picked it up with fingers that she could not keep from trembling and cradled it against her heart. 'Thank you, Saint Anthony,' she whispered. Had he helped or was it all silly superstition? She did not care. At last she became aware of the numbing cold and she struggled to her feet. She welcomed the gathering darkness, for she knew that her clothes had to be stained by the mud and rotting leaves at the base of the steps. Not only her head but also her whole body ached and it was an effort merely to put one foot forward after the other. Outside the wood the sleet seemed heavier and was driven by a wind that capriciously changed direction, now sending icy sleet into her face and eyes, now pushing her along from behind. It skirled along at her ankles, swirling her cloak up and away, so that sometimes its volume was more hindrance than help. The wind pummelled her and pushed her along and she was exhausted when she reached the house, too tired to do more than drop her cloak to the floor and stagger forward to fall into a chair.

She woke still aching from top to toe and with a raging temperature, but instinct took over and forced her up the stairs and into her beautiful room. With hands that fumbled and shook she tried again to peel off her clothes and perhaps because they were dry she managed to get out of her skirt and her jumper but the zippers on her boots still defeated her and once more she crawled under her covers with her boots on.

She wept, from exhaustion, from illness, or from worry over her beloved grandmother's sheets, Bryn's watch tightly clasped in her hand.

Father Benedict noticed that her curtains were not drawn and that no lights showed. He worried but assured himself that she had gone out and that he would meet her on the beach.

He did not. He could not settle. Some instinct told him that all was not well but he thought, What do I know of this woman and her life? Perhaps her friends are still here. Perhaps she has gone away for a day or two. On the next day as soon as he possibly could he took the great dog and walked quickly into the village and looked again at the windows of Abbots House. The curtains were open but perhaps she had closed them after he had walked past and now had opened them again. He was worrying needlessly and there were so many other things he should be doing.

He went, however, to the door and knocked lightly. Nothing. He opened the letterbox and, feeling extremely stupid but slightly uneasy, called, 'Miss Buchanan? Kate?' Again there was absolutely no sound from the silent house. He turned to leave but saw that the dog, Thane stood, a silent sentinel at the door. 'Home, Thane, let's go home,' but the deerhound, who had never once disobeyed a direct command, remained at the door. Benedict believed very strongly in animal instinct and although a rational part of him could say, 'Perhaps he smells food,' he knew his dog. It was not in Thane's nature to disobey; there had to be a good reason.

For a moment Benedict stood on the doorstep, ideas swirling around in his brain: call the police, an ambulance, and then he did something that he had never in his life before ever considered doing. He peered through a window of someone's home. The Venetian blinds, even though they were open, made it very diffi-cult but vaguely he could see a huddled shape by the door, a coat or, no, that all-concealing cloak. So unlike the fastidious Kate to drop her clothes, surely, on the floor.

He knocked again. 'Kate? It's Benedict.' No answer. He crossed himself, said a quick but fervent prayer and tried the handle. The door opened. 'Jesus, Mary and Joseph,' he prayed again and stepped inside, the dog at his heels. The cloak was damp. He did not notice the elegant beauty of the room but followed the dog who stood, ears pricked and eyes bright, looking up the stairs. 'Kate,' he called. 'It's Father Benedict. Is everything all right?' No answer. He looked round and saw the Christmas crib with its two babies. Had she gone away without remembering to lock up? Then he remem-bered the damp cloak and went back to the staircase where Thane still stood eager and anxious to climb it because his instinct and his nose told him that there was trouble at the top.

'Jesus, help me. Mary and Joseph, pray for me,' the monk prayed as he climbed the stairs, the dog racing ahead. A door was open and Benedict hurried in to see Thane standing at the head of the bed. Kate was lying very still. She was breathing but it was very shallow. He touched her forehead gently and she moaned.

He turned to find a telephone. He found one downstairs; its presence had registered unbeknownst to him while he had looked round quickly and he had missed the extension on the table between the bedroom doors.

The local doctor, who had on his National Health list all the monks at the priory, had just finished his Sunday lunch. 'You should have contacted the emergency services,' he said gruffly. 'I'll come this time.'

'What shall I do in the meantime?'

'Nothing. Keep her warm. Pray, I suppose. I'll be ten minutes.'

It took him eight.

Benedict had prayed and he had hung up the damp cloak. Then he had filled a kettle and switched it on. Why, he had no idea, but he had done it. He let young Dr Jarvis in and waited at the foot of the stairs while the doctor made his examination.

'She'll pull through but if you hadn't found her, Father . . .' The doctor left him to finish that sentence for himself. 'She's had some rough times and she's not strong. A bit of hypothermia, under-nourished, I would say, but I need to see her notes. What do you know about her? She's never been registered with the practice.' 'Young' Dr Jarvis had taken over completely from his father three years before but was still referred to as the young doctor since the two men had worked in tandem for a year or two.

What did he know? thought Benedict. That she had been a great actress. He said nothing.

The doctor looked annoyed as he pulled a prescription pad from his pocket and began to write. 'I'll give her something for her aches and pains but she's not my patient, Father, and it's obvious that she's had serious trauma at some time. You knew that surely or why are you here? Do you know anything about her? Friends, family?'

Had Kate Buchanan a family? All those friends. There must be someone still who knew. 'I know nothing about Kate Buchanan, Doctor, but she knows Maggie Thomson.'

The doctor looked at him shrewdly. 'We're in the same business, Father, and we abide, more or less, by the same rules. Mrs Thomson is a good woman. I could put Miss Buchanan in the nearest hospital, and I should, but at this time of the year we're stacking patients as it is. Maybe Maggie will know about relatives.' He was dialling as he spoke.

Fifteen minutes later Maggie arrived and two days later Kate woke and was surprised to see her sitting there.

'How are you feeling, Miss Buchanan?'

'Have I been ill? Am I in hospital?'

'No, you're in your own bed. You were quite ill. Thank goodness the monk found you.'

Kate gasped sharply and looked down at herself.

'Don't worry. You were still in your clothes, nicely covered up. It was the dog, that big hound that goes with the father everywhere; he sensed you were ill and the monk came in, saw you were running a fever and rang the doctor. Animals are amazing, aren't they?' Maggie stopped talking. There was so much she wanted to say, had to ask, but it was so difficult. Miss Buchanan was a very private person but there were worries. 'I put that nightie on. Hope you don't mind my going through your things. The doctor examined you, but you wouldn't mind that?'

Kate was puzzled. Doctor? Which doctor? Simon had been here but he had gone, hadn't he, and he had not examined her; he was not that kind of doctor. Father Benedict? When had she last spoken to Benedict? Think, Kate, think. You are well now. Think. She dredged it up with relief. Midnight Mass. I spoke to him then. No, I did not speak. I watched and listened. Father Benedict, Guardian of the abbey. She could hear his voice, quiet, gentle, but when? That must have been part of the nightmare. Hugh had been here, and Simon. No, that was before. It had been snowing. He had kissed her in the snow.

Kate slept.

When she woke it was almost dark, that lovely blue-grey time between late afternoon and evening proper. This together with early morning was Kate's favourite time. She lay still, for she was warm and comfortable; nothing hurt, not even the thought of Maggie having seen the damage the fire and various surgeries had done to her anatomy. Maggie's face was like the beautiful face of Sister Mary Magdalene, although it was not fine-boned and aristocratic but was round and rosy; like Mary Mag's face it said, I am the personification of human kindness. I will never hurt you.

As if thinking of her had conjured her up, the door opened quietly

184

and Maggie peeped in. 'How lovely, you're awake. That's the best cure of all I always tell my Jim, a good night's sleep, although you've had yours during the day. Still, day or night doesn't much matter when you've been ill, does it?' She was advancing into the room as she spoke and Maggie did advance rather than enter. Her large bosom seemed to come first, followed by all the other bits that eventually made a delightful whole that stood smiling at the foot of Kate's bed. 'I'd love covers like this if I could get my Jim to accept it. He puts up with most things but lace . . . Have as much as you like on your knickers, he says.'

She stopped in some confusion and Kate smiled inside to see Maggie blush.

'I shouldn't be mentioning such things to you,' she said.

'Why, Maggie dear, because I'm a maiden lady of indeterminate age?'

'No, Miss Buchanan, because you're a customer.'

'A customer, Maggie. Do you wait hand and foot on all your customers? I would like you to call me Kate and then perhaps you won't feel so badly about telling me about your lacy underwear and I might feel a little better about accepting your kindness.'

Maggie laughed. 'What a silly thing to say, Miss Buchanan. Why you'd do the same for me.'

Kate looked at her in astonishment 'I have never waited on anyone in my life.'

'Not much call for it in your line of work. Me now. Always someone with the snuffles. I'll just pop down and get you a little supper. I made you some soup – very nourishing. You lie there and relax. By the way, there have been no phone calls while we've been here. Anyone you want to ring, to tell them you're poorly?'

Kate shook her head and wished she had not. Kate closed her eyes. Why was Maggie Thomson in her house? What was her own family doing without wife and mother? How was she to pay her? She had a strong feeling that any talk of money would ruin what might become a real friendship. A friend. Me and Maggie? Why, she has to be ten years younger than I am and we're so different. God, am I sounding like a snob? I don't mean to but I'm not used to friendship, only Mary Mag and Sister Aquinas in recent years.

I'm out of the habit of making friends. And they must not tell Hugh I've been ill. Dear Hugh, he would come but he must not see me an invalid again. I'll ring him when I'm feeling a little stronger.

Maggie returned. For a large woman she moved very quietly and all her movements were deft and sure. 'How did you get yourself into such a state?'

How? The snow. No, it wasn't the snow. My watch. 'My watch, Maggie. Where's my watch?'

'There there, don't get upset. You were holding a watch. Dr Jarvis put it on the dresser. Shame about the bracelet but it'll mend, won't it?'

Mend? Most things mend. 'May I have it?' She tried to struggle up but was too weak to sit up by herself.

Quickly Maggie brought the broken watch and then she sat on the bed and supported Kate with pillows while she fed her like a baby and tried not to think of why anyone would cling to a broken watch, even though it was gold and very pretty. 'The father from the monastery had the prescription filled. It's a liquid; easier than pills, I always say.'

'Tastes worse,' said Kate. 'Maggie, I don't quite know what happened and why you're here.'

'Don't worry about it tonight. I'm going home for a few hours to see to things there but Stacie's coming down.' Was this the time to speak about the tutoring or coaching or whatever it was? No. Maybe that was all over now. 'She'll sit downstairs and you call if you need her. Then I'll come back. Would you like a cup of tea before I go?'

Kate shook her head and relaxed back against the pillows. She was too tired to think. She was aware, however, that she had regressed frighteningly. She was back in the care of an attendant, albeit a nice one, powerless to do anything for herself. Better not to think. Best to lie back and rest and try to rebuild her strength. A doctor had been, but not Simon, and Ben had found her. What fear for one of God's creatures had made him open her door? I must have left the door unlocked. I suppose that was lucky. Otherwise, perhaps I would have died. Would I have slipped effortlessly into nothingness? Was that what I wanted? Oh, Ben, why did you open the door?

He did not tell her because he did not return to Abbots House while she was ill. Dr Jarvis visited regularly and he was not so circumspect as Maggie.

'Feeling a bit better today, Kate?'

'Yes, Doctor. Thank you for all your care. I know I'm not your patient and you have been very good.'

Dr Jarvis interrupted. 'I need to let your family know that you are ill. Who is your doctor? He needs to be informed.'

'My lawyer is my family, Doctor, and he will not expect to hear from me. I see no point in worrying him when you and Mrs Thomson have everything so beautifully under control.'

'Perhaps Maggie Thomson has other things to do with her time; she does have a business to run, you know, and a family.'

Kate gasped. How cruel, but he was right and she was selfish and self-centred. She bowed her head and her hair fell forward over her face. 'I'm so sorry, Doctor. You're right; I didn't think. I have learned nothing in these past few months and yet I hoped that I was learning so much.' She looked up at him and her eyes were wet with unshed tears. 'She is a lovely human being but I have taken advantage. May I ask you for one more thing? Can you find me a nurse and I will tell my lawyer that I have . . . what shall I call it, a rather severe winter cold?'

Dr Jarvis pulled a chair up to the bed. His young face was troubled. 'Where is your doctor, Miss Buchanan? Professional courtesy demands that I inform him that I'm treating you.'

So many doctors: Scottish ones, English ones, even French ones. 'My last doctor lives in France, I'm afraid, and I forgot to register when I returned to Britain.'

'You should register with someone. Lucky that Father Benedict caught me at home and at a time when I wasn't up to my ears.'

'I will, as soon as I'm well. You will try to find me a nurse. I can afford to pay one.'

Could she? Where did the money come from? Hugh had always talked about investments and trusts. Her tired brain could handle no more. Kate closed her eyes and tried to shut out everything.

She woke during Sunday night and saw Maggie, with her coat over her like a blanket, dozing in a chair by her bed. Dear God, I can handle no more guilt. 'Maggie, wake up, Maggie.'

Maggie sat up and blinked. 'Oh, there, must have dozed off.'

'It's the middle of the night: you must go home. The doctor will find me a nurse. I can't impose.' Despite herself she was becoming more and more upset, out of control.

She was not allowed to finish. 'You're not imposing. My Stacie told us how kind you've been to her. It's no problem for me to stay here for a few nights.'

Kate tried to push herself up and Maggie helped her. 'Now, that's not doing you the slightest bit of good. Jim agrees, and I'm going to pop in and out during the day and Stacie will come and do her homework, if you'll allow her, that is, just for a few days. You're getting better all the time.'

Kate lay back and looked up at her. So much guilt and here is more. 'Maggie, if you insist on staying, you must sleep in the guest room. Take one of my nightgowns.'

Maggie burst into wholesome attractive laughter. 'You've got to be joking. Can you just see me in your nightie?'

In spite of her exhaustion and frustration, Kate had to smile. 'Lovely image. You are very kind but I have already . . .' No, she could not say, imposed. Maggie did not like that word. 'Your family need you more than I do,' she finished lamely.

'No, it's very good for my family, my being here. Spoiled them a bit, haven't I? Well, you do, don't you?' She looked carefully at her patient. 'My Cameron offered to help with the tea last night and he made his own bed, pulled the duvet up, but it's a start, right? Now, I'll just pop down and warm up some soup; it's hours since you ate, and then I'll take myself off next door.' She turned at the door and began earnestly. 'Let me do this little bit for you, Miss Buchanan. Stacie's told us, you see, about the coaching and this could be our way of paying, if that's all right.'

'May I at least be Kate?' She lay back and, taking this for agreement that she was to be allowed to nurse her, Maggie went down to the kitchen and Kate lay and tried to remember everything about Stacie – she had met her in the wood once, she remembered that – but she was too tired and was in fact asleep when Maggie, who had been practising saying Kate, bustled back up the stairs.

Maggie covered her patient's shoulders very gently with the

lovely covers. So feminine. Her Stacie would love covers like that but for herself, really, when you got right down to it, she was more the toile de jouy type; she'd definitely have to get a cushion or two for the bedroom. She left the door ajar in ease her patient should wake and then she tiptoed into the guest room. Such a lovely cover. She would have to tell Jim; he did like boats.

13

There was something about Stacie that Kate wanted to say but she could not remember what it was and was too tired and confused to ask. We have been here before, Kate, and so we'll wait and what I want to say will come in its own time. Don't rush it, or it will fly away for ever.

Dr Jarvis came back and again asked about friends. 'If the monk hadn't found you it wouldn't have been hypothermia.'

'True.' She had looked steadily at the doctor who had looked back just as steadily and Kate capitulated. 'Very well, I have two friends in London. Their numbers are stored in my telephone. One and two; you may ring them – should real need ever arise.'

'And a doctor?'

'He is one of them. Your examination has told you all you need to know, Dr Jarvis. I was badly burned and have had plastic surgery. Otherwise, apart from a few internal problems caused by the fire and smoke inhalation, I am quite healthy.'

'He'll send your records, no doubt.'

'You have been very kind, Doctor, and I have taken a great deal of your time.' She closed her eyes dismissively.

He stood up and his bulk blocked out some of the light. She had forgotten how tall men did that and how annoyed it made her. Petty.

'You're very foolish, but I can't force you to tell me anything.'

'About what? My burns? Where I have spent the past few years? I suppose you have the right.'

He sat down again and, much to her surprise, took her hand. 'I'm interested only in your medical history, Miss Buchanan.'

'In 1972 this house burned down with me in it. A man died in that fire and I was accused of murdering him. I was suffering from complete loss of memory and was badly burned, therefore unfit to stand trial. Instead I was admitted to the psychiatric wing of a hospital specialising in burns. I was there for years. Do you have any experience of severe burns, Doctor?'

He shook his head.

'I hope you never need to learn. When I was well enough to leave hospital, my stepbrother, who is also my lawyer, arranged for me to live as a paying guest in a convent in Provence. I returned here to re-build this house in a – so far – not too successful attempt to rebuild my memory completely. You have not released my hand.'

He laughed. 'Should I have? In outrage or shock or perhaps distaste?'

She looked at him. His eyes were smiling. 'Button number two will reach Mr Simon Whittaker. He's a psychiatrist; he'll tell you all about my head, Dr Jarvis, but to him, my body is a closed book. Please do not dial one; that is Hugh and he will worry and come flying to me and I owe him too much already.'

'I'll pop in some time tomorrow.'

'I'm fine, Doctor, thank you. It's not necessary.'

'It is for me,' he said and left.

Her next visitor was a girl in school uniform, a not unattractive uniform; a pseudo-tartan skirt, she supposed, since she had never seen the pattern before but that meant little these days, a regulation white blouse and a blazer that was grey with yellow stripes. It looked like something Bryn had worn boating once. Kate smiled. What an ass. He had no skill and tipped them into the water, but perhaps he had intended to do that; one could never tell with Bryn.

'I'm going to get you some lunch, Miss Buchanan. Would you like an omelette? I make great omelettes; it's the only thing I make really well.' She came closer. 'It's me, Miss Buchanan, Stacie.' She looked worried and a little upset.

'Stacie, of course.' The tabs were open and the light gauze that was hanging across front of stage to create a hazy effect was lifting. 'But it's a school day. Shouldn't you be at school?'

'Mum said I could come and see you on my lunch break; I've been so worried about you.'

Why would this girl be so concerned? What was nagging there

at the edge of her consciousness? Stacie. Stacie. She almost cried out in her joy. The play. The girl was in a play. 'The play, Stacie. How is the play going?'

'I was so scared that you'd forgotten. The auditions are this week. But look, I'll pop down and make you an omelette: plain, or with cheese, or ham?'

Fines herbes. 'Plain is perfect.'

The girl turned and Kate heard her clattering down the stairs. She did not move so gracefully or quietly as her much larger mother but then Maggie was not impeded by those ghastly school shoes. Restful, that was it. Maggie was restful. Kate lay back a little happier than before. She had remembered something, not perfectly, but she had remembered. Stacie was in a play, no, she was auditioning for a play. Why do I know so much? And then it all came rushing back, the girl at the tomb, the girl in her garden, and then, oh no, I promised to help her.

'Stacie, how much have you told your parents?' Stacie had returned very quickly with a delightful tray on which sat a most delicious looking delicate omelette on one of her own sea green plates. There was a smaller plate with two tiny pieces of fresh bread spread with golden butter and the invalid smiled with anticipation. 'This looks appetising, Stacie, but your parents.'

'Didn't Mum tell you? Oh, she wouldn't bother you while you were ill but we talked on Christmas Day. Did you have a nice Christmas? I know your New Year was lovely with Mr Forsythe, but Christmas . . .'

For a moment she forgot Kate as she relived those awful hours. At last Craig had telephoned and they had had a blissful chat. They had said goodnight and they had made arrangements for the party. She had gone through the next few days in a warm glow and the party had been more wonderful that she could ever have dreamed. Then it had gone wrong again - until they had met in the street. She touched her lips brushing them gently, softly as Craig's lips had done. He had promised to ring her, by eleven, he had said, and he had just gone away without telephoning.

She remembered waiting in a fever of impatience for school to start. She smiled at Kate. 'Did you ever wish a big slice could be taken out of your life . . . ?' Oh, dear God, what a stupid thing to say. 'I'm so sorry, Miss Buchanan,' she began but Kate lifted her hand wearily.

'Everything all right now?' Kate was tired and the girl was exhausting her with her energy.

'First day of school I cried all over Craig's jacket. Sophisticated women don't get snot on expensive jackets.'

In spite of her weariness, Kate laughed. 'Poor Stacie. Love is never easy.'

Happy again, Stacie smiled at Kate. 'Christmas Day was the worst day of my entire life . . . until New Year's Day which was a stinker. I tried to hide my misery from Mum and Dad but I couldn't in the end. He promised to ring me, you see, and they went off skiing and never even thought about me. Growing up is so awful sometimes. Oh, you're not eating your lunch. That's my fault. Look, I'll go and make you a nice cup of tea. Mum brought down ginger with a burst of lemon. Fancy that? It's really tasty.'

Sister Aloysius had made tea out of the strangest mixtures of flowers and herbs; that was all tea was really. 'Sounds lovely.' Anything to get the girl to go. Clatter, clatter clatter. Kate, this child's mother has saved your life. Or was that Ben? Why did he not come to see her?'

My sanctuary has been invaded and I did not want that, or did I?

It had been a perfect hide-away, so far from London, so difficult to reach. Only a few of the gilded people had even known of its existence and how happy she had been to hug her secret to her. She remembered her conversations with Simon and Hugh.

'Kate, you're ready to live on the outside, but not there.' That was Simon.

'Of course, there. It's mine and I was so happy there.'

'You nearly died there, Kate.' That was Hugh. Simon was never brutal.

She had smiled sadly. How often I have wished I had. 'But I didn't,' she said, 'and there are ghosts there. I must lay them to rest.'

'I can't advise it. It's . . .' Simon had stopped in time.

'Insane?'

'Not very sensible.' He had become very professional, almost detached. 'I can't advise it,' he had said again.

Hugh had been more animated. Poor old Hugh, so worried, so fretful. 'You need to get away from those memories, Kate. How can you even contemplate rebuilding a house where you almost burned to death? I'm absolutely terrified for you.' He had been walking up and down, up and down. That was because his instinct was to hold her and he was afraid. She was so frail, her bones looked so brittle. 'Everywhere you look you will be confronted by memories.'

She sighed. 'Memories travel with you, dear old Hugh. They walk step by step wherever one goes. They're here, my darling. I didn't leave them in the ashes of the fire.'

He had no idea what to say, what to do, and she loved him for it. 'It'll be worse, bound to be.'

She had got up painfully from her chair and walked stiffly to the window that looked out on to lovely lawns. 'England does well by her loonies,' she had teased herself but she could not say that to Hugh who had never understood her sense of humour and would be unnecessarily upset.

'Perhaps life will be easier if I confront them head-on. That's part of the plan, my dear. Can I compel myself to confront my demons? Here with you, calm and safe, I can say I want to remember everything, no matter how ghastly it was. Someone hated me enough to try to burn me to death. Talk about Method acting; I would have done a fantastic Maid of Orleans had I not been too, what shall we say, indisposed.' She turned round from the window: *persona*, Latin for, no, not person, mask. She was wearing one of her masks, the jolly one. She almost sparkled. 'I want to have fun with the rebuilding, Hugh. You must tell me how much money I can spend and everything will be different, almost everything will be new, no memories that belong to me attached.'

Had she been right? Perhaps. Probably. The nightmares were no worse here than they had been in the clinical surroundings of the hospital.

Clatter, clatter. Stacie with a tray of tea. 'Oh, good, you've eaten your omelette. Was it good? Mum taught me.'

'Perfect.' Not really a lie. It was not so good as Sister Aloysius's omelettes but then the nun had been making them for at least thirty years. She smiled. 'You have so many talents, Stacie.'

The girl beamed. 'I have to go. Chemistry first thing. I'm giving it up at the end of this year. I shall have a party, a "thank God chemistry is over" party. Want to come?'

Kate laughed. She really was a nice girl and besides, she remembered another girl who had not been overly fond of the sciences.

'See you later.' Clatter, clatter, clatter. The front door closed.

The house itself seemed to sigh in relief.

How exuberant the young are, but it was nice to see her happy. Christmas Day the worst day of her life. Poor child, but probably the day he happily went skiing was even worse. Kate drank her tea, which was surprisingly refreshing, and she managed to put the cup and saucer down on her bedside table without knocking anything over. Stacie had left the tray at the end of the bed. It should be safe there unless she fell asleep and had a nightmare. Should I ring Hugh? What if he telephones and I don't answer? At first he will assume that I'm out walking but if he rings twice, he'll worry. I'll ask Maggie to get me a telephone unless I can get out.

Hugh did intend to be in touch with Kate as soon as he had finished the work he was doing, work that had absolutely nothing to do with his law practice. His office, usually hot enough to hatch eggs, was rather chilly today – windows open too long to let in some fresh air. Fresh air in London: there's a contradiction in terms although, to be fair, it was not nearly so bad nowadays as it had been. He moved over to the fireplace where a politically correct fire burned brightly. At this time of the year he liked a real fire and why not? In the country he did not have to chop the wood or clean the fireplace, and neither was any labour expected of him here. The flames cheered him and warmed him and he sat and went over his interaction with Kate over the Christmas holidays. In his head he heard her scream and he shook it in an unsuccessful bid to rid it of the sound. Since he had returned from Scotland dreams of that scream had disturbed his sleep. The stomach-churning sound ricocheted around his brain and he shook his head in a vain effort to rid it of the pitiable noise that conjured up for him the picture of a woman who is desperately trying to help or protect. Was he making himself believe that, because he loved Kate and had loved her in one way or another since they had become such a mismatched brother and sister, the ethereal will-o'-the-wisp that was Kate and the solid rather dull character who was Hugh? As always, Hugh undervalued himself: others did not.

He tried to remember the casual conversations he had had or had overheard at the time of the trial. The actual transcripts were available verbatim but it was the throwaway remarks that people made in casual conversation or in press interviews when they were taken by surprise that were really interesting. What had Rose, poor, distraught, weeping, totally lovely, and always, always prepared Rose said? *He told her it was over. He said he had been insane.*

Their affair had lasted for years. How long did such insanity last and how did it manifest itself? Kate, when she had been well enough to speak, had said nothing, denied nothing, and had been quietly and with as little publicity as possible pronounced insane. Her horrific injuries had kept her hospitalised for over two years and she had gone from hospital to mental institution with little fuss.

'*Kate, help me to help you.*'

'*Poor old Hugh, what does it matter? Bryn is dead: nothing else matters.*'

It did matter. Hugh got up and went to his desk over which were spread maps and train and air timetables and soon he was compiling rows of figures in his punctiliously neat scholarly hand. He also had a complete dossier dealing with Rose and another one covering the hearings. To his amazement he had even found articles about either Bryn or Kate and sometimes both, written in the past few years. There were also articles covering Rose's career and one or two had, appallingly, to Hugh, intimate details of her private life. She had certainly met some interesting people, he thought diplomatically, as he had looked at photographs of Rose on yachts, in private villas and even in a castle, weekend home of her third husband, another man she had married hoping 'to forget'. It would be quite enlightening, decided Hugh the lawyer, to discover exactly what it was that Mrs, no, Baroness, no, wrong again, Ms Rose Lamont really wanted to forget.

He folded up some of the maps and pushed them aside. Then he unlocked the drawer that he had begun to fill over ten years before and he sat in his well-appointed room that smelled of lemon polish, soft leather, wood smoke and affluence, and he read and reread every word that had been spoken or written about the tragic death of Bryn Edgar.

He looked at the press photographs. Bryn as Hamlet, as Macbeth, as Trigorin, as Ivanov, as Arthur Loudon, as everything and anything, and not quite so many photographs of Katherine Buchan. There was another cutting from a newspaper. Rose Lamont marries Clint Roberts. He had been the cattle baron one and not the 'real' baron who had been German or was it Dutch?

I should never have married again. I am still in love with my Bryn. I keep looking for him.

Five times she had looked. Where was she now? Hugh shrugged. He had never been fond of Rose, probably because she had dismissed him.

Hugh Forsythe, Kate's tame little lawyer.

Almost fifteen years after the fire the tame little lawyer looked at the clipping, at the beautiful face and the expensive hair. Are you still as beautiful, Rose? Are there lines and hollows that show what life has done to you or, perhaps, what you did to life? It would be quite interesting to track you down, if you are still alive. His last cutting about Rose was a small article that said that the tragic actress was leaving Britain and memories of Bryn for ever. Only in Spain could she find inner peace. What on earth, wondered the very simple Hugh, was inner peace? Serenity? Mary Mag had it: she was serene; and Kate awake, that was serenity, was it not? But as always he saw only the face she chose to show him.

Hugh picked up his pen, always a fountain pen, and went back to his calculations.

Stacie, thrilled to have been allowed to make Miss Buchanan's lunch, hurried up through the village, trying not to be seen eating a sandwich in the street – an activity frowned upon by the powers that be at school – and, for a totally different reason, by Maggie who thought such sloppy ways of eating led to indigestion. Stacie was happy. Craig was well and they had coffee together every day, Miss Buchanan was getting better and she, Eustacia Thomson, was allowed to let herself in to Abbots House, to sit in the serenely lovely sitting room, and to run up and down stairs looking after Miss Buchanan. She had hoped to be allowed to study in the garden; being welcomed into the house and even given a cup of cocoa had been a dream, but to be there, to be allowed to cook for her, to make her tea, to think of small delicacies that might tempt her appetite, it was bliss.

She could hardly wait to tell Craig. Her heart seemed to swell inside her as she thought about him. How sweetly he had explained the mix-ups that had led to his not getting her messages. Poor Craig; he did not want to believe that his mother deliberately 'forgot' to tell him, but Stacie knew better. Never would she say anything to him, of course. After all, her own parents were none too keen on her seeing Craig; they just were less devious than the sophisticated Sinclairs. And our friendship, our feelings for each other, are nothing to do with our parents. They can think what they like. Craig loves me; he has told me he does, and I love him. Miss Buchanan is getting better; the world is a totally wonderful place. Stacie almost skipped like a little girl as happiness bubbled away inside her.

She met Craig for just a heart beat while they were changing classes. He was in a much more advanced chemistry class and so she did not see him there but they passed in the corridor while he was on his way to the changing rooms and she to 'double French'.

'How is she?' he asked.

'Much better. I'm going to talk to her tonight.'

'Great.'

He touched her hand as he passed, just a touch, a brushing together of skin, but she felt it, a pleasant sensation all over her body. Was there anything more beautiful than falling in love for the first time, for ever? she added quickly. Irregular verbs brought her down to earth a little but she was still in a happy frame of mind when the last bell sounded all over the school and its grounds. After-school classes did not begin for another week and so there was no opportunity to find Craig, still being picked up at the door by his hyperventilating mother, but there were other friends to greet and to chat with, and Cameron to avoid, easy really because he did his best to avoid her too.

At last she was free and she hurried off. Maggie would have popped in to see Miss Buchanan for a few minutes during the afternoon, leaving Ciss to mind the shop, but she would have been able to stay only for a few minutes. Stacie looked at her watch and worked out that Miss Buchanan would have been alone for at least an hour and a half if Mum had been able to get away at three. What if something had happened to her in the interim? How awful, for instance, if she had fallen out of bed on to her wooden floor. Stacie would quite like to rush in some way to Miss Buchanan's aid, do something memorable for her, but for that to happen the poor woman would have to be hurt and there had been enough of that, had there not.

She was annoyed to find Dr Jarvis making himself comfortable in Miss Buchanan's beautiful white bedroom. He looked quite relaxed sitting there in that beautiful chair, completely at home. Nothing could have happened while he was there and she herself could hardly rush to the rescue with a more than competent doctor sitting there.

'Hello, Miss Buchanan, I popped in to see if you'd like a cup of tea.'

'How kind. You see what good nurses I have, Dr Jarvis. I am totally spoiled but I'm perfectly fine for now, Stacie. Dr Jarvis, however, has other calls to make. Perhaps he would like something before he goes?'

The doctor hauled himself to his feet. 'No thanks. If I drank all the tea I'm offered in a day, Miss Buchanan, I would never get any work done. Now, Stacie, my patient is pleased to see you but don't let her get tired. She still needs plenty of rest, and peace and quiet.'

'I'll show you out, Doctor,' said Stacie, deliberately playing the part of very refined housemaid in a West End production.

She led the way downstairs and opened the front door and he went out but he turned on the step. 'You're a good girl, Stacie, but I mean it. Don't tire her; she's still quite frail. I think she'll ask you to bring her the telephone and it is time she contacted her family, but take it away again once she's done. All right?'

'Yes, Doctor,' said Stacie who was Stacie again.

She closed the door happily and went back upstairs. Kate in a practical blue nightgown with the minimum of lace at the neck was sitting cautiously on the side of her bed. I could kill for those sheets, thought Stacie happily. 'Is there anything I can get for you, Miss Buchanan?'

'Would you mind helping me to walk over to that chair, Stacie. I must ring my lawyer.'

'Lean on me; I'm very strong, but are you sure you should be out of bed?'

'Have you ever been ill, Stacie?' asked Kate, slipping her feet into her slippers. They were soft mules, made of some material that reminded Stacie of the curtains. How fab: co-ordinated slippers.

Stacie saw the marks on her patient's feet and looked away and then, ashamed of herself, looked back again. 'No, Miss Buchanan, healthy as a horse.'

'Long may it continue, my dear, but nowadays the medical profession have their patients on their feet as soon as possible. Dr Jarvis just doesn't want me up too long. I promise to go back to bed as soon as I've finished.'

Stacie settled her in the chair beside the telephone table and then went back to the bed and brought Kate's dressing-gown. It was blue and it was made of silk and Stacie loved the feel of it against her fingers. 'My mum wears candlewick.'

'I have one of those too. This is my "being visited by the doctor dressing-gown". I won't be more than fifteen minutes, Stacie. Make yourself some tea or coffee and if there's anything to eat, you're welcome to it.'

Lights were on all over the house. Stacie tutted with annoyance. Had her parents never heard of the ozone layer, pollution, saving the earth's natural resources, saving the whale? Of course they had. She and, to give him his due, Cameron told them several times a week if not every day. So simple to flick a switch as you left a room but her parents canoed through life on a river of electricity.

Saving the planet, however important, was not the issue at this point. Being the lead in the play was. Going to drama school instead of university was. She stood at the gate and looked at the house. Cameron's room was at the back and so she could not see if his light was on. Her parents' room was lit and yet at this time of the evening it was highly unlikely that either of them was anywhere near it. All the downstairs lights were on and the curtains in the sitting room – rarely used and never during the week – were not drawn. Any burglar who happened to be passing could see, quite clearly, Maggie's Lladro figurines in the cabinet, several pieces of very nice sterling silver, and an original McIntosh Patrick, which Jim had bought before the artist had become astronomically famous. Jim, no sophisticated art lover, liked paintings of trees.

'Well done, Dad,' said Stacie and opened the gate. She hurried up the neat path and into the house, taking off her lovely red jacket as she did so. She threw it on a peg on the hallstand.

Her parents and her brother were in the kitchen. 'You're late, Stacie. You know I said I was going down to do something for Miss Buchanan this evening and so we have to eat early.'

Stacie dropped a kiss on her father's head. 'She's fine, Mum; she says not to worry about her.'

Maggie stopped stirring and turned to her daughter, dripping spoon in hand. 'I said you could go at lunchtime. Who gave you permission to go again?' She looked down at the floor. 'Now look what you've made me do. Cromwell, get away from there.'

'Quicker than washing the floor, Mum,' Cameron said. 'Is the chilli good, Cromwell? At this rate you're the only one in the family who's got a hope of getting any of it.'

'Don't be silly, Cameron, and go and get a damp cloth to wipe that up. Stacie, we thought you were at one of your after-school clubs.'

'Big deal, Mum. French club starts next week so I popped down to see if she needed anything and she did. The doctor was just leaving and he said I should stay until she'd finished her phone call.' Stacie sat down at the table and picked up one of her mother's home-baked bread slicks. 'I'm sorry if I'm late but tea isn't ready anyway.'

'It damn well is, young lady, and has been for half an hour. I'm fed up with you and your mother waiting on that woman hand and foot.'

Jim was rarely angry but he was now and Stacie hung her head and sat quietly and it was Maggie who defused the tension. 'Now, now, Jim, we're not waiting on her hand and foot. Just a wee bit of Christian charity.'

'I'd like a little less charity outside the home and a little more here where it belongs.'

'Hear, hear!' said Cameron, and that was the wrong thing to say because his father turned on him while Maggie stood fussing and tutting and muttering over her pots.

'Mum, Dad, please,' said Stacie. 'I have so much to tell you. Mum, come and sit down.'

But Maggie refused until she had filled the plates and Stacie waited, with her heart beating unpleasantly quickly. The chilli was excellent as was the hot apple crumble that followed it and, according to family rules, no controversial subjects were discussed while they were actually eating. School, homework, dating and Miss Buchanan – all were controversial, and so, as usual, Jim and Maggie talked about the shops and the odd ways of their customers. Stacie and her brother told such heavily edited tales from school as they felt would go down well with their particular adults.

Her heart still racing, her stomach churning and the palms of her hands clammy, Stacie waited until her father sat back and smiled, his pudding plate empty. 'That was good, Maggie. Now Stacie, pet, tell us what you wanted to say.'

What did she want to say? So much, so many different things. 'I told you I went down to Abbots House and Dr Jarvis asked me to stay for a while; Miss Buchanan is allowed out of bed to use the phone but she's a bit shaky on her feet. While she was on the phone I went down and made myself a coffee.' She looked at her father who was glaring belligerently. 'She told me to; I wouldn't make myself free like that. You should know that, Dad,' she added chidingly. 'Anyway, after about twenty minutes, she called me up and I helped her get back into bed and . . .'

'Do I have to listen to this?' Cameron was bored.

'No, but that doesn't mean you can watch television or play computer games. Homework till at least nine. Go on Stacie.'

'She told me about the fire.'

'Stacie, you saw my feet; rather ugly, aren't they? And your wonderful mother has seen almost everything else.'

'She hasn't said anything, Miss Buchanan, to me or to anyone else.'

Kate sat up straight and clasped her hands in front of her on the beautiful lace edging and so her hands, usually hidden, were quite visible. 'I was hideously burned in this house or at least in the house that stood here in 1972, that's fourteen years ago. It's taken a lot of time and talent to do these repairs.' She looked directly at Stacie. 'I'm assuming you have read all the newspaper reports.'

Stacie blushed. She had wanted to read them, would have relished reading all the stories, not in a voyeuristic fashion, but merely to find out more about this fascinating woman. 'I haven't actually, Miss Buchanan. I was going to Edinburgh to look you up, not for the scandal.' She stopped, blushing furiously again. Oh, God, she hated being young and unsophisticated. She wanted to be cool and serene, and look at her, she was gibbering like a monkey and would be thrown out and never allowed in again. 'I wanted to read about plays and the theatre and reviews and all that sort of stuff and it's so exciting to be able to speak to a real actress, never mind a bona fide star, someone who has done all the things that I want to do, that I know I can do if I get the chance.'

'Why didn't you read it?' asked Kate gently.

'Craig was ill and so we didn't go.'

Kate reached forward and patted her hand, the scars on the back of her own hand showing quite clearly. 'You're a nice girl, Stacie,' she echoed the doctor. 'I didn't really want to help you, you know. I wasn't sure that I could, but now, if your mother wants me to, I will at least try. But first I have to tell your parents who I am – they have to know everything, that I've been in jail and in a mental hospital. I cannot allow you to come again without your parents' express permission.'

'Dad said it would be fine; he wanted to pay you. He's very proud. He's worked so hard, you see, so that we can have all the advantages, but Mum told him . . .' She wanted to cry, for once again she could feel the hot tide of shame sweeping up her neck and on to her face. Perhaps Miss Buchanan could teach her not to blush.

'Go home, Stacie, and when your mother comes down later this evening, perhaps you will be free to return and I can tell her the whole, rather sordid, story.'

'So that's where we are, Mum, Dad. Can I come with you, Mum? I did some of my homework while I was having my coffee and I can easily do the rest when we get back.'

'"Sordid story." My God,' said Jim. 'What is my wee girl doing in the house of a woman who has a sordid story to tell? And you, Maggie, running after her since the minute she moved into the village and this past week, leaving me and Ciss to mind the shops and the kids and the house and all the time she was . . . what the hell was she doing, Stacie?'

'Jim, calm down. You're purple. We'll have Dr Jarvis in looking at you in a minute.'

'All she ever did was help me to breathe,' Stacie said quickly.

'Breathe. You've been doing that for nearly seventeen years on your own. You're not going back there.' Jim was so distressed that he flung his chair back and it went flying across the kitchen and banged into the Aga and Stacie and Maggie watched it and turned only when they heard the kitchen door slam shut behind Jim.

Maggie slumped in her chair and Stacie moved to sit closer to her and groped for her hand. 'Dad really doesn't like Miss Buchanan.'

'At the moment he doesn't know what to think.'

'He can't mean it, Mum, please. He'll never give permission for me to go to a stage school: he's so set on a university. My daughter, the university student. Why can't he be proud of "my daughter, the drama student"? Mum, you know Miss Buchanan. She didn't mean sordid the way Dad thinks she means sordid. She's lovely, a real lady.'

'Thanks.'

Stacie shook her head in affectionate understanding. 'Oh, Mum, you're lovely. It's just that she's different; you know that. Mrs Sinclair thinks she's a lady but she's not; she's just a woman with a posh voice and money. I want to be like Miss Buchanan. I want to speak like her, to move like her, dress like her, have my house just like hers.'

Maggie took her daughter's hand and held it very firmly. Her usual smiling happy face was pale and serious. 'Stacie, have you been asking her questions?'

'Aw, Mum, she doesn't invite you to ask her personal questions. She knows everything about breathing and voice production and she is so good. I thought I was doing really well and then she said the lines. I know it sounds all arty or airy-fairy but it was almost as if there was a new person in the room. I stayed in the light and she sat in the shadows; she didn't want me to see her face but I don't even think of it any more. I hear her voice and I know she's beautiful. Today she was different, completely free. I think, because you undressed her and saw all her scars, she feels she has nothing to hide. She told me some things, about her granny who brought her up when her father died, in a car crash, I think. She never mentioned her mother. Her grandmother thought women should be able to play the piano and do embroidery. She laughed when she told me that. "I never did learn to cook. Thank God for your father's wonderful pies." Her laugh is lovely too, like her voice. I said, "You have a lovely laugh," and she went very still and said, "No, Stacie, Rose has the lovely laugh." I never asked her who Rose was.'

'Well, this isn't getting the dishes washed,' said Maggie as she stood up. She reached for her apron and tied it round her ample waist. 'Better if you go off to your room and get some studying done. I suggest chemistry. I'll clean up here.' She looked steadily at her daughter. 'Then I'll talk to your dad.'

Tears welled up again. 'But aren't you going to see Miss Buchanan? You must go. Oh, Mum, please make everything all right.'

Left alone in the kitchen, Maggie methodically began to clear the table. 'Mummy, make it better.' How many times had little voices called that in the past? It would take more than a bit of Elastoplast and a kiss to fix this problem. She scraped the spoonful of leftovers into Cromwell's dish while the dog tied himself up in knots with excitement.

The door opened and Jim returned. 'Thought I'd help you with the dishes, love. I've overreacted again, haven't I?'

'Sit down, Jim.' Maggie thought hard before answering. She wanted to say exactly the right thing for all of them, for Jim, for Stacie and for herself. For Cameron, life was still fairly uncomplicated but Stacie? She squeezed herself in beside him and then leaned against him, side by side, the way they had been for over half her life now. Funny thing, marriage. You sat down one evening and realised you had lived half your life with someone. Would she even remember what her blood relations looked like in twenty years' time?

'I can pay for a tutor.' Jim stood up and glared at her. 'What the hell am I working all these hours for? So if they need tutors I can provide them,' he answered himself. 'I don't need some woman with a past coaching my daughter.'

Maggie smiled to herself.

Jim struggled to get the words out. He had never said them before although they both knew he thought them often. 'I love her so much, Maggie. She's everything to me. She's pretty and clever and she's kind. She's great in the shop, friendly and helpful. I want her to go to a university. I want to sit in Edinburgh in that big grand McEwan Hall in my best suit, you with your hair done, and see some clever professor in black robes say Eustacia Thomson, MA. Can you imagine my mother's face if she could see one of her family getting a degree?'

'Our wee lassie could get the best part in the school production, Jim. The star. Joan of Arc. I think I'd burst with pride to see her on the stage in the star part. And she's not setting out on a life of crime, love. She's never done a play before. Angels in Christmas plays are not exactly the same thing. Maybe she'll find it too much work.'

Immediately he jumped to the defence of his daughter's capabilities. 'Too much work? Since when has my Stacie been afraid of hard work? She'll be great.'

'She has been finding chemistry a problem this year; you know she intends to drop it and specialise.'

'She'll manage.' He looked at her and laughed. 'You think you're leading me along by the nose, Maggie T . . . Well, let me tell you, madam, you can lead me only where I'm willing to go.'

'I never doubted that for a minute, pet. Are you going to help here so that I can go down to Abbots House?'

Jim took the dishcloth off its peg and moved over to the sink. 'I'm saying yes to the play and a bit of coaching if you think it's a good idea but I will never give my permission for her to go to acting school. It's university and a degree for my daughter.'

'Thank you, Jim.'

'And I'll send a pie down to Abbots House every Saturday and there won't be a bill.'

'Whatever you say, dear.'

14

She moved to pick up her coat but he stopped her. 'Kate, don't go. Don't leave me.'

Kate looked at him. He looked lost, alone, an orphan in the middle of a storm. Dear God, what was real and what 'the stuff that dreams are made on'?

'I have to leave, Bryn. My rehearsals start tomorrow and this is so important; this is the dream part.'

'What has a rehearsal got to do with you and me?' He pulled her into his arms and kissed her lips, gently, then more demandingly, forcing her lips open and, despite herself, Kate responded. At last he drew away from her but kept her tightly held in his arms. 'Face it, Katie, you want me as much as I want you. Stay with me. I'll have you up and out of here before nine.'

'Bright-eyed and bushy-tailed?' She tried to joke.

'Believe me, darling girl, you'll feel wonderful.'

Had he not said that she just might have given in to her body, which was sending her heart and her brain strong messages, but he was so damned sure of himself. She pushed hard and she was as tall as he and quite strong. He let go. 'Go practise your charms on Rose.'

'Too easy, Katie. Besides, damn it all, it's not just sex. There's more between you and me than overwhelming urges.'

'They're not overwhelming, Bryn. I can't take risks, not now I've got this part.'

'For God's sake, what risk is there in having a good fuck? If I remember rightly your precious Maurice was the first to recommend it.'

Kate slapped him and in his surprise he let go and she threw open the door and rushed out. Clatter, clatter, clatter, down the stone stairs. 'Damn it, he is so sure of himself. Why do I let him affect me? Why? He's vain and arrogant and, damn him, the most exciting man I have ever met in my life. Let there be a taxi.'

London, centre of the universe, where one can buy a pint of milk or find a taxi at virtually any moment of the day or night. She did not need milk but she did hail a taxi within a few minutes of leaving Bryn's flat and was especially thankful, for she had left her coat and could not possibly have gone back for it. He would win then as he almost always did. She sat back and since the driver seemed as disinclined for small talk as she was herself she was able to let her thoughts roam. Bryn, such a complex character, and easier to analyse when they were not sharing the same space. When he was, all she could think of was the emotional pull as if he were the magnet and she the helpless iron filing.

It's easy to understand the attraction when he is on stage. To play opposite him is as exciting and frightening as if . . . oh, I can't explain. There's a buzz like an electric current in the air around him and there's his charm. There has to be a better word than charming but he does have charm and it's real, unlike some of those other smarmy actors.

The voice. I cannot be in love with a voice but everyone in the theatre is when he speaks. How can I describe it? Melting honey on hot toast; it warms and cajoles and soothes. Oh, how it woos. Who could resist? But it can be razor sharp too or harsh. And his eyes. He maintains eye contact throughout; he's never *the* Bryn Edgar waiting for his moment: he's the character, whoever it is, he stays there throughout, and everyone thinks that he is looking at them, speaking directly to them. I've heard people outside in the crowds that line up waiting for him to appear and they say, 'He was looking at me all the time he was delivering that speech,' but I know he was looking at me, not me, Kate, but me Ophelia or Juliet.

But that is Bryn, the actor. What is it in Bryn, the man? The same animal magnetism, for he does not pull it on with his tights or his sword, the voice murmuring in my ear or my neck or my hair, and the eyes that look at me and say, Katie, you know my weaknesses; I'm totally honest with you, only with you. Take care of me, Kate, don't let me down.

She paid the taxi driver and let herself into her own little flat, bought with her own money earned by her own talent, and she leaned against the door and the first thing she saw was a picture of Bryn, a picture that few of his fans, and they were legion, would recognise. Bryn, in an old jumper and even older trousers, sitting in the snow. His eyes were saying, Isn't this fun, Kate, my love, my heart, you and me together playing in the snow?

They had gone to Abbots House for a few days of peace and quiet. They had not expected quite so much peace. 'The snow fell softly through the night, and we awoke to find the garden white.' Not just the garden, but the carse, all the way as far as they could see. Even the sea seemed to run right up to it on the beach, perhaps determined to wash the sand, to rid it of impurities, to make it flat and smooth.

Bryn, as he always did, had got up to make coffee and Kate had luxuriated in lying alone in the nice warm bed and spreading herself all over his space, smelling him on the pillows and in the sheets. He had erupted up the stairs again. 'Kate, Katie, come and see. Snow. Snow everywhere, on the wall, like little hats on top of the milk bottles, all along the branches of the trees, and against the windows. Look, Katie,' and he had thrown aside the curtains and shown her snow on her window like the arc of a hyperbola and beyond it a wonderland. 'Now, isn't that beautiful?'

She turned over lazily and looked at him. 'Yes, it is,' she agreed.

'Silly cow. Keep your eyes to yourself, you hussy, while I put some clothes on. There's a tiny matter of no electricity and so your coffee, madame, will take a little longer this morning. But I'll light a fire and boil a pot of water.' He turned to look at her again and his eyes danced with mischief. 'I'll be a real Boy Scout, *cariad*, and fill the pot with snow and then we'll put on all the clothes we have with us and we'll go and make angels.'

She pulled the down-filled quilt over her head and snuggled inside the covers. Angels? She used to make snow angels with her cousin, David, and once surely with Hugh, or was he too dignified for snow angels. Dear Hugh. Well, she was definitely much too dignified for them now. No electricity. The underfloor pipes would not be heating and they would be unable to cook, but the hunter-gatherer who had just gone racing downstairs seemed capable of lighting a fire and so they could at least have hot drinks. What was there to eat in the house? Very little but it did not matter. It would only be for a few hours and in the meantime they could be cut off from the world, alone in the snow. The world could not reach them. Paradise.

'That's not you asleep again?' Bryn was back, two steaming mugs in his hands. 'Here, sit up, *caru*. Instant coffee but, unfortunately, the bottle of milk at the door is frozen. I've put it in the sink to defrost.' He climbed on to the bed beside her. 'I haven't been snowed in since I was seven. There's not a light to be seen from the top of the hill to the bottom. No shops. The chip shop closed. What a tragedy. I shall have to catch a rabbit.'

'God forbid.'

He laughed. 'You've been in the big city too long, Kate Buchanan. Drink up and then I'll make toast. Did you ever make toast, Katie, with a piece of bread stuck on the end of a fork? My mam had this gadget with a little hinge so that you could turn the bread round and it would toast first one side and then the other. Very up-market, a gadget like that was. I bet your granny had the old toasting fork, green, wasn't it, and held so close to the coals it singed your eyebrows. See that's what happened to mine.'

'You have perfectly splendid eyebrows.'

'I know, like my perfectly splendid voice. Shall I boil you some water for your very dirty face? A slovenly face it is, Kate, like the face of a woman who fell into bed with her love without resorting to her creams and potions.'

'And it was wonderful.'

'So it was. I go to make toast.' He struck a pose. 'I may be some time.'

He made toast, black on one side and barely warm on the other but they covered it in marmalade and it was a feast fit for a king, and then they dressed as warmly as they could and went outside and walked down to the sea.

It was bitterly cold. The sun was a blazing red ball way down in the sky, and several pompous seabirds strutted up and down the slender line, the frontier, between land and sea. Sometimes a wave hit their large flat feet and they would jump, squawking, a few feet into the air and then settle down again to their perambulations; and Kate and Bryn, arm in arm, would strut up and down with the birds and they too would jump into the air with indignant screeches.

They tired of playing with the birds and ran instead down the carse. 'Shall we go all the way to the end of the Sea Green, Bryn, and perhaps into the woods? I think there's an old ruin there, an abbey or a castle or something.'

But Bryn was practical. 'I would go with you to the ends of the earth, my love,' he said seriously, 'but if there is still no electricity, then we had best get to building up our fire. What can you cook on a fire, Katie, for the burned offering we had for breakfast has gone long ago?'

'There's bound to be electricity now,' began Kate, turning round and looking towards the village, 'but do you know, Bryn, I see no lights.'

'It's the middle of the morning.'

'There's usually at least one light somewhere, wouldn't you say?'

Because they were almost the same height they were able to walk as if between them they had only three legs. Kate stood on Bryn's left and they strode back to the village like rather tall children at a Sunday-school picnic and when they reached Abbots House they forgot that they were stars of the West End stage and made angels in the snow. Bryn lay down first, legs close together and arms stiff and straight by his side and then he began to open and close his legs like the scissors of a demented tailor, and co-ordinated his arms, sweeping them up to touch above his head and then down.

'Leave me some snow, leave me some snow,' yelled Kate and threw herself down beside him.

'What a baby you are,' said Bryn at last as they lay on their backs in the snow, snow angels evident all over the garden. 'Ruins the garden; we should have made them on the Sea Green.'

'And had all my neighbours talking about that strange actory woman from London. Help me up and we'll see about lunch.'

Lunch was bread and cheese, followed by bread and marmalade, and they ate it in bed wrapped up in quilts while their clothes dried on the pulley in the kitchen. Bryn got up and padded downstairs to put more coal on the fire and when it was hot enough to make the living room pleasant he called for Kate and she joined him. He opened wine while she lit candles and then they sat in front of the fire and sipped wine and recited pieces from plays or favourite poems. When it grew dark they opened the curtains and saw that it was snowing again, and so they sat and watched the snow fall, obliterating the angels, and they were as happy as they had ever been. They made love there on the floor of the living room, in front of the fire, and Kate knew she would remember every minute of the day for the rest of her life.

'It's snowing again.' Maggie's voice broke into her reverie. Had she been asleep or dozing or merely luxuriating in some of the pleasanter memories? 'Would you like to look at it?' She was already reaching for the cord that controlled the blinds.

'Yes, I like watching snow.'

Maggie opened the blinds and then pulled Kate's easy chair from beside the table and put it near the windows. 'The doctor says for you to get out of bed for a few hours. I have to open the shop but Stacie's downstairs if you need her.'

'Let her come up if she'd like to, Maggie. She can let me hear how her piece is progressing.'

'You mustn't get tired.'

'Maggie, my dear, surely my long sad story has shown you how many hours I have spent in bed over the past fourteen miserable years? It will be lovely to listen to her. Perhaps I could go down-stairs.'

'Not yet. Maybe tomorrow. There.' She finished tucking in a rug. 'Are you quite comfortable?'

'Maggie, have you seen Benedict?'

'I did forget after all. Hold on a minute; I have something for you in my handbag.' Maggie left Kate sitting at the window and hurried downstairs and returned a few minutes later with a small parcel. 'This is from me and Jim, a wee thank you for coaching Stacie. Even her dad says he can hear a difference.'

Kate took the little package and opened it carefully. Inside was small bird, a puffin, exquisitely carved. Benedict's work. 'Oh, Maggie, how lovely and how very kind. Thank you both. So you have seen Benedict?'

'He comes in every few days to ask how you are. I've told him you'll soon be strong enough to take short walks. Now, I have to go. Stacie'll bring you up a nice cup of tea.'

And she was gone and Kate sat in the chair and looked out at the falling snow. She saw Maggie, bundled up in a warm blue coat and a red hat and scarf, emerge from the house and hurry, head down, up the road towards the main street. She peered as hard as she could through the snow, hoping to catch a glimpse of a tall thin figure and a long grey dog but Benedict was nowhere to be seen. He wouldn't be, would he? I must telephone or write him a letter. Perhaps that's the better way to say thank you.

A timid knocking on the door admitted Stacie, not in her school uniform today but in a pair of grey trousers and a lovely pink sweater. She had lost weight and it suited her. She put a tray down on the little table by the window. 'A cup of tea, Miss Buchanan?'

'Thank you, Stacie. How nice you look. Pink's a good colour.' Kate picked up the teapot and reached for a cup. 'Stacie, why don't you join me, if you have time?'

'Lovely.' Stacie hurried out, clatter, clatter, and was back in a few minutes with a mug.

Kate, aware and unconcerned that her scarred hands could be seen, poured tea. 'Have you come to tell me how the drama group is doing? Sit on the bed.'

Stacie, looking a little unsure, perched on the bed. 'Tomorrow is the big day, D-day. I'm so nervous.'

'You'll be fine. You know the words. You know the whole play; that is vitally important. And, since you've lost a little weight, you look more like a Joan. That's not terribly important, just think of the huge sopranos who can make their audiences believe they're wasting away, but you'll feel more in character, and that's vital. Have you seen the costume?'

'No, the mums make them after the plays have been cast.'

'No matter; it certainly won't be as flattering as that sweater.'

'Craig gave it to me. I was quite surprised because it's sort of an

214

intimate present, isn't it? I think he wanted to make a statement, to his parents as well as to me.'

'It's lovely. You wouldn't like to try for Juliet? She could wear something in a nice pink.'

They both laughed and, feeling emboldened, Stacie leaned closer to her patient. 'Miss Buchanan, could I ask you something?'

Kate stiffened and then relaxed. The girl was bound to be curious and she and her family had been unbelievably good to her in this past week; without them she would probably be in a hospital somewhere and that was something she really did not want. 'Of course, Stacie; if I can answer, I will.'

'It's just that, you were famous, top of your profession. If I were famous I'd want to live in London or maybe New York. New York must be fabulous. What brought you to Friars Carse?'

Kate laughed aloud in her relief. Whatever she had expected, it was not that question. 'I fell in love with a ruin, but I think I found the ruin at the right time. I loved the theatre, Stacie, I liked my life, learning lines, rehearsing, performing. Believe it or not I even loved travelling; New York yes, very stimulating, Moscow, Paris, Sydney, even Tokyo. Paris. Paris with Edith Evans; can you believe it? I used to pinch myself. How lucky we were. People all over the world were so kind. The bad part, what they call the downside now, was that there was no privacy. Some people, not many, seemed to feel that – I don't know, that they owned us, I suppose, that having paid for a ticket which was going towards our salaries, that they had a right to intrude, to ask questions on planes or trains or in restaurants. Our photographs were on the covers of magazines – *Vogue* and *Harper's Bazaar* – and society hostesses used to ask us to dinner: so silly. What if we'd eaten our peas with a knife? Bryn Edgar' – it did not hurt to say his name aloud – 'used to threaten to do that. "It's what they're hoping for." He got very Welsh when his dander was up. I was at the Edinburgh Festival when I found this place; I have never once regretted buying it although twice it has cost a fortune to restore.' She made a mental note to ask Hugh, once again, about money. After all, she had not earned anything for years. What investments were there? 'I came here alone, or with my stepbrother, my lawyer.' She turned from her contemplation of the snow. 'You met him – Hugh. When I first bought the house I invited several friends, even had an enormous party. Latterly I came only with a friend.' She stopped talking and turned again as if fascinated by the large soft flakes dancing past the window.

'Bryn Edgar, the actor?'

Kate nodded. 'He was the greatest actor of his generation. Had he lived he would have surpassed Gielgud or even Paul Scofield. We used to say that Scofield would be acknowledged as the best and he was such a decent human being too. Private, reserved. I was rather like that. Every night we stood in the wings, all of us, all the fledglings, and watched the emerging wonders, actors like Maggie Smith and Peter O'Toole, Glenda Jackson and Judi Dench, established greats like Gielgud, Redgrave, Guinness, Sybil Thorndike, Peggy Ashcroft, Margaret Rutherford. What an incredible woman she was: a great star, but always so interested in encouraging young actors. She was a good listener. "Tell me, dear," she would say, and I always felt she really wanted to know. But Bryn was unique and he was my love.'

'I didn't mean to pry.'

Kate patted her hand. 'You didn't, my dear, but thank you. I have not said his name out loud for many years. He's dead, you see, and they said I killed him and I didn't know. I remembered nothing. Have you any idea how frustrating it is to be without a memory. They insisted that I could remember if I tried, but when I tried I remembered only horror and pain.' Suddenly she realised that she was talking to a young impressionable girl. 'Your parents would be very angry if they could hear me. I think you should go now but do come and tell me the good news tomorrow.'

Stacie tidied up the cups, picked up the tray and, after promising to return the next day, went off downstairs. Kate listened to her shoes on the wooden floors and smiled. 'Bryn Edgar,' she said aloud and listened to the sound. 'Bryn Edgar.' Such a lovely name.

She waited until she was quite sure that Stacie had gone and then she pushed herself up out of the chair. Her writing materials were downstairs in her lovely desk and all day she had been thinking about her goldwork. Time to get back to normal. She closed her eyes for just a moment at the top of the stairs and then opened them again. No dizziness. One stair at a time, and holding on to the banister, she went down. She smiled as she looked at her sitting room. It was as if she were seeing it as the work of someone else and for the first time. It really was a lovely room.

It was also perfectly clean. Maggie or Stacie had been dusting: there was not a speck of dust anywhere. Her embroidery frame was where she had left it and she walked slowly over to it and sat down but she had no energy to sew. For now it was joy just to see it; yes, she was pleased with it. It reminded her, as always, of Sister Mary Magdalene and she decided to write a letter to Provence. That made her smile a little. Kate Buchan writing two letters and each of them to a religious. That would have made Bryn smile. 'Bryn.' She said it again to listen to the sound in the empty room and then, more calm and at ease than she had been for some time, she sat down at her desk and wrote her letters. But first she took the hand-carved puffin out of her dressing-gown pocket and put it in pride of place on the desktop where she would always be able to see it as she was writing.

15

Hugh Forsythe decided to have a few days in the sun. It was January and so, for a short break, Spain seemed the best option. He pretended to consider the possibilities: Madrid, the capital, but not a good bet for sun in January; Seville, my goodness, everything the cultured man could want could be found in Seville, architecture, history, music, to list but a few of its delights, and the climate was perfect. Was there anyone who did not know that the great Mozart set his sublime opera, *Don Giovanni*, in Seville or that Beethoven, perhaps the greatest composer of them all, set *Fidelio* there? The first feminist opera, Hugh always thought. In another time and place he could have seen Kate, like the Fidelio of the opera, fight for her love, but her time and place had not been right. He decided to go to Málaga, a city on the Mediterranean coast, much loved by the expatriate communities, and a few hours' drive from Seville should sun and sand prove too mindless.

Hugh wondered whether or not to ring Kate before he went but after weighing up all the pros and cons he crossed every toe and finger that he possibly could and decided to go without telling her. After all, it was her wish. They were not to live in each other's pockets; he was not to treat her like an invalid. If he went abroad for a few days he was to bring her olives or lavender honey, serious addictions, unwittingly fostered by the delightful sisters at Le Prieuré. And besides, he was only going for a few days.

Hugh was not a brave traveller and had opted for the Parador Málaga-Gibralfaro, a luxury hotel on the hill, the Gibralfaro, that dominated the city centre. He believed, and he was quite correct, that the views and the accommodation would be superb. Already he could feel that he was on holiday; it was more than warm. Hugh removed his summer-weight jacket and, for just a fleeting part of a moment, wished that he was in Spain to make merry – but he was not. He took a taxi to his hotel, showered, changed clothes, went down to the dining room, but on the way he stopped at the desk and asked for a car and a driver for eight o'clock the next morning.

He ate well, noted a few dishes that he would like to try to recreate for Kate or that he would like her to try when he could persuade her to leave Abbots House, and left the rather grand dining room before eleven, remarkably early for sunny Spain. But Hugh Forsythe had come to Spain with a not so hidden agenda. Once back in his room he spread maps out over the huge old-fashioned wooden four-poster bed and studied them. This entire area was beloved of English expatriates but, possibly more importantly, several film studios had used an area in the east of the province to make films, usually westerns. Rose had been a somewhat unusual star of many of these films and he believed it to be highly likely that she lived somewhere between Málaga and Almería which was about a two-hour drive to the east along the rather ghastly coastal road. The photographs in the magazines he had seen had convinced Hugh that it was distinctly probable that Rose was in the area around Málaga where there was an ideal all-year-round temperature; the area was also being much touted by savvy developers and travel agents. 'Buy before the boom.'

His driver, Marcelo, was outside the hotel well before eight. He was a tall, handsome sunny-faced young man who spoke excellent English and who was studying astrophysics at university. 'In Spain it is too expensive to go to another town or country to study, señor, and so I have to live with my parents which is nice because my *madre* washes all my clothes, but I try to earn extra money to help. I am a good driver and I speak Spanish of course, Italian, French and German.'

'And you're studying physics.'

'In Spain we are told what to study, señor. All depends on the grades, but don't worry, I will like astrophysics.' He smiled at Hugh, a beautiful smile that showed perfect teeth. 'And see, next year I go to Frankfurt for a work-study programme and already I speak serviceable German. It's perfect. No?'

'It's perfect, yes,' said Hugh, who wondered fleetingly what he would have been allowed to study in Spain. 'Now, this morning I want to see a few of the areas where the British live.'

'The expats,' said Marcelo, thus displaying his idiomatic knowledge.

'Exactly. And this afternoon and maybe tomorrow some of these places I have marked on the maps.'

Marcelo looked at the circles on the map. 'But there is nothing there, señor, the desert only.' Then he smiled as if suddenly he understood. 'Unless you want to see the big houses and then you want to build for yourself but out there is not a good idea, I think.'

'Nerja first, please, Marcelo, and then towards Salobreña and on towards Almería.'

'It's your car, señor.' Marcelo shrugged.

They spent the morning driving from one development to the next. Hugh was not too sure why he was doing this but he had an idea that perhaps, just perhaps, if he was very lucky, he might spot Rose Lamont sunning herself on one of those immaculate sunbeds beside the perfect pools in the meticulously landscaped gardens. Marcelo had given him an idea for a cover story should he need it. The rigours of the British winters were too much. He just might want to live in the sunny south, at least for part of the year. Surely Rose had not known him well enough to know that apart from London, Hugh felt that France was the only civilised place for a cultured man to live.

Marcelo was perfectly happy to drive and he kept up a running commentary on Spain, its royal family, its educational system, its football teams – which seemed to begin and end with Real Madrid and Málaga's own team – its cuisine, its culture, and anything else that came into his head, for his employer merely grunted from time to time, and very occasionally asked him to drive past the same wedding cake of a building twice. They stopped for lunch, superb fish dishes chosen by Marcelo, and paid for by Hugh, an arrangement that suited them both and then, after buying two bottles of mineral water, they drove out into the desert. Hugh blinked a few times as they drove through canyons and rocky wastes. Had he not known he was in Spain he could have believed himself in Arizona.

'Many films were made in this area, señor, but a long time ago. Now it's a, what you call it, tourist attraction, lots of sets. They even do a bank hold-up. But you know *The Good, the Bad and the Ugly,* or maybe *The Magnificent Seven;* oh, I like to watch that one. The big stars came here, real big, like Clint Eastwood. *"Go ahead, make my day."'* he said in a respectable American accent. 'Look, there are several little airports or runways. You can be in Madrid or Paris or even your London in just a few hours.'

'Should astrophysics not work for you, Marcelo, you have a future in the travel industry.'

'Thank you.'

'You're welcome. Marcelo, I'd like to stop at one of the film studios and perhaps a small airport.'

'Desde luego, of course. You want to see the bank hold-up?'

God forbid, thought Hugh, but he merely said, 'I don't think so, Marcelo. I'd like to visit an airstrip.'

They drove on and stopped at a small private airfield. There was an immaculate little waiting room with a coffee machine and a water cooler and a few very out-of-date magazines lying on a table. The wall was covered with rather old black and white photographs and Hugh recognised Charles Bronson and Clint Eastwood and, with a sigh of nostalgia, Raquel Welch, but there were no shots that he could see of Rose Lament. Two leather-covered settees stood facing each other and a healthy and large pot plant stood in a corner where it threatened to take over the wall. A small remarkably burly man in overalls was sitting behind the reception desk drinking water and wiping his neck with a rather soiled handkerchief. Hugh wondered why on earth he did not remove the overalls since he was so obviously uncomfortable.

'Buenas tardes,' Hugh began.

'Señor?'

End of conversation on Hugh's part. The Spanish words for hello, goodbye, thank you, and morning, afternoon and evening were the sum total of his linguistic skills. 'Ask him if he speaks English, Marcelo.'

Marcelo laughed. 'Perhaps you should have spoken in English right away, señor.'

'One is always told to start a conversation in Europe with a polite greeting, Marcelo,' said Hugh gravely, 'and so I did.'

'It's okay to be polite in English and he speaks English.' It was obvious to Marcelo that the man was following the conversation and enjoying Hugh's discomfort.

'Good afternoon. My young friend says you speak English.'

The man shrugged, a shrug that said a great deal. 'Enough, señor. What I can do for you? You want to hire a plane? We have two beauts.'

'No, not at this point. I was merely interested in how long this airport has been here.'

The Spaniard turned and said something to Marcelo in rapid Spanish.

'Since 1937,' answered Marcelo. 'He's not so great with numbers.'

'And I wondered if the film studios used your services.'

'In the sixties and seventies all the time. Our pilots flew everybody. Why you ask, señor?' He pushed himself up out of the chair and his stocky stance and belligerent look were threatening. ' All the books are good.'

Hugh cursed himself for his stupidity. 'I'm sorry. I'm just interested in films. You see, some of my favourites were made around here.' He remembered Marcelo's spiel. '*The Magnificent Seven*, for instance. I found myself wondering what the stars did for recreation. Dinner in Almería, perhaps, or weekends in Seville.'

The man shrugged again. This shrug said, None of my business.

'Could a plane fly from here to London, for instance?'

'*Claro*. Of course, we fly to London all the time, and to Rome, and Madrid and you name, we can go there too maybe.'

'Edinburgh?'

'*Por qué non?* Why not? It has an airport we can fly. Now, I'm busy. You want to fly someplace you talk me. Otherwise, *adios*.'

'Goodbye, and thank you.'

Hugh, feeling slightly stupid, walked out into the warm dry air and Marcelo followed. 'Let's find another one, Marcelo, and this time I'll try not to antagonise the office manager.'

'Especially if he's the pilot too, señor. That was – what you call it? – a one-man band, pilot, mechanic, office manager.'

'You will go far, Marcelo. One more airstrip and then we'll return to Málaga. I feel in need of a tall cool beer.'

'I know the very place.'

'My hotel will be fine. Let's find another airstrip or a studio.'

They drove for fifteen or twenty kilometres and reached another airstrip. Again there were the studio publicity shots all over the walls and this time Hugh thought he recognised Rose in a crowd scene. 'Wow, Rose Lamont,' he said in the tones of an excited fan. 'I loved her pictures. Did pilots here fly her around, señor?'

To his surprise the receptionist, who had been very friendly and had even offered them coffee, spat loudly on the floor and went into a tirade in Spanish, which thankfully Hugh could not understand; what was obvious was that he wanted them out of his airport.

'He wants us to leave and he says he spits on her and all her friends and family to the sixth generation,' said Marcelo, closing the door behind their retreating figures.

'Good heavens; she wasn't that bad an actress surely. Go in and ask him why he dislikes her so much, Marcelo.' He gave the driver several large banknotes. 'He's too young to have known her.'

A few minutes later Marcelo slipped into the driving seat. 'You know that lady, señor? He says she's the daughter of a pig and several other things I won't translate but I think he says she screwed . . . no, how you say, she cheated his uncle out of a lot of money. He was the original owner, pilot, mechanic, you name it. Not a nice lady and he says her acting stinks too.'

'And his name, Marcelo?'

'Felipe Santa Cruz.'

They were much later returning to the hotel than Hugh had intended. Marcelo had not complained; after all, he was being paid by the hour but, still, he was a young man and was possibly late for a date. 'I'm sorry if I'm making you late for something, Marcelo.'

'No problem, señor. You know in Spain we all hang around together. I can catch my friends later. My girlfriend might be there or maybe she went out with her girlfriends or maybe with her parents and the grandparents also.'

Hugh, who was an only child and who had grown up with a much-married mother, several stepfathers and, for a few months, a step-sister who became the light of his life, was quite jealous of all this family. 'You choose to go out with your grandparents?'

'*Más o menos,* more or less. Maybe they choose to go with us. It's okay. The old ones stay in the back of the room, then the parents and in the centre all the young ones. It's a sensible arrangement, I think, and your father can't say, where were you till one o'clock because he was there too! Where do you want to go tomorrow? Seville is just a few hours on a better road. Nice place to stay.'

'I think I'll stay around here, Marcelo; a few more of the expat places, maybe to the west. Now, how about a beer before you join your friends; maybe this "in" place you were talking about.'

'Great. Everybody goes there, señor, everyone who has money, that is. They do fabulous *tapas*, you know, little things to eat with your fingers, but it's expensive.'

'I think we've earned it.'

Marcelo drove to a newly refurbished restaurant on Plaza de la Malagueta, facing the beach. Being new and brash it was not Hugh's type of place; he much preferred atmosphere and could sense none, but it was early by Spanish standards. Hugh smiled. By British standards the prices were reasonable: by Spanish they were high. The bar was attractive, light and airy with marble flooring and heavy wooden tables with rather splendid glass tops. Marcelo ordered some *tapas* and they sat and sipped their cold beer while they waited for them and they looked around. The room was already quite full. People were meeting for drinks and then perhaps, going on to restaurants and nightclubs. Although there were some very young customers like Marcelo, most of the clientèle were not only older but they were foreign.

'Here are some expats, señor, not all, the two tables nearest the fountain are Spanish – maybe they been since lunch, but the foreigners like to come here. See the beautiful ladies at the table in the window there; they are all famous people.'

Hugh looked. Twelve or so extremely well-dressed and well-preserved people were sitting at a large glass table in one of the huge bay windows. The women wore what Hugh's very sophisticated, elegant and rich mother had called cocktail dresses – in fact one or two reminded him of his mother and her own circle of high-maintenance friends in Grasse – and the men wore white dinner jackets. Hugh smiled with nostalgia. He had a jacket cut exactly like the one on the rather florid old man on the right of a striking woman in emerald green.

He was so busy looking at the jacket and trying to work out whether or not he and the ruddy-faced old man shared a tailor that for some time he did not look at the woman. When he did he liked what he saw. She was small, tiny in fact, and her hair was a neat, carefully coloured cap that caressed the neck and curled around the ears. It was not blonde which would have looked ridiculous – she was not a young woman – nor was it white, which possibly it should well have been, but a lovely pale colour that somehow looked quite natural. Not for nothing had Hugh spent countless holidays driving his mother to and from beauty salons. The woman in the beauti-fully cut green silk dress held a champagne glass in her right hand which sported the obligatory large diamond and bright red finger-nails. She swung her foot as she sat, her high-heeled toeless green mules revealing her toes, the nails also bright red. Hugh applauded the woman's hard work and diligence; he had met many like her since his mother had returned to her holiday home on the Riviera some years after the end of the war, and in fact the colour of the nails reminded him of his mother. Red had been in fashion when she was young and since she liked the colour and it suited her colouring and her temperament she had never deviated from it. Perhaps he had spent too long in silent admiration, for, as if at a suggestion from the man beside her, the woman turned and looked straight at Hugh. It was Rose Lamont. He had spent much money and the greater part of the day driving around in the heat and the dust in what he had felt from the beginning was a rather immature and ineffectual attempt to trace her and here she was in a night-club that he had almost not visited. She had not recognised him; she laughed as if she were used to such quiet admiration, and turned back to her companions.

Hugh recovered, calmed his beating heart and stood up. Marcelo was looking at him in amusement. 'Cute *chica*, señor,' he said and Hugh managed to stifle the words, 'Don't be impertinent.' Instead he smiled and walked across to the table.

'Miss Lamont?'

'Take yourself off, sir,' said the florid gentleman, but Rose had turned again and this time she gasped a little and lifted a delicate hand to her throat.

'It's all right, Cyril. This is . . . I'm sorry.' She smiled, put down her champagne glass, and held out her hand. 'I can't quite remember.'

And Bryn and Kate had always said she could not act. Hugh took the hand, noting as he did so the quality of both the diamond and the manicure. Both were excellent. 'Hugh Forsythe, Katherine Buchan's lawyer.'

Rose recovered. 'Of course, Hugh. How extraordinary to see you and what a delightful surprise.' She reeled off the names of her companions who immediately asked Hugh to join them.

'Any friend of the baroness is a friend of mine,' said the florid and portly Cyril.

'Yes, do join us, Hugh. It's been such a long time, and Cyril, darling, I'm no longer a baroness, as you well know, naughty boy.' She turned and smiled directly at Hugh, her large blue eyes no less beautiful than they had ever been. 'Are you living here now?'

Although a chair was pulled out for him Hugh remained standing. 'No, just felt like a few days in the sun. I won't join you but I would love to see you, Rose, for a little chat – old times.'

'How exciting, Rose darling, to meet such a delicious old friend.' One of the women spoke. Was it Marilyn or Mary-Lee? Hugh could not remember but he did recognise predatory eyes: he had seen too many over the years.

'Tomorrow, Rose, lunch perhaps or morning coffee?' he said. 'I'd love to hear what you've been doing. Good gracious it must be ten years, more perhaps.'

'So long?' Rose was searching in her handbag and she found what she was looking for and Hugh smiled. His mother had had one too. How delightful: a small silver-backed notebook with a tiny silver pencil. Where did she get the fillings for them these days?

'Naughty Rose,' said Predatory Eyes, 'to let such a divine figure of a man out of your sight. May we all come to lunch tomorrow? Pretty please.'

'Absolutely not,' said Rose. 'I shall keep him all to myself; this first visit at least. Here's my address, Hugh. It's quite a way out of town although it is being developed, and I'm on the top floor – such views over the sea.'

Hugh bowed to the table – it seemed the easiest way of edging out of the group – and went back to Marcelo. 'Eat them all,' he said to the young man who was patiently waiting with the plates of *tapas* in front of him. 'I've lost my appetite.'

Ten minutes later they were on the way back to Hugh's hotel. 'Early again tomorrow, señor?'

'No. Marcelo, drive me past this address just now please, and tomorrow pick me up in time to get me there for around eleven.'

Marcelo stole a quick look at the note. 'Oh, these are classy places, señor. Mostly English and Germans living there, no Spanish, I think, maybe one or maybe two.'

Hugh said nothing and sat quietly until his driver pointed out the building where Rose said she lived. It was one of the buildings that they had driven past twice that morning. Hugh congratulated himself on his perspicacity. 'My hotel, Marcelo, and tomorrow, maybe get me here for ten. Looks a nice place for coffee.'

Later he enjoyed dinner sitting in his hotel, watching other people. He stayed late; he was in Spain and so, for one night, he would dine as the Spanish do. He could scarcely believe the coincidence of meeting Rose in the bar but since Marcelo had described it as the 'in' place, perhaps he should have realised he was bound to see her there sooner or later. His date with Rose Lamont was for lunch but he had been reading Rose's body language as well as listening to her and he was sure that she had not been too pleased to see him. He had therefore decided to go to the apartment building early to watch the elevators just in case Rose 'forgot' that he was coming.

Several times during the evening he had wanted to ring Kate. What would he have said? 'Hello, Kate, you will never guess who I bumped into,' but he realised that he wanted to tell her not for her sake but for his own. Kate had never once mentioned Rose of her own volition. As far as he knew she did not even remember Bryn's wife but then how much did he know of what was going on in Kate's head? Rose had known of the affair. They had tried to keep it quiet but for a time they were the only people who did not know that their entire world was aware of their love. It had been so beautifully, painfully obvious: the way Kate, strong and independent, seemed to melt into something softer whenever Bryn was in the room; the way that Bryn, acknowledged as a rather trying self-centred genius, became kinder, gentler, more thoughtful when Kate was near. The way their faces lit up when either entered a room, even though each studiously looked away and focused on someone else, had been particularly hard to swallow.

Why am I here? He asked himself question after question. Rose had been here in Spain on the night of the fire. That was an undisputed fact. Ergo, she could not have been in Scotland. But the belligerent pilot had said they could fly easily to Edinburgh. Was there perhaps a small private airstrip even closer to Friars Carse? Harder, indubitably, to check a passenger manifesto on a private plane than on a commercial flight. Were such records even kept and if they existed were they kept for over ten years?

'God dammit,' Hugh shouted at himself in the mirror as he was cleaning his teeth. 'You're not a detective; you're an English lawyer who likes both his comfort and the south of France and so why are you driving around playing . . .' He could not think of the name of a detective and then exploded with: 'Perry Mason?' Perry Mason would have got the name and address of the man who disliked Rose Lamont and might be sitting down chatting with him over a few cold beers right now. Hugh was not pleased with himself. He sighed. First Rose and then, depending on what she had to say, another drive out into the desert for a further chat with the charmer.

Next morning, in a lightweight blue suit and a rather natty pale blue shirt, he drove with Marcelo to the address Rose had given. The desk clerk did not know a Miss Lamont but assured him that Mrs Bryn Edgar did indeed live on the top floor. Hugh persuaded her not to ring up and alert Rose. He had arrived a little early, he explained. Rather than disturb his hostess, he would wait in the lobby. Marcelo, as cheerful and friendly as he had been the day before, was sitting outside in the car. Hugh sat and looked through a few magazines, not unlike the ones he had seen in the hotel in the Lake District. The elevator doors opened once or twice but there was no sign of Rose. Hugh relaxed. Just after eleven the elevator opened again and several people came out. In the middle of them, her hair covered by a pale lilac scarf, was Rose. Glancing fearfully around, she walked quickly towards the doors and Hugh blew a sigh of relief that he had had the foresight to hold the magazine before his face. He waited until she had left the building and then hurried after her.

Marcelo, bless that boy, he certainly deserved a rise, was right outside the door and the engine was running. Hugh got in and almost lost his balance as the driver, thoroughly enjoying the situation, sped away. 'Take it easy, Marcelo, the lady may have gone for a bottle of milk.'

'There's a, how you call it, *una tienda,* a shop in the basement, señor,' answered Marcelo as he swept out on to the main thoroughfare. A few cars in front of them was a daffodil-yellow Mercedes convertible and Hugh could see a lilac scarf blowing in the wind.

'Don't get too close, but don't lose her.'

'I know the drill.'

Hugh looked at the back of his driver's head. From the set of the ears he knew the boy was grinning. 'I'm glad this is making you happy, Marcelo, but where did you learn the drill, if I may ask?'

'Cop shows. This is the first time I ever got to follow a suspect.'

'Good heavens. It's not a suspect; the lady is merely someone whom I wish to meet for lunch.'

'Because you like her so much? Señor Forsythe, I'm a Spaniard and so I can tell you don't like her one bit. Is she the lady in the picture? Are you a policeman, señor?'

'Keep your eyes on the road.' The young man, Hugh thought, had a brilliant future ahead of him. He was, he supposed, handsome – any young woman in the restaurant last night and not a few older women had certainly watched him – but he had a charm, an exuberance, and he was also, as some of Hugh's clients might have said, as sharp as a tack. Was astrophysics the correct place for him? Hugh mused, as he found himself in the ridiculous position of following Rose Lament who was probably, whatever the shop in the basement held, merely doing her shopping.

She was not. She drove for miles along the bumpy beach road

until Hugh, bumping along behind her, began to feel ill, but she pulled in at last to the grounds of a large hotel. She parked the car and went in and Hugh followed as quickly and as secretively as he could, all the time assuring himself that he was making a complete ass of himself. He was absolutely delighted that none of his friends and colleagues could see him, skulking around a Spanish holiday resort, spying on a well-preserved widow.

'This is going very good,' Marcelo encouraged him as if he could feel his employer's unease.

'Very well,' Hugh corrected automatically. 'Marcelo, you go in and see if you can find the lady. Perhaps there's a coffee shop.'

Marcelo, well pleased with his role, went off, and returned a few minutes later. 'There's a very expensive, what you say, boutique. She's looking at dresses.'

Clothes? Surely she was not buying something new to wear at lunch.

'There is also a coffee shop, very nice.'

'Good. Let's go in.'

Marcelo followed him into the hotel and, sure enough, across from the entrance to the boutique Marcelo had mentioned was a very attractive little restaurant. They went in and Hugh insisted on sitting at a table from where he could watch the boutique and about ten minutes after they had sat down Rose, carrying a dress bag, walked out of the shop. They could hear her high-heeled sandals on the tiles as she approached the coffee shop, and Hugh, wondering if acting genes ran in families even where there was no actual blood relationship, jumped to his feet and said, 'Good gracious, Rose, how lovely to see you here. Marcelo and I were just having some coffee before heading for your apartment. I'm so looking forward to lunch. Do come and have coffee. We have time, don't we? We actually didn't say an exact time.'

Rose, obviously startled, looked at them in consternation. 'What are you doing here?'

Marcelo, the soul of discretion, took himself off to sit at the counter, leaving Hugh to lie on his own. 'We were driving around and I thought, time for coffee before I head for my delightful *rendezvous*. Do sit down.'

He looked at his watch. 'We could have lunch here unless it's frowned on to lunch so early.'

'It is rather early,' said Rose, who was beginning to look a little more relaxed. 'That's why I'm here. Lunch in Spain is usually around one, one thirty. I thought I'd pop out and see if this gown was still here. One should buy when one sees something because often it's gone when one goes back.'

'Absolutely.' Hugh ordered, hoping that the waiter, who seemed to speak good English, had understood him and would not bring the short black coffee, *café solo,* of which Hugh was not overly fond. A large cup of rather milky coffee was eventually put in front of him and what the waiter called *cortado,* a small cup of black coffee with a little milk, in front of Rose. Hugh would have preferred that but was grateful to recognise what he was drinking.

'This is an unexpected surprise, Rose,' he began.

'I told you I came out to shop,' said Rose defensively.

'I meant to see you after all these years.'

Rose sipped her coffee. 'Apart from a disastrous marriage to an Italian and an even more ghastly but shorter one to a Hungarian baron – or was he Polish – I have been here since Bryn died.'

'What a tragedy that was.'

'Yes, my life was blighted.' She closed her eyes for a moment and then opened them wide and gazed at Hugh over the top of her tiny coffee cup. The effect was meant to be disarming but Hugh had dealt, all his working life, with professionals: he was not moved. 'And the loss to world theatre – incalculable. Such a great actor.'

'Two great actors, Rose. Kate's career burned to death in that fire too and she is still living with the effects of it visible in her mirror every day.'

Rose gave her head a little shake. 'I never think of her. Forgive me, she was a client, wasn't she?'

'She is my sister.'

Rose's right hand was playing nervously with her demitasse spoon and her fingers tightened round it so that Hugh would not have been surprised to see it bend. 'Sister? I had forgotten. I'm so sorry. Does she, does she ever mention me?'

'Never.'

'She is in an insane asylum? The best place really; even you would have to agree with that, Hugh.'

Hugh clenched his hands so tightly that he could feel his well-manicured nails trying hard to pierce the skin of his palms. 'While she was so gravely ill as a result of her horrifying experiences, Rose, a hospital was the best place, yes. But she has not been hospitalised for many years. Her recovery has been slow: not only were there life-threatening injuries, there was the psychological trauma of seeing the man she loved burn to death.'

Rose gasped and at last she was not acting. She jumped to her feet, sending the little cup and saucer sliding across the glass table and on to the tile floor. 'She did not see it, she could not.' She covered her face with her hands and began to sob, and Marcelo and the waiter came rushing to assist.

Hugh could not have touched Rose had his life depended on it but Marcelo put his arms around her tenderly and led her to a table at the side of the room and all the time he murmured soothingly in a mixture of Spanish and English.

'I want to go home,' Rose sobbed into his shoulder. 'How could you, Hugh, how could you remind me of that awful night?' She took a moment to pull herself together. 'Poor Kate, poor dear Kate, all these years I have prayed that she knew nothing, but to be told so baldly that all the time she realised what she was doing. She said nothing at the time, never, never has she said anything and I was so glad. Her mind was so upset, poor Kate, because Bryn was going to end it all, fly out to me and we were going to start again. That's why she killed him, whatever she says, that's why she killed him.' She began again, a violent paroxysm of grief-stricken weeping shaking her tiny body and the waiter began to argue forcibly with Marcelo who still held Rose.

'*Ay Caray*, señor Forsythe, I think I pay you for this.' He yelled something at the waiter. 'I've asked him for a brandy, and coffee for us. He says we're scaring away his customers. Maybe you have to drive your car and I take this poor little lady home in her car. You can't drive, señora, you're too upset,' he finished soothingly to Rose who was now sitting dabbing ineffectually at her eyes. 'Don't worry, señora, the tears make the beautiful eyes bright.'

God, how can she swallow that? thought Hugh. The tears make her look like a raddled old woman. 'Rose, I didn't mean to upset you. Of course, everyone knows that you were abroad filming on the night of the fire. Kate did lose her memory but it's coming back, very, very slowly . . .'

'There is nothing for her to remember. I was in Spain, no more than thirty kilometres from here. Ask anyone.' She drank the brandy in one swift gulp, threw off Marcelo's comforting hand, and walked quickly out of the coffee shop. They heard her shoes again on the tiles and then she returned, glared at Hugh, picked up the dress bag she had forgotten in her hysteria, and, despite her impossibly high heels, walked gracefully out.

Hugh and Marcelo were left looking at one another. 'This lady is the daughter of the pig, I suppose. Wow, what a temper. I guess you don't get lunch, señor.'

Hugh laughed. He really was an engaging and enterprising young man. 'I think this establishment has seen enough of us too, Marcelo. I want to go back to Mini Hollywood; on the way we can stop somewhere for some lunch.'

'Great. I know the best place in the whole of Spain for *paella*.'

'I thought you might.'

Three hours or so later they were back at the second airport they had visited. 'How good is his English, Marcelo?'

'I doubt he can discuss astrophysics, but his English is good, not like mine, you understand, but good. And señor, you'll need lots of pesos.'

The office looked just as it had looked the day before; the same photographs, no, the one with Rose in it had been torn violently from the wall, the same plants, the same armchairs, and the same Jack-of-all trades sweating behind the counter. He did not look pleased to see Hugh, who began by taking out his wallet. That did seem to lighten the atmosphere.

'When in Europe always greet the inhabitants politely before engaging in business."

'Good afternoon,' said Hugh and received a shrug and a grunt in reply. 'I'm sorry to have offended you yesterday but I was very interested in what you had to say about Miss Lamont.'

The pilot turned his head and spat loudly on the floor.

'Miss Lamont is not a friend of mine but I am sorry if she has caused trouble to your family. I am a lawyer . . .'

'*Abogado?* Good, you are here to get our plane back?' The pilot was looking a great deal more cheerful.

'Your plane? I'm sorry, I know nothing about a plane but I am very interested in your dealings with Miss Lamont.'

'There is money?' A large, rather dirty hand was extended.

Hugh produced his wallet. 'Your uncle, señor, Felipe Santa Cruz; you say he lost money to Miss Lamont. Did he perhaps fly her somewhere and she has not yet paid?'

The man laughed. 'Fly her? He was her *enamorado,* her how you say it?'

'Lover?' Surely not, thought Hugh. She had been crazy about Bryn; there had never been a hint of scandal attached to Rose.

'*Si,* lover. He was crazy for her. He flew her everywhere. In fact he was so proud she bought a plane for him and they were going to get married; not easy to do in Spain since he was married, but for her he became a crazy man, and then she said, "Marry you; you must be . . . *chiste,* how you say, make the joke," and off she went and some guys came for the plane and the papers were in her name and what could he do?'

Hugh was tense and excited and he just knew that he had to speak to Rose's former lover. He, if anyone, would know where and when she flew. 'Your uncle,' he said, handing over a fat roll of paper, 'I must speak to him. I'll make it worth his while.'

The pilot carefully put the money into his rather slim wallet and carefully buttoned it into a pocket of his jeans. 'He's dead, señor, ten years.'

'Damn. I'm so sorry, of course I'm sorry but his records, his flight plans.'

'No point to keep them, señor. We burned them, three maybe four years ago.'

16

Maggie brought a lunch of chicken breasts in a delicious saffron sauce, which she warmed up in Kate's oven while she prepared a little rice and some simple vegetables. 'The sauce is so rich, Kate, we don't need anything fancy with it.'

Kate agreed and she and her new friend sat upstairs at the small table and ate and chatted until Maggie had to rush off to reopen the shop.

'Stacie's corning down to make you a cup of tea after school – that all right?'

'Of course; I'll be delighted to see her.'

When Maggie left Kate decided that she felt strong enough to return to her sewing and so she made her slow way downstairs and went to her chair beside the embroidery frame. She sat back for a moment and looked around the room. How lovely it was, serene and welcoming. She would have to thank Maggie for dusting it. A picture of the room as it had been superimposed itself on reality and she welcomed it, embraced it. If ghosts were there let them come. She was stronger; there was nothing she could not handle. But no spirits came, not even the best beloved, only the memory of the flames. She shook her head to clear her vision but still she saw them, eating up the curtains, racing across the so carefully chosen rugs, and devouring . . . She hid her face in her hands but the pictures went on just as vividly and she tried to rid herself of horror by focusing instead on delight.

He had arrived, by train and then taxi. His visit was unexpected; she had been in Russia and he was in a West End production. They had not seen each other for weeks and she was hungry for his presence, for his voice, his smile, his kiss, his body. She offered to prepare a meal, as usual something simple and plain, but he could wait no longer either and hungrily, thirstily, they had flown into each other's arms. They had not even had time to go upstairs to use the beautiful bed with its lace covers and white pillows, the moonlight invading and lighting up the marriage bed.

'Oh, dear God, what a fool I was,' he moaned as they lay sated on the sofa before the fire.

And she had tried to comfort him. 'We have this, Bryn, this special place where the world can't find us.'

By the world had she meant Rose? Or had she meant those others – the vampires, he called them – who tried to suck him dry?

'It's not enough, *caru*. I want to acknowledge our love. I want to marry you, fill you with my children.'

She stirred under the weight of his body but pulled him back when, courteously, he attempted to move. 'No, I love to feel the weight of you against me.' She lay there uncomfortably but happier than she had ever been in her life. 'I'd love to have a baby, Bryn, now that the subject has come up again. What do you think he'd grow up to be? Would he inherit our talent such as it is, your beautiful, glorious voice?'

'Do you take after your parents? I don't. Our poor little sprog would probably end up a dustman.'

She shifted again. 'Someone has to be a dustman and, although I would like my children to be very successful, I suppose if he was a really excellent dustman—'

'Who quoted Shakespeare,' he interrupted as he pushed himself up on one elbow. 'The fire's going out and I have other plans for you, madame, before I let you put some clothes on.'

He got up and threw some logs on the fire and squatted there watching while first sparks danced and then flames began to creep up along the edges of the logs. She was cold without the shelter of his body and she went to him. He pulled her into him and held her close while the flames ran races along the logs and jumped haphazardly from one to another. Then he put her down on the rug and began to love her, methodically, seriously and she responded dizzily, leaping with him every step of the way. When she awoke she could not feel his weight and she reached out a hand but he was not there.

'I hate this memory, I hate it. I don't want it, not even the loving. Why won't it leave me in peace? I want to remember something nice, the way Bryn's eyes creased up when he smiled, Hugh, sunlight through leaves.' But her mind refused her commands and she was back in the graphic memory. She remembered now, clearly. She had gone to have a long hot bath and Bryn, hungry now for food, had promised to make coffee and omelettes.

There was something wrong. She had expected to be enticed back downstairs by the smell of perking coffee but she could smell smoke. At first she supposed that it was the fire, a log that had refused to burn and slowly slumbered sending out smoke that was unpleasant, acrid. She coughed; how it stung her eyes, her nose, her throat. Blast. The last thing any actor wanted was a rasping throat. Couldn't Bryn smell it? She got out of the bath, wrapped herself in a towel and hurried into the bedroom. A pink satin robe, a gift from Bryn, was on the bed, and she dropped the towel and pulled it on and ran, in her bare wet feet, down the stairs.

There was no smouldering log, only embers. Damn it, there is smoke but we lit no other fire. And then she heard the voices but still thought nothing, only that it was a nuisance that someone should visit so late at night. Bryn was talking, arguing, shouting.

Kate jumped to her feet. She could bear no more; she did not want to relive this nightmare. 'I'm awake,' she sobbed. 'I'm wide awake in my house and I do not want to relive that night.' She shook her head as if to clear it, paced up and down for a few minutes and sat down again. 'I'm so close, so close, and I must remember, for Bryn's sake, for Hugh. When did I smell the smoke, not while I was in the bath? Concentrate, Kate, pretend it's a part in a play.' She closed her eyes and breathed, calming herself, and then concentrated with all her might. Focus, focus on the sounds, the smells. Not smoke, not yet. Coffee: that was it. He was making coffee. I heard the voices in the bath and I laughed, yes, I did, I laughed because I wondered if Bryn had dressed. I was not frightened, only rather annoyed; someone had interrupted our one precious night together. Concentrate on the other voice, Kate, a low, impassioned

237

sound. A woman but what woman? No Maggie in those days. Mrs Balakirev? No.

I remember walking in the dark towards the dining room end of the house. I heard Bryn's voice, a cry, strangled or cut off somehow. I called to him and now I was frightened. I opened the kitchen door. The omelettes were burning and I went forward and turned off the stove and I called him again. There was a form, a shadow, something in the dining room door.

'You slut, you whore. Now look what you've done. It's all your fault, all of it. I never meant to hurt him.'

The words from the past hit Kate as cruelly as they had done fourteen years before. 'My God, my God, I can't bear it.' She felt faint and put her head down between her knees for a moment. She straightened up. 'Come on, Kate, you have come this far, not much more. "I never meant to hurt him." That proves it, at least as far as I'm concerned. I did not kill Bryn, not even by accident, but the fire, I have to remember the fire. How did the fire start? I was on the kitchen floor. I was cold and my head ached. She hit me, no, she pushed past me and I banged my head on the doorjamb. It was deathly quiet except for crackling; that's all I heard, a crackling noise as if Bryn was lighting the fire again and I smelled smoke. That's when I smelled it, when I regained consciousness. What did I do? I got up and I was dizzy and it was so dark. I called him again. I pushed the dining room door open and there was a loud woosh, just like the noise when a big firework goes off. Then smoke was billowing towards me making it difficult to see anything. Flames, dear God, flames, not creeping lazily but bursting furiously to devour the curtains. I panicked; I wanted to get away but Bryn, Bryn, where was Bryn? I had to find him. I was coughing and choking and spluttering. My eyes smarted and it was almost impossible to force them to stay open so much did they want to close against the attack of the smoke and I got back down on my knees close to the floor and there, there I saw him. He was lying quite near me and was half in half out of the fireplace and, oh God, the flames were reaching for his hair. On all fours, like a wild animal, I scrambled to him. I was screaming, "Help me, help me."'

'Miss Buchanan?'

Someone was calling her name.

'Miss Buchanan, it's Stacie.'

Kate pushed her hair out of her eyes and tried to stand up but her legs refused to hold her and her voice disobeyed her orders to answer the girl. She was still frighteningly tied to the past by that too real dream, hallucination, memory, whatever it had been. She was cold, and yet the room was warm enough, the expensive central heating obediently heating centrally as it should. The room seemed to echo with the sounds of her demented voice. How could the girl not hear it, or had she heard it? Was that why she still stood at the door? Kate gave up the unequal struggle and fell back on the plump cushions; after a few minutes she was sure she heard the gate open and close. Stacie was gone.

Later Kate would be sorry for her, would wonder why she had come, but for now she lay waiting to regain control of her unwilling muscles. 'Oh, blast, oh, damn, double damn,' she said when she was able again to stand. 'She was coming to make me some tea and this was the day of the play; she wanted to tell me about the play.'

She tried to remember the tone of the young voice. Miss Buchanan? Had it been excited, happy, full of eagerness to share?

Kate looked at her watch. It was not yet two thirty. Stacie was still in school. But I heard her voice; I tried to call out to her when she knocked. Kate put her head in her hands and tried to think. Why had Stacie knocked at the door? She had a key; she never knocked but came straight in. Kate stood up so clumsily that she banged against the embroidery frame and almost knocked it over. She went over to the door and opened it. Outside it was dull and grey and there was a strong wind blowing from the sea: an east wind, cold. She breathed deeply, emptying her lungs that still seemed full of that damaging smoke. Her lungs, even after so many years, bore scars; she dare not walk to the gate to try to see if a grey-skirted figure was hurrying away.

She closed the door against the greyness and took some warmth from the colours of her embroidery silks that she had knocked to the floor when she stumbled. 'Leave them, leave them. You are not so well as you thought you were. But hearing voices, imagining voices. I never did that before. In the dream I always heard voices,

Bryn and hers.' She felt sick. Of course it had to be her. I was wearing something, something flowing. Oh, God, what is true and what is false? Am I mixing different times, different experiences? She went into the dining room and tried to see it as it had been. 'The fireplace was over there to the left, and the table, the table was more or less where it is now. There was a crystal vase and roses, white tipped with pink. Bryn brought them. A painting there on that wall, a McTaggart. Damn: I loved that painting. Hugh told me it was foolish to hang it in a house that was empty most of the time. The curtains: my trademark toile de jouy, blue, with shepherdesses. They were drawn.

'Think I'll let her have you . . . slut . . . whore . . . I keep what's mine.'

The words struggled out of the ether that seemed to be swirling around in her brain and it was Rose, Rose who was screaming at Bryn, Rose who was in Spain. 'No, I saw her. She spoke to me. She said it was my fault.' Kate stumbled forward until a dining room chair caught her hip and the sharp pain cleared her head. She lowered herself into the chair and pushed her back against the hard wooden slats; she needed contact with something concrete. Rose. Rose killed Bryn. No, impossible. He was her husband. She loved him.

'I keep what's mine.'

The bile rose in her throat again. Maggie's saffron chicken. Oh, dear Maggie, how insulting if I were to lose your wonderful chicken.

She hauled herself to her feet. She had to get upstairs away from this room that seemed to be echoing with voices, her own, Bryn's and now, so clearly, Rose's.

She was on the stairs when the door opened. 'Miss Buchanan, what are you doing out of bed? Aren't you glad it's me and not Dr Jarvis? He would be very cross.' The happy young voice with its soft Scottish accent successfully banished Rose's strident tones.

Kate took a firmer grip of the banister and turned and looked down. Stacie's face was glowing, with cold and happiness. 'I got it, I got Joan, and Craig is doing Burgundy. I'll get you back into bed and then we'll go mad and celebrate. Hot chocolate all round.'

She was there beside Kate, her firm young arm holding her round the waist, giving strength and courage.

'Stacie dear, you weren't here earlier?'

'No, sorry I'm a bit late but I knew you'd want to know. Had a few minutes with Craig,' she said with a slight blush.

Thank God. She did not hear my maniacal screaming but I heard her voice so clearly. What is real? Dreams, nightmares, the stuff of dreams. No, actors are the stuff of dreams or is it humankind?

Gratefully Kate allowed herself to be helped into bed and lay back, propped up on her pillows.

'You're sweating, Miss Buchanan. This nightie is wet. You can't wear this.' Stacie went to the dresser. 'Which drawer?' But before Kate could pull herself together and answer the second drawer yielded up a nightgown. 'Let's get you changed.'

Kate managed to smile at Stacie and patted the side of the bed with her scarred hand. 'Never mind the wild celebration or my silly nightie. I'll change in a minute. Tell me all about it, and say your audition speech for me. Let me be there in the room with you.'

'First things first. You'll be ill again. Let me help you.'

That she could not possibly bear. 'Stacie, dear child. You run and pop the kettle on while I change and then I'll hear your speech.'

Stacie hesitated.

'I can manage.'

The girl turned and whisked out of the room and clatter, clatter, clatter down the staircase. What a lovely sound. A few moments of peace and then she was flying up again but Kate had managed to change.

'Gosh, you were quick.'

She managed a smile. 'Years of practice. I feel so much better. Now all I need is to hear your speech.' In truth she wanted the girl to go away, not to have come at all. She had to make sense of her memory, of the new knowledge. She needed time, peace, not an excited teenager.

'And you'll tell me how I can improve?'

'When is the production?'

'End of summer term.'

'My dear, you will be ready for Drury Lane by the summer.

Come along, pretend I'm Miss-what's-her-name, and audition for me.'

She tried to relax while her brain seethed with implications but she allowed the girl to speak and she tried to concentrate on her eyes and the language of her body as Joan of Arc harangued her countryman. Then there was a silence that stretched too long for Stacie.

'What do you think? Would you have given me the part?'

'I haven't heard the opposition,' Kate said and then she laughed. 'You were wonderful, Stacie. Were I Burgundy I would be thoroughly ashamed of myself.'

Stacie moved forward and before Kate knew what was happening, had leaned down and kissed her cheek. 'That's the nicest compliment I have ever had, Miss Buchanan. Thank you. I'll go and make tea; you'd prefer that to chocolate?'

Kate felt that a large brandy would probably go down even better but she smiled and agreed and when the girl had gone she put her hand up to her cheek. Such a long time since she had been kissed like that, naturally and freely.

Down the stairs Stacie went and after the clattering of those ghastly school shoes there was silence for a while and then singing and then another lower deeper voice and Kate felt a glow of pleasure. Benedict. Her friend Ben was there. The voices went on for a few minutes and then there was silence again until Stacie, more slowly this time, came back upstairs, carrying a tray.

'The monk from the monastery came. He wouldn't come up, looked quite horrified at the thought actually. My dad's a bit like that with sickbeds. He brought you some books; he says they're novels and he hopes you like them.' All the time she was pouring tea. 'He also hopes you'll be well enough to go for short walks soon and says he'll go with you to the beach, if you like, and Thane. Thane's a lovely dog, isn't he? Our Cromwell is such a feisty wee thing; he'd be quite useless with anyone who'd been ill but my dad just loves him. We all do, I suppose, but Thane is a real dog somehow, isn't he?'

'Beautiful, dignified,' began Kate.

'You could hardly say that about Cromwell. It's nice the Father wants to look after you; he's nice, isn't he?'

'He saved my life, Stacie. I will honour him for all that is left of it. When I was burned, you know, I really wanted to die. Dying is easier sometimes than living. I should not be saying that to a young girl like you with the entire world ahead, but I tried to die. People I loved fought me, they fought for me, they fought my desire and they won. My stepbrother, Hugh Forsythe, has loved me since the day his mother married my father. I don't understand it, for years I took it for granted and now I thank God humbly for it. Never take love for granted, Stacie; it's a precious thing. Sometimes we are so caught up in *love*, you know, the pulling out all the stops kind of love that we forget the bricklayers that shore us up: people like Hugh who do so much and ask for nothing. Benedict. What a man of courage. And there was a nun in France. I lived in Provence for several years after the fire.' She stopped for a moment. 'After I was released Hugh found this convent where they took paying guests. Sister Mary Magdalene taught me to sew; she spent hours with me, Stacie. She massaged my hands into new life; she believed when I did not know whether to believe or not.'

She was silent thinking and at last Stacie could bear it no longer. 'Believed in God?'

Kate laughed. 'No, my dear. Her knowledge of God's existence is a part of her. No, she believed that I was not responsible for the fire, and this was at a time when I hardly knew myself. The mind is a powerful thing; mine had blocked out things it could not bear to see.' Rose, my friend Rose. Bryn's wife, Rose. What am I going to do? Hysteria was so close. Fight it, Kate, fight it. 'Now, what are we going to do with you, dear Stacie, to see that you are the best St Joan that Friars Carse has ever seen?'

'I wish I sounded like you.'

Kate looked at her in amazement. 'Why? You have a very nice voice.'

'But it marks me as Scottish and . . .' She blushed in embarrassment. 'People respect people who sound like you.'

Do they indeed. Sometimes they hate merely because of the sound. 'I didn't sound quite so plummy as this growing up. Those were among our first lessons: getting rid of the regional accent. I'm not sure drama schools do that nowadays. Accents are in. You will learn to adapt, Stacie, to colour your voice as a singer colours hers so that you will have the right sound for any part. It's fairly easy to sound like me; it's all in the vowels and the breathing.'

'Vowels please, and breathing. Help me to breathe.'

Kate laughed. 'You do it all the time. It's easy. It's the first thing a newborn baby does and no one teaches him and it's the last thing a dying person does. Even plants breathe. Did you know that?' She was tired and she wanted only to lie down while she tried to assimilate what she had just learned but Stacie was looking at her, yearning in her eyes. 'Let's see. Do you know the Latin word for breath? No. *Spiritus*. And the word for to breathe? *Aspirare*. Isn't that fascinating? To aspire, to reach for the highest, and breath as spirit; breathing out we breathe out all the toxins and breathing in we breathe in – life.'

'I'll take a deep breath,' began Stacie as she refilled Kate's cup.

Kate smiled as she took the cup. 'Why? You don't "take" breaths. You breathe. And you have to learn to breathe properly but we can't do it all today. All you need to know at this point is that the amount of breath you let in and out, and the way it goes in and out determine the quality of your voice. I could go on and on with theory but you'll do enough of that at school. Right, lesson one. I want you to hold your breath for as long as you can. Now, just don't breathe out.'

After a few moments when her face got rounder and rounder and redder and redder Stacie exploded in a loud exhalation.

'Well done. What happened?'

'Nothing, I held my breath and then popped.'

'And then what happened?'

'Nothing.'

'Nothing? Stacie, the breath you expelled was immediately replaced by, I hope, fresh air. Your lungs did it all by themselves. You did not take anything. Now I want you to practise breathing; expel all the air out of your lungs forcefully with your lips open, completely emptying the lungs and that will include that massive store chamber of residual air at the bottom of your lungs which is very rarely if ever, in the average human, changed. Do this in front of a mirror and watch what happens to your body as breath rushes back in. If your chest rises you are not breathing everything out. You should see your sides push out as the lungs are filled with lovely clean non-toxic air. Be excellent for exams and studying too: clears the head amazingly. Do it at your bedroom window, do it on the way to school.'

'What's residual air?'

'Next time you come I'll draw a diagram.'

Stacie noticed the dark shadows under her patient's eyes. 'Oh, golly, Miss Buchanan, you are absolutely exhausted and here I am tiring you even more. I'll go but I'll see you tomorrow. And I shall breathe all the way home. Will I bring up Father Benedict's books?'

'Not yet.'

'Okay. You lie down and have a nice nap. I think Mum's making pheasant casserole. Craig went shooting. I'm talking too much again.' She took the cup back and lifted the covers up round Kate's neck. 'I love this room, feminine and dead sexy.'

'Thank you. I think that was my plan.'

'Naughty.' And she was gone.

She really was a nice child. Kate closed her eyes and thought of the lungs. Dear God in heaven, how can I draw lungs? Can I even remember the layers? I'm remembering so much; it's beginning to resemble a flood. Nothing, then a trickle and then a deluge, like the little boy with the hole in the dyke. Do I want to stick my finger in the hole to stop the flood? Rose killed Bryn deliberately. No, she said she did not mean to hurt him. And then came another startling revelation. She had smelled smoke but it had been cigarette smoke. Rose smoked. The fire had gone out before she went up to bathe. Could a dropped cigarette have caused the fire? There will be records. Perhaps Rose did not mean to burn the house down. And she said she did not mean to hurt Bryn. She must have hit him in anger, taken him by surprise. I saw her and I struggled with her. Pain, I remember pain and then nothing. She was in Spain. Did she come to see me, to argue with me and found him? Did she suspect that he was going to leave her? Did he tell her that we had decided? Everything was going to be out in the open. We wanted to get married, to have children. We were going to have it all, each other, children, a flat in town and a cottage in the country. We could have made it work.

Kate wept; she wept for herself and for Bryn, that wonderful talent snuffed out like a burned candle, and she wept for her unborn children. She turned her head into her lace-trimmed pillowcases and at last she slept.

There was a picture. Rose was wearing a dress that looked to be made of various sizes of rectangles in alternating colours. Possibly it was just black and white; it was difficult to tell with newsprint. She looked, as usual, quite beautiful and, for once, unbelievably happy. It was, thought Kate, the look of happiness that might be worn by a lioness that had just caught the biggest antelope in the herd.

'What a bitch you are, Kate Buchanan. Katherine Buchan had better be seen at Harrods shopping for a vastly expensive wedding gift.'

She refused to analyse the look on Bryn's face. She would see there what she wanted to see. I refused him. I didn't expect him to rush from my flat to Rose though. Would it have made a difference? I don't know. It might have.

'Do you love me, Kate?'

'Of course I do.'

'Then marry me.'

'Why? Why can't you be happy with what we have now?'

'Because I want it all. I want you, and babies.'

'And your career.'

'Of course.'

'And what about mine?'

'You can have one too, Katie. Women have always managed to have it all.'

But she worried. Marriage would give Bryn too many rights and her too many responsibilities. 'It's too soon.'

'*Ach y fi*, Katie! Lord, save me. Are we going to wheel ourselves up the aisle in bath chairs? What are you afraid of, for God's sake? I won't get in the way of your career.'

'You're going to have the babies too, are you then? Can't you

246

understand? I want to be the best actress in the world. When I have a baby I want to be the best mother in the world.' She tried to picture her own mother who at least had not meant to leave her child. 'Good mothers don't leave their children for weeks at a time, so how can I be a great actress and a good mother?'

'Other women do it all the time.'

'I'm not ready.'

'I am.'

Kate was the first person Bryn rang when he and Rose returned from their short honeymoon in Rome. 'The Eternal City, Kate, eternal like marriage. Are you happy for me?'

What could she say? That she was devastated? That she had felt that she might die of grief? 'Ecstatically. Now you'll stop all the lovey-dovey nonsense and concentrate on your career.'

He did not answer for a moment and she thought he had gone; then she heard him sigh. 'I've made a terrible mistake. I'm coming over.'

Her heart behaved in a ridiculous way and she realised with a mouth gone dry and a stomach that was lurching unpleasantly that she wanted to see him more than she wanted anything else in the world. But she pulled herself together. He had rushed off in a bad temper and he had married Rose. Perhaps he had been drunk or possibly he was so angry that he could not think straight but he was married to Rose. She wanted to scream, to cry, to tell him she had not meant to refuse him but it was all too late. Feeling worse than she had ever felt in her entire life she said, 'Don't be silly. You haven't been married a week yet and besides, I'm busy. You disturbed me in the middle of dressing for dinner. And there's a rehearsal tomorrow. If you weren't wonderful, Bryn, you would have come back to the sack and unemployed actors shouldn't get married.'

She hung up on him and thought wildly. She had to go out but where and with whom? Bryn was perfectly capable of coming around to the flat and although she longed to see him she would not. He belonged to Rose. It was as simple as that. Her fingers had been dialling and she heard a voice before she even realised that she was using the telephone. Damn you, Bryn, leave me alone. 'Hugh darling, I'm famished. You couldn't feed me, could you? Somewhere fearfully grand with lovely food?'

'My flat is quite grand and I'm preparing *Gratin printanière au Brie*, just the way Mother used to make it, exquisite new vegetables in a casserole with a crust of melted Brie. You may share that if you want. Why the sudden hunger?'

'I've been studying all day and just realised.'

'Bryn's back, Kate. Has this sudden desire for my company got anything to do with that?'

'Hugh, when did I ever need an excuse to see my oldest friend in the entire world?'

'So you do know they're back. You saw the news item on the six o'clock news, I suppose.'

Here at least she could tell the truth. 'I didn't have time to do anything today but work.'

'But you know they're back. Get a taxi, Kate. I'm putting it under the grill right this minute. Perfection won't wait.'

How right he was. She should have grabbed what was perfect and right when it was handed to her. 'You're perfect, Hugh, you do know that?'

'I'm opening a nice little Sancerre; help you drown your sorrows.'

Next day a chastened Bryn arrived early at the rehearsal rooms. The director had telephoned him as soon as he saw that his missing star had returned.

'Awfully good of you to return,' he said sarcastically and Bryn almost grovelled as he apologised. It would be the first and last time he apologised to anyone, except Kate.

'Aren't you going to congratulate me?'

She looked at him and felt her heart shatter into tiny fragments. How often could it do that? 'Congratulate you? For what? For attempting to ruin the play?'

'There is an understudy.'

'And you damn well know he's not capable of filling your shoes.'

'Oh, Katie, he can act.'

'So can my grandmother, damn you, Bryn. What do you want

me to say? That you're unique, that no one holds a candle to you? That the play won't work unless you're there to inspire us, fire us, forge us into one great white heat?'

'That you love me.'

She looked at him and she had never loved nor hated him more. 'God forgive you, Bryn Edgar, for I doubt that I ever will.' She turned and walked away and part of her prayed that he would come running after her, and part was afraid that he would not and all of her was aching for what might have been and never would be.

He stood on the stage and watched her leave. He noticed the long slim line from waist to ankle and the way her cap of hair clung to her head. 'Damn you, Katie,' he yelled after her. 'I begged you often enough. What did you want from me? I love you. Isn't that enough?'

She heard his voice but she could not understand what he was saying, for there was a strange buzzing in her ears. He had married Rose and yet he looked the same; he sounded the same. God damn it to hell, he smelled the same. And he had the audacity to blame her for pushing him into Rose's arms.

She went to the director. 'I want out.'

'No.'

'I'm ill.'

'Get over it.'

And she did, didn't she: she did recover. One always recovered from illness – unless one died.

17

Dr Jarvis reluctantly gave Kate permission to start taking short walks.

'Doctors are supposed to want to get rid of their patients as quickly as possible,' said Kate, laughing at him. 'The word mollycoddle springs to mind.'

'Doctors want to make sure their patients are really well, Kate.'

'Oh, I am. I am so well, and I'm grateful to you and to Maggie and her family.'

'I've heard about the coaching. Don't take on too much.'

No, she would not take on too much. Stacie was thoughtful and she was also a very busy teenager with too many other things to do; it was unlikely that she would wear out her welcome. Kate gave some thought to lungs, structure of . . . At the narrow top, tidal air, that shallow flow that goes rhythmically like the tide on the shore at Friars Carse, next the reserve and at the bottom the residual. Did Stacie realise that her lungs filled the chest cavity from neck to waist? Would she even care? Kate had found it fascinating, had taken long walks in London parks experimenting and inadvertently discovering that by exercising that belt of muscle around the residual air chamber she guaranteed herself a slender waist.

'I'll go out now, and pretend I'm young again and in love. No, I wasn't in love with Bryn then, or was I? Something momentous did happen that very first day in class and I had not the sense or perhaps the maturity to recognise it. Would everything have been so different if I had? Would Bryn still be alive? Would my face and body not bear these scars? No, Kate, that way lies madness and I have been mad, mad with grief, mad with pain, mad with despair. I did not kill Bryn or light the fire but ultimately I am responsible.'

Out, out. How wonderful the world is. Look at the light on the water, the ever changing patterns in the sky. Look, look there, at that bird, see how perfect is the structure of its wings, how beautiful the colours of its feathers. The snow is gone. Did I take joy in the snow? Yes.

She did not think she had consciously gone looking for him but there he was on the sand a few hundred yards down the beach. The dog, Thane, paced at his side, occasionally stopping to investigate some alluring smell. What was the attraction in a discarded bottle? For Thane there was joy in everything.

She had to catch up, had to thank him face to face.

Thane became alerted to her first and he pranced back to see her. What a thing of beauty he was, his beautiful head, his bright, kind, all-knowing eyes, his long graceful legs. She had never noticed before just how magnificent an animal he was. 'Hello, friend Thane,' she said and held out her hand to him.

The monk had turned back too.

'Friend Benedict, how nice to see you.'

He smiled. 'Kate, wonderful to see you up and about.'

She thanked him again and he brushed her thanks aside. 'If you must thank someone, thank Thane. Dogs are amazing creatures: he sensed that all was not well.'

'It was still good of you to follow his instincts. I am grateful, for so much, Ben, for Dr Jarvis and Maggie and Stacie. I had been considering abandoning my house, you know, and going back to Provence.'

'And now you will stay.'

'May I walk with you?'

He turned and they began to walk slowly along the waterline, saying nothing for a few minutes, aware of each other but also of the perfectly shaped little sand piles created by worms, and of the tracks of birds in the sand.

'Good heavens, a webbed footprint. See, Kate, how wonderful; such a large print. A Canada goose, perhaps, blown off course and dropping down for a rest.'

'And a snack. I didn't kill Bryn, Benedict. Rose did.' The words were out. She had not meant to say it, or had she? 'Words unexpressed may sometimes fall back dead, but God Himself cannot kill them once they're said.' She did not exactly believe that. God could do anything, could He not, but would He bother with such nonsense when there was so much else to worry about?

'What are you going to do, Kate?'

'Do?' She stopped and so he had to stop too and she looked at him in puzzlement and the dog stopped, looked at them both and then, perhaps slightly exasperated with these lovely humans who could neither smell nor see the wonders laid out before them, went off to examine some seaweed. 'Why, nothing. What should I do?'

'A serious crime was committed against you and against Bryn Edgar, Kate. I saw you both act, you know, several times. That talent was murdered too that night, and you, my dear, you went to prison. Don't you want revenge?'

She looked up and with eyes full of tears, laughed. 'What a strange thing for a priest to say. Don't you believe in "Vengeance is mine, etcetera, etcetera"?'

'What I believe is irrelevant, Kate. Can grave injustice be cured by vengeance or righteous wrath?'

'Christ showed the other cheek.'

'He also lost his temper and whipped the moneylenders out of the temple. There is such a thing as righteous anger.'

They began to walk again and a little breeze whipped up the hems of their cloaks and ruffled the brindle hairs along Thane's spine. Kate watched and tried to feel and to be aware of precious small ordinary moments. 'I deliberately had an affair with a married man, Father Benedict.' She did not try to explain the months of self-denial and unhappiness. 'Therefore the initial fault, would you not agree, is mine?'

He bent and picked up a stone and threw it as far as he could and they watched the long grey dog race after it and jump into the air to catch it. Kate had been thinking Lippizaner to try to describe the dog's grace, but his speed and elegance surprised her again. Mind you, the beautiful horses from the Spanish Riding School perform the complicated 'Airs above the Ground', and all four legs are off the ground then. Yes, Thane was the Lippizaner of the canine world. She smiled at the monk, silently begging him to answer her.

'We could speak all morning in cliché, my dear. Two wrongs not making a right, etcetera, but the decision has to be yours.'

'I can prove nothing. My memory, I believe, is completely restored. I remember the smallest of things, moments of incredible beauty, and I'm glad they have been restored to me and I remember things I would rather forget. I do not want to forget Bryn or my love for him but, at this time, after so many years, what would be the point of reopening the case? God, I almost said old wounds there. Another cliché. To hound Rose would not bring Bryn back to life or give me back either my career or my love.'

'What about your reputation?'

'My reputation as an actor stands unsullied. My reputation as a human being, that's different. I have remembered so much selfishness, so much unwitting use of others. Perhaps helping Stacie, if I can help her, if I have not lost my talents, might expurgate my failings.'

'The Church says one must make reparation to the person hurt.'

'I cannot bring Bryn back to life. What can I say to Rose? I took your husband and you left me to burn alive so let's call it evens. And actually I don't remember how the fire started. I do know now that somehow, although she was supposed to be in Spain, Rose Lamont was in my house, and she hit Bryn. I shall ask Hugh how the fire started. Hugh, my stepbrother, my lawyer. I can begin to show him that I value him. I took his love completely for granted.'

'One does with family.'

'My father was married to his mother for about three months and I cashed in on that relationship all my life. All these years, friend Ben, Hugh must have been paying for my upkeep. I made lots of money in the sixties but I spent it. I had a small flat in London and this house. The house cost nothing to buy but, my goodness, even then it cost oodles to renovate, and someone paid my bills in Provence. Hugh, patiently, quietly, devotedly, has been supporting me since I was a small child. People don't come much better than Hugh.'

'I'm sure he knows you feel that way.'

'I'm not sure and so I'll tell him. In fact when I get back from this walk I'll ring him and then I have to try to draw a lung or even two.'

He expressed a fascination with lungs and listened to her while she went on and on about clavicular breathing and residual chambers and then wandered on to resonators.

'You're a good man too, friend Ben, listening while I tried to prepare something to say to Stacie.'

'Ah, but I assure you I was quite enthralled,' he said and she knew that she would never know whether or not he was telling the truth but somehow it did not seem to matter.

They walked back to Abbots House, all three of them together, and the man and the dog waited patiently while she unearthed her key from the depths of her pocket and then let herself in. 'Would you like a cup of tea?'

He smiled. 'Thane and I are already late. Take care of yourself, Kate, and we'll look for you on our walks. Remember your phone call.'

She watched them go down the path. Both turned at the gate. She raised her hand and they were gone. Feeling remarkably warmed, she went into the living room to ring Hugh.

Hugh too was feeling guilty. All the way from Malaga he had gone over and over everything that Rose had said and done and he had remembered and tried to note down all his reactions to the place, to his conversations with the pilots, and even with young Marcelo, and especially his conversations with Bryn Edgar's widow. She was guilty: every atom of his being told him that; but incontrovertible proof that she had been in Scotland on the day of the fire had disappeared in another fire many years later. Any pilot could confirm that it was possible to fly from Malaga to Scotland and return on the same day, but the pilot who had flown Rose from location to location in those days was dead, Hugh could prove nothing but he wanted to ring Kate, to hear her voice. He wanted to tell her something splendid and he could not.

'I don't believe it,' he said when he picked up his receiver and heard her voice. 'I was about to ring you.'

'That's nice, Hugh. I have a lot to tell, my dear, to confess.'

'Me too, but ladies first.'

She sat down and prepared to enjoy herself. What could he have to confess? He had received a speeding ticket. Could he possibly have had one over the eight? Not Hugh, never one to kick over the traces; he had spent too many years trying to anchor his glorious mother. 'No, you first. Fess up,' she added, reminding him of their shared childhood.

'Kate, I've been to Spain.'

'Spain, but you never go to Spain. How unlike you. I hope it was somewhere lovely and hot.'

'I went to Mini Hollywood.'

'Good God, how absolutely revolting. Why on earth would a man of discern—' No, it was not possible. Had his mind and hers been working in the same way? Stupid. Ties of blood did not connect him to her, only affection. 'Hugh, why did you go to Spain?'

'Mainly to see if it was possible in 1972 to fly privately from Spain to Scotland and back again without being missed.'

She sat back, spine straight against the back of her chair. She tried to remember the four-inch rule – four inches from the bottom of the ribcage to the waist, the breath belt. She was sitting properly, breathing properly, and her lungs were full of good clean air from her walk. She would remain calm. 'And is it, possible, I mean?'

'Yes, it is. What I can't find out is whether or not it was done.'

'Oh, but it was, dear old Hugh. I have remembered. Rose was here. I saw her. I spoke to her. How did the fire start, Hugh? Was it a cigarette? Neither Bryn nor I smoked although almost everyone else smoked in those days. Anyway, she was definitely gone by the time the fire got a hold. I saw it race up my dining room curtains. I loved those curtains; I had made such a blooming good job of them.'

'I'm coming up. We have to talk.'

And he would not allow her to refuse and she did want to see him. Perhaps this time she could introduce him to Ben; he would like Ben. She should rest now; were those not Dr Jarvis's instructions? Her goldwork panel, so nearly finished, still stood securely attached to the embroidery frame. Kate sat and moved the frame so that it was squarely in front of her. It was as if she had never seen the work before and had absolutely no idea what she had meant to do next. She sat and looked at the design and saw where she had last worked. It was beautiful, one of the loveliest designs she had ever created. She felt that faint stir of excitement, almost an itch to start work.

255

She would concentrate on filling that leaf pattern with sweeping lines of couched Jap gold and then she would scatter gold purls over that padded area and watch it catch the light. Purls were so easy to use, threaded on a needle like a bead. First she must find her tough little nail scissors to cut the original gold wire into the right lengths, a quarter of an inch perhaps or even smaller.

There was no room to think of anyone or anything else. Later she did not hear the gate and neither did she hear the faint knock at the door and was startled when Stacie was there in the room with her. She was wearing her school uniform and looked very young and rather pretty, and – difficult to do in a school uniform – she was elegant.

'You haven't touched your lunch, Miss Buchanan.'

Kate looked at her watch. 'Good gracious, I've been working for hours.'

Stacie sat down beside her on the sofa and looked at the embroidery. 'You've done absolute masses. It's wonderful. I wouldn't have the patience and besides, I am such a klutz with sewing or handwork. Shall I make you a pot of tea and I'll warm up the soup and freshen the salad a bit?'

Kate stood up. 'We'll do it together and now that you have reminded me, I'm very hungry. I went for a long walk with Father Benedict, met him on the beach, and somehow I forgot to eat. There was drama class today, wasn't there? Tell me all.'

They were in the kitchen and Kate insisted on preparing her meal while Stacie talked and then they sat at the table but Stacie would eat nothing and drank only some tea.

'Actors eat like horses, Stacie. A play is like a mini marathon, every night of the week and twice on Wednesday and Saturday. You need your strength.'

'Oh, I know and I'm not being silly, just careful. Mum is at home cooking for Scotland and it's better if I have a decent portion – keeps them happy. If I eat something with you, I'll be too full. Besides, face it, I did look like the village butcher's daughter. I prefer being a bit thinner.'

'And what does Craig think?'

Stacie looked down into her cup and Kate saw the faint pink flush.

'He says he doesn't mind what I weigh but he did like my party dress and I'm even thinner now.' She looked up squarely into Kate's eyes. 'Don't worry, Miss Buchanan, I'm not going to be foolish; health first.'

'Good. Now tell me all about class today.'

Stacie poured herself more tea and Kate smiled with delight at this evidence of how at ease the girl was.

'I told Craig about breathing. We've been practising. I'm better than he is at the moment: he's asthmatic, you see.'

'Good breathing habits can only help.'

'That's what he thinks and his mother.' She looked surprised as if she had thought it utterly impossible that anyone could impress Craig's over-solicitous parent. 'She'll be inviting you to cocktail parties next.'

Kate ignored that and Stacie blushed again. 'Let me get you a little more salad.'

Kate stood up. 'It was lovely. Let's go back to the sitting room and you can talk while I work.' She was already leading the way and so Stacie followed.

In the sitting room Kate sat down in her usual place in front of her frame. 'Now, Stacie, you have the play. Let's read the pages. You are doing the whole scene.'

'Yes, so many small parts, gives lots of people a chance. There's Charles, the Dauphin, and the Bastard of Orleans, imagine that for a title, and a tiny part, Alençon and Joan gets lots to say, and Craig is doing Burgundy, which isn't a huge part.' She stopped and blushed furiously. 'Oh, what am I saying? I'm so sorry; you know it so much better than I do.'

'Can't remember a word, except La Pucelle's big speech and God knows where that came from. How much have you learned? Stacie, Joan of Arc would not be completely put off her stride by the notion that she might just have offended someone. Get into character, give me the play and we'll do from the entry of Burgundy. I'll prompt should you need it. Now where are you?'

Stacie breathed deeply and properly. 'I'm outside a large tent on the plains near Rouen. There's a breeze, which is moving the robes and flags, and it's disturbing papers on a table.'

'Good Lord, did Shakespeare write that?'

'No, I made it up; is that all right?'

'Fabulous; you're directing too now. I'll be the trumpets. Toot de toot. "Who craves a parley with the Burgundy?"'

'"The princely Charles of France, thy countryman."'

They carried on, Stacie reciting and sometimes stumbling over Joan's speeches and Kate reading or reciting Burgundy and occasionally Charles. 'Let's try it again and this time I'll stand with my haughty hand on my splendid sword and you will look into the arrogant face of one of the most important men in Europe.'

'You know Burgundy's speeches.'

'So it would appear,' agreed Kate nonchalantly. 'Here, you take the book; the second great speech is still rather dodgy.'

Stacie decided not to point out that she had had only a few days to study the speeches and that several other subjects had to be studied at the same time. They read the scene several times, Kate suggesting where there might be emphasis or pathos, gentleness or force, and then she gave the girl some articulation exercises. 'It's an old chestnut but it works and you can do it everywhere without being sent to the funny farm. Say red lorry, yellow lorry.'

'Red lorry, lellow yellow lorry, led lorry,' began Stacie.

'No, stop, stop. I'm giving you too much. I took years to learn all this and I find myself wanting to share it all with you, and you'll learn it in college anyway. We had such wonderful teachers.'

'What was it like, being on the stage? Was it always exciting? What was your first part? I'm sorry; my mother said I was absolutely never ever to ask you any personal questions.'

'Dear Maggie. But it's natural to be interested in others, Stacie. For instance, I find you absolutely fascinating.'

They laughed and Kate said, 'Come and sit down for a few minutes and then you really must go home.'

Stacie sat down beside her on the sofa and, if a moment before she had been Joan of Arc sternly regarding the recalcitrant Duke of Burgundy, now she was looking with eyes full of hero-worship at Kate.

'Being on stage was like being really alive. Even though I was playing a part, I always felt real. I don't know how to explain. It's as if everything else was the shadow and this part of my life was the substance. My first part, after graduation, was Miranda in *The Tempest*. Everyone was so kind. But next I had a tiny part and I used to stand in the wings and watch – magic. Watch and learn, Stacie. I watched Gielgud, and Olivier, and Peggy Ashcroft, not all at the same time, but that was an education in itself.'

'And Bryn Edgar?'

Of course she wanted to know. 'Oh, yes, I watched him too. We all did.' She did not add that the many who stood to watch Bryn also stood to watch and learn from Katherine Buchan, Katherine Buchan who could, one critic said, 'convey even her very thoughts and this with her back turned to the audience'. 'We were students together, and we became friends. At least I thought we were friends but we loved each other, only we didn't really realise it until it was almost too late. He said I was too utterly absorbed in my career, that I took everything too seriously but so did he. When he was on stage no one looked at anyone else, even when he was quiet. His stillness was riveting. He wasn't really tall, average, I suppose one might say, but he had a beautiful face, good bones and lovely mountain-water-coloured eyes, slate blue, or should it be slate grey. It depended on his mood and what he was wearing. His voice was quite remarkable, so musical, to hear him speak verse was such a joy and privilege. Sometimes I would close my eyes and just listen to the voice and I would see streams of clear cool water running down mountain crevasses; at other times I could hear thunder and lightning, or I would think of sweet wild honey. He played his voice as a violinist plays his violin and he took just as much care of it. He affected to wonder what all the fuss was about. "Doesn't everyone in Wales sound like me?" he'd say, but he knew no one else did. He was unique; "such stuff as dreams are made on". Time to go, Stacie. I can't have your parents worrying.'

Stacie stood up immediately. 'They don't worry when I'm here.' Off she went and Kate heard 'red rorry, red lorry, yellow lolly,' as she hurried up the path.

She returned to her sewing. If she continued at this pace it would be finished within a week and could be sent off and then she might just take a small break from commissions. That reminded her of money and of Hugh. He was coming up, her knight in shining armour, to tell her about Rose and Spain, but she would ask him about money and she would not allow him to fob her off. She would demand to see facts and figures. In the meantime she had best see if the guest room was in order since he was coming as soon as he could get a flight. That gave her the rest of the day and most of tomorrow, since Hugh liked his comfort and was highly unlikely to rise with the dawn to fly, in February, to Scotland. She had better ring Jim too and ask for some venison or perhaps a brace of pheasants.

The guest room was immaculate. Maggie had changed the bed and put out fresh towels; it was as if she had never been.

Hugh arrived by taxi before eleven. Kate was still in her little breakfast room. She had been for a walk on the beach and although she had not met Benedict she had not been lonely. Her strength was returning or perhaps such strength as she had, had returned. She was smiling at this thought when she heard the doorbell and Hugh's cheery voice calling her. Her heart lifted. How wonderful and how humbling to be so much loved.

'Hugh, my dear,' she said as she welcomed him into the hall and helped him off with his extremely heavy old tweed coat. 'I didn't expect you before this evening.'

He stopped her and put his hands on her shoulders, holding her away from him so that he could see her clearly. Then he pulled her forward into his arms and held her close against him for a moment. He released her, perhaps embarrassed by his show of emotion. 'You're very naughty and you can think yourself lucky that I haven't yet rung Simon.'

'Flu doesn't affect the mind, darling old Hugh. Come and have some coffee. I make a very passable cup these days.'

'You're thinner, Kate, and you can't afford it but you do look well, happy even.'

They were sitting at the table looking across at each other as they had done many times for nearly forty years. Kate drank in his face, his still thick but silvery hair, the laugh lines around his eyes, the worry lines on his forehead. 'It's wonderful to see you and thank you for going to Spain; must have been quite ghastly for you.'

260

'Actually, it wasn't. I'm in a rut, Katie: Provence, Provence, Provence. The almond blossom in the south of Spain at this time of year is absolutely breathtaking; we must go together to see it. Next year, perhaps, although some time in the sun would do you the world of good.'

'You didn't drive north?'

He stood up. 'Not this time, not fast enough. Kate, shall I take my things upstairs and then we can sit down for a proper talk.' He raised a hand to stop her as she stood up and made housewifely gestures to the kitchen. 'Fortnum's have done us proud, my dear, and I shall go to see that wonderful butcher of yours. In fact will you take me to meet him?'

'I don't go much into the village, Hugh.'

'Then it's time you did. This Maggie person and her daughter have accepted you; I want to hear all about the coaching and perhaps sit in on some. You have your friend Benedict, and this doctor seems a real salt-of-the-earth chap. If he's put you as a private patient I need to see him to settle up.'

Settle up. That was it. 'Sit down, Hugh, for a moment, dear. That's actually something I wanted to talk about – finance, my finance or lack thereof.' Did he look uncomfortable? Difficult to tell.

'Your finances are fine, Kate, and we'll discuss them later if you want. Right now I need to talk about Spain and I need to talk about the fire and I need to know that I don't need to ring Simon.'

She smiled at him and it was a smile such as he had not seen in years, relaxed, open, loving. 'I know about the murder, Hugh. I know everything but perhaps I don't fully understand the why or the how.'

For a split second he thought of his trip to Spain, of drives through mountain canyons and dried up rivers, of surly pilots, and of Rose. 'Tell me,' was all he said.

Kate was wearing a long grey-blue skirt and a blue shirt, and her hair hung around her face in an attempt to hide the faint scars of which she and no one else, was so aware. She was stunning. As usual, everything looked as if the finest designer had spent hours fashioning his shirt or his skirt to her shape.

'It's all come back,' she said. 'Someone pulled a plug, Hugh, and I can't stop the memories even if I wanted to stop them. I was ill, stupidly. I went out in ghastly weather and got soaked and sick. Ben, his dog Thane really, found me. You'll love them, and they sent for Dr Jarvis who's quite young and frightfully correct and he doesn't really know what to do with me but he listened to me when I said no hospital and he brought Maggie. Ben said Maggie was my friend and she is, she is. It's lovely. She stayed here for a few days; can you imagine? An almost stranger and she stayed here to see that I was all right. She likes your room, by the way, mine is too girly for Jim but yours is just right.'

'I'm thrilled for her.'

'Good, because I've had some thoughts and while you're here we might as well talk about them.'

She was flitting like a butterfly and it was cruel, but he had no alternative other than to pin her down. 'Tell me about the murder.'

If she had wings they would have been fluttering. As it was her hands were restless. 'What is there to tell?' She looked at him, calmer now. 'It's the dream, Hugh, the nightmare, but I saw it through, went right to the end: no holds barred; I saw everything.' She bowed her head and her hands fussed with the material of her skirt front. 'I didn't kill him,' she said quietly and she looked up and smiled at him, a lovely happy smile. 'After all these years, to know, not to feel or to think or to believe but to know. It's wonderful.'

He stood up now so that he was looking down at her. 'Kate, I saw Rose.'

She pushed her chair back and stood up and she was tall enough to look in his eye or even over his head. 'Rose? How odd. Is she well? You must have some lunch, Hugh, such a flight and then a taxi. My goodness, what will my neighbours think, a taxi from Edinburgh? How wildly extravagant.' Bryn had done that too, she remembered.

He snatched her hand and felt it tremble and he went at once and put his arms around her. 'Katie, it's me, Hugh, dear old Hugh, your lawyer, your brother. If it makes you feel better then we'll open the Fortnum packages and we'll eat but you must talk to me and you must listen. You have to decide what to do about Rose.'

262

She pulled away and walked almost wildly around the room for a moment and then she went into the kitchen, moved a pot on a shelf two inches or so and then walked back. 'You must be hungry. Let's have some lunch. What do you have? Lobster, salmon?'

'Quail stuffed with figs: I know how you adore figs; and skewers of sausage all served on little pieces of toast.'

She reached for her green glass plates. 'I was thinking along the lines of biscuits and cheese. You learned all this from Tante, you know. She used to tell the most ghastly stories about being on trains in India during riots with nothing but digestive biscuits and Horlicks.'

'My mother never drank Horlicks in her life,' said Hugh as he rummaged in a drawer for cutlery.

'I agree; she was always prepared. Hugh, dearest Hugh, I don't want to do anything about Rose.'

'Where's your bottle opener? It was in this drawer at Christmas.'

'No, it wasn't, except when you put it in there.' She opened a drawer in a small cupboard on the opposite side of the room and handed him a corkscrew, and, as she expected, he took it, telling her what a daft place she had chosen to hide it in.

'Kate,' he went on, 'Rose murdered Bryn. The fire started in the carpeting under the dining room curtains. It wasn't a spark from the fire and so it must have been a cigarette, tossed down in anger. Perhaps she thought it was out, but it smouldered and, I don't know, it had a good hold and then when you opened the door, it exploded. Doesn't matter. What matters is that you know you didn't hit him or start the fire. But if Rose saw the fire start, she left you to die.'

'How she must have suffered all these years,' she said simply.

He bowed his head, took a deep breath, and decided to open his wine. He poured her a glass. 'A terrible crime was committed. Great injustice was done.'

She sipped. 'I know. But what good would there be in sending Rose to prison? It won't bring Bryn back; it won't take these ghastly scars and puckering off my skin, would that it might. It won't resurrect my career, won't give me back the lost years.'

'She should be punished.'

She handed him a plate. 'Remember these? I bought them in Provence. She has been punished, Hugh, believe me. Every minute of every day she has been waiting for a knock at the door, for a telephone call. That's no way to live.'

'And the way you've lived?'

'There's Mary Mag and Sister Aloysius and here there's Maggie and Stacie, Benedict and you. I've really learned to value you.'

He looked across at her and she smiled back with her loving sister, best friend in the whole wide world smile. 'The wine's gone to your head,' he said. 'Let me open this and we'll have something to eat.'

While they ate the delicious food and sipped their wine, they talked and talked and argued and grew heated and then grew calm. Kate was adamant. To her, enough pain and distress had been caused already, but to Hugh it was not quite so simple. His brain told him that there had to be closure; Rose, to him, had escaped scot-free. She had lived a charmed life in the south of Spain, gaining worldwide sympathy as the bereaved widow drowning in grief. Her career path, always a tad dodgy since she possessed little other than her English rose looks, had really taken off and for almost ten years after Bryn's death she had starred in one epic after the other. Despite the hot Spanish sun and the dry winds from the deserts Rose had remained quintessentially English and hard work and strict discipline had allowed her to keep her figure and little else was needed in such films as *Desert Bride,* or *Empress of Outer Space.* Since her appeal had depended solely on her looks and not her talent. Only the long-held-back advance of years had put an end to Rose's career but she had obviously made enough money to live more than comfortably.

'You'd have hated to live the ageing film star life, Kate. Rose and her chums reminded me of some of the women Mother used to entertain – or did they entertain her? Dyed hair, facelifts, tucks here and there, and far too much jewellery. Terribly empty life.'

'Haven't I just said that, and besides, I have quite enough tucks here and there of my own.'

'Humour, that's what she lacked and it's the only thing you never lost.'

Kate stood up. 'Oh, I lost it, Hugh dear. Found it in Provence.

Come on. We've had far too much to eat and drink. I want you to see my monastery and, if we're lucky, we'll meet Ben and the beautiful Thane. I should have had my picture taken with straining deerhounds wrapped in furs. Deerhounds wrapped in fur.' She began to laugh and Hugh had to join in. 'Wicked Hugh, I'm squiffy.'

He put his arm round her and led her into the sitting room. 'I'll make coffee and then we'll walk.'

But when he returned she was sound asleep and he lifted her feet very gently on to the sofa and then sat across the room drinking coffee and watching her as she slept.

18

Stacie had almost mastered 'red lorry, yellow lorry' by the time she had climbed the hill. She had to share it with Craig and so, instead of rushing into the kitchen where she could hear Maggie at work, she took the telephone and shut herself into the little cupboard under the stairs. She and Craig had decided on a code. She would let the telephone ring twice, hang up, let it ring twice again, and then let it ring until, she was assured, Craig would answer.

'By the second time, Mum will be fixing another G and T and saying, "For God's sake, Craig, see who that is." It won't fail; she is easily frustrated, my mama.'

'What about your father?' Stacie had asked and Craig had looked at her in utter astonishment.

'He never answers the telephone. He pays people to do that. Most of his calls are business and so they go to his office and I suppose his girlfriends ring him there.'

Stacie had looked at him with wide saucer eyes. Girlfriends? This was living. 'Girlfriends?'

'I'm joking, Stacie. He'd be terrified and besides he quite likes Mum, but he still never answers the telephone. Twice, twice and then let it ring.'

And so she did and it worked. 'I have had the most fabulous meeting with Miss Buchanan. She told me all about Bryn Edgar.'

'Everything? Wow.'

Stacie scrunched herself up even more tightly and tried to edge deeper into the cupboard, pushing the vacuum cleaner a little further into the darkness. 'I wish you could meet her, Craig. She's super. We read the scene today – about ninety times – and although she used my copy the first time the words all seemed to come back and she did all the extra bits including you, I mean Burgundy, without it.'

'Wouldn't it be fab if you could get her to come to drama club. Can you ask her, Stacie, a real live actress who acted with all the greats? We looked her up in the library.'

Stacie felt cold. 'You did what?'

'It's only what we were going to do that day in Edinburgh. Dad and I looked her up. Mum was going a bit hairy about murderers in the village and Dad searched through all the old newspapers. There wasn't a real trial.' He hesitated and then went on. 'Stacie, she was . . . mentally ill and so she couldn't tell them anything. What was clear was that they were having . . . they were in love. Dad thinks it was accident.'

'She's my friend, Craig. She didn't kill anyone. She loved him.' Stacie started to cry. Miss Buchanan had loved Bryn Edgar and someone had killed him and tried to blame her. It was all too awful.

'Stacie, Stacie, it's all right. Please don't cry.' But all he could hear on the other end of the line was weeping. He had very little experience but he knew that for some inexplicable reason he had made a vital error. 'Stacie, I'm coming. Right now, Stacie. Don't cry.' He hung up and rushed into the drawing room where his mother was sitting reading a newspaper. 'Mum, I have to see Stacie. Can I take your car?'

And he would not listen to her when she spoke about homework and asthma and his father coming home in five minutes expecting to see his son and so eventually she said, 'One hour, Craig, no more, and for heaven's sake drive carefully.'

Maggie had prised her daughter out of the cupboard after hearing some rather uncontrolled sobbing. She led Stacie gently into the kitchen and had enough sense to say nothing until the sobbing died down to an occasional hiccup. 'Wee problem with Craig?'

Wrong question. Stacie burst once again into uncontrollable sobbing.

'We'd best go into the sitting room, Stacie, for your father'll be here in a minute and what he wants in the kitchen is hot soup.' She manhandled her sobbing daughter out of the kitchen across the hall and into the sitting room that had not been much used since Christmas. 'Sweetheart, I take it you went to see Miss Buchanan and then you dived into the glory hole to ring Craig. What on earth happened after that?'

'It's an invasion of privacy: he looked her up in old newspaper files. He said we were going to anyway, so he and his ghastly mother or, no, it was his father . . .' And she began to cry again.

'Very little wrong in parents wanting to know about the people their child is consorting with; that's a bad sentence, isn't it?'

'Mother?' And Maggie knew from the tone that she was damned but luckily the doorbell rang at that point and it went on ringing as if someone was standing outside pressing the little white button flush against the wall. Craig was.

'I'm so sorry, Mrs Thomson. I'm Craig and I upset Stacie and I'm frightfully sorry.'

Maggie opened the door wider. 'How nice to meet you, Craig. Come in; Stacie's in the sitting room.' She pointed to a door and motioned for him to go in and then she went back to the kitchen and put on the kettle.

In the sitting room Stacie, with a red nose and swollen eyes, was not too thrilled to find Craig standing there, but Craig had been working out a plan of action all along the dark road from his home to the village and he pulled her up into his arms and kissed her soundly.

'I'm so sorry I upset you, Stacie.'

She mumbled something into his neck, which he took to be favourable, and so he gently lifted up her head again and smiled into her eyes, bent his head and kissed her again and this time Stacie responded. They spent several very pleasurable minutes doing this, kissing, one or other murmuring soothing things the other could not catch and kissing again. 'I love you, Stacie Thomson. How many times do I have to tell you? I think you're beautiful and clever and kind and funny and I would never ever ever deliberately hurt you. Dad's very pragmatic and he says Miss Buchanan has a right to live here and Mum's impressed; she pretends she isn't but Mum likes her celebrities.'

Stacie had listened to nothing after the words I love you. He loved her. Craig Sinclair, whom she had absolutely adored from the minute he walked through the classroom door, loved her. She could listen to him tell her every day. 'I love you too, Craig,' she whispered and then, naturally, they had to kiss some more and they were still pleasurably engaged when Maggie knocked discreetly on the door.

They sprang apart and Maggie pretended not to see the flushed faces or the untidy hair. 'I've made a cup of tea in the kitchen. We usually have our meal about seven, Craig, and you're more than welcome to stay but in the meantime a wee cup of tea and some shortbread or a scone won't take the edge off, will it?'

'Oh, Mother.' Stacie was embarrassed. 'Craig doesn't eat in kitchens. He won't want to have a meal with us.'

'Oh, but I will, Stacie. I'd love a cup of tea, Mrs Thomson. Shall we come in now? I can't stay for a meal this time, too short notice for my mum, but I'd love some of your shortbread. Everyone says you're the best baker in the area.' He held out his hand to Stacie who ignored it and so he smiled at her and followed Maggie out of the sitting room and into the kitchen, and Stacie had perforce to take up the rear.

Craig sat down seemingly quite happily in the chair to which Maggie had directed him and then he stood up again and waited while Maggie and Stacie sat down.

'Now don't get up and down every time I do, Craig, or you'll wear yourself out. I'm like a yo-yo when I'm cooking; your mum'll be the same? I won't call Cameron; he's in the middle of his home-work.'

Stacie had almost bowed her head and thanked God that she was to be spared sharing Craig's first visit with her brother and she did pray that her father would not arrive home before Craig had gone. She smiled at him tentatively over her cup, noting how at ease he was, how he fitted in, so much more comfortably than she had done, she felt, when she had visited his home; but the kitchen. Just this once Mum could have taken the cups into the sitting room. She had, Stacie noticed with gratitude, used cups, even though they were not the best ones kept for special occasions in the display cabinet. Mugs would have been too awful. She was aware that her mother and Craig were chattering away as if they were lifelong friends instead of having met for the first time less than fifteen minutes before and Craig was even laughing.

'I think I'll ask Mrs Thomson to let me work in the shop next Christmas, Stacie: some of her stories. You should have been a diplomat, Mrs Thomson.' He waved away the offer of a third cup of tea and stood up. 'I'm sorry but I will have to go. Mum said an hour and it'll be longer than that by the time I drive home.'

He continued, saying all the correct things to Maggie as he headed for the door and Maggie stayed in the kitchen to clear the table and left Stacie alone to see him out. 'Nice lad; just the kind we want Stacie to meet.'

In the hall Craig was asking Stacie to walk him to his car. It was parked in the dark little lane well away from any streetlights. Craig put his arms around her. 'I'm coming to tea after drama club next week. Have to hear some more of your mother's politically incorrect stories. I wonder if she has any about my mum?' He tightened his arms around her. 'I've wanted to do this for absolute ages,' he said as he kissed her again. 'Since my first cup of tea.'

'"Brave Burgundy, undoubted hope of France. Stay, let thy humble handmaid speak to thee."'

'"Speak on, but be not over-tedious."'

Stacie laughed. It was difficult to be serious with Craig trying to steal kisses that she was only too happy to give. 'Say red lorry, yellow lorry.'

'Red lorry, yellow lorry.'

'Aha, you're cheating, say it quickly.'

'Red yorry, lellow lorry.'

They dissolved in giggles.

'Miss Buchanan gave me that as an articulation exercise.'

'I shall practise all the way home. See you tomorrow. I like your mum.'

'See you tomorrow.' She said nothing about his mother.

When Kate woke the house was quiet, the only sound being the very faint ticking of the clock in the hall. There had been a grand-father clock at Granny's house. It had stood on the first landing and so was almost outside the room used by cousin David and often by Hugh. Hugh had loathed the clock. 'Every bloody fifteen minutes,' he had complained to Kate, who slept like a log and would not have heard it had it been in the room with her. David had never complained or, if he had, that was one memory still locked in Kate's unconscious. It had not been among the loved pieces inherited by Kate and must therefore have gone to Australia with her cousin, or, heaven forbid, it had ended up in an auction house. That was, she supposed, marginally better than going up in smoke.

'Hello, sleepy-head.'

'Hugh?'

'I popped up to the village for some fish, lovely Dover sole. Fabulous smell of fish and chips. Demarco's is still there. I wonder if it's the same family.'

'I have no idea.'

'Had I smelled the chippie before I bought the fish we would have had a fish supper in a nice Styrofoam box for supper.'

'Not in a paper? They always came in the *News of the World*. Got all my serious reading done over a fish supper.' She was looking on the floor around the settee. 'Where on earth are my shoes?'

'I took them off and put them on the shoe rack in the hall but I brought you a new pair of slippers. They're over there on the chair.'

Kate's face lit up. 'A present, but it isn't Christmas. Why are you staring at your fish?'

'I'm thinking, and it doesn't have to be Christmas. I was in Fortnum and Mason's buying some new towels and there they were, toile de jouy, a colour I've never seen and I thought, Kate will like these.'

He went into the kitchen and began to search in Kate's meticulously tidy cupboards and Kate followed him, unwrapping her present as she went. 'Gosh, how perfectly lovely. Lilac slippers. Thank you, Hugh, you are so thoughtful.'

'Don't wear them on the stairs. I didn't think about mules being a bit silly.'

Since she was still in her stockinged feet Kate slipped them on. 'Perfect. Thank you. Is it suppertime already? It seems as though we just had lunch.'

'Do the table, Kate, while I do this. It will take fifteen minutes at the most. You slept for three hours. You must have been tired.'

'Nonsense. It was the alcohol with which my house guest plied me. I've been sleeping well and no nightmares lately. I don't need to dream to work things out; everything is coming back. Things I'd completely forgotten but didn't know I'd forgotten, if you understand. Time with Granny and my father, though heaven knows I saw very little of him, and you and dear Tante. And I remember plays I was in and actors I knew, and even theatres. I remember New York and Paris and even Moscow. I worked in Moscow, Hugh, and, of course, Edinburgh. I remember Edinburgh and the Festival and finding this house and fighting with you about restoring it. And that reminds me, you said we'd talk about finance.'

'Not while I'm preparing food. Kate, it's so wonderful that your memory is back. That means that we will have a light supper and then we will talk about the murder and what we are going to do. I want to tell you all about my visit to Spain.'

'Tell me about the food,' she interrupted him.

'You're not interested in food. Did you know that it's possible to fly from the south of Spain to Edinburgh, say, in about four hours? Where did I put the parsley?'

'I don't have parsley.'

'I know; that's why I brought some. I have one clean shirt with me; the rest is food.' He espied his pot of parsley and soon was busily chopping and Kate went back and forth with plates and cutlery and glasses, one wine glass for Hugh and a water glass for herself. Serviettes, prettily embroidered ones she had bought in Provence – not the vast linen squares she had inherited from Granny which had gone with the immense linen cloths – and leather mats, bought who knows where, completed her arrangements.

'I couldn't remember where these mats came from. Perhaps my memory isn't so good as I thought it was.'

'No one remembers trivia. The human mind can only hold so much. Now come along and then we'll talk.'

Kate sat down. Hugh joined her and they spent several minutes just enjoying the excellent fish but at last came the moment that Kate wanted to put off. This was so pleasant, sitting here with Hugh, eating together, laughing and remembering. Only now that her memory had returned – she crossed her fingers superstitiously – did she realise just how diminished she had been as a person for all these painfully sad years. Incomplete, made less not only by the loss of Bryn, her love, but even by her memories. She had an urge to go to the crusader's tomb and tell him her life story.

'Could we go for a walk?'

'Of course, my dear, but I can still walk and talk at the same time. I'll get my coat.'

It was a perfect February evening. The night was dark but the stars were clear and bright and the moon was almost full. Hugh, used to London streets, if one can call running from the door of a taxi to the door of a theatre or restaurant familiarity, was quite taken by the peace of the village. Just as he was about to say so a motor-bike roared out of nowhere, and flew past them, emitting a series of loud and probably unnecessary roars as it went but that too died away into the distance.

'I was about to say that it was so different from London and then civilisation thrust itself upon us.'

'It's not really too much different from the sixties, as far as noise is concerned. The same boys hang around outside the chip shop, under lampposts, the same girls laugh too loudly.' She looked up at the roofs of the houses. 'More television aerials.' She frowned. 'Let's walk down towards the sea.'

He objected. 'These shoes cost an absolute fortune, Kate. I'll walk along the beach but not on wet sand.'

'I love to see and hear the sea but I'll be considerate about your shoes and walk along the path. There is a paved one that runs along the road through the carse. Breathe, Hugh, fill your poor city lungs with Scottish air and the smell of the sea. You can see the roots that ground me to this place, can't you? I feel an affinity to the abbot who first built my house. Some of his stones are still there in the garden: that's where the connection is closest. And even when I was still in Limbo-land I felt the pull of the house, the carse, the sea.' She was looking at him, begging him to understand and he did and smiled at her and tucked her poor scarred hand into his arm and together they walked along the road, not talking now but listening to the hushing and shushing of the waves as they played games on the sand.

'Can you hear the stones?' She stood still and he stood beside her and tried to distinguish the various sounds of the sea and there it was; a faint tintinnabulation as the receding waves displaced the pebbles buried in the sand, pulled them backwards and then threw them forward again up on to the shoreline.

'Do you think waves play games, Hugh?'

'No, I don't, and don't think I don't know what you're doing, Katie, because I do and we are going to discuss Rose and the irrefutable fact that she murdered her husband, tried to murder you, burned down your home with you in it, and let you be tried for it. This is Forsythe, the lawyer, sworn to uphold the law of the land. A crime has been committed, and I'm obligated to tell the police what I know.'

'Darling Hugh, telling them that I have remembered being pushed against the doorjamb by Rose or proving to them that a long dead pilot who left no logs could have flown to Scotland from Spain and back again without being discovered will not go down well with an overworked police force. It's all too late, don't you understand? I'm just so relieved to know, really deep down know that I didn't do it: I don't need vengeance.'

'The crime does. Perhaps Bryn does. From what you've said, Kate, it wasn't an accident: she lost her temper and her control. Perhaps it wasn't murder but it's manslaughter and what she allowed to happen to you was evil.'

'If she deliberately dropped a lighted cigarette, but I think the whole sad business was accidental. She was a tiny person, Hugh. She couldn't have killed Bryn with one blow.'

'Good evening.' The voice from the darkness startled them and then the cold nose pushed into Kate's hand alerted her first to Father Benedict and then to Thane.

'How lovely,' she said. 'Hugh, this is Father Benedict from the monastery and this beautiful creature is Thane. My stepbrother, Hugh Forsythe.'

The men shook hands. 'I believe you saved Kate's life, Father. You have my gratitude.'

The monk smiled. 'If Kate was really ill then it is Dr Jarvis who saved her, but perhaps this fellow here could take a share.'

Hugh looked down into gleaming dark eyes and an open mouth

with a long pink tongue and two very fine rows of strong teeth.

'Hugh's used to gundogs and the silly little things his darling mother used to have. Hold out your hand, Hugh. He's an absolute darling, a gentleman.'

'Splendid animal,' agreed Hugh, who was thinking that although the great jaws did look faintly menacing the eyes were beautiful. A dog with eyes like that had no temper in him. 'We were just going back to have a nightcap. Father Benedict should join us, Kate, and perhaps he'll listen to the arguments. Would you join us, Father? It is rather important.'

'I'll walk along with you, if I may, Mr Forsythe, and if I can be of any use I'll do what I can.'

'Hugh is a lawyer and has some silly idea of reopening my case. My memory, as I told you, has returned and I know I didn't kill Bryn. That's enough for me but not enough for Hugh.'

'Did she tell you she knows who did kill Edgar?'

Benedict stopped. 'I am overjoyed that her mind is at rest. Now she must do what she thinks is right.'

Kate felt the dog leaning against her, giving her quiet support. 'What do you think, Thane? Shall I ruin Rose's life as she ruined mine? Brother Ben has reminded me that there is justified anger and I am angry, angry that Bryn is dead, that the world believed me guilty of his murder. Perhaps if I were younger and had not spent all these years in some kind of limbo I would be angry that my career was over before I played all the parts I wanted to play but I cannot think of that. I am content.'

'I'm sorry,' said Hugh, and his voice was full of suppressed anger, 'but I am not.'

They began to walk again and Kate tried to gather strength from the beauty of the late winter sky, purple and pink and dark grey clouds gathering on the horizon. She looked at the men, one on either side of her, and was glad that they were there but could they not see that she was unable to bear more trials, more media spotlight? Could they not see that she preferred anonymity here with the few friends she had and the new ones she was slowly making?

'I think there is a difference between a personal affront, Kate, and a major crime,' said Ben. 'Would you have wanted Rose caught and convicted all those years ago?'

'Of course, but this is now. Agree with me, Ben. Rose has suffered, not so painfully as I have, and she has not lost so much but she has suffered. Why make it worse now? For what? For revenge? I want peace; I have struggled so hard to achieve it and I don't want it taken away now.'

They were almost at the house. Its lights beckoned them, welcomed them. The Abbot's House.

Ben was very pragmatic, 'I have met criminals whose crimes have caused them no suffering at all, Kate. I can have no opinion of Rose since I have never met her.'

'Will you come in?'

'Another time, perhaps, while Mr Forsythe is here.'

They watched his tall slender figure move quietly up towards the town, the dog, head down and tail down, at his side.

'Even Thane looks depressed,' said Kate.

'That's because he agrees with me.'

They argued long into the night, Hugh laying out his case as clearly as he could and Kate refuting all his arguments.

'She's living in luxury in the sun, Kate.'

'And I'm living in luxury here. Which reminds me . . .'

And on and on they argued about justice and money, and Hugh was so clever that Kate was really no further forward with his talk of trusts and investments, until finally Hugh remembered that Kate was recovering from a serious illness and he suggested that it was time to agree to differ for the moment and to go to bed. He lay for some time in his own room waiting with fear for sounds of grief from the room across the hall. What a burden as well as a joy love could be.

The house was quiet. Kate slept and eventually Hugh slept too.

Kate woke first. She slipped out of bed, put on her new slippers – so that he could see that she really liked them – and her old dressing-gown and crept downstairs, just in case Hugh was still a light sleeper, but perhaps only the grandfather clock had had the power to disturb his slumbers. She opened the blinds and the curtains and saw that the world outside was full of brilliant spring sunshine. She opened the back door and went out into the walled garden. There was a biting wind and so it was much too cold to sit on the iron garden seat; she would stand on the concrete path and breathe.

When did I last look here? Flowers, flowers everywhere. Round the statue of the little girl there were millions, don't exaggerate, Kate, of snowdrops. Some of them – Kate found herself on her knees looking at them – had more than one set of pristine white petals, one set with a tiny ruff. Elizabethan snowdrops, she laughed to herself as she examined them. Why didn't I see them before – for they were past their best? Snowdrops at Granny's had flourished for several weeks, beginning in very early January and dying away in mid February. The big argument every year was what came first, the snowdrop or the aconite. Next year, God willing, I will watch and note. Another memory stirred. Aconite. It was poisonous, was it not? The name monkshood popped into her head. She could see Granny weeding among her plants. *These hooded aconites, Kate darling, monkshood, poisonous.* Kate looked around. Her aconites all had flat little yellow faces held up now to the strong spring sunshine or was February still winter? She struggled up from her knees. The stone was very cold but there was no monkshood that she could see in her monk's garden. There were sweeps of crocuses though, buffeted by the unkind wind, their petals tightly shut although the sun was so bright: they were white and purple and bright bright gold and there, under the tree in the corner, oh how utterly beautiful, scillas. It was spring, she decided, even though it was still so cold. She would pick some snowdrops if she could find enough that would not die on their way to a little vase for the table but the scillas she would leave alone to enjoy. Every day when the weather was fine she would wrap up and come out here with her beautiful little stone girl and her scillas and if she remembered rightly, under the same tree there would be lily of the valley, the lovely *muguet-de-bois*. No wonder she had loved it so much in the nuns' garden in Provence: it had touched a subconscious memory. She shivered; she could linger no longer and so she returned to the kitchen and thought about breakfast for Hugh.

She opened the fridge door. Eggs, bacon, perfect. She would begin to grill the bacon. Hugh liked his crisp. Carefully she laid the slices side by side on her grill, put on the kettle and stood to watch both of them. Feeding Hugh could scarcely compare to the abbots of old extending hospitality but she liked the idea of being a link in a long and powerful chain. She had grilled bacon and sausages for Bryn in this house. No, not this house but Abbots House. He came often; it was the only place where they could be totally alone. No one in the village saw them and if they did they ignored them. It was the sixties. By that time she was acting with all the greats, John Gielgud, Richard Burton, another Welshman but one more loyal to the silver screen than to the stage, Olivier, and with delightful greats such as the American, Rod Steiger.

Kate stood in her kitchen while she waited for the bacon and let herself remember Steiger, actor before anything, totally absorbed in his character, but always kind, thoughtful and overwhelmingly generous. She had been absolutely thrilled when she was told that she was to be auditioned for an ingénue part in a play that was to bring the actor back to the West End stage. How nervous she had been and how encouraging Bryn had been as he took her step by step, word by word through the speech she was to give. She had, as always, been far too early for her appointment and had walked up and down outside until exhaustion forced her to find a seat on a park bench. At last it was time. Convinced that she would never pass muster, she had gone into the rehearsal rooms to meet Steiger who had charmed her. He did not do it consciously; the warmth of his personality, the smile in his kind eyes had made her feel she was with an old friend and she had, as she told Bryn later, acted her socks off. When they were finished Steiger had looked at her and said, 'How did I do?' She still could not believe it. Had he really believed he was there to audition to appear with her? Surely he could not have been so modest.

The kettle intruded and she made a cup of herb tea, lemon and ginger, and stood leaning against a counter as she held the cup in her hands and inhaled the aroma. Oh, and since we're facing the ghosts, there were some bastards too. What was the name of that ghastly little man who stood so far upstage that I had to

278

throw every line away, so the entire female lead was inaudible to the frustrated audience? What a power trip he was on, such an ego. Ego is necessary. I must encourage Stacie to develop hers, but too big an ego is destructive.

She laughed. Good heavens, I was going to sit quietly in my little house and sew and I have become a teacher.

She turned over the slices of bacon, carefully, slowly. She wanted them just exactly right for dear old Hugh.

Who can Stacie watch? I must start to read and find out. Scofield must be working yet. The joy of watching him, a joy reserved now for Stacie. Names, names? Maggie Smith, Judi Dench: they must still be working. To see them again? No. I'm so happy, as happy as a girl in love for the first time. I'm interested in the world again; I want to know and to learn. Katherine Buchan used to stand in the wings and watch and learn. She watched Gielgud, a joy to look at even when he was not speaking, but when he was, his lyrical voice, his intelligence: everything about him was thrilling. And there was Bryn, not so physically beautiful as Gielgud had been but nevertheless a meteor, a star flashing brilliantly across the stage. His stage presence so immediate and exciting that even when he was silent the entire audience looked only at him and at no one else. They knew he was shining with greatness, and she? She cared only that she loved him.

He would have rejected this bacon.

Another burned offering, Katie. Thank God for that chip shop on the High Street.

Kate sighed. She turned down the power on the grill. Hugh liked it crisp and it would soon be past perfection. She would do nothing with eggs until he appeared. She took the cup to the table that was covered in a deep blue cloth skirted with white and sat down. Stacie should have it.

Good heavens. It must have been the late-night far-ranging conversation with Hugh that had made her think of the future of such possessions as she had. Whatever he said, Hugh had paid for everything all these years. She had spent money as easily as she had earned it, and there had been little in the bank when the fire had changed her life for ever. David would not thank her for the table or the house with its scandalous memories but Hugh should have the house to dispose of as he chose and Stacie should have any furniture that Hugh did not want. He might want to take the desk. She was laughing again. She had no intention of shuffling off her mortal coil any time in the near future and Hugh was only a year or two older. She would have to think of something for Mary Mag and the convent but for the rest, such as it was, yes, Stacie should have it. She would talk to Hugh.

She made the mistake of mentioning money when he was enjoying his late breakfast. 'You're out of your mind, Kate. You hardly know this child.'

'Do you want it, dear old Hugh?'

He did not deign to answer.

'I thought not and I have no intention of discarding my shell yet awhile but when I do I think it would be rather nice to let Stacie benefit from it.'

'We'll talk about it later. There's plenty of time. You can think about it. For now we have to decide about trying to have you exonerated.'

'Hugh, if you want nothing from the house then it's little enough to do for them after . . .' She forgot that she had not told him just how much she felt she owed Maggie, much more than could be paid for with a little coaching.

He put down his knife and his fork. 'I want the whole truth, Kate, not a doctored synopsis of the play.'

She told him and waited for his wrath.

Hugh looked blindly at his plate. She had been gravely ill and he had not known. No instinct had told him that his love needed him. How many times over the years had he wanted to tell her how he really felt about her; much too late now, for both of them, and he would neither do nor say anything that might jeopardise the relationship they had. 'A beachfront property is a little over the top for payment for a few days' nursing, Kate.'

'I said the furniture, Hugh. The house is yours by right.'

His good intentions flew out of the room. 'Damn it, Kate, I don't want your house. Do you think, if you weren't here, that I could bear to be anywhere near this place? Have you any idea how much it hurts that strangers cared for you, that you didn't trust me enough to tell me, to ask for my help. God in heaven, Kate, I've loved you since I was . . .' He shook his head. What was he saying? Now he had ruined everything.

Kate felt herself grow cold. 'How could I have been so blind? I'm so sorry. You were my brother; it simply never crossed my mind. I love you, Hugh, I always have. You know that.'

'And it's enough. I knew you loved Bryn before you did, silly Kate, and I've learned to live with it. I know I can't replace him and I don't want to.' As he said it he knew it was true. It was too late. He really did not want the stresses of being in love, not now. He liked his life, just so long as his sister, his dearest friend, was in it.

'He never took anything that was yours, darling Hugh. You have always been you, special, unique and I have thanked God for you so many times. Can we forget we've had a shouting match? We were always very good at forgetting and forgiving.'

'Can you promise to let me know, from now on, at the first sniffle or bump or whatever?'

'I wanted to spare you, Hugh.'

'I have never wanted to be spared, Kate.' He held up his cup. 'The least you can do, my dear, is pour me another cup of coffee.'

19

Hugh had bought some ground venison from Jim's shop and was anxious to try to cook an Italian dinner and so Kate decided to go for a long walk. The atmosphere in Abbots House was not so happy as it had been. The words 'I've loved you since' hung in the air between them, moved from room to room with them, and it was better for an hour or two for them to be apart, for the words, beautiful and sad as they were, to fade, as the petals fade on the most perfect of roses leaving only a trace of what has been. You can discard the withered rose or you can add it to a compost heap; Kate would try her hand at composting.

Remembering the chill in the garden she dressed warmly, hauling on another jumper, wrapping herself in a scarf and then topping everything with her cloak. She pulled a knitted hat down over her ears, and took some mittens from a drawer in the kitchen. 'There,' she said as she strove for nonchalance, 'better dressed than Scott of the Antarctic.'

'Probably,' said Hugh. 'The beach will be cold and blustery, Kate. Don't you adore the smell of crushed garlic? I think I'll do garlic bread too.'

'Sounds, and smells, wonderful. I thought I'd walk to the crusader's tomb; it's sheltered. I've got into the habit of lunching on oatcakes and cheese there. I'll commune with my crusader for a while and walk back; I won't be too long, Hugh, a few hours at most.'

'Enjoy. I'll enjoy myself here. That butcher should be bronzed, he's so good.'

'But then we'd never get his lovely meat.' She kissed his cheek, which was turned away from her, and went out, closing the door very quietly behind her and worrying about kissing Hugh for the first time in her life. Did he usually turn towards her? No, surely not. She had kissed him on his forehead, on the back of his neck, on his cheek; it all depended on what he was doing.

She stood for a moment on the doorstep, acclimatising herself to the cold. Too cold for snow or not cold enough for snow? Which was correct?

She looked around trying to discover the source of a rhythmic creaking sound and it took her some time to realise that the wind was blowing in such a way that leaves of the holly bush in the corner of the garden rubbed together, protesting. Did I know that holly leaves made that sound or am I just aware now? Have all my sleeping senses wakened with my memory? Everything is more intense: the taste of wine, the smells of food, the joy of awakening, the pain of hurting Hugh.

Thought of unwitting pain sent her scurrying with some trapped leaves along the path and on to the little road. She turned from habit down towards the sea. No friendly sleeping giant today but angry surf and galloping white horses and she revelled in its power but still turned away from it along the inner shore and headed for Templehall Woods. The paths were frozen hard: the earth was asleep. The trees were quite bare, except for, here and there, a holly with bright green leaves or a rhododendron where buds, despite the cold, were already beginning to show.

I must visit in the spring. What colour are their flowers? Purple, probably, but who knows.

She walked on under the swaying branches of the tall rowans, beeches and sycamores until at last she came to the clearing. She had taxed her strength and was more tired than she had expected to be. She leaned against a stone wall, which was seriously in need of some educated conservation, and closed her eyes to listen better to the silence. The peace, the serenity, enfolded her.

Hello, Sir Knight. I have neglected you but it was not my fault. Your steps are worn, but I forgive you for my accident. I have made new friends, real friends who worry about me, Kate, not about Katherine Buchan, the actress. Mind you, not good form to blow one's own trumpet, Sir Knight, but she was jolly good, and had some superlative reviews, but Kate, who was Katherine, is remembering all the triumphs and disasters and is so enjoying being whole again. It's not total joy, Sir Knight. Can you relate? The pain of losing Bryn is like a knife in my side every time I think of him; and the hurt of realising that perhaps Rose hated me enough to leave me to die, I'm finding that hard to bear. You took life, Crusader. Did you think? Did they mean anything? Bryn was her husband. What God has joined together . . . I tried, Sir Knight. I loved him but I tried to be strong for both of us. We had been so blinded by our success that we had not realised the depth of the feeling between us but when he married Rose, I tried to stay out of his life. I kept my promise; I acted with him when contracts brought us together but I never allowed myself to be alone with him, not for two whole miserable barren years. Granny would have wanted that. Tante? I don't know about Tante. Would she have urged me to snatch what happiness I could?

How different this visit to Edinburgh was. Kate was booked into the Caledonian Hotel at the west end of Edinburgh; Bryn was in his favourite hotel on George Street.

It was Saturday night at the end of the first full week of Enid Bagnold's delicious comedy, *The Chalk Garden*. They had done both a matinee and an evening performance and were exhilarated and exhausted. They could almost see the reviews. For her: 'Miss Buchan is brilliant – she is possessed of an instinctive technical talent, an engaging sense of irreverence, and, most unfortunately for her legions of admirers, a honed predilection for absolute privacy.' For Bryn: 'This was a definitive performance; he possesses powerful physical magnetism and a Stradivarius among voices; played by the consummate master it can be heard without any effort at the furthest reaches of the house.'

The cast looked forward with eager anticipation to an entire day off, time to wander around this lovely city, to sleep late, to eat, perhaps even just to do laundry. Voices echoed around the emptying theatre.

'Good night, darling. Monday.'

'Fabulous performance, Angel. Monday.'

'Have supper with me now, Katie, or dinner with me to-morrow. What harm can there be in that?'

'I don't date married men.'

'Who's asking you for a date, you conceited woman? Come on, Kate, think of the play. If I have room service I'll drink too much.'

Kate looked at him. With all her might she wished that she could stop loving this man but she could not. She had no control over her feelings. But I have control over what I do with my emotions, she reminded herself angrily. 'No, you won't,' she told him, 'because the play matters to you and you want to be good and if you're hung over you won't give your best and that's really all you care about, Bryn, not Rose nor me, nor any of those silly little chits you encourage to massage your enormous ego. Goodnight, Bryn.' She almost ran from the theatre, her feeling for Bryn more of hate than love.

Her overnight bag was in the car that she had hired for her time in Edinburgh. She did not care how late it was; in a little less than an hour she would be in her sanctuary, Abbots House. She was ravenously hungry but there were enough tins in the cupboard, surely a bottle of wine in the rack. She would manage. Once she was out of the city the roads were relatively clear and, keeping an eye out for a police car, she drove as quickly as she dared, her heart stirring more and more strongly with excitement the closer she got to Friars Carse. One day, she promised herself, she would have an entire month to spend in her lovely home. Hugh would come, no one else, and together they would get to know the area. They would research Friar Carse's connections with whichever religious order had settled the area, had lived in the monastery or priory that she had occasionally seen among the magnificent trees and, more importantly, she would find the name of the monk who had commissioned the building of her house. Each time she visited the house she stood in the hall and solemnly said, Thank you, Father Abbot,' but he must have had a name, and she would discover it.

She had reached the village. A crowd of teenagers stood on the pavement outside Demarco's, and the glorious smells of frying fish, chips and vinegar drifted inside her open windows to bid her welcome. She hesitated; she was hungry and practically salivating but at the last minute good sense prevailed: a huge fish supper, which was what her taste buds demanded, would merely keep her awake. She drove on, down towards the sea, her heart swelling with joy as she drove. She was almost there, home, her Abbots House. She parked neatly on the street outside and retrieved her suitcase from the boot and then she stood quietly for a moment and let Friars Carse wash over her. She could hear the sea, fairly calm tonight; she could hear the young people, laughing and joshing, harmless. She could smell the sea – how she loved the smell of the sea – and what was that? She could smell honeysuckle. Good heavens, when did I plant that? But it has bloomed and it is lovely.

Thank you, Father Abbot. One day, I promise, I will know your name.

She dropped her bag on the floor beside her, stood in the hall for a moment, and let the atmosphere settle around her. She liked to believe that even though the house was merely a reconstruction of its original self some vestiges of early inhabitants remained. She laughed out loud, for all she saw were dust mites dancing in the air current from the opened door. How she loved this house. She had her flat in London and she loved it, had spent time and money decorating it, but unless she was working in London she spent very little time there and when she was working it was a place to bathe and to sleep. Abbots House, however, was a place to curl up and relax, to unwind, and that is what she would do. A whole day without Bryn's beloved but disturbing presence would be wonderful.

Food first. Soup would do and crackers; oatcakes, there should be an airtight tin, and wine. Yes, Hugh had left wine and she opened a bottle while her soup was warming up on the stove and poured a glass. Health and thanks to the best of brothers.

She finished the soup: delicious. Such nonsense that women should be able to cook. Why? There were perfectly adequate meals in tins. She rinsed the bowl and her wine glass, stuck the cork back in the bottle, turned out the lights and took her bag upstairs to her lovely feminine bedroom. She had cleaned her face in the theatre and so now she cleaned her teeth, and climbed into bed. She would have a long bath in the morning. She decided to recite the party piece she was learning, a speech from John Mortimer's *What Shall We Tell Caroline?* 'I'm only a small guy, not very brave . . .' And the effort of thinking herself a man, and faking what she called a tough-guy American accent put her, as it always did, immediately to sleep.

She was wakened by a pounding on the front door and jumped up, for a moment not sure of where she was. She was in Abbots House and someone was banging on the door.

'Kate, please, we have to talk, please Kate.'

Bryn.

Damn him, damn him. Her knees turned to jelly and her stomach began to churn. 'Stop banging,' she yelled but he paid no heed. 'Thank God I have no near neighbours.'

She pulled on her dressing-gown and tied it tightly at the waist, slipped her feet into her slippers and hurried down the staircase, turning on lights as she passed them.

'Katie, I'll stand here all night . . .'

She opened the door and he did not finish his sentence. Bryn looked terrible: his eyes were bloodshot and he badly needed a shave. 'Come in, for goodness sake. You have probably wakened the entire village and my reputation will go out with tomorrow's tide. What on earth do you think you're doing and how did you get here at – she looked around wildly and saw the clock – three o'clock in the morning?'

'I took a taxi.'

'From Edinburgh! My God, the driver must have thought he had died and gone to heaven. What are you doing here? I asked you to leave me alone.'

'I can't, Kate. There isn't a minute of the day or night when I'm not thinking about you.'

They were still standing in the hall and Kate turned away from him and went into the kitchen. She switched the lights on and pulled down the blinds. No one would be walking outside at the time, would they, but best to be sure?

He laughed, a harsh unpleasant sound. 'Guarding our reputation, are we? Being alone with me in the middle of the night hasn't bothered you in the past.'

'You were not married then, Bryn. You should not be here.' She reached for the wine bottle that still stood on the table and then turned back to him. 'You've been drinking? I'll make coffee.'

He sat down at the table. 'I'm sober. I've never been more sober. I poured it in but it had no effect tonight. Kate, we have to talk. I've made a mistake, a terrible mistake.' He stood up and went to her where she stood beside the counter waiting for the coffee to perk, put his hands on her arms and pulled her round to face him. 'I love you, Kate. I have loved you since that first term and I will love you till the day I die.'

Kate wanted nothing more than to throw her arms around him, to bind him close and never let him go, to look into his eyes and see herself reflected in them, but she stiffened. 'How is Rose, your wife?'

He let go as if her silk-clad arms had suddenly become red-hot. 'Damn it, *caru*, Rose is fine. You know how damned fine she is. She's in Hollywood' – he said it as if it were two separate words, emphasising each one – 'and at this particular moment I would imagine she's lying in her bikini painting her toenails and making every man around her sweat.'

He sat down again and Kate poured the coffee and put it in front of him, and then as if she had relented and changed her mind, she poured a cup for herself and stood with her back against the counter, looking across at him. 'Give your marriage more of a chance, Bryn.'

'It doesn't deserve it. I don't love Rose, damn you, I don't think I even like her, and she doesn't love me. She loves the idea of me, Bryn Edgar, actor.' Again he split the word into its two syllables, and for once the rolling R sounded very Welsh. 'Some idiot wants us to make a film together. Can you believe it, some insipid costume drama starring Bryn Edgar and his Barbie doll.'

Kate laughed, 'She's not so bad as all that, Bryn. Surely you just say, no.'

'My mam warned me about women who keep at you and at you, like water falling on a stone will eventually wear it away. If you don't get away from them you give in to them to shut them up.' He looked over at her and his desperation showed in his eyes. 'I was a damn fool, Kate. I married her to make you unhappy and now we're all miserable. You are unhappy, aren't you, *caru?*'

'I'll adjust.' She was lying and she could not look at him because he would see the truth in her eyes. He would see that the love, passion, desire, whatever it was that was between them was still there. He must not see it, for if he stood up, if he smiled at her with that sweet almost lop-sided diffident smile, if he touched her . . . Her stomach churned, desire rushing through her veins as the waves rushed over the Sea Green, devouring all in its path. If he touched her, everything she had learned, had believed about the sanctity of marriage, would be swept away as easily as the tides swept the beach, leaving nothing in its wake but small bubbles and eddies.

He was there. Her eyes were closed but she could sense his body close to her blocking the light.

'Are you all right, Katie?' His voice was gentle as if he feared that she were ill.

'I'm fine,' she began but then she was looking at him, at his eyes that looked into hers with such concern, such caring, such love.

'Bryn.'

'Kate.'

They spoke at the same time, the names more like moans than words and then his arms were around her and his lips were on hers and she felt mad with love and everything that she had ever been taught evaporated like mist on a spring morning, and she put her hands up on his neck and twined his dark curls around her fingers and she responded to him with every fibre of her being. It was like their first time when everything had been so new and so beautiful and unspoiled but their knowledge of each other's bodies and likes and dislikes, and their abstinence from each other made their feelings sharper and even heightened their pleasure until Kate felt that she could bear no more.

They were on the floor in front of the empty fireplace. How they got from kitchen to sitting room Kate would never know and she did not care. She laughed, suddenly becoming aware of carpet burns.

'Ouch,' she said and had to explain and he laughed too.

'My stinging backside is the furthest thing from my mind at the moment, Miss Buchanan.' He looked at the fireplace and saw that as usual Mrs Balakirev had left paper and kindling just waiting for a match. 'We'll have a fire, Kate, and we'll talk.' Reluctantly he helped her up. *'Cariad,'* he said, looking appraisingly at her naked body. 'You're thinner but more beautiful than you have ever been.' He kneeled down at her feet and bowed his head. 'Forgive me, Kate. I'll make it up to you. I love you with my whole heart and I knew it the moment I stood there in that register office in my flash new suit. Poor Rose, I looked at her as I said, "1 do", and my brain was racing. I don't, I don't, it was screaming. I love Kate, have always loved her, will love her till the day I die.'

Kate shivered, but was it from the feelings aroused by her memory or by the cold air seeping through her warm sweaters? Would you have understood, Sir Knight? I gave in, no, I rushed in, and loving him and being loved were the most beautiful parts of my life. We wanted to marry but Rose refused to divorce him, and I didn't want scandal so I played along. And look what a scandal I got for myself. I'm almost grateful that I lost my mind, my memory. Could I have borne all that pain? Could you? Hugh wants revenge. Is it his lawyer's brain or his lover's heart, for he loves me, and I never knew? The person closest to me in the entire world for most of my life and I never even suspected. For a time I thought he was gay, and I hoped he was happy. I owe him, Crusader, for the roof over my head, for the clothes on my back, for the food I eat, and I took it all for granted.

Kate bowed her head as if in prayer and then she straightened up and looked around in a silent farewell. There were snowdrops all over the clearing and in drifts under the trees and she had not seen them. Snowdrops, like rainbows, had the ability to lift Kate's spirits and she felt her heart sing. Winter was almost over and spring was on its way. The darkness of her life was almost over too. The pain of loss would never go but it would become bearable. She had not killed him, even accidentally, and although she cared nothing for her lost reputation – after all, apart from the people in this village, who even remembered her and her scandalous past? – it would please Hugh to have the record set straight.

Hugh fussed, of course, when she returned much later than she had promised, and in fussing they got over the edginess of their morning meeting.

She breathed in the smells of onions and garlic. 'Mouth-watering, Hugh. I didn't take my oatcakes and I'm suddenly absolutely starving.'

He frowned. 'You've been ill, Kate, and you must learn to take better care of yourself. Simon—' He stopped as she interrupted him.

'I was about to say, I must tell Simon. What were you going to say?'

'Just that Simon's main worry is that you don't take care of yourself.'

'I do, perfectly well. I went out when I was already wet through because I'd lost my watch. It's all I have left of him; I had to find it.' She looked away, fearful that such a remark would hurt him.

'I can understand that, Kate, and I'm glad you found it. Look, why don't you ring Simon while I get us a drink and something to keep body and soul together until this *sugo* is ready.'

'Lovely, but I'll talk to him tomorrow when I'm sure he'll be in his office: I hate disturbing him at home. Rae must really resent the amount of home time he gives to patients, and especially to former patients.'

'Then she shouldn't have married a doctor,' said Hugh brutally, but he was smiling as he went into the kitchen.

Kate went upstairs, took off the top sweater and tidied her hair. She looked out of her bedroom window. Five thirty and still light. How quickly spring was coming. She obeyed an impulse and went to the telephone, dialled a local number and stood with her fingers crossed. 'Hello, Maggie, it's Kate Buchanan. How are you?'

'I'm fine, Kate. Is something wrong?'

'No, nothing, quite the opposite. Maggie, I'm so grateful for all your help and for your trust in me, allowing your daughter to come here. I do value that and I wanted you to know that . . .' She stopped. How do you tell someone that you are not a murderer? Straightforwardly. 'Maggie, I know now, absolutely, that I did not murder Bryn Edgar and burn my own house down.'

'I know that'

'No, you didn't know it, dear Maggie. Perhaps you felt it, as I did, but being ill again has actually been good for me. All, I think, all the gaps in my memory have returned. Some memories I welcome and will treasure and some are fearful and I will attempt to sublimate them with happy memories, but I have quite clearly remembered all the events of that night and, more importantly, who else was there.'

Maggie's voice was trembling as she spoke and Kate could almost see her. She would probably be cooking and she would be wearing an apron and her round pretty face would be shining with effort and happiness. Oh, yes, Maggie would be happy for her. 'Oh, Kate, I'm so happy for you. Can I tell Stacie?'

'Of course, but, Maggie, I'm not sure that I can prove anything or whether or not I want to prove it. My lawyer, Hugh, is here with me. He came up when I confessed I hadn't been well. I'm very lucky with family and friends, Maggie. Hugh has been doing some sleuthing on his own. I'll keep you informed, and please send Stacie down at any time. It doesn't matter if Hugh is still here. She can practise on him.'

They chatted happily for a few more minutes and then hung up and Kate went down to find Hugh back in the sitting room. He handed her a glass of red wine. 'Build you up.'

'I told Maggie about my recovered memory and so we may well have a visit from Stacie.'

'Are you trying to avoid talking about Rose?'

Kate was eating a cracker with some unknown but delicious topping and so it was some time before she was able to answer. 'No, I found myself agreeing with you, Hugh, but I need time to think of all the ramifications. I don't particularly want every newspaper in Europe sending reporters to my front door. And they would. What will the village think? Perhaps they won't want such intrusion.'

'No, but if you're not here the newspapers will get fed up eventually. It will be yesterday's news.'

She reached for another cracker. 'And where would I be?'

He smiled at her, a smile that was as wicked in its way as any of Bryn's had been. 'Provence,' he said.

20

Rose Lamont had been unnerved by Hugh's arrival in Spain. Until the moment he had thrust himself upon her pleasant little party she had allowed herself to believe that the past would not catch up with her. For a few months after the fire the world's press had besieged her and her poignant representation of grieving widowhood had solidified her fan base and made her, for a time, extremely commercial. She had read each and every account of the tribulations of Kate Buchanan, for, of course, Kate had been arrested under her legal name, and she had breathed a very deep sigh of relief when Kate had been pronounced unfit to stand trial and had been incarcerated in the psychiatric wing at Carstairs prison. It would have been much neater, she often thought, if Kate were to die but the hideously burned woman had clung stubbornly to a thread of life. The media interest had faded and Kate had disappeared and so eventually had Rose. Her film career was almost as transient as her marriages. Desperate attempts to recreate her beloved Bryn, was how she explained them to the journalists who showed interest. For fourteen years she had lived on the Spanish Riviera, rarely leaving the area and these days she was grateful for an invitation to appear at a premiere or even a fashion show. Unlike Bryn and Kate, Rose's finances, and marriages, had been astutely managed, and she was very comfortable surrounded by a coterie of admirers who could be trusted to say and do the right thing. Of course she had thought about Kate, always surreptitiously and nervously scouring English-language newspapers for any word of her, but she had found nothing and had even begun to suspect that Kate had indeed died in prison.

And now Hugh Forsythe, Kate's lawyer and stepbrother was here. Whatever he said she knew he had not just happened to come to

Málaga. Even she, who had little interest in anyone except herself, remembered that he had maintained a home in Provence. 'He was a colossal bore about his precious France, never went anywhere else. He was an insular little sod,' said Rose, who had very rarely left Spain in fifteen years. 'Why did he come? What did he want? Kate is alive but she's got to be gaga; she can't have got better. If a person is a loony they stay that way, don't they?' Rose tossed off another very strong martini. She had learned to drink martinis in the 1960s – Bryn had bought her first one – and they had worked then and worked now. She kicked off her impossibly high-heeled mules and began to pace up and down her tiled floor. 'What did he want? What did he learn? Thank God Felipe is dead. That Neanderthal nephew of his would want to get back at me. If Forsythe saw him he's probably learned about the plane. So what? Everyone used planes. We needed them to get to locations quickly. There are no records of any flights Felipe made with me. I saw to that. Men, how easy they are to manipulate. He destroyed all records dealing with me. "*Querido,* don't keep any records. I have to have some privacy. How they hound me. And, maybe better your wife doesn't know where you are sometimes."' He had been like a salivating pup and had actually thought Rose would become his lover when she had recovered from 'her great grief'. An affair with a Spanish pilot with one dodgy little plane? As for his ridiculous notion that he might defy his Church, divorce his wife and marry '*querida Rosa*': 'I don't think so.'

She had financed a new plane for him though – expediency. He had thought it was love; she had seen it as a business proposition. She had not known that the house was on fire. She did not like to think about what she might or might not have done. Fire killed evidence and Bryn was dead, or she had thought he was, and she had been terrified that she would be discovered. Thank God Felipe had rented the car. He was dead. No one could ever get him to talk and he had believed her when she had said Bryn and Kate were alive when she left. 'You should have seen them, *querido,* she had said. 'Half dressed, wallowing in their sin. I had to get out. We were already airborne when that fire started; you know that.' That part at least was true. The cigarette she had thought she had thrown into the fireplace when she was arguing with Bryn had smouldered for some time before erupting with such awful consequences.

Now Rose found herself wondering if perhaps it would have been better to let the family keep the plane, even though its purchase price had made a serious dent in her bank accounts.

She would think better after another martini.

Stacie Thomson no longer needed to hide in the under-stair closet in order to talk privately to Craig and she was delighted that his mother greeted her with 'Hello Stacie' the one and only time that she actually answered the telephone.

Maggie had called her down to tell her about Kate's call and they had hugged each other and danced a little crazily around the kitchen.

'I knew it, I knew it. I knew it.'

Maggie was determined to be calm. 'Yes, dear. But we'd better not tell anyone. Miss Buchanan didn't actually say it was time to tell the world.'

'I have to tell Craig; she knows I would want to tell him and then that snooty mother of his can really eat humble pie.'

Maggie was not quite sure of Stacie's reasoning here but sometimes it was better not to get too involved in her daughter's thought processes. 'Ask her first, just to make sure. She wants to see you; she says to go anytime even while her lawyer is here.'

'Mr Forsythe. He's her stepbrother too and he has the yummiest voice. Mum, let me go now before tea. I won't stay long.'

Maggie knew the war was lost before she started the battle and so she reduced the heat under her pots and went off to indulge herself by reading a magazine that had been waiting for her for two days. Stacie grabbed her jacket and ran all the way to Abbots House.

Hugh opened the door. 'Ah, the divine Miss Sarah Bernhardt,' he welcomed her, in a way that made Stacie blush with a mixture of embarrassment and pleasure. 'Come in. Kate's sewing in the sitting room.'

He took Stacie's jacket and ushered her into the room where Kate was sitting in her usual chair, her embroidery in front of her. The lights shone on the exquisite gold threads and on the tiny seed pearls. 'Wow, you're nearly finished and it is absolutely stunning,' said Stacie after Kate had welcomed her.

'Thank you. I'm rather pleased with it myself. Everything has been going well for the past few days. Do you find that, Stacie? Something goes wrong, everything goes wrong and the opposite seems to be true, too. Perhaps it's merely expectations.'

'Being relaxed or tense would have something to do with it too.'

'Good point. How was school?'

'Great, everything's going well there too.' She sat down where Kate indicated on the sofa so that she could see both Kate and the lovely panel. 'Mum shared your wonderful news with me and I wanted to tell Craig. He never believed you were a bad person either. May I tell him?'

Kate stood up and moved into the centre of the room and Stacie saw that her long velvet skirt, which she had thought to be brown, was in fact a lovely claret red. It whispered softly as it caressed the carpet and, for the first time, Stacie was aware that she had never seen Kate in trousers or anything short. But, she decided, the long elegant skirts suited her and she wore them as if she were a queen.

'I can prove nothing and, more than that, I'm not sure that I want to prove anything. Can you understand that, Stacie?'

Not prove that you were not a murderer? Not want to see every newspaper in the land print stories about your innocence? Compensation? Wrongful arrest. Brilliant career cut short. Oh, surely she would want the world that had reviled her to admit that she had been horribly wronged. 'I'm not sure. I think I would want everyone to grovel.'

Kate laughed, a delightful young laugh, one of the many pleasant things about her and Stacie had to smile too. 'It would not bring Bryn back, dear, and I am content to know. I feel better in myself and that is important.'

Stacie wanted to question, to find out what her friend had remembered. If she knew that she had not set the fire then, was it obvious that she knew who had? Was there indeed a murderer on the loose? Her doubts and misgivings wrote themselves on her expressive face and Kate took pity on her.

'I have not yet decided what to do, Stacie. Mainly I want to be allowed to live here in Friars Carse in peace.'

Hugh popped his head round the door. 'Dinner in ten minutes, ladies.' He looked at Kate and received an almost imperceptible nod. 'Stacie, you are welcome to join us.'

To join them, to have dinner with Miss Buchanan and Mr Forsythe, to listen to their beautiful voices. She would love it. 'I can't, I'm afraid. I promised Mum I'd be right back.'

They did not press her. 'There will be other times, my dear. Now we have ten minutes. What can I tell you about the theatre in ten minutes? Perhaps that I found it easier to learn lines the way I learned French verbs, by writing them down, over and over, like learning to spell when you first go to school. Is that helpful? Or should I prepare you for disappointment, tell you that you have to learn to make and accept choices. The day will come when, like almost every actor before or after you, you will be desperate for a part, any part so that you can eat, pay your rent, have new heels put on your only decent pair of shoes, but no parts are on offer and then just before you expire from hunger you get a tiny part in a play off, off, off the West End and the day you sign the contract you are offered something else, a better play in a better theatre and with ten bob a week more, but you have to turn it down. There, does that discourage you, Eustacia Thomson?'

'No.'

'But you have never been hungry, my dear. Go, Stacie, but come tomorrow and we'll think about voice production more. If Hugh is still here, stay to supper. He's a fabulous cook whereas I can only heat things up.'

Stacie flew up the brae, convinced that her shoes never touched the pavement and when she reached her home she dialled Craig's number straight away and, as if he had anticipated her call, Craig answered. 'Craig, I've just been down to see Miss Buchanan. She's got her memory back and she didn't set fire to the house.'

'Wonderful, but gosh, poor woman; how absolutely awful for her. If she knows she didn't set the fire does she know who did?'

'Yes, at least she hinted that she did but she says she can prove nothing.'

Craig thought for a moment before speaking. 'The police can do fabulous things nowadays that they couldn't when it happened; forensic science has come a long way. I just bet they could find something to help her.'

'She's not sure that she wants them to find out. She says she wants peace. I told her I'd want the world to grovel and she laughed.'

'I think I'm with you, Stace. What a way to resurrect a career. Mega interviews in all the papers and on the telly. Every theatre she appeared in would be sold out. Book deals, the sky would be the proverbial limit.'

'All she wants is peace.'

'She has peace in Friars Carse. If this place were any more laid back it would actually fall over. That's my mum over drinks just now: she's bullying Dad into going back to London.'

Stacie's heart, which had been in serious danger of climbing out over her collar bone, fell to the furthest pit in her stomach. Craig gone, living in London. She would die. 'You can't leave.'

His voice deepened, soothingly. 'I'm going anyway this year; you know that, Stacie.'

'But you would be back at the holidays and mid-terms and odd weekends, you said that.' She had always faced the fact that since he was a year older Craig would go to drama school before her and she had given herself lots of reasons for thinking positively. They could work very hard while they were apart and then they could be together with no stress of worry about learning lines or studying for exams while they were together. But the idea that he might not come back at all – that was not to be borne. She tried not to cry. How excited and happy she had been and now it was all spoiled.

'Don't cry, Stacie. Mum's talking over the second G and T. Dad loves this house and has sunk a fortune into it. But the way property is, if he sold it and tried to move back to London he'd be lucky to find a one-bedroomed flat anywhere that Mum would want to live. It'll work out, honest. Come on, smile.'

'I can't.'

'For me.'

'Come and see me.'

'I can't, Stacie. We're about to eat and I still have masses of homework to do. Look, I'll get Dad to drop me off a bit early tomorrow and we can go for a walk.'

She agreed to that; after all, she had promised herself that she would not become so dependent on him that she could not do without him. She was not going to turn into a hysteric: bursting into tears every time they spoke had to be the quickest way to disgust him.

Wonderful smells were coming from the kitchen. Stacie had a suspicion that her mother had opened the door a little just to tantalise her. It had worked, she thought ruefully as she followed the smell of basil into the kitchen. Italian food, yummy, and Italian was what Miss Buchanan was having too. She had definitely smelled the mouth-watering aroma of garlic, tomatoes and onions and who knows what spices at Abbots House. She wiped her eyes, blew her nose, and fixed a smile on her face. 'Hi, everybody, guess what? I got invited to dinner by Miss Buchanan; they're having Italian too,' she said cheerily as she slid into her seat.

'I minced some venison for Mr Forsythe and he bought some sausages too,' said Jim. 'Seems like a good cook, Maggie. You certainly won't be needed while he's there.'

'How come you're slumming it here, Stace?'

His parents and his sister glared at Cameron. 'Your charm, Cameron,' said Stacie.

'Watch your mouth, Cameron,' said Jim as he poured an enormous ladle of sauce on to his spaghetti. He winked at Stacie. 'Five gets you ten your mum's a better cook, pet.'

Stacie's good humour was restored.

At Abbots House, Kate and Hugh were enjoying their meal and Hugh had opened a rather robust red wine to complement the venison. Kate drank sparingly; she had always preferred to be fully in control. 'This is delicious, Hugh,' she said when she had finished a rather large piece of sausage. 'I wonder why I never learned to cook and you did.'

'Simple. You were never very interested.'

'That's not true. I loved my food.'

'I don't deny that but that's not exactly the same thing. Remember that little place on the Riviera that boasted what – fifty different ways of cooking *moules.*'

'Fifty-one, but that's really false advertising. It was mussels in fifty-one different sauces, *moules à l'estragon, moules avec sauce piquante,* see spicy sauce. I can't remember what *estragon* was. Tell me.'

'Tarragon. We should go back, Kate, and see if he's found sauce fifty-two.'

'Not good enough a reason, and besides, I can't afford foreign travel.'

'Yes, you can. The legal shenanigans that wouldn't allow me to sell your flat for years did eat up some of your capital, Kate, but you do have some sound investments – for your old age.'

'And what's this, pray?'

'Early middle. Have another sausage.'

She shook her head. She ate more in a day when Hugh was staying than she did in a week on her own. 'Hugh, I really need to think about what happened. I need to come to terms with Rose's hate. I was trying to think why on earth she suddenly decided to come over. Maybe she thought I was alone. Perhaps she rang their London flat and Bryn wasn't there. We'll never know, but I think the shouting I heard was her reaction to him saying that I would live with him openly, marry him if she ever agreed to a divorce but if she didn't then I'd still set up home permanently. I do remember the word slut was used quite a lot.'

'If you remembered everything you've forgotten all at one fell swoop, old girl, the top of your head would come off. Blast, have you spoken to Simon?'

Kate looked at her watch, her hand automatically caressing the bracelet as she did so. 'I forgot. Damn. I suppose it could wait until tomorrow because I really hate ringing him at home.'

Hugh got up and went out into the hall, returning with the telephone. 'Ring him now and chat while you have another nice glass of *vino.*'

Rae was never happy to have her husband telephoned at home by his patients but she was used to it and only the most sensitive or perhaps the most paranoid of people would have detected any of this from her voice. Kate, in fact, detected a faint note of warmth and she was touched because she knew she made Rae uneasy. It was not her mental health but her fame that worried Rae, who knew that Kate Buchanan had never been just another patient. 'Kate, how lovely to speak to you. It seems ages since New Year. You're well, I hope. Simon had a beastly cold. Hold on, here he is.'

'Kate?'

'Hello, Simon, I am sorry to ring you at home. I meant to ring you at the office earlier but got side-tracked.'

'You know you may ring me at any time, Kate. Are you well?'

'My memory has come back, Simon. I've remembered every-thing up to the moment I was hit. No, I wasn't hit. I slammed against the doorjamb. That knocked me out and did the damage to my ribs, I think. Everything after that is a bit of a jumble and memo-ries are coming back in no particular order. I just find myself remembering things. I didn't kill Bryn.'

'You slammed against the door. How?'

'She pushed me. Rose Lamont.'

'But wasn't she abroad somewhere?'

'Spain. That's four hours away today, Simon, obviously rather longer in the seventies. She was flown to, I suppose, some small private airport near here. Mind you, it could just as easily have been Edinburgh, but records would probably be kept there. Her pilot was, we think, a lover; he certainly was the pilot who flew her to locations in Spain.' She stopped and waited for him to decide what to say. He would be thinking, analysing.

'How are you?'

She smiled; she had almost expected, 'What now?' 'I'm fine, wonderful in fact. It's even more indescribable than getting out of hospital or leaving the safety of the convent. Have you any idea how losing memory diminishes the sufferer as a person? You don't remember bad things but you have no recall of all the special moments, moments that you didn't think about when they were happening because they were so small, but which, later in life, have great significance. Christmas memories, visits to France with Hugh's mother, food on the beach at St Raphaël, snowdrops. I saw them each spring in the hospital but until today I didn't remember the feeling of joy that their first appearance gives, their exquisite white heads forcing their way upwards through the earth towards the sun. Life-enhancing, that feeling, Simon, and perhaps it's silly and I'm imagining things but food tastes better. It can't be just because Hugh is a better cook; I've had a wonderful cook looking after me for a week or two, but I'm savouring being alive, I suppose.'

'That seems enough to handle for now, Kate. Have you made any decisions about trying to clear your name?'

'I doubt that a retrieved memory would stand up in court.'

'Depends on the barrister a good lawyer would find for you. Hugh knows everyone; he'll find the right person.'

'I don't think. I want him found.'

'You must make that decision for yourself, Kate. Was there a trigger?'

'It's a long story. Are you in the middle of dinner and please tell me the truth because now that you've got the main news I can tell you the story tomorrow in office hours.'

'This is much too exciting. Rae will understand. Take your time and tell me everything.'

She was still talking when Hugh came back with coffee. He poured her a cup, put milk and sugar in it and set it down in front of her. She looked up and gave him a dazzling smile and went on talking. Hugh poured his own coffee. He had bought the latest blockbuster whodunit at the airport and this seemed as good a time as any to read it.

21

Stacie yelled, 'Goodbye' and hurried out before either of her parents could see her – and stop her. Maggie, who was usually not quite so antediluvian as most of her friends' parents, frowned on make-up at school but, thought Stacie, this is before school and it's a date and so she had applied a little discreet enhancement, some mascara on her too fair lashes – one day she would have them professionally tinted – a judicious application of colour to her brows and a lady-like but flattering lipstick. This one was called Desert Sunset and was a rosy pink. A quick squirt of her carefully hoarded Chanel No. 5 eau de Cologne – enough that Craig would be captivated by its subtlety but not so much that Maggie would smell it as Stacie sprinted for the front door – and she was in the lane.

She met Craig just short of the school gates. They had twenty minutes before classes began and so they crossed the road and walked away from the school back out towards Craig's home. They held hands and Craig squeezed Stacie's every few seconds and that sent delicious tingles up and down her spine.

'It looked like rain this morning and I was so terrified that we wouldn't be able to meet.' The skies were still very grey and overcast with no hint of blue anywhere.

'What's a little rain to us?' Craig said bravely, although he knew perfectly well that if there had been the slightest hint of inclement weather his father would have driven him practically to the school steps. 'If every single one of your parents' customers weren't driving along this road, Miss Thomson, I would show you how sorry I am for upsetting you.'

Stacie squeezed his fingers back. 'I'd never see you again if your dad sells up and I couldn't bear that.'

'He won't, not yet, anyway,' added Craig honestly. He knew that once his mother started complaining then eventually whatever was necessary to make her happy again would be done. 'Poor Mum. She had so many friends in London, and was out almost every night of the week. There's nothing here. What on earth do your parents do for amusement?'

'The Women's Rural Institute; my mother likes that, and they have friends they see for drinks or to go to see a film with and Edinburgh isn't too far away for more exciting things,'

'What Dad does will depend on where I get accepted, if I get accepted.'

He would be accepted. All the colleges would want him; Stacie just knew it and he would be gone, out of her life.

'You'll just have to see that you get to the same college, Stacie.'

It was almost as if he were reading her mind. She squeezed his hand again. 'Dad is still going on about university.'

He had already thought this out. 'Not the end of the world. You could go to uni in the same city and we could see each other. Where did Miss Buchanan train?'

'RADA.'

'Boy, I bet an introduction from her would do wonders.' He turned her towards him and stole a quick kiss since there seemed to be a slight hiatus in the cars carrying schoolchildren. 'You look fab by the way. How do you manage?' Another slightly longer embrace. 'We'd better turn back. The last thing we want is a detention.'

As it was they had to hurry and the school bell was ringing before they reached the school gates but Craig was a sportsman and he ran, dragging Stacie along beside him. 'You're getting faster,' he said and smiled into her eyes. 'See you at drama class.'

The rest of the day flashed by and twice Stacie was reprimanded for 'wool gathering'. She tried to concentrate on the subject she was being taught but sooner or later her thoughts would go back to that walk with Craig, to her hand in his, to those swift kisses. His hands were large but well shaped and his nails were neat and, unlike Cameron, the cuticles were pushed back and a nice half moon could be seen on every nail. Tells you a lot about a person, the way they take care of their nails, thought Stacie, who had begun to nourish her own nails the day Craig had walked into the school. And his kisses? Perfect, exactly right.

'Saw you this morning,' teased two of her friends. 'A little subtle messaging to any other interested parties, was it, hand in hand in broad daylight?'

Stacie blushed in spite of herself. Damn, she was sure no one they knew had seen them, certainly not at the moment he kissed her. Nothing sordid must touch that. 'Why not? We have nothing to hide. Craig had tea with us the other night. He's got my mum eating out of his hand.'

'Blushing? What haven't you told us, Stacie Thomson? Besides, your mum loves everybody. She even tolerates my brother. What's Craig's mother like? She seems a bit frozen.'

'Oh, she's not at all,' Stacie exaggerated and was relieved when the bell for the next class went.

At four fifteen the drama class met in the school hall. The stage was at one end but, with assembly chairs folded up and stacked against a wall, there was plenty of room for role-playing, which is what Miss Galbraith said she wanted them to do this afternoon. Miss Galbraith wore business suits during schoolhours but, as usual for drama class she was wearing trousers. *Why,* no one knew. They had hoped that she was going to climb on chairs or swing from ropes but there would be no fun in that, for them, if she were wearing trousers. Perhaps she felt that trousers freed her from her everyday starched and prim teacher-of-English look. The children could not imagine her young and gay. To them she had been born an English teacher who had never married but most of them loved her, for she taught very well. She loved her subject and infected even the most recalcitrant of students with her interest in the theatre. Then surprisingly, they had thought at the beginning, but now took for granted, she was amazingly talented. She could imitate almost every accent and she could be an old crone one minute and a swashbuckling hero the next. They had stopped saying things like, 'Wonder if she's ever heard the word hairdresser?' or, 'Where does she gets those awful suits? Must have been made for her by her mum.' She was Miss

Galbraith and she opened up vistas that some of them would otherwise never have known existed.

'Have you all learned your parts?' She looked round at them trying to make eye contact with everyone. Those who did not meet her eyes, she marked. She would watch them carefully. 'We'll warm up today by moving. You have to learn to use your body' – for the moment she ignored the one or two who made lascivious gestures – 'because the voice is dependent on the body. It is not in a little voice box all on its own. We'll spend a few minutes being trees in a storm; that will give you an opportunity to stretch every muscle and then I want everyone on the floor being sinuous. You do know what sinuous means, Barry, Charlie?' She addressed the group clowns. 'Fine. Show me a tree.'

Stacie liked being a tree. It allowed large movement and there was plenty of room. She decide that the branches on the left side of her trunk would move completely independently of the branches on her right but it was actually more difficult than she had imagined. Craig stood beside her thrashing about, throwing his arms all over the place. 'This is daft,' he whispered. 'It would have to be a hurricane before anything in our wood would move, except small fine branch ends.'

'Then be branch ends.' Stacie laughed. Oh, she loved this class.

Miss Galbraith was clapping her hands. Sinuousness was wanted. Mum would have a conniption fit at the state of this blouse.

At last they worked on their parts. 'I want you all to find a space; there's plenty of room here. Now you have to start saying your lines while walking at the same time and at every punctuation mark, change direction. I know, I know. Some of you have only a few lines but just repeat them. Barry, you're Alençon. How does he start?'

Barry, too tall and too thin, had become a class clown because subconsciously he needed to deflect attention from the ghastly awareness that he had an Adam's apple that bobbled about in his throat like a small boat that has lost its moorings. To his eyes his wrists were nothing more than great knobbly bones that always, no matter what, jutted out from under shirt or sweater. His insecurities, however, were not so big that he had spent any time at all on his assignment. 'Em; something about a statue of someone.'

'Of whom, Barry, that is vaguely important, you know. Read it, boy, and for next week have read the whole play, not just your two lines.'

'I've got more than two lines,' began Barry in an aggrieved voice.

'The magnificent seven,' joked Miss Galbraith but, although perfectly accurate, that too was wasted on Barry. 'Never mind, Barry, read it.'

'"We'll set thy statue in some holy place,"' began Barry and was startled to hear Miss Galbraith bellow, 'Change.'

'Change what?'

'Direction, oh Brain of Britain. Go on.'

'"And have thee reverenced like a blessed saint:"'

'Change.'

'Gotcha,' laughed Barry who had changed direction, 'but you know, Miss Galbraith, this is a bit daft, why on earth would he change direction when he's saying this? Surely he'd be looking at the person he was talking to; he'd not be pacing around his tent or the council chamber or whatever.'

'No, he wouldn't, but where did Alençon deliver this speech, Barry?'

'Haven't a clue. I will learn it all off for next week.'

'Good. Everyone else, do you all understand the importance of knowing everything, the what, the why, the who, the where, the when? Who came before, who comes next and why they're all in that place. An actor doesn't learn just his own lines and he doesn't learn them in a vacuum. Right, we'll have you, Burgundy.'

Craig went through his word-perfect first speech, changing direction at every punctuation mark and was smiled at and dismissed.

'Barry's right, this is daft,' he whispered to Stacie as they watched another classmate stumble all over the floor and the lines. 'Burgundy would have been too tired to fight if he'd done all that changing direction.'

'She's read it in a book and ought to tell us the point. I'll ask Miss Buchanan.'

'Wish she'd come up and teach this.'

'I've thought of asking, but I don't feel I know her well enough. Maybe, one day, if she gets her reputation back.'

'Stacie, Craig, go to opposite ends of the hall; you are not here to catch up on all the gossip you've missed since last week.'

'Sorry, Miss Galbraith.' A smile, a special look. Heck, being reprimanded was almost worth it.

Then there was time to read through the parts.

'Soon we will move to plotting the moves and blocking the play; you will all love that but it's better if you know the lines. Those of you who are having difficulty, write them down, read them quietly again and again just to get the gist. You do know what gist means? Barry? Craig?'

'The general idea.'

'Yes. Stacie?'

'Is it the essence of the idea?'

'Exactly. Now sometimes read aloud but not trying to act it, just read it, or say it. Hear the words aloud in a room. How many of you are doing that?'

Hands went up. 'My mum listens every time I practise,' confessed the Juliet and was horrified and a little miffed to be told that it was unlikely that her mother would be a good critic.

'Who hears you?'

Miss Galbraith had rounded on Stacie who said, 'Miss Buchanan,' before she had time to think.

'Miss Buchanan?'

'She's the murderess, Miss Galbraith: she's out of prison and she's living in the village.' Most of the drama class were delighted to share this local knowledge.

'She never murdered anyone,' yelled Stacie before Craig could get to her.

The hall erupted with a babble of talking.

'She killed her lover, and tried to die with him.'

'She was in the funny farm . . .'

'She was in the loony bin . . .'

'She was in jail for years . . .'

'Stop it, stop it.' Stacie was in real distress. She wanted to punch someone, anyone who would say anything nasty about her friend. 'She's wonderful, beautiful, and she didn't kill him, she didn't.'

'My dad says . . .'

'My granny says . . .'

'Class, class.' Miss Galbraith held her arms up. 'Enough. Stacie.' She approached her Joan of Arc as one might approach a shrine. 'Is Miss Buchanan, your Miss Buchanan, the Katherine Buchan?'

Stacie, trying desperately to control her anger, but comforted before the whole group by Craig's hand, nodded.

Miss Galbraith patted her. 'Class, Katherine Buchan was undoubtedly the greatest actress of her generation. Had she lived' – she looked at Stacie and a smile such as they had never seen lit up her rather plain countenance and made her for a moment lovely – 'how wonderful, she has lived. I saw her once, only once and I was very young.' The drama teacher looked so coy when she said this that everyone knew she was lying through her teeth and was probably a mere year or two younger than the actress. 'She was, she was a vision from another world. Even when she was silent everyone looked at her, for she was always in her part. Her voice, her breath control? Girls and boys, I cannot tell you what she was like. She carried the energy of a speech through to the end. Can you understand that? It means that her breath grew stronger right through to the last word, something I have occasionally heard the very best of operatic singers do. Remarkable control. I would pay to know her secrets. Stacie, dear, Miss Buchan lives here in Friars Carse?'

Stacie nodded.

The rather plain middle-aged woman beamed. 'How wonderful. She is a family friend?'

Stacie felt dreadful. Never had she wanted to make Miss Buchanan a subject of discussion. It was one thing to talk about her with Craig, but for the class, some of them as heedless and thoughtless as Cameron, to be discussing her, was an anathema. The words murderess, funny farm and loony bin still seemed to hang there. But she had been brought up to answer truthfully and so she said, 'Yes.'

The headlight beam burned to a steady worshipful glow and

Stacie understood it. Did she not feel the same way herself? 'Stacie, do you think she would consider visiting the class? Oh, to have an actress of such eminence talk to us, perhaps to see you all perform, what a privilege, what a pleasure.'

'I don't know Miss Buchanan,' began Craig, since it was obvious that Stacie was having difficulty saying anything, 'but I believe she is a very private person and has been quite ill recently.'

Stacie looked at him gratefully. 'Craig's right: she has been ill.'

'Boy, I'd love to meet a murderer. Ask her, Stacie, tell her we'd all love to meet a real live mur— actress.' Barry smirked.

Stacie looked at him as if at some rare species, something she had never witnessed close up before, something to be dissected and analysed. His eyes were bright and she was sure there was saliva on his chin. Baying for blood. So must the crowds have been around Joan, La Pucelle. Humanity at its worst. Never would she allow Miss Buchanan to be subjected to it. 'You are totally gross, Barry.'

There were other calls, some agreeing with Barry, most with Stacie.

'Children, children, we are wasting precious time. And please remember, Barry, that whatever Miss Buchanan did, she has paid her debt to society and should be allowed to live as she chooses.'

'No,' yelled Stacie. 'You're all wrong. She never killed him. I know she didn't and she's had such a ghastly time and she's innocent, and she's got her memory back and knows who the murderer was.'

Craig's hand on her arm brought her back to earth. What had she done? What had she said? Oh, it was all too awful. She had been told implicitly that it was too early to say or do anything and she, Stacie Thomson, who was supposed to be Miss Buchanan's friend, had just told the entire world. Not for the last time in her growing up, Stacie felt the ready tears start. She would not give in; she would not. She could almost hear Barry's jeers and soothing noises from more sensitive souls, and what would Craig think, that all she ever did to end a difficult situation was bubble over like a boiling pot of soup. Ghastly image. His hand was still on her arm and he pressed it encouragingly. Stacie gulped, blinked, and looked directly at Barry. 'I'm sorry, everyone. I had no right to break a confidence. Please, could we just get on with the class.'

'Well done, Stacie. Right, everyone, let's have a quick read through and if you can do without your script, even better.'

The class overran and one or two irate parents were pointedly just outside the hall when Miss Galbraith dismissed them with instructions to 'learn your lines'.

Craig's father was there but not at all irate. He had used the waiting time to make some business phone calls, being the only person most of the villagers had ever seen who had a telephone actually in his car.

'Hello, Stacie, how are you?'

Stacie, who felt dreadful, managed to smile, especially since Craig did not let go of her hand when he saw his father. 'Fine, thanks, Mr Sinclair.'

'She's not fine at all, Dad. Can we drive her home?'

Stacie protested. Her home was nowhere near Craig's and was only a quick run down the hill into the village but Mr Sinclair was quite good-natured about going a long way round and seemed genuinely interested in her unhappiness.

'Can I tell Dad, Stacie? He won't tell anyone.'

Stacie nodded and listened quietly while Craig went through the whole sorry story.

'I can't see that any real harm has been done, Stacie. All you did was stand up for a friend. Miss Buchanan would applaud.'

'She would prefer not to be championed at all, Mr Sinclair.'

They were outside her house already.

'You're a nice girl, Stacie. Don't worry. What can happen? Nothing. Poor Miss Buchanan's life history is there for all to read in any decent library. Friars Carse isn't suddenly going to learn who she is. Believe me, there are no secrets in small villages and I think Miss Buchanan knows that too. She made a conscious decision to come back here; she went to a great deal of trouble because of her affection for the place. If she decides to fight to prove her innocence, good luck to her. If she wants to keep a low profile, that's fine too. She must be delighted to have such a stalwart champion.'

But Stacie could not be cheered. A champion would have kept

her mouth closed. Now she had brought Miss Buchanan back to everyone's attention. If only Barry had had pneumonia or had broken his neck or something, it would be easier. But he definitely was the 'You'll never guess what I heard at school' type. She said goodnight and stood outside the gate until the car was out of sight.

22

Hugh flew back to London after promising Kate that he would do nothing about looking for barristers or informing the police about her newly recovered knowledge. He kept his promise, but he had not promised to leave the matter alone. He would not defy Kate and make public her memory return but there were still little things that he could find out. It would be a simple matter, surely, to pinpoint the locations of all private airstrips, within a prescribed radius of Friars Carse, that existed in the 1970s. A few telephone calls should answer such questions as, 'How long do airports keep records?'

If Rose Lamont had flown from Spain to Scotland on that fatal night a record had to exist somewhere. All planes had to be given landing permission; that information would be filed. There was also the question of records in Spain. The particular pilot's notebooks might have been destroyed but surely the aviation authorities would be legally bound to keep information on all flights somewhere. Another visit to Spain might be a good idea. With young Marcelo to drive and to translate it should be easy and this time he did not have to look for Rose: he knew exactly where she lived.

Stacie had thought of a list of excuses for not visiting Miss Buchanan in the days following her drama class. Miss Buchanan would be exhausted from having had a house guest. She herself had to catch up with some schoolwork she had let slip a little. She was quite sure she was coming down with something or so she told her mother who asked her why she was not rushing through her meals in order to fly down the road to Abbots House.

Maggie looked at her. 'It wouldn't have anything to do with the story I heard in the shop yesterday?'

'Story?'

'Aye, the one about you telling the class that Miss Buchanan is about to reveal "all" about the murder of Bryn Edgar.'

Stacie felt the colour drain from her face and she sank down into a chair. Maggie handed her a glass of water straight from the cold tap. 'What possessed you? Barry's mum told me first thing Wednesday morning and then Sheila's granny and her auntie were in. The whole village is talking.'

'What did you say, Mum?' Stacie was really frightened. A quick true answer to a fairly innocuous question had landed her in the soup. And, she had asked herself harshly a thousand times since Tuesday evening, had it really been a quick true answer? She could easily have said, 'My mum hears my lines,' which was true.

'I said it was a load of nonsense, that Miss Buchanan was a lovely quiet lady who wanted only to be left alone in this village which she loves.'

'Do you think they believed you?'

'Well, it's the truth, isn't it? You can't do much better than the truth. I take it you haven't told Kate what a big mouth you have?' Maggie's usually soft face was stern and hard and she looked down, with absolutely no pity, on her daughter. 'Now, madam, you go down to Abbots House and you tell her what you've done and if she doesn't forgive you, then that's something you have to live with.'

'But, Mum, she won't find out; she never goes out and no one goes to visit her. Why distress her? It would be different if Mr Forsythe was still there but she's alone.'

'All the more reason she should be prepared.'

'Miss Galbraith asked and I just said, "Miss Buchanan". It was automatic. Please, Mum. I don't want her to hate me.'

Maggie had been drying cups that were already quite dry and she folded her not even slightly damp dishcloth and put it down beside the sink. She patted it as if she were pleased with it and began to hang the cups up on hooks. Without turning around she said, 'She's certainly not going to be crazy about you if someone knocks on the door to ask her about it.'

Stacie's heart, which had been beating quickly, seemed to jump and then plummet to the pit of her stomach. She jumped up quickly but stood, undecided, in the middle of the kitchen. Maggie stood, arms akimbo, beside the sink and watched her. 'Stacie, love, it's better that you tell her. Maybe no one will say a word, maybe it will all die down but with Sheila's auntie knowing . . . Who knows, maybe it's been semaphored to the fleet by now. That woman's tongue embroiders with as much genius as Kate's fingers.'

'Thanks a lot. I thought Barry would be the problem.'

'There's no malice in Barry; there's mischief but no malice and his family is the same. Change out of your school clothes and go.'

There was no way out. Stacie walked upstairs with less gusto than some French aristocrats had exhibited on their way to the guillotine but she could not pretend she was an unfortunate mademoiselle. This was not acting out a daydream. This was real. She took her uniform off and although she usually flung everything on to the bed to sort out later she took her time, hanging up her skirt and her blazer and putting the blouse into the laundry basket in the bathroom. Her mother was right as usual. It took no longer to be neat than it took to be untidy.

Her pink sweater. Miss Buchanan liked her in that. 'Let it be clean.' It was. She reached for a pair of jeans and then changed her mind and took down a calf-length brown woollen skirt. Black boots completed her ensemble. At least she would look nice.

Maggie met her in the hall and proffered a nicely wrapped package of her home-baked scones. Stacie recoiled in horror. 'A bribe? You're asking me to take a bribe. My own mother. How could you?' She grabbed her red jacket and went out, slamming the door behind her, and Maggie sat down to reflect on the mixed pleasures of having teenagers in the house.

Stacie stuck her hands deep into her pockets and hurried along the path, out of the gate and into the lane. She felt sick. What trouble an unguarded word could cause. 'I would do anything to protect her.' She felt the tears at last begin to run down her cheeks and, hands still clenched in her pockets, tried to shake the tears away. There was a rather used tissue at the bottom of one pocket and she took it out, wiped her face and blew her nose. 'I would do anything for her,' she said again, 'and yet, I'm the one who is bringing the attention she doesn't want. No, calmly, Stacie, calmly, nothing has happened yet. What can Sheila's aunt do? What could any middle-aged woman still living with her mum in a village do? Nothing. She can talk but she'll get tired.'

There was Abbots House. How lovely and serene it looked: there was a light on in the front bedroom, another in the hall – she could see it through the window in the top of the door – and yet another in the sitting room where Miss Buchanan usually sat when she was sewing. Stacie sniffed. Miss Buchanan was as profligate with electricity as Stacie's own parents were.

Kate did not come to the door immediately. Thinking perhaps she had not heard, Stacie rang the doorbell again. She heard it chime inside the house but nothing else. Then a voice said quietly, 'Yes, who is it?'

'It's me, Miss Buchanan, Stacie.'

She heard the sounds of keys and chains and then the door opened just enough for her to enter. 'Oh dear, Miss Buchanan, what has happened? Are you all right?'

'Yes, of course, but I had a visitor today and that took me by surprise. Why didn't you tell me, Stacie?' She was standing, her hands clasped together in front of her and resting lightly on her long black tweed skirt. With it she wore a long-sleeved old gold cashmere sweater with a wide boat neckline. She looked both wonderful and totally unaware of the fact.

Stacie prayed, as she had never prayed before, for the ground to open and swallow her up, or that, just this once, time had gone backwards and it was before drama class and she had never said the words. But she found herself still standing just inside Miss Buchanan's home, aware that, for the first time, she had not been asked to take off her coat and sit down. 'I'm sorry. Your name just came out. It was the answer to the question and I never even thought.' She dried up and stood and was aware of Miss Buchanan standing just looking at her and Stacie could say absolutely nothing in her own defence. She wondered for a moment who the visitor had been but it hardly mattered. Miss Buchanan was furious.

Kate turned away from her and walked into her sitting room. 'Hang up your coat, Stacie, and we'll talk.'

Stacie had been unaware that she had been holding her breath and it now exploded from her with an audible whoosh. She took off her jacket and hung it beside Kate's cloak on the back of the door to the garden. She felt weak with relief. Miss Buchanan was at least prepared to speak to her. If she were still her friend, no, even if she were not, Stacie would never mention her name again.

Kate was sitting in her usual chair but the embroidery frame was no longer there. Kate saw her looking around. 'It's finished, Stacie. Hugh took it to London to send it to its owner.'

'Do you miss it?'

'No. It was mine for a time and now it's right that it should be where it belongs.' Kate looked at her hands, still in her lap. 'A rather flustered hyperventilating woman presented herself on my doorstep this afternoon, Stacie, a Miss Galbraith.'

Whatever Stacie had expected, it was not this. 'Miss Galbraith? What a cheek.'

'My sentiments entirely.' Kate paused, remembering the feverish and embarrassed but hopeful tones at her door. Words like great honour, never forgotten experience, greatest living exponent, chased themselves around in her head. What was it Bryn had said? *Goes with the job, caru. Smile, let them take your photograph, sign their bits of paper.* Goes with the job. It bloody well doesn't. 'She issued an invitation to speak to the drama group. Whatever possessed you to say I might be willing to do that, Stacie? Surely you know me better than that.'

Anger came to Stacie's assistance. 'And you should know me better too, Miss Buchanan. I never said you would. I never said anything about even asking you. She was asking who heard our lines and I know I should have said, my parents, but Miss Buchanan popped out before I could stop it and it was wrong and I'm sorry. Craig asked me if I would ask you to talk to the group. I don't remember his exact words; he said it in a sort of 'it would be fabulous if she would talk to us' way and I told him I didn't know you well enough. Miss Galbraith asked, and I said you'd been ill. Honestly.

The hated embarrassing tears were streaming down her face and she badly needed to blow her nose but, horror of horrors, she had no tissues, no handkerchief. God, how much more awful could this get?

Kate handed her a delicate handkerchief with more lace than fine cotton. It was not meant for mighty nose-blowing but it would have to suffice. The handkerchief was a sodden ball in Stacie's hand and she stood trying to master her tears and her sobs.

'Who told her I was Katherine Buchan?'

Stacie was flustered. How could she say, they all started yelling? 'I'm not quite sure.' Was it Charlie? It was one of the boys. 'Barry, I think, but Mum says Barry's got no malice in him.'

'Neither, I think, has your Miss Galbraith.' She looked up at Stacie for the first time. 'Is she any good?'

'I used to think she was wonderful, till I heard your voice at the tomb.'

Kate laughed. Stacie had no idea how sincere a compliment she had just given her. 'That must have been quite a surprise. You handled it very well.' She had too. She was such a mixture of little girl and sophisticated young woman. Was I like this at sixteen? Kate could not even remember herself at that age.

'She saw you on the stage once.'

'You see me here, at least twice a week.'

'But on the stage; that must have been something. The atmosphere, the sets, the costumes.'

'If I can't make you believe they are all in this room then I have lost my touch.' Kate spoke lightly.

Stacie blushed again and Kate sighed. When would she grow out of that?

'I think you're wonderful,' said Stacie and began to cry.

Kate looked at her in astonishment and fought an almost overwhelming need to laugh. She was quite pleased that it was laughter she felt, for earlier she could quite easily have joined in the tears. Gossip, hateful ill-informed gossip. What were they saying behind their curtains? 'Tea, I think,' she said and went off to the kitchen and Stacie followed her when she was calmer.

Is this what Maggie handles day in day out? Could I have borne it? Kate sighed. Yes. Oh yes. 'Stacie, I think we deserve best cups. There are two very old, very lovely cups in the sideboard in the dining room. Bring them in for me.' Best way to handle hysterics is to work them off. Who had told her that or had she just made it up? It seemed successful, for Stacie came in reverently carrying two fragile double-handed cups with matching saucers.

319

'These?' she asked breathlessly as if she were afraid to speak too loudly for fear that they might shatter.

Kate waited until they were safely on the table. 'Yes. Yesterday's inexpensive cottage china, today's valuable antiques. These are from a British firm, Champion's Bristol, and are at least two hundred years old.'

'My God. You can't use them. What if I drop one?'

'Why should you? Have you suddenly developed co-ordination problems? I bought these with my first salary, Stacie, and I use them often' – and then she smiled at the girl – 'but only for very special people. They were made to be used and, if you're nervous, pretend you're one of Jane Austen's well-brought-up young ladies and hold both handles.'

Stacie had not heard much after special people. She watched while Kate poured tea and Kate saw that she no longer noticed the scarring on her hands.

'I almost expected them to shatter.'

'Had they not been well used they would have. I remember my grandmother telling me about her own mother's twenty-fifth wedding anniversary. They owned an exquisite tea set of fine Chinese porcelain in a lovely pale aquamarine colour, quite rare, no pattern at all and they had lived in a display cabinet for all those years. They were brought out every now and again, washed, dried and returned and then Great-Grandmama decided to use them at a silver wedding tea party and each and every one exploded as it was filled. Had they been used over the years they would have been tempered and there would have been no problems.'

'But some of them might have got broken.'

'Life is all about risk, Stacie. Surely it's better to enjoy four or even two lovely cups than to have none at all. Using these cups cheers me. My grandmother brought me up because my mother died when I was very young and my father travelled a lot. She always used her best china but taught me to take care of it and to appreciate it. I was a careful little girl and so I don't remember breaking anything. Perhaps I did.'

'Mum has all her best things in a cupboard. Gosh, tea even tastes better in a lovely cup.' Stacie dared to smile for the first time. 'I am so sorry that I have caused you pain.'

'Miss Galbraith has gone off swearing that she understands my inability to speak to her drama group. She has invited me to the performance but I have refused. I will hear you here and enjoy it all so much when you come to tell me about it. Tell me the entire truth, Stacie; that's the only way that we can be friends. Apart from Barry, was it, Barry who has no malice, who else spoke to Miss Galbraith?'

'I'm not sure. One or two. Not Craig. I think he said something about you being a private person.' What could she say about Sheila and her ghastly aunt?

Nice boy. She might just include him some day but Stacie was withholding something. 'Tell me, Stacie. It's the only way I can handle this.'

Stacie returned her beautiful white cup with its delicate perfect roses to its fluted saucer before she spoke. 'There's a girl in the class called Sheila, nice enough but her auntie was in the shop and Mum says she wanted to know everything. Mum soon sent her packing and she's just an aunt who lives at home here in the village taking care of her mother. I'm sure it will be fine. Everyone in Friars Carse has accepted you, Miss Buchanan. They know you're not an evil person but if you could prove it . . .'

Kate had stood up and Stacie trembled, for she looked like a Valkyrie ready to strike. 'I do not want to prove *it*. I do not want to prove anything. All I want is to live quietly, here where I was once very happy, and if my doorstep is to be cluttered up with silly women or . . .' But she could say no more. She could not tell Stacie that her fear was that one of these so nice people who wished her well would contact a local newspaper, for it would not end there. She knew the parallel of the little acorn that, before you know it, becomes a mighty oak, and she had no desire to see her name, once again, and for all the wrong reasons, splattered across the national and international press. 'Better go home now, Stacie. Perhaps, in a day or two, when we see how things are going, you can come down and practise. I would like to meet Craig, one day, not yet. Will he understand?'

'Yes. He's a really fabulous person.'

'I wouldn't expect you to choose less than fabulous.' She went with Stacie to the door and when the girl had put on her jacket, the door was open, and she had already stepped outside, she said, 'I know it took courage to come. Thank you.' She leaned forward slightly and touched her lips to Stacie's cheek. 'Goodnight, my dear.' And she closed the door.

Stacie on the other side stood for a moment as if transfixed and then, hugging her pleasure to her, she ran up the hill. Ignoble thought, but it was almost as wonderful as when Craig had kissed her.

Inside Abbots House, Kate took her cups and washed them and returned them to the dining room. She tried to remember all the people in her life who had been judged wonderful enough to use her special cups. Bryn? But he had always said, except at dinner parties when she used a Sèvres coffee service, 'For God's sake, Katie, give me a mug that isn't more valuable than I am.' Granny? Yes, thank God, she had lived to use them, to see her granddaughter on a West End stage, and Paris, and had Granny not come to Moscow? Yes. Oh, what joy to have a memory. Had darling Tante ever used them? Hugh, yes. Hugh. Should she ring and tell him that she was absolutely terrified that some silly woman was going to make a bid for two seconds of fame by trying to interest a newspaper in yesterday's heart-breaking news?

She could not sew. Her material from Monsieur le Duc had not yet arrived and she had no thoughts of creating anything for herself. Automatically she went to the door and wrapped herself in her cloak. It was still dark at seven in late February; she could walk for miles and no one would see her. Where would she go? Follow your nose, Kate, she told herself and went out, locking the door behind her.

As usual, she turned left at the gate and walked down towards Sea Green and the beach. In a few short weeks it would be light at this time and there would be other people about, boys playing football, or people throwing sticks for dogs. For now it was all hers. She struck out straight across the green, not worrying about her shoes as Hugh had done, but splashing through puddles and squelching in some mud, and just as she began to worry that perhaps it would be too unpleasant underfoot, she had walked through the marshy part and was on harder, drier ground.

The condition of her footwear was the least of her worries. Although she had tried to be fairly positive with Stacie she very much feared that the woman known only as Sheila's auntie might prove to be quite a nuisance. What if, what if; the different scenarios went around and around in her head. She had never sought or even particularly liked any type of publicity when she was a working actress. She had embraced it because it was a necessary evil. She had been a personality and the public liked to read about the lives of those they admired. Bryn had courted the media, not so Kate. Like many actors she had been shy and only really relaxed on the stage. She thanked God that she had never been aware of the worldwide media frenzy at the time of the murder. There, she had called it a murder; she was accepting it. Before she had always referred to the accident or to the fire, but Bryn had been murdered and Rose Lamont was his murderer.

What if Sheila's aunt rang a newspaper? Would there be any interest in an ageing woman who had once been Katherine Buchan? Surely not. Even if a journalist got wind of the fact that Kate had said she now knew that she herself had not killed Bryn Edgar, would his editor give him permission to follow up on such an unsubstantiated piece of information? Highly unlikely, Kate decided, rather naïvely.

She was well out of the village environs now and automatically kept on towards Templehall Woods. She was not thinking of her 'friend Ben', her mind was busy with Miss Galbraith and Stacie. Miss Galbraith she had not allowed in to the house. In fact she had not even opened the door but she never did. People who were allowed in were people she had invited and that meant Hugh, Father Ben, Maggie, Stacie, Simon, of course, and Dr Jarvis who still popped in occasionally but, knowing her fear of being accosted on her own doorstep, he rang to alert her that he was coming.

I should have been much stricter with Stacie and not been concerned because she was so upset. She deserved to be upset and I should have made her go over and over what had happened in the drama class till she remembered exactly what she said. Did she tell me she had told them I knew who had murdered him? She stopped dead, shuddering. What an ugly hard word murder is and she could hear herself say it, accepting it, murdered, so 'trippingly on the tongue'. Oh, Bryn, my darling Bryn. Had I married you when you first asked . . .

Enough, Kate, enough of what if. We have to deal with what is.

She began to walk again, quickly, forcefully, as someone walks who knows where they are going. She was in the woods and it was dark and what if – there was what if again – what if she tripped again but now in the dark? Foolish Kate. She was at the crusader's tomb, so still and peaceful and somehow serene in the darkness. Oh, Crusader, what a mess I am in. She leaned against the cold stones of the tomb for a few minutes but knew that she should not rest there. It was too cold and she had been ill.

Did you recover quickly from wounds or illness, Crusader, apart from that final blow, of course? As we get older, we heal more slowly. Perhaps you never lived long enough to find that out, and besides, there was no wonderful National Health Service in your day, my friend. What did you rely on, herbs and potions? I am much more sophisticated but the years become the enemy rather than the friend. Goodnight.

She left the clearing where the tomb stood but she did not retire but instead went on until she stood in front of the monastery itself. Last time she had been here the windows had been alive with light and sound, the joys of Christmas. Now it stood dark and unfriendly, closed against her. No, it was a holy house and welcomed all who came seeking succour. She found herself tugging the bell pull on the stone wall and wished she had not, for suddenly she wondered if monks went to bed when the light faded so that they could rise early to begin the work of a new day. She heard the bell reverberate along stone corridors and then, eventually, the sound of sandals on a wooden floor.

A grille opened in the great oak door and a voice said, 'Yes?'

'I'm so sorry. I wanted to see the Guardian. I'm so sorry. I'll telephone tomorrow,' but she heard the rattle of keys as the door was unlocked.

A monk stood with head bowed and arm extended as if to show her in. Inside the door was a lobby with a flagstoned floor and beyond that a long wide corridor lit by small flickering lights high up on the stone walls. When Kate stepped in the silent monk closed the door behind her, but he did not lock it, and then walked ahead of her down the corridor. The floor was highly polished wood and her shoes embarrassed Kate. She prayed that no mud from the Sea Green adhered to them but was terrified to look down lest she see it sullying these miles of evidence of hard manual labour. Her eyes adjusted to the minimalist lighting and she saw that the corridor was very imposing, great stone walls with beautiful windows at regular intervals. It was not so empty as she had thought, but had some fine oak tables, also highly polished, under several of the windows. There were also carved doors set into the walls and she wondered idly where they led. Then the monk stopped at a door, knocked, opened it and ushered Kate in.

Ben was sitting at a table not unlike the ones in the hall. He was reading or writing by the light of a strong lamp, and although he looked surprised momentarily, he stood up and smiled at Kate. 'Thank you, Brother. Some tea for my visitor. Kate, what a pleasant surprise.'

The monk, still silent, withdrew just as noiselessly and Kate found herself sitting on a hard wooden chair. 'I'm so sorry, Ben. I have no idea why I'm here and there's mud on my shoes; how dreadfully embarrassing, and I don't want to cause you to break rules.' She petered out.

'I won't. I take it Mr Forsythe has gone home.'

'Yes, and we argued about reopening the case and then something happened at the school yesterday or the day before and I'm worried.'

Another discreet knock and the silent monk returned with a tray on which reposed a very fine tea pot, cream jug and sugar basin and a matching cup. What would Stacie make of these? 'Meissen?' she queried. 'Quite lovely.'

'Brother Sebastian approves of you; usually only bishops get this one. Do you want to tell me what happened at school?'

Kate realised that she was expected to drink tea alone; there was only one cup and so she fussed for a moment pouring tea that she did not want, but at last she had pulled herself together enough and was able to speak quite normally. 'I am so sorry about imposing myself like this.' She stopped again.

'You do not impose, friend Kate. Have you considered that you were sent?'

She smiled. 'You have a very calming effect on me, friend Ben. Stacie inadvertently mentioned my name at her drama class. The teacher had seen me act once and seemingly got quite excited and from reading between the lines of Stacie's rather hysterical confession, I think the children told the teacher, Miss Galbraith, all about me. One of the students has an aunt who was gossiping in Maggie's shop.'

'She would get little encouragement from Maggie.'

'I know, but it occurred to me later that Maggie is not the only person with a shop in Friars Carse. What if. I keep hearing myself say "What if", but what if someone rings a newspaper with this rather wild idea that Kate Buchanan says she saw Bryn Edgar murdered.'

'Isn't this rather crossing a bridge before you have come to it?'

'Possibly, but I always do better if I'm prepared. I keep saying that I'm yesterday's news. No one will be interested and so I'm worrying for nothing but I really do not want reporters at my door asking questions, taking photographs. I want to live out the rest of my life in peace, Ben. Is that too much to ask? I know that I did not kill Bryn. Whether or not I am responsible for his death is another matter.'

'You're too hard on yourself, Kate.'

'If I had married him when he asked me or if I had been strong and not had an affair with a married man the murder would not have been committed.'

'Have one of those biscuits. We have a monk who bakes almost as well as Maggie. Kate, you cannot know that. Murder is a crime in the eyes of man as well as of God and perhaps justice should be done. Many would say that the murderer deserves to be punished even after all these years. Perhaps you deserve justice. You have suffered so appallingly, both because of the bodily pain of the fire and all its effects, and because of the loss of reputation; you were wrongly accused and some learned judge released you, after some years. I read that there was little real evidence; the verdict in a Scottish trial would have been Not Proven. Is it not so? And what of Bryn? Does he not deserve, even after all these years, that the person who took his life should be punished? Only you can answer these questions. If Rose has suffered for her crime, if she has waited breathlessly for a phone call or a knock at the door, perhaps she would welcome discovery. At least then it would all be over. No more waiting. And if she has spent the last thirteen years or so happy in the knowledge that someone else was being punished for the crime she committed, then perhaps she deserves to be found out.'

'You're telling me to reopen the case.'

'I'm telling you that only you can make that decision. God knows that Rose murdered Bryn Edgar and tried to kill you, and He knows that she allowed you to be found guilty of this heinous crime. She will be punished.'

'If I start proceedings, even if the police would look at the case after so long, I would find myself in the public spotlight again and I really do not think that I could bear that.'

'Then retreat from the world for a while, Kate. You hid well in Provence, did you not?'

'That particular convent is no longer taking paying guests. That was one of my reasons for giving in to my impulse to return here.'

'Then consider coming here. We are a retreat house. Where better to retreat from the world until the dust settles?'

23

When she returned from the monastery Kate telephoned Hugh. After a few minutes of chit-chat she told him that Stacie had told the drama club about her and that she feared there would soon be a reporter knocking on her door.

'Dash it all, Kate. I'll come up to fend them off for you but I had intended to pop back over to Spain, just to check some facts with Señor Cruz's nephew, not to pre-empt you or force you,' he added quickly, 'but it's always good to have as many tricks up your sleeve as possible.'

Kate made herself more comfortable on the sofa. Gosh, she missed having something to work on. She hoped her French commission would arrive soon. 'I had a long chat with Father Ben this evening, and the more I think about it, the more I believe that I should try to set the record straight.' She heard him making grumpy agreeing noises. 'Before I lay myself open to all that brouhaha, however, I wanted to ask you if talking to the police would be worth while. It's all so long ago. If they won't reopen there seems little point in making myself miserable being photographed, scar tissue and all, for national newspapers.'

'Oh, they'll reopen, Kate. Of course they will. If they don't, they'll get flak from some quarters saying that they are protecting a big name – Rose. She was very famous for a while after the fire. Grieving widow in all the papers, struggling to cope. She made at least one film a year. I never had to see any of them, thank God, but she was box-office. On the other hand it would be a nice coup for them to net a big one and show that the law has no favourites, so yes, Kate, I'm in no doubt at all that the case will be reopened.'

'Just on my say-so.'

'Yes. Simon will have to say something, memory gone, slowly

returning, returned. And you're a big name, Kate. Clearing your name would be great public relations. And forensic science has moved light years since 1972. You'd be surprised what they can find out.'

Kate looked around her lovely room. There was nothing of the past there, only memory. They could not dust memories for fingerprints but she was prepared to heed Hugh. 'I'm still not totally convinced that I want to do it. I don't have to have Rose convicted in order to be happy, you know. It might be enough for Rose to know that I remember. Go to Spain by all means. I'll manage.'

'I couldn't possibly leave you to face reporters, even the nicest of them. I can ask young Marcelo to help me out or I'll contact a Spanish lawyer. There's bound to be someone in the firm who knows a good one in the area.'

Kate laughed. 'Dear Hugh, I have a plan, and it's such a clever one. Ben thought of it. I shall go to the monastery as a paying guest.' She stopped. She had no money.

'Wonderful idea. I shall speak to Father Ben and give him some telephone numbers.'

'Hugh, I know I'm penniless.'

His voice was very calm and measured: lawyer addressing client for her own good; the client could trust that voice, would trust it. 'Like everyone else in the world, the value of your shares portfolio has gone up and down but you still have some nice little earners. You're not my pensioner, Kate. I do wish you would disabuse your mind of that idea.'

She had a happy thought. 'I've finished the panel. A nice little cheque will pop through the letterbox any day now and I have told Monsieur Le Duc that I am free to work for him now.'

They talked long into the night and by the time Kate went to bed she had decided on her plan of action. At the first sign of any media interest she would contact Father Benjamin who would arrange for her to be picked up and taken to the monastery. The only people to know where she was, apart from Hugh and Simon, would be the Thomsons. She would need to ask Maggie to collect any mail that came; she wanted that cheque in her bank account.

She slept peacefully for almost five hours; apart from drug-induced sleep, she did not remember when she had last slept for so long. Remembering everything seemed to have laid all her ghosts to rest. Her poor overworked brain no longer needed to work over-time trying to put her life in focus and in order.

As usual she showered quickly and then, wrapped in her long blue dressing-gown, she went downstairs to make coffee. How still the house was. She loved the particular stillness that is early morning, but this one felt slightly different. She opened the kitchen blinds and peered out. How unexpected. There had been a slight snowfall in the night. Even one of the garden spiders had been taken by surprise, for it had carefully constructed a web across the top part of the window and now it hung there catching snowflakes and not tasty flies. Kate watched it for a time, wondering at the strength of the web which sagged alarmingly in the middle but which refused to break. The sun, if it came up, would melt the snow and perhaps a breakfast would appear. Kate, however, would have to prepare her own. Instant coffee and some toast with some of Hugh's fig jam. Ambrosia.

The day stretched ahead and, with no sewing to do, it could be empty. She relished this feeling of worry that she would be bored; for too many years she had drifted like a leaf blown along in the gutter by a playful wind, sometimes pushed up against a solidity that held her prisoner and at other times thrown violently hither and thither. Instead of wondering idly what she could possibly do before it was time to try to sleep, hours of excitement stretched ahead. Had she a commission she would sew. She would walk, of course. What a cheek I had, she thought, as she recalled her visit to the monastery. What a surprise I must have been to them and yet, how wonderfully they welcomed me, especially Ben, my friend Ben. But today, what shall I do today? I don't want to waste a minute.

And then the idea came and it was so overwhelming that she had to sit down while she assimilated what she planned. She would open the box where Katherine Buchan lived still. Hugh had kept programmes, newspaper articles, magazine features and who knew what else and he had put them in a box hidden at the very back of her linen cupboard.

'One day you might like to look at them, Kate, remember old friends, great moments: who knows, my dear, some might make you laugh. Your hats, charming though they certainly were, might raise a smile today. Remember the little black and white Robin Hood one; I tell you now that every time you lunched with me in that one and leaned across the table towards me with a delicious piece of gossip, I feared for my eyes.'

Tears welled up in her eyes. 'Oh, Hugh, my dearest friend, if I hadn't loved Bryn I would surely have loved you. And I do, I do.'

She wiped away her tears. No more feeling sorry for herself. Hugh knew she loved him as much as she possibly could. She would look through the box and see if there was anything that Stacie might like, a good luck token, a signed programme perhaps.

She went upstairs to dress but the cupboard door stood there, daring her to pass or to open. She stood for a moment undecided and then turned the key. Of course she could face the past; she had challenged it already and had won. Kate Buchanan was in full possession of her history; all that lay in the box was detail. The box was, as Hugh had said, in the furthest reaches and she had to move several other things to get to it. One was a large lamp of rather strange design.

'Now, that I do not remember but I could never have bought it myself; it's just too ghastly for words. What on earth is it doing here? It's not a Hugh-type lamp either, or a Granny lamp and certainly not a Tante. Bryn? Bryn at a coconut shy?'

She admitted defeat. That memory, if it was a memory, still eluded her. Another box, large, bulky, and sealed with wide tape. Kate's furs. 'Good God, I do have a winter coat. Wicked hedonist Kate. You bought a floor-length mink in nineteen sixty-something. Oh, God, and you've got Tante's little foxes, all those sad little heads and little tails. What on earth will I do with those? The drama club! Next year they can do *Hedda Gabler* or something.' She could prevaricate no longer. There was the box, almost as large as the one holding the mink but not so tightly wrapped.

Kate pulled the large cardboard container out on to the landing, noting with joy that it had originally contained extremely fine French wines, and knelt down beside it. Her past was in that box.

331

Should she open it? Were there other nightmares just waiting to jump out? Silly Kate. Hugh packed this box. On the very top was a neatly typed list and so she could see exactly what the box contained. She was pleased to note that they were not souvenirs that Hugh himself had collected; that would have been just too sad. Tante's memories were here. 'Little Kate's first part at RADA; charming.'

'Ha,' said Kate. 'I doubt that I was ever charming.'

There were a few, so few and therefore so precious, scrapbook mementoes from Granny: a few programmes. Dear God, the first *Tempest*.

'"Ah pray you, work not so hard."'

Gloves. Where did they come from? Were they mine? My first dance? Did I wear them in a play? Kid. But of course.

Kate tried one on. It slipped over her hand and then she pulled and tweaked and eventually the glove settled over her elbow. She gave up trying to button the five little pearl buttons. How on earth did one wear those? She had a vague memory of unbuttoning them and slipping her very hot hand out so that she could eat supper, and did one fold them back while one was dancing? No, men wore gloves then too and no dandy would like to hold hot sweaty hands in his immaculate and expensively cleaned kid gloves. She wondered when she had last attended a party. Such a long time ago but she found that she had not missed them at all. Going to a party had been a little like going on stage. One had enjoyed it once one was over the hurdle of actually getting there in the first place. Would Stacie feel terror? Would she learn to cope with nerves, with nausea? Kate could not remember a single great actor who had not suffered terribly while standing in the wings waiting for the word or gesture that would catapult them into the limelight.

What was this? The fan. *Hedda Gabler*. How exquisite. Bryn had given that to her. He had asked her to marry him, told her that the fan was damned expensive but cheaper than diamonds. She held it to her face for a moment. The perfume was still there. Gardenias. He had bought her gardenias because she had complained that her bosom was too small for the orchids that everyone else was wearing that season. She opened the fan, black ostrich feathers. It was lovely. Again she lifted it to her face and she became Ibsen's flawed creation. Bryn had brought the fan on her third night. He had been away. Where? *Hamlet* in New York. That was it. Then he had come and he had the fan. New York. Of course. Anything and everything was available, he said, in New York. He still talked of moving there. The offers were phenomenal but he was, first and foremost, a stage actor, and he rejoiced in the traditions and history of English theatre. He revelled in being part of it but another side of him, the Welsh boy from the valleys, sometimes thought he should sell out for adulation.

'*Aye*, Caru, *penthouses they call them, on the top of the world and a swimming pool alongside. Isn't that the way to live? But I worry,* cariad, *for water flows down not up. How does it get up there, tell me, to those fancy pools?*'

'*Engineering.*'

'*It's not natural though, is it? However you look at it, water is meant to go down, and maybe it will one day and all the swimmers with it.*'

It was impossible to tell when Bryn was serious and when he was playing poor little boy from the mountains of Wales but he never did move to New York. He never lived long enough to move anywhere.

Kate sighed, put the fan aside and went on with her box. Next came programmes tied up in a rubber band. How many there were. She would have to read them some time. The next group consisted of her own early copies, her parts underlined in red, and each one signed by any member of the cast of whom at the time she had not been afraid. The hesitancy to speak to the great actors was her weakness, not theirs, for almost every one had been warm and welcoming, and in many cases helpful. Most seemed to have the attitude, there's room for us all if you're good, if you keep up the standards. One or two had become distant and unfriendly as her own fame grew. Jealousy, she supposed. Had she herself ever eyed an ingénue with worry? No, she did not think so.

'But Katherine Buchan did not live enough to become a *grande dame.*'

Good heavens, a battered and rather tawdry silver rose. It was not silver, of course, or even silver plate: something that had been

333

made in a theatre workshop, but for whom and why? Kate closed her eyes to think better but no play came to mind where a silver rose had been part of the props made in a theatre workshop. Opera. *Der Rosenkavalier*. There is a rose, a silver rose, in that opera. Kate had seen it only once. If the rose came from that performance why do I have it? She did not know the opera, hearing it once is no more than that. She remembered some glorious soprano singing and surely the rose was given by that fat old man to a girl.

She sat back on her heels. She had remembered and her memory did not fill her with pride in herself. After Bryn had married Rose, in defiance she had agreed to have dinner with an admirer who also happened to be a singer, not a very good one if she remembered correctly. He had had a bit part in *Der Rosenkavalier* and had begged, borrowed or stolen the prop rose to give to her as a romantic symbol. Later, back in her flat, having successfully extricated herself from verbose protestations of undying affection, she had laughed at the operatic gesture and tossed the rose aside. Where was the singer now and what on earth was his name?

Kate stood up and stretched. She was cramped from kneeling so long.

'Well, Mr Tenor, I really do hope that I meant as little to you as you did to me.' She looked at her watch and was shocked to see that it was after one and here she was, without the excuse of illness, still in her dressing-gown. She went to her bedroom and, managing to avoid all mirrors, dressed for her walk. The rose had upset her. It proved, did it not, that she had used and discarded people. She had dined with the unremembered tenor merely in order to pretend to herself that she cared nothing for Bryn. Had he been hurt or was she putting too much emphasis on one dinner and one flamboyant and possibly rather charming gesture? She hoped there were no more nasty surprises for her in her recovered memory.

She was reflecting on this too much; she knew that. Dating a man on the rebound or accepting a date from someone who made no bells ring was merely part and parcel of growing up. Surely as long as one was totally honest, then no harm was done. The box, with half of its contents spilled out on to the landing, was still outside the linen cupboard. Should she tidy it up before she went?

She shrugged and went downstairs. She had forgotten to open the curtains and was thankful that she had few visitors, for anyone calling would have assumed that she was still in bed. The snow had gone and the world outside her windows looked cold and unwelcoming. The spider's web, still intact but now glistening with melted snow, had no little parcels of wrapped lunch waiting for the hungry spider. Kate could go to her kitchen. She would warm some soup and eat some bread and cheese before she faced the rigours of the beginning of March on the east coast of Scotland.

She was just sitting down to enjoy it when she heard the sound of her gate and then the rattle of her letterbox. Letters were rare and so she left the soup and hurried into the hall. Two letters lay on the mat, a veritable bonanza. She gathered them up, noting the postmarks and the stamps, and hurried back into the breakfast room. A letter from Sister Mary Magdalene and a thank you note with a generous cheque for the delivered work deserved to be savoured slowly. The cheque necessitated a walk into the village or she could prepare it for deposit and leave it in the depository after dark. Either way, she could pay for a few weeks at the retreat house should she need it. Soup with bread and cheese was a perfect accompaniment for a letter from a friend. It was an apology for not writing earlier to thank Kate for the good things delivered by 'the so kind Monsieur Hugh'. Everything, of course, delivered in Kate's name.

The telephone rang and, because so few people knew her number, she assumed it was Maggie or Hugh with something he had forgotten to say. 'Good afternoon,' she sang out.

'Is that Katherine Buchan?'

She did not know the voice but later would be pleased that some instinct took over, for she heard herself saying, quite calmly. 'Katherine Buchan? No, there is no one here by that name.' And she hung up.

It had started.

Kate sat down mainly because she suddenly felt faint. She put her head down between her knees for a moment, sat up straight and breathed out with short sharp barks. Hah. Hah. Then she breathed deeply and slowly, trying to picture the breath making its way down

335

through all the levels in her lungs, tidal, reserve or complemental, and at last the residual, the air seldom renewed save in moments of severe physical stress. 'That's now, buddy.' She was calm. Now she could think what to do.

It would ring again. She sat looking at the receiver for some time. Nothing. It had worked. He had gone away. But Kate had been only too familiar with media interest and she knew that no self-respecting journalist would give up so easily. How had he got her number? It was a mistake but no, he had asked for Katherine Buchan. Someone had given him the number but who knew it? Hugh, Simon, Maggie and Stacie, possibly Father Ben; she could not remember whether or not she had given it to him. And Dr Jarvis but he would never give it to anyone. No matter what any caller said, the telephone companies would not release an unlisted number, would they? No, of course not.

Kate looked down and was horrified to see that she was actually wringing her hands and she drew them apart in some annoyance. 'Next I'll be having the bloody vapours. So, someone has discovered or uncovered me but he does not know my real name. Finding it out, however, will take a second if he is a reporter, merely by looking in his newspaper's files. Therefore I can assume that in no time at all he will be knocking at my door.'

She got up and went to the blinds, closed them and then peeped through. Nothing stirred.

She could not, however, risk going out for her walk. She could not take her cheque to the bank. 'Bloody hell. I'll go out if I damned well choose to go out.' Wearily she sat down again. Such bravado, Kate. You do not want to risk the knowing eyes, the whispers, the direct or indirect antagonism; you are making a prisoner of yourself. What will he ask? Is it true, Miss Buchanan or Miss Buchan, that you did not kill Bryn Edgar? Is it also true that you know who did? Then will you allow us to reveal this to our readers for you? Might he say they would, what was the phrase, make it worth her while? What the hell was a while? A unit of time, the years since the fire, and Bryn dead so horrifically. Was that a while? So what could they give her that would make it worth it?

★   ★   ★

336

Rose Lamont carefully inserted tubes of sponge between her tanned toes and picked up her nail polish – red. It used to have a different name but was now Classic Cayenne. It looked absolutely nothing like the colour of cayenne pepper; perhaps the makers meant it was red-hot. Then why didn't they call it Red-hot Red? Not for the first time she wished that she had gone with Rose as a colour; it would have been a signature but surely red, scarlet was her colour? Her friend Edna was wearing pale aqua this week; there was a fashion to co-ordinate with one's clothes but it was a fad that Rose would allow to pass without comment. Red made a statement. When had she ever worn anything as insipid as pale aqua anyway? Bryn used to ask her about that? 'Why don't you buy a gown in something a little less strong? Kate wears some lovely blues, Rosie.' She might have tried blue if he had not mentioned the perfect Kate, perfect woman, perfect actress, perfect dresser, perfect lover, absolutely imperfect friend. What kind of friend steals your husband? The little voice to which she very rarely listened told her that Bryn had only ever been hers legally. She had known the day he asked her to marry him that he was coming from one rejection too many from his precious Kate.

But I loved him, didn't I?

After two martinis Rose knew that she had absolutely adored Bryn Edgar.

We were made for each other. His Celtic masculinity, my Saxon fragility, and besides, we were the right size for each other. Kate was far too tall and gawky for him. When she wore heels she looked right into his eyes. What man likes a woman who can eyeball him? They prefer to be looked up at, and usually adoringly. Kate never adored him, did she? But he couldn't keep away. From the very first day at RADA I knew she was a problem; she wasn't so pretty as I am; no figure to speak of, indifferent hair, but he couldn't take his eyes off her and only relaxed when she was in the room. I made him relax after we were married though. I kept him busy; everything he wanted. No little tarts anywhere, none of those simpering wannabees with their, 'I just die when I hear you speak.' I died when he spoke too, especially when he spoke about the wonderful Kate. I could have been good too if he had coached me but right from the start he had time only for Kate. He laughed at my parts in soaps; he ridiculed the spaghetti westerns even though they made more money than he ever dreamed of making. What was that he said to me when she got her first audition and he spent hours coaching her? 'Leave it, Rose, you don't need talent to sell soap.' Damn it all, I was the best actor of the three of us and they were too wrapped up in their love of each other and their damned classical stage to see it.

She reached for the nail polish remover. There was perhaps a tad too much polish on her toes. Eyes swimming with tears did not augur well for seeing with accuracy. Rose blew her nose delicately, folded the handkerchief carefully, and wiped her eyes, taking care not to stretch that delicate area of skin just under the eye. Should she apply some cream in case she had been too rough? No, much better to get these toenails perfect.

Rose concentrated. Concentrating meant that she did not have to think of the phone call from Javier with his implied threats. What trouble could he cause? He had been a young boy, fascinated by planes and film stars. He asked everyone he met two questions. 'You know Senor Eastwood?' 'You know Raquel Welch?' If the answer was 'no' then his victim was left alone. Surprising the number of actors who seemed never to have heard of them. Rose had acted with Clint in a western, a good-hearted saloon girl. 'It was a small part but I was terrific. It's not easy to play someone so different from one's own personality. Not that I'm not good-hearted,' she reminded herself quickly, 'but I know nothing of low life in bars and saloons. I had to dig deep within myself to find that character.'

'Money for old rope, so it is.' That was Bryn. She jumped up and threw the nail varnish remover away from her and as hard as she could. It sailed across the still surface of the pool, raining drops of remover on to aquamarine perfection and then crashed against a terracotta pot containing an orange tree, full of blossom and ripe oranges. The scent from the orange blossom was soon battling with the acid smell of what she supposed was acetone. 'He deserved all he got.'

'What am I saying, what am I saying?' Rose looked around to see if she had been overheard and began gathering her things together,

her nail polish, her book, her spectacles. Where was Pilar and did the pool boy come today? He spoke no English, but Pilar did, although she was sly enough to pretend that she did not. That way, thought Rose, she heard things that she shouldn't and passed them on. Had she ever said anything? No, there was nothing to say. While she was filming north of Benahadux Bryn had been murdered in his mistress's house in Scotland: their love nest, the paper had called it. She had been, and still was, completely broken-hearted, no matter what anyone said.

24

Kate was still sitting in her sitting room when Stacie arrived for a lesson. As usual she knocked, then opened the letterbox, and called, 'Miss Buchanan, it's Stacie.' Since Kate had recovered from her recent illness neither Maggie nor Stacie entered the house without knocking.

Kate rose and unlocked the door and Stacie, who had been about to launch forth with her usual exuberance, was immediately concerned. 'Miss Buchanan, is everything all right?'

Kate ushered her in and waited until she had hung up her favourite red jacket. Then she smiled at the girl, a rather strained smile. 'Forgive me, Stacie. I quite lost track of time. It's been rather an odd day; I had a telephone call, you see, and it rather perplexed me. "Discombobulated" was Bryn's favourite word. I think he made it up or, now that I think about it, it was a slang souvenir from his first trip to New York, But he'd say, "You're all discombobulated, Katie," but he meant upset, worried. Let's have a cup of tea before we start because I think I have to ask you a very big favour, and maybe Craig too, and I'll need to speak to your mother, your parents, in fact.'

They were moving into the kitchen and Stacie took down some of Kate's pretty green cups, while her hostess made tea. 'What have you been doing this week, Stacie? Have you learned everything?' It would be better to chatter normally for a while, to get herself functioning properly. She could never tell anyone that she had spent the entire afternoon sitting in a chair praying that a telephone would not ring. Usually people prayed that one would, that an agent would be on the other end, or an impresario, or a lover. Her prayers today had been answered: the telephone had not rung again.

'Miss Galbraith was on great form. She told us about movement, that we should move only when we absolutely have to get somewhere. And she spoke about not fidgeting when someone else is speaking.'

Kate nodded while she filled the two cups. 'Excellent. The audience will be distracted by the fidgets and miss your best line. It has been known for some actors to do it on purpose.'

'Like upstaging?'

'Yes, there are small people in every profession, Stacie, and you will meet one or two, but mostly the people you meet in the theatre will be there to cheer you on, to wish you well.'

'Oh, I've remembered something I wanted to ask you; it's something I read in a book about stage directions. What's my upstage arm?'

'First, where is upstage?'

'The back of the stage.'

'Right, and so whichever arm is nearer the fixed back cloth, the curtain that stretches across the back of the stage, is your upstage arm. If you gesture with the other one it tends to hide your body and it looks clumsy. Simple but effective trick of the trade. What else did you learn?'

'We're blocking moves; we used masses of tape tonight to show where Joan stands and Alençon, and Burgundy and the Dauphin, etcetera. Seemingly the trick is to use the whole stage. Miss Galbraith says amateurs tend to cluster together. It's very exciting, isn't it, although, would you believe when we were actually on the stage today, Craig, of all people, forgot his lines, and Emma, that's Juliet, said her lines so quickly that we missed almost every word.'

'Happens to everyone,' commiserated Kate as she led the way back into the sitting room. She took her usual seat. 'When I was at RADA we found that the people who galloped their lines were usually afraid that they would forget them before they were finished and so they raced to get the speech out, forgetting everything they'd ever learned about projection or meaning, or significance. As for poor old Craig, everyone forgets from time to time. That's why there's a prompter. Now I have to talk to you about what happened today and my great plan but I have a hint, if you haven't discovered it yet, for you and Craig and anyone else who's interested. Do you have a tape recorder?'

341

'Yes.'

'Everyone tapes their lines, Stacie. Read all the parts with the correct timing; act them all out, and then do it again and leave the right space for your own lines. That way you get used to knowing what goes before you and what comes after. You cannot study lines in your own little vacuum.'

Stacie gazed at her and Kate recognised the admiration, adulation, in her eyes and she smiled, almost knowing what was going to come next.

'Miss Buchanan, could I tape you doing it with me, when you do all the parts?'

She had not meant to bring her plan up at this point but Stacie's question innocently led straight into it. 'I think that could be arranged, Stacie, and we could get your Craig to do his bit. Bryn and I used to do that all the time; he would do the male voices.' She smiled reminiscently. 'Mind you, he made a marvellous Lady Bracknell too, and the nurse in *Romeo and Juliet*. We had so much fun.' She stopped. Her recovered memories seemed to gallop around in her head as fast as poor Emma had delivered her lines. She would not impose them on Stacie. 'I'm sorry, but I'm remembering so much without even trying these days and it's wonderful but I shouldn't inflict my ramblings on you.'

'Oh, Miss Buchanan, I love hearing it. The more I hear you speak, the more I want to be an actress too.'

'There's disappointment too, Stacie, and hard work.'

Stacie smiled and this time it was she who showed her growing maturity. 'But there's disappointment and hard work in everything, isn't there? It's how one handles it.'

And for some there is horror. Let there not be horror for this child.

Stacie picked up the now empty cups. 'Let me wash these.' She walked into the kitchen and Kate sat and listened to the sound of water running.

'Craig would love to meet you.' Stacie was back, drying her hands on paper towels. 'Can I really bring him to meet you?' She tossed the wet towel behind her, cursed softy and returned to the kitchen to put it into the wastebasket. 'I was sure I could make a basket. Never was much good at games though.'

Kate smiled at her but carried on with her conversation. 'He has to have permission from his parents. I really do understand their point of view, you know, as I know your dear father is not totally happy. Has he noticed how you are improving?'

Stacie thumped herself down into the chair, a sure sign of emotional stress. 'He will never agree to drama college before university.' She sat up straight as if mentally shaking herself. 'You mentioned a phone call that upset you.'

'Discombobulated me,' said Kate with a lopsided, not quite genuine, smile. 'It was a man, early afternoon, I think. I had been upstairs going through a box.' She was silent again, thinking of the box and of the telephone call. 'He asked for Katherine Buchan. Now who would ask for her and more importantly where did he get my telephone number?'

'You don't think . . . Oh, Miss Buchanan, you can't . . .'

'No, Stacie, I'm sorry. I know it simply would not occur to you or any other member of your family. Anyway, he hasn't called back so it's possible he thinks he got the wrong information.'

'No one at school has your number. Mum has it at the shop and Dad at his but I'm sure none of the assistants would give it to anyone. Goodness, they've all worked in the shops since the day they opened.' She looked at her watch. 'I have to go but your plan; you were going to tell me about your plan.'

Kate stood up. 'Let's get your jacket. For now my plan is to keep my head down and wait. I'll ring your mother and talk to her, and as for you and young Craig, if you bring one of those recording machines we'll tape the scene. Craig is welcome; otherwise I'll do the other parts.'

When Stacie had gone she locked and bolted the front door and closed all the curtains and blinds. Once again she was pleased that there was a streetlight just outside on the narrow pavement that ran along beside the house almost down to the Sea Green. Its golden light lit up her front door extremely well and if she lay in bed with her curtains open it lit the room almost as well as a lamp. She liked its soft glow nearly as much as she enjoyed the light of the moon; moonlight was perhaps more romantic. She felt slightly sick but realised that she had eaten nothing for hours and so she went into her tiny kitchen and opened the refrigerator. She stood looking in at its pristine cleanliness. Refrigerators do not fill themselves. She would need to ring Maggie and Mr Morrison as well as Jim. Jim provided her with beautifully trimmed lamb chops that she had learned to cook. There would be some of Maggie's wonderful packages in the small freezer but she was hungry now. The cupboard yielded oatcakes, tinned beans and tins of soup. Nothing appealed. 'I'd absolutely love one of Demarco's fish suppers. What joy just to put on my cape and walk up, like any other villager, to stand in line and ask for extra vinegar on my chips.' She could feel herself salivating and, after all these years, she felt she could taste the crisp light fish in its secret award-winning coat. 'Dare I, dare I?'

She reached for her cape. 'Everyone recognises the cape. I'm the batty old woman in Abbots House who walks around at night in a cape with its hood up.'

She left the cloak where it hung and went upstairs. She had to have a coat somewhere, apart from the mink. Would she have dared walk into a fish and chip shop in Friars Carse in a floor-length mink, even at the height of her fame? Her real fame, that is, not the infamy that had followed the fire. The box with half its treasures strewn around was still on the floor outside the linen cupboard, and she was in the middle of repacking it when the telephone rang again. Kate felt her heartbeat speed up. Should she answer it? Would she answer it? She could see it from her kneeling place on the carpet. Nothing in the way it sounded to tell her whether friend or foe was on the other end.

She dragged herself to her feet and walked over to the table and reached out tentatively. Get it over with, Kate. 'Hello.'

'I was about to hang up.'

She had her left hand on her heart as if to attempt to slow it down and she deliberately commanded it to move and to push her hair over her ear to hide the scar there, her least favourite scar. 'I've been looking through the boxes. You caught me on my hands and knees tidying up.'

'Good,' said Hugh in the tone of voice used when one has found someone doing something recommended for 'your own good'. 'Which ones?'

'The life and times of Katherine Buchan and I found my furs. Why on earth didn't you get rid of those?'

'Couldn't give furs away a few years ago and I don't think it's much better now. You can wear the mink walking on that blessed beach of yours. Either that or use it as a blanket when the north wind blows.'

'My central heating is adequate.'

'Good, how was your day? Have you started some new work?'

'No, although, if Stacie is "new work", she was here for a while. I thought I would give her something as a good luck charm and I found that rose. Do you remember the tenor? Gosh, I've just remembered he used to sing to me under my window. I'd be as embarrassed as hell now but in those days, apart from losing sleep, I took it all as my due.'

'And so it was. I'm going off to Spain tomorrow to Almería, a decent flight to Madrid and then an internal flight to an airport that is a few miles from the town. My young physics student is meeting me; I don't think his heart is in astrophysics to be honest. You'd like him, Kate, and, more importantly, so would your Stacie.'

'Stacie is in love with Craig.'

'Meeting a good-looking young Spaniard will do her allure no end of good.'

'What on earth are you talking about, Hugh, and what do you intend to do in Spain; not harass Rose?'

'No, I have an appointment with a lawyer, an associate of one of the partners here, and I plan to visit the little airports out at Mini Hollywood again. Money talks, Kate, and I want you to have as much ammunition as possible. Now tell me what else you did today.'

'Got my first phone call; some man asking for Katherine Buchan.'

'That's strange. Accent?'

'Undistinguished. In no way remarkable. Scots certainly.'

'What did you say?'

'I said that no one by that name lived here.'

'Well done, Katie. Has he rung back?'

'No.'

'Then he probably won't.'

345

'You don't believe that and neither do I. He rang early afternoon but not again.'

Anxiety was in his voice as he said, 'You didn't think I was him?'

'No,' lied Kate, who even managed a light nonchalant laugh. 'I took time to get to the phone because I was on my hands and knees, Hugh, and I have made a plan. It's obvious to me that someone somewhere has got hold of my number. Sooner or later they will turn up on my doorstep. I don't intend to be here, but I need help from Maggie's family and possibly young Craig.'

'I'll cancel my trip.'

'No, I'm actually looking forward to the next few days,' and she told him her plan.

When her conversation with Hugh was over, Kate went downstairs. She had eaten so little since early morning that she no longer felt hungry but from experience she knew that she would cope better if she ate something; going to Demarco's for a fish supper was merely a dream; it would have to be beans with oatcakes on the side or oatcakes with beans on the side; she opted for the first. While the beans were warming she spread butter thickly on the oatcakes. One of the absolute joys of being thin was that she could indulge her love for real butter without putting on any weight.

She ate an oatcake; she savoured every mouthful of thick grainy oats and unsalted butter. Food fit for kings or gods even. How wonderful to be able to enjoy a relatively simple pleasure. She would butter another one and by then the beans would be ready. The telephone rang just as she sliced the butter with her knife. She put it down and hurried to the telephone. It would be Maggie; had she not told Stacie that she would ring her mother?

'Hello.'

'Miss Buchanan?' It was the same voice.

Her mouth seemed to dry up, her heart began to race and her palms felt clammy. Should she slam down the receiver? No, then he would know that he had Katherine Buchan in his sights. She closed her eyes for a moment and then raised her head and opened her eyes at the same moment. 'Yes,' she said very calmly into the receiver. 'This is Kate Buchanan.'

'Miss Buchanan, my name is Terry Webster; I work for the

Borders Town and Country Gazette and I'd like to do a story on you and your really remarkable recovery from death's door.'

'I haven't been at death's door as you call it, Mr Webster, for almost fifteen years, and I have no desire to tell the world about it. Thank you.'

He shouted so loudly that she held the receiver away from her ear; that is probably what saved it from being hung up. 'No, don't hang up. I can help you, Miss Buchan' – so he did know that she and Katherine were one and the same – 'I'm a great admirer of yours; at least, my mother was; she saw every film you made, two and three times some of them.'

He was not a very good journalist. She and Bryn had boasted of their strength in turning down lucrative offers of films; a few plays for television, that was her entire celluloid output. 'That's nice, but I have nothing to say to you that your readers would want to read, Mr Webster.'

'On the contrary, they would love to hear that you did not murder Bryn Edgar, possibly the greatest young English actor of his time, and that you know who did. They'd love to hear that.'

'He was Welsh, Mr Webster, and there's no possibly about it.' And that's when she hung up.

She was exhilarated. Stupid oaf. His mother had seen every film she had made. What kind of a journalist relies on that kind of poor research and lashings of soft soap? At the accusation of being English Bryn would have floored him; he was not always the most civilised of Welshmen. Thank God he was not a journalist from a reputable or even well-known paper. Who had ever heard of the *Borders Town and Country Gazette*? And that, if his standard of research was anything to go by, was where he would stay. Nevertheless he would probably end up on her doorstep and possibly with a camera.

She was calm, if a little excited, but she was not afraid for once, rather stimulated. The smell of burning alerted her to her kitchen and she found her supper reduced to a brown crust. 'Damn,' she said loudly as she flung the pan into the sink and filled it with cold water, remembering too late that one should always fill a pan with hot water.

She rang Maggie. 'Maggie, I'm so sorry. It's Kate Buchanan and I do hate to impose on you but something rather nasty has happened and I may need your help.'

'No bother, Kate.' Maggie still got a small thrill from calling her famous customer by her Christian name. 'I'll come down or, look, would you like to come up here? We have a spare room and you're more than welcome.'

Like a good wife a good friend is a pearl without price. 'Maybe one day, Maggie, but is it possible for you and Jim, and Stacie if it's not too late, to come here this evening?'

'We'll be right down.'

Kate never learned what Maggie had to say or do or promise but less than ten minutes later the Thomsons were at her door and Kate opened the door wide to welcome them in. Maggie and Stacie walked in as old friends, people who knew the ropes, who had been welcomed countless times before but Jim was ill at ease and Kate set herself, not to charming him, although unconsciously that was what she did, but to making him feel at ease in her home, welcome. Maggie and Stacie accepted a glass of wine but Jim refused, although he did stop sitting rigidly on the edge of his chair and settled himself more comfortably into the seat of it.

'Stacie told us you were a wee bit upset when she got here, Kate,' said Maggie. 'Do you want to tell us a bit more about the telephone call?'

'It's really the ramifications, the effects of the call that are worrying, Maggie, and then he called back, just a few minutes ago. This time he used my real name; he wants to do a piece on my recovery and this story that's going around that I know who really murdered Bryn Edgar. He will be on my doorstep tomorrow morning, if I know my journalists, although this Mr Webster is the kind that gives other journalists a bad name. Tried to soft-soap me, can you believe, with some cock and bull story about his mother loving my films. My films, can you believe it? He hasn't done five minutes of research, has obviously just heard some story, probably from this woman who lives in the village.'

'What paper?' asked Jim.

'The *Borders Town and Country Gazette*.'

348

Jim made a rude noise. 'That's no much of a paper.'

'They sell a lot in this area, Jim. But what's your plan, Kate? We'll help if we can.'

Kate proffered the bottle for refills but they were rejected and she took her time, putting the bottle back, marshalling her thoughts. 'I plan to go as a paying guest to the monastery; it's a retreat house and they do have basic accommodation for non-religious. No one is likely to find me there and even if some newspaper traced me, they surely can't get into a cloister.'

Stacie stood up and took Kate's empty glass away; she looked upset. 'But it's wrong that you have to leave your lovely house. Maybe it will all fizzle out.'

'I can't take the risk, Stacie.'

'But what does Hugh, Mr Forsythe say?'

'He's off to Spain tomorrow to consult a Spanish lawyer and to make further enquiries.' She turned to Maggie and Jim. 'Hugh is my lawyer and he is also my stepbrother; I may have told you about him. I really would prefer to stay here until he gets back, to see if we have grounds to reopen the investigation.'

'That's so exciting,' said Stacie.

Kate smiled at her enthusiasm. 'Yes, but ghastly for me. Reporters will descend like locusts and I just couldn't handle the stress. You understand, Maggie, Jim?'

'Aye, and how can we help?' said Jim, while Maggie nodded vigorously in agreement.

'I'd like to dress up as Stacie and, if it's possible, have young Craig drive me to the monastery while Stacie stays here pretending to be me.'

Stacie was on her feet again. 'Fab. An acting role. I'll be great. I'll sit in your chair pretending to sew. We could leave the blinds open a little.'

Jim watched his daughter entering into the spirit of the plan and his heart sank into his boots. 'I've no objection to you doing anything that won't get you into any trouble, Stacie, but that won't mean I'm changing my mind. Would you mind explaining your plan a wee bit, Miss Buchanan?'

★   ★   ★

Hugh arrived in Almería and now that he was comfortably and safely there wished that he had used a direct flight even though it was an airline with which he was unfamiliar. 'Too comfortable for your own good, Hugh,' he told himself, but had to admit to feeling happier when he saw young Marcelo standing in the arrivals hall.

'Señor Hugh, good to see you.'

'Marcelo, you're not missing classes to drive me around?'

'Yes and no, señor. My best friend, Ignacio, takes the same classes. I'll borrow his notes just this once. I miss no class today and tomorrow only one. So I get the class in the second hand, I help you investigate which is bound to be good for my future and I make a bit of money. This is all good, señor.'

He was, as usual, pragmatic. Hugh admired his insouciance. He had little experience of young men but he thought that if Marcelo was an example of Spanish youth, or youth in general, then there was hope for the future. 'You had better end up as Prime Minister, Marcelo. For now, just take me to the hotel.'

The young man laughed. 'No *parador* this time, but the Torreluz is three star, pretty good, no, and you can walk to the *abogado*, the lawyer. Not much choice for restaurants but if you like good Spanish sherry there's a great bar, Bodega Las Botas, but maybe there's better *tapas* at Casa Puga, or there's the Torreluz belonging to your hotel. You won't starve, Señor Hugh.'

'That's good to know,' said Hugh as they arrived at the hotel. He arranged to meet Marcelo at two the next afternoon to drive out to the airport, checked in and went upstairs to prepare for his meeting the next morning.

The lawyer suggested to him by one of his own colleagues was of the stereotypical Spanish grandee class; he was average height with a fine aristocratic face dominated by a rather splendid almost hooked nose. His immaculate suit fitted as if it had been fashioned on his spare frame and his shoes, like Hugh's own, were hand-made. There was, as was immediately obvious, nothing of the dilettante about him and his mind was as razor sharp as his nose. Two hours in his company flew past, speeded along, it must be said, by the enjoyment of a glass of rather fine sherry. Hugh took his leave of him with some reluctance; it had been so good to be back at the coal-face again, but he did have the name of the sherry supplier and an invitation to return at any time.

He lunched at the Casa Puga, even though, by Spanish standards, he was far too early, and he sat long over his lunch making notes of his conversation with the splendidly named Señor Diego Hernandez Dias. A good, reliable and discreet detective could be found who would do all the legwork regarding the flights made by Miss Lamont in Spain in 1972. He could also uncover details of the relationship Miss Lamont may have had with her pilot. The fact that Miss Lamont denied a relationship, even although the pilot's nephew swore to one, was immaterial. Long forgotten or mislaid details of unheralded flights out of the province of Almería could also be uncovered.

'As you say in England, señor, money talks but I can make a few calls from here to get us started. The firm, as it happens, has its own aircraft.'

He dialled a number, and spoke at some length punctuated by long periods of silence. When he was silent he listened but at the same time he was scribbling furiously and, Hugh thought, doodling. He sat back, letting both the silence and the flood of Spanish flow over him as he saw little aeroplanes and outline maps take shape on the notepad in front of his colleague. Señor Hernandez eventually put the receiver down and sat back with an expression of complete satisfaction. 'You hardly need hire a detective, Señor Forsythe. There is indeed an airfield a few miles from your Friars Carse. It's called West Hatton and there is now a museum but in the seventies many planes flew in and out, very active like many small airfields along that coastline in the war. Our plane would make the journey – less than twelve hundred miles – I can tell you exact, in *más o menos,* two hours and twenty-nine minutes. In those days, at most five hours; plenty of time to fly there, commit murder and arson and fly back.'

'My God,' said Hugh, who was feeling euphoric. 'And can we prove it?'

'Relax, I have more. The pilot files a flight plan with both airports, the one from which he is flying and his destination. He takes off, he lands. His passenger gets out, goes through immigration, and leaves. He refuels and sits and waits for whatever: in this case, his passenger. They have a prearranged slot. You know, maybe he has said, I fly back to Spain at such and such time. His passenger returns, a short taxi ride, and they take off, all laws obeyed.'

'So the flight plans are there.' Hugh was almost hopping with excitement.

'A little more sherry, *amigo*. I regret, no. The Civil Aviation Authority says, "How can we keep all these records for ever?" They would have gone in a few months, a year at the most. There are no records.'

'Damn. I was so sure.' Hugh got up and walked around the beautiful modern office, so different from his own. 'So there is absolutely nothing I can do.' Poor Kate. He should never have awakened hopes. So unlike him to be impetuous.

'You can reopen the case, Señior Hugh. There is enough reasonable cause. We lawyers, and yes, the police too, we are, how you say so well in English, damned if we do, dammed if we don't. The law has to be seen to be impartial, to be fair to all. If we refuse to reopen this case, someone, a powerful newspaper perhaps, can say, "Look, they are protecting this big film star. The law is selective." Now, your client, Miss Buchanan, was also very famous and the world has seen her horrific suffering and you say she was not guilty. She was unfit to be interviewed; her poor mind and body shattered by ghastly experiences, and now you say, after nearly fifteen years, the mind has healed itself, and she remembers the truth of what happened on that summer night. Every barrister in Britain will want to take this case, no?'

'Every barrister will want to take this case, yes. I have one other avenue to pursue. Perhaps we could have dinner before I return to Britain?'

'It will be a pleasure.'

Hugh strode back to his hotel, conscious of the fragrance of the ubiquitous orange blossom. He was euphoric. A word had crushed his spirits and then another had lifted him to the heights again. His gut instincts had been correct; the case would be reopened. The best barrister in the country would fight for his Kate. Just one more piece of even the slightest circumstantial evidence, that was all, he felt sure, that was needed and he crossed his fingers superstitiously and prayed that it would be available at the little airfield in the desert. He wanted to dance, to shout, to throw out his arms and embrace Spain. What a wonderful country: fabulous sherry, inexpensive wine that was immensely potable, the climate, so far, was delightful and the scent of orange blossom was almost exactly the same scent as Kate's favourite jasmine. He would bring Kate for a lovely restful holiday. This area was a little touristy perhaps, but then so was Nice in high summer.

Marcelo, having attended morning classes, was waiting for him and they took the road north towards Benahadux and then beyond into a landscape of canyons and rocky wastes. Javier Santa Cruz was not at the airport.

Marcelo correctly read the look of disappointment on Hugh's face. 'He may still be having lunch somewhere, señor. This is southern Spain, remember, where it's too hot to eat in the middle of the day.'

' "Mad dogs and Englishmen," Marcelo,' said Hugh.

'Así es. Efectivamente. That's true.'

Marcelo, it seemed, had been forearmed and had eaten what he called a *bocadillo* or little sandwich in the car while he waited for Hugh and so they decided to wait to see if Señor Santa Cruz would eventually turn up.

He did, at four thirty.

'Spain, Señor Hugh,' warned Marcelo.

Hugh, wondering how long he would have stayed in business had he returned from lunch half an hour before his staff went home, got out of the car and followed Marcelo into the office. It did not look any happier than it had looked on his last visit. Business, obviously, was not booming. He said, 'Good afternoon', in Spanish and then stood patiently while Marcelo talked. The conversation became more and more animated on both sides and just when Hugh feared that the two men would come to blows, Santa Cruz started to laugh.

'I hope you brought a lot of money, señor. According to Javier here, the lady bought a plane for his uncle in 1972. She said his old crop sprayer was too uncomfortable and so she bought a nice little twin-engined job and they assumed, from the way his uncle spoke, that it was a *regalo*, gift. But when Señor Felipe died, her smart lawyers from Madrid turned up with paperwork that they said showed the plane belonged to Miss Lamont and had been just for the use of his uncle while he was flying her. But he says they flew lots of people in it, film crews, crazy people who wanted to hike in the canyons, and that he can prove. He's a little hazy about flights out of the country but he says his mother, who is his uncle's sister, was thrilled because he told her once that he had just been in Scotland. She doesn't remember the exact time but it was just after his little sister made *La Primera Comunión,* her First Holy Communion and that was when this little Noelia had seven years. The day is always sometime in May but maybe in June, before the feast day, Corpus Christi, so that has to be summer of 1972. If that's your date, señor, then you're in business.'

'We're in business,' said Hugh and took out his wallet.

25

Someone rang the bell of Kate's house just after nine o'clock a few mornings after her meeting with Stacie and her parents. She peered through the blinds and saw a man she did not recognise and so she made no answer. It had to be the newspaper reporter but she would not speak to him and she would not allow his presence to upset her. She went back to the sitting room and went on carefully and methodically setting up her embroidery frame. The bell rang again. Tension. Get it right. A rattling at the letterbox.

'Miss Buchanan, I know you're in there. Please open the door. Miss Buchanan, my paper just wants to help you.'

With hands that, despite her best efforts, had begun to tremble, Kate went on with her tightening of the tension. She wanted to transfer her pattern to the fabric and for that she needed steady hands. She had already traced the design she wanted to use on to greaseproof paper, her preferred medium, which she would then place on the fabric already in the frame. When that was done she planned to tack through the outlines with a contrasting colour. Today it was red; red was Kate's favourite colour, although she never wore it, and she used it for tacking stitches except when the fabric was red. Next step was to scratch along her nice big stitches with a pin in order to tear the paper that would then lift off. Sister Mary Magdalene never used this method because she was so secure in her artistic ability that she never needed to change her design. Kate was made of feebler clay.

She attempted to thread her needle but her right hand was wavering slightly.

Damn him, she thought. She got up and went into the hall. 'Mr Webster, is it you, Mr Webster? Go away and leave me alone or I will call the police and tell them that you are harassing me.'

'Harassing you? Couldn't be further from the truth. I'm only doing my job and my civic duty.'

Since he had bent down to shout through her letterbox, Kate could see his mouth. What would he do should she push a broom handle through? Who will be harassing whom then, Mr Webster? But she didn't. She could not remember prison. But she had been there, had she not? She knew instinctively that it would not be a pleasant place to be.

She rang Maggie to ask if Stacie could visit that evening and when Maggie agreed, the rest of the plan was put into action. First Kate rang Father Benedict and asked if she might come to the retreat house that evening and then went upstairs and packed a small suit-case. She tried not to dwell on the fact that she was being driven out of her home; it would not be for long, just until any furore blew over. Perhaps this man would be the only annoying gnat buzzing around her head and, to look positively on the experience, she would enjoy listening to the calming sound of plainchant echoing along the monastery corridors. The ugly lamp was still standing outside the linen closet. She looked at it, striving to remember if it had been something from Granny's house or Tante's, a gift from someone she liked, from the operatic tenor perhaps. Had she felt so guilty about her treatment of him that she had once given houseroom to it? 'I could never have felt that guilty.' She closed her eyes and furrowed her brows and concentrated, but no pictures regaling her with the history of the lamp swam into view. She would ask Hugh. He had put it in the cupboard; surely he had a reason.

When she returned downstairs, carrying her little suitcase, she rang Hugh's London flat but she heard his telephone ring and ring and there was no answer. She had forgotten that he had already gone to Spain. She hung up and then she remembered that Hugh hired a faceless voice, an answering service, who would take messages. She pictured the woman: she would be very thin and her blonde hair would be in a neat French twist; her skirt would be as pencil thin as she was and her blouse would be very starched and very white. She was choosing a lipstick for the faceless voice when she realised how silly she was being. No doubt the woman was a perfectly nice middle-aged mother who needed the money the job brought. If she left no message for Hugh he would not know that she had gone to stay at the monastery. If he rang and rang her number he would worry. Steeling herself, she dialled his office and waited, almost calmly, for a pleasant voice to tell her that Hugh Forsythe was unavailable at the moment but if she cared to leave a message he would return her call as soon as possible. Panic. She hung up again. She would have lunch and try again. Lunch?

She had defrosted one of Maggie's pies and she popped it into the oven. There was actually enough for Mr Webster too and he had to be hungry standing there on her cold doorstep. She would do as the jailers of old had done in the Middle Ages. She would hold the cooked pie at her opened letterbox. That would teach him a lesson. Her idea of modern-day torture made Kate laugh and she sat down to eat her piece of the pie in a very light-hearted fashion. Light-hearted is better than light-headed. Never had Maggie's cooking tasted so good. Perhaps it was because she was no longer sitting, waiting for calamity to overtake her. Was it because she was facing it head-on, and she had such stalwart troops had she not? There was Maggie the indomitable, Jim the stout – in the nicest possible meaning of the word – Stacie the mettlesome, Benedict the . . . he had better be the spirited, and had she not Craig on her side, Craig the dauntless? Oh, Bryn, *cariad,* how you would have liked these people. Would the pain of losing you be less if I had even been aware that I had lost you? 'Just as well,' people had said. She could hear the voices in her head, different accents but the meaning the same. Because she could not remember she did not feel. But oh, she did, and now almost fifteen years later and fully aware of the awfulness of what had happened that night she felt his loss yet more keenly in every fibre of her being. She wanted to curl up small and hug her stomach in some primal scream of anguish. My love, my love, you are gone, and your suffering was so acute. I remember the flames in your hair and your scream. It drowns out the sound of your voice, the sweetest music that ever fell upon my ears.

Another memory surfaced just as a log that has been pulled down by quicksand will often pop to the surface years later. No, Kate, Bryn was dead already. You tried to pull him out and the scream was yours. You saw him through the smoke, that ghastly choking smoke that beat you down to the ground. You crawled then and touched his bare foot. Remember.

She had found him, one foot, and she felt forward in the swirling smoke to try to find his head, his dear face. He was on his front and was so still. She tried to scream his name but only choking sounds came out and she panicked. Dear God, how could she rouse him, how could she get him out before the house went up like a Halloween bonfire? She groped for his legs and forced herself, still gasping and wheezing, to her feet. She would pull him to the door. She had to get him out. His inert body did not move, for she had no strength and she collapsed on top of his legs sobbing, desperately thinking. No good, no good, she was not strong enough. Again she lurched to her feet, and again grasped his ankles and pulled. An inch. Had he moved an inch? The door, she would get to the door. Everything would be all right if she could get to the door. The house and everything in it could burn but she had to get him out. The door. If she could open the front door air, lifesaving air would come in. Again she tugged but he did not move and she dropped his legs and crumpled for a second beside them. She had to get out. She turned and began to crawl to the door. It was hotter now and she could see the flames creeping, creeping, preparing to devour everything in their path. With an almost superhuman effort she got to her feet and stumbled forward. The door. She had reached the door. It was unlocked and she grappled with the handle and pulled. It opened towards her and as the outside air rushed in there was the most terrifying sound as the house around her exploded into flame. Her beautiful silk robe went up like the most spectacular of candles and she forgot everything but fear and pain.

Kate lay forward weakly on her tabletop as she relived that nightmare. The memory explained why she had been found half in and half out of the burning house. Falling on to the doorstep was what had saved her face, she supposed, from the dreadful burns that had affected the rest of her body. Perhaps she had rolled, she did not know and did not really care. She had left Bryn to die in the flames but they had said he was dead from the blow to the back of his head, the blow struck in anger by Rose.

I can survive, my love, if I believe I did not cause your death. I remember feeling always that the initial fault was mine, *caru*, but I have paid. I remember looking at my body in my ugliness and trying to find the piece that was not there. I could feel a void, a great painful aching emptiness. Did I have my arms, my legs, my feet and my ears? Something had been torn from my body and soul but, although ugly, it seemed to have its full complement of bits. The mourning has not lessened with the years, it has grown, for now I know for what I grieve. I grieve for your horrible and undeserved death, and I grieve for the great actor who never played his finest roles, and I cry for the woman who loved you and would not marry you and is doomed to live her life alone, and scarred, her all-important career in shatters around her. She deserves her pain, Bryn, but she did not set the fire and she did not strike you down. Rose did, Rose, your wife. Poor Rose. You should never have married her and certainly not to punish me. Would I be different had I the chance again? How I would love to say that I would have realised the value of true love and that I would have held my nose and jumped whole-heartedly into the swirling pool of love and children and the theatre. I could have done it all, Bryn, but I fear I would have acted just the same.

She got up from the table, the half-eaten pie cooling on the table in front of her. She went to the window and peeped out. Webster was still there. He saw her, or saw the twitching of the blinds.

'I'm staying here till I get an exclusive, Miss Buchanan.'

'Then you'll starve to death, Mr Webster.'

She went back to the table and took the pie to the oven, covered it with a piece of tinfoil, as per Maggie's instructions for reheating, and slid it back in.

'Mr Webster,' she called through the letterbox, 'I have no intention of speaking to you but I would prefer that you not expire on my doorstep. This is Abbots House, a refuge for the poor, the downtrodden, the hungry, since the fourteenth century. In five minutes, I will put an absolutely delicious and nourishing serving of haddock and smoked salmon pie on the doorstep, with a fork, Mr

Webster. You may eat it, but you will only get it if you remove yourself to the gate while I open the door.'

'You're joking.'

'I've forgotten how to do that.'

'I'll go to the gate, but I'm still going to stay here until I get an
exclusive.'

'We must all do what we must, Mr Webster. The pie, I think, is
warmed through. To the gate.'

She peered through the letterbox and saw him walk quickly up
the path. She should have given him coffee too; it was bitterly cold
out there but that was his problem, was it not? She hurried back
into the kitchen, slipped the pie out of the oven, picked up a fork
and hurried back to the door. Peering through the letterbox, she
saw that he was indeed at the gate. He would have to be an
Olympic sprinter to get to the door before she closed it again. She
stood up. One, two, three. Open the door. Dump the pie rather
unceremoniously on the doorstep and whisk back in, closing the
door and locking it. Bravo. Mission accomplished. No journalist
would die on her doorstep, no matter if he deserved to starve. A
pang of regret that she had not put the pie on a plate – what would
Granny have said? She was back inside her lovely home, back
against the door, gasping for breath like a fugitive.

Her euphoria raced away like water through a sluice; she was a
fugitive, from the prurient gaze of her fellow man.

Hugh. Ring Hugh and, with luck, she would hear his dear calm
voice. She dialled and almost immediately the receptionist's voice
announced the firm's name.

'Anstruther and Forsythe.'

When did I last ring Hugh at his office? 'This is Kate Buchanan,
I'd like to leave a message for Mr Forsythe, please.'

'One moment, please, Miss Buchanan. Miss Currie will be happy
to take a message.'

Miss Currie. Was that the name of his secretary? 'Thank you,' she
managed and soon was speaking, not to a faceless answering service,
but to a real flesh and blood person who spoke to Hugh every day.
Hesitant at first but growing in confidence she left her message.
'Will you tell Mr Forsythe that I won't be at the house for a while.

Can you tell him that the man's here and won't leave till I speak to him and so I'm going to Benedict. He's not to worry but he can ring me at Benedict's or Maggie, Maggie will know.'

The secretary calmly repeated everything as if she heard such messages every day. Perhaps she did. Lawyers must deal with some strange people.

'Thank you,' said Kate when Miss Currie finished. 'By the way, could you ask him if he knows anything about the ghastly lamp in my linen closet?' She hung up, feeling that she had done rather well, apart from asking about the lamp. Miss Currie must think her an absolute idiot.

Kate sighed and washed her dishes; she could not leave an untidy house. Then when everything was spotless she went to her sewing. She was making a burse, veil and stole for the godson of one of her patrons who was soon to be ordained as a Roman Catholic priest. Her theme was the Holy Spirit and so she had drawn representations of the dove and of fire on her wonderful emerald-green satin. The fire had frightened her for some time but the more she had drawn and traced other pictures the more her mind had told her that it had to be flame to show the purifying spirit of the Holy Spirit and she had given in and sketched leaping flames that really did not look too amateurish. She had decided to outline her sketches in varying sizes of gold thread but she would use some other techniques: the breast of each dove would be padded white kid and the flames would be varying shades of red, gold and even lilac padded shot silk. Then she would embellish the wings and the hearts of the flames with tiny beads in the same colours so as to give depth and also to catch candlelight in the churches in which the gifts would be used. A church, Kate had decided, was really the only place where goldwork could be seen in its magnificent entirety since all the techniques had been developed over hundreds of years to take advantage of flickering flame. Here in her own sitting room she herself, the creator, could not appreciate the work fully; she could only imagine how it should and perhaps would look and that was one of the challenges of the work and was perhaps why she found it so enthralling.

She did not know whether or not Mr Webster stayed on her doorstep all afternoon, for she was lost in the physical and mental activity of creating. The house was still, only the clock keeping her company with its soft ticking and gentle chiming and she was somewhat startled when she heard the doorbell. She stopped sewing, head up, alert.

'Hello, it's Stacie.'

Kate went immediately to the front door and unlocked it. Stacie and a tall slender boy with blond hair were standing together on the doorstep. The newspaperman stood hesitantly on the path close to the gate and firmly Kate closed the door. He should have no doubt that he was unwelcome, whatever the history of the houses that had stood on this spot.

'This must be Craig,' said Kate, holding out her hand and realising at the same time that she had no compunction at all these days of showing her scarred hands to new people. Her heart lifted again with another surge of joy at the beauty of life.

Craig had a cool, firm no-nonsense grip and again Kate smiled. 'Welcome, Craig, it's so kind of you to come.'

Stacie with, 'Mum made a casserole and I'll just warm it up,' had disappeared into the kitchen.

'I'm quite thrilled to meet you, Miss Buchanan. It's fabulous of you to help us. I brought a tape recorder.'

Kate looked down at a compact silver box. 'Good heavens, it took three men to carry the ones we used to use,' she said, exaggerating more than slightly. 'Does it give the same quality of sound?' She led the way into the sitting room. 'I didn't expect a party but the more normality the better, don't you think?'

Stacie saw that her embroidery frame was back in place. 'Wow. Do I get to sit and sew?'

'I don't want to offend, my dear, but not on that material. But your skill will be in having our visitor assume that you are. You must both be very hungry, just out of school. I should have thought and how typical that Maggie did.'

Stacie laughed. 'I don't think she was thinking about us; she doesn't think monks eat and is worried that you'll fade away completely unless you add a layer of fat before you go.'

'The monks will take good care of me. Craig, you have your parents' permission for this?'

'Yes, the car is just outside. Dad got quite excited. Said he's sure it's a bit like an SAS mission, not that he has any real idea of what the SAS do. Still, it showed willing, don't you think? I have a feeling he was a little miffed not to be asked to drive.' He stopped talking and looked at her and then he said earnestly, 'Miss Buchanan, we will have time to work with you, won't we?'

'As soon as we've eaten Maggie's wonderful food. In fact you can tell me all about yourself and your aims and goals and what studying and reading you have done and, possibly more importantly, what you plan to do if you're not immediately accepted by a good drama school.'

They sat around the little table in the kitchen with its elegant blue cloth and they ate and talked and laughed and Kate realised what a joy family life could be; she had never before eaten a meal with two teenagers and this one exhilarated her. They were so young, so arrogant and yet unsure at the same time, so full of their hopes and dreams and so anxious to listen to her, to be advised, to learn. They were an attractive pair and obviously fond of each other and yet their backgrounds were so different that Kate foresaw battles ahead if their young love developed into deep abiding love. The stumbling block, she felt from the little she knew, was Stacie's father. He had an inbred wariness of what he called the upper classes and it would take all Craig's charm and personality to win him over. His father, on the other hand, seemed to accept Stacie; it was his mother who might attempt to scupper the burgeoning romance. Maggie, on the other hand, accepted each person she met at face value, a simple philosophy that not only made her happy but also went a long way to making her business successful. Stacie and Craig were very young but she and Bryn had not been much older when their friendship and respect for each other's abilities had grown into real love.

'I'd almost forgotten my visitor,' she said as they cleared the table. 'How nice that we finished the casserole; I might have been tempted to feed him.'

Kate could not resist peering through the blinds as they went back into the sitting room. Mr Webster was standing in the light from the streetlamp; it was not becoming to his skin that was quite blue from the nip of the cold air. Serves him right, she thought as she bent to turn on the lamp beside her chair. Its soft glow shone on her threads all assembled waiting for her skill to transform them into a thing of beauty.

'Now, Craig, let's hear your speeches. You don't have too much in this scene, of course, because it's really a show-stopper for La Pucelle, but you'll know how to make the very most of it.'

'Shall I turn on the machine?'

She shook her head and he went into the centre of the room and stood, already a great warlord, faced Stacie and began almost immediately.

'"I am vanquished; these haughty words of hers . . ."'

When he finished he turned to Kate and suddenly the soldier was gone, so too was the captain of the rugby team and a small boy seeking approval peeped hopefully out of his eyes. Kate smiled. 'Well done, my lord. Now let's run through it from the beginning and I'll do everyone but Joan and Burgundy.' She stayed seated in her chair and so Craig was totally unprepared for the complete change of voice and presence that came from the frail woman on the sofa as she played Charles to Stacie's Joan.

'"We have been guided by thee hitherto . . ."'

Then without moving a muscle she became the Bastard of Orleans and Craig could see that she spoke the words of two different men.

'"Search out thy wit for secret policies . . ."'

Stacie started to laugh and Craig blushed to the roots of his hair.

'Why are you laughing, Stacie? I thought I was doing rather well,' teased Kate.

'It's Craig's face. He looked around as if he thought someone else was here. See the difference, Craig? Isn't she just totally fab? Sorry, Miss Buchanan, but there is such a difference between Miss Galbraith, good as she is, and you.'

'Years of training, and years of experience,' said Kate matter-of-factly. 'Now let's go on from there, Craig, and we'll ignore our funny friend here.'

'She's right, Miss Buchanan. The hairs rose on the back of my neck.'

Kate's eyes filled with tears. 'Ah, my dear, what a compliment

364

after all these years. Thank you but to work. We'll miss out Alençon and start with Joan's, "Then thus it must be." You be the drums and the trumpets, Craig.'

They worked for over an hour and the time passed so quickly that none of them noticed its passing. It was Kate who looked at her watch. 'The recording, my Thespians, for it's time for Stacie to be driven home. Don't look so solemn; I'm thoroughly enjoying myself and look forward to being with you both very soon. Now, off you go and stand in the kitchen door, Craig, and this time I'll be the advancing army. The machine is running? Good. Remember to look at Joan when you're addressing her, and look at each of the others in turn. Ready. *Henry VI, Part 1*, Act 3, Scene 3. The plains near Rouen.'

She allowed a complete run-through and although there were points that needed to be made she decided to write them down – after all, she was going to have plenty of time and privacy in which to do it – and Craig agreed to make a copy for Stacie.

'It needs work, but you are both very talented. Now, let's get Stacie's coat.'

Ten minutes later Craig opened the front door and the waiting journalist saw the two school pupils on the steps, turning back to call goodbye and thank you to the shadowy figure in the hall. Craig put his arm around his companion and hurried her past Webster. 'Leave Miss Buchanan alone,' he said fiercely. 'She doesn't want to speak to you.'

'Oh, she'll speak to me, laddie. She'll get fed up having me here on her doorstep.'

'Don't count on it,' argued Craig and he opened the passenger door and closed it behind his companion. Then he put the bag he was carrying onto the back seat, got in, and drove off, leaving the reporter to his solitary and very cold vigil.

Twenty minutes another car drew up at Abbots House and Jim Thomson, the local butcher, got out. 'Have you nothing better to do with your time?' he asked as he passed the reporter.

'I'm doing my job, trying to let the great British public know the truth.'

'At the cost of harassing a frail woman who's done no harm?'

'That's the whole point. She's done no harm; she's brought a lot of pleasure to people. Will she talk to you? Tell her I just want to set the record straight, help her get the apology she's due.'

'Maybe she doesn't want an apology. Maybe she just wants to live in peace in her own home and the likes of you have driven her out of it.'

Webster looked astounded. 'Me? I've not driven her out. She's sitting there sewing. I've peered in the wee chink in the blinds a few times.'

Jim laughed and pressed the doorbell. 'Silly fool. That's my wee lassie acting. Middle-aged woman defying the press, I think she told us she would call it when we saw her practising. Method acting, I think it's called,' he finished as Stacie opened the door.

'Hi, Dad. Thanks for coming. I've locked up. Goodnight, Mr Webster.'

The reporter was at first speechless and then when he realised that he had been fooled he almost danced in a rage on the path. 'Bloody hell. Do you mean to tell me that damned kid helped her walk out past my bloody nose?'

'Method acting,' laughed Jim who was now enjoying himself mightily. 'And I don't want to see you anywhere near my wee lassie. Understood?'

Stacie linked arms with her dad and almost skipped down the path. 'It was great, Dad. We were great. Everything's great.'

They got into their car and drove off, leaving the poor hapless reporter fuming and swearing on Kate's doorstep. But there was no one there to hear him.

26

Rose Lamont repositioned her sun-lounger and lay down again. The turquoise stripes on the pads were almost exactly the same colour as the clear water in the pool. She considered slipping into the pool for a moment to cool off; she could almost feel the cool water caressing her sunburned shoulders. Getting up again, however, required effort and so she reconsidered, thought better of the idea, put on her huge diamanté-studded sunglasses and wriggled again until she was perfectly comfortable. She could see her feet and she lay for a while admiring the pedicure that Teresa had given her. Really the girl had such clever hands; not a speck of polish anywhere that it should not be and every nail perfect. Why she had ever thought to do it herself, she could not imagine.

She had needed a little pampering after the dreadful experience with Felipe's nephew.

'So you thought you could rob from us and get away with it, Rose Lamont, but the English lawyer is going to prove your guilt. You killed your husband, we all know that now, and you stole back the plane you bought for my poor uncle to try to buy his silence. Death silenced him but his voice speaks from the grave.' God, how melodramatic Spaniards were.

And all in front of the bridge group too. Thank God none of them really spoke Spanish. Living here in this glorious birthday cake of an apartment building they had no need to learn the language. Rose had fobbed them off with tales of disgruntled staff who complained, without the slightest justification, that they had not been paid. That had started a discussion about the good and bad habits of the serving classes in Spain, in Italy, and anywhere else that these expatriates had ever lived, and so Rose's unpleasant, loud-mouthed and belligerent visitor had been forgotten. Not by Rose.

She could not stop worrying about the English lawyer, Hugh Forsythe. What could he find out all these years after the fire? There were no records; the house had burned down to the ground and been razed and built on all over again. Surely the police had kept nothing from the scene? Why should they? It had been, as the papers had said, an open and shut case. Katherine Buchan had murdered her lover, and tried to kill herself in their secret love nest. Even if she spoke now and said that she remembered a different scenario, who would believe her and how could she prove anything? I remember: therefore it must be so. No, the law needed more than the recovering memory of a woman who had spent years in psychiatric care. She should damned well have rotted in the funny farm, thought Rose viciously and tried to relax while she toasted her still amazingly flat and unwrinkled stomach.

She dozed off but was startled to find herself being shaken awake by a frightened and hysterical Pilar, her own maid.

'Señora, policia, dos guardias. The police, two policemen.' She was holding one of Rose's lamentably sunburned shoulders and shaking her.

'Damn it, Pilar, let go and stop screaming. Do you want the entire south coast of Spain to hear you? What are you saying, now quietly, or you're out of a job?'

'Dos guardias. Policia.' Tears were streaming down Pilar's cheeks and she was blowing her nose and rubbing her eyes on the ends of her little apron. 'They want to see you and they won't go away. They're in the sitting room.'

Conscious of all the interested eyes and the hushed comments and even of the friendly remarks, 'Speeding again, Rosie?' Rose tried to hush the crying girl and to get up from the sun-lounger in as unconcerned and elegant a way as possible. Unconcerned? Her stomach was churning and she knew that in just one minute she would be violently ill in the bloody pool. That would really give them something to talk about.

'Parking,' she said with a shrug rolling her eyes up to heaven to be her judge. 'Five gets you ten I'm in El Jefe's spot again.'

She picked up her animal-print towelling robe and slowly, to show that she was completely at ease, tied it on over the matching bikini.

Then she slipped on her mules, collected her magazines, and, followed by the sobbing Pilar, returned to her own apartment.

Kate sat down in the ancient deckchair and covered her lower half with a blanket. Thane, who was lying beside her, edged his way under her legs into the shelter.

'You have a friend there, Kate.' Father Benedict was weeding a vegetable bed while he and his friend Kate chatted. They did this almost every morning. Ben would work and Kate would sit in the late spring sunshine and look out to where she knew the sea rolled in and out, twice a day. Even though, from a supine position, she could not see it, Kate knew that it was there and, as always, its music gave her comfort.

'Cupboard love of the non-food kind, friend Ben. He likes his comfort.'

Ben, who knew perfectly well that if Kate were not there the great grey dog would stay beside him on the path, merely smiled. The dog's heart had room and more for two. He finished what he had planned to do, dug his fork into the ground, wiped his hands on the old piece of sacking tied round his waist, and went over to sit down beside Kate but in an even more rickety deckchair. 'Some days, Kate, if the wind is in the right direction you can smell the sea from this patch of the garden.'

'I see it from my room. I open the window and listen to it before I go to bed.'

'But you miss walking there.'

'This nightmare will be over soon, friend Ben, and for ever. Hugh doesn't think they'll send Rose to prison. "Mitigating circumstances." She'll be placed in secure accommodation.' She sighed. 'I don't think I wanted vengeance, did I, Ben? I didn't want Rose to suffer just because I had suffered. I'm glad she confessed. A trial would have been so much more exciting for the Mr Websters of this world.'

Ben bent down to scratch Thane who had inched his way forward until he was lying between the two of them. 'He won't give up. Statements from your solicitor are not nearly so exciting as words from the horse's mouth.'

369

She laughed and he reflected as so many men had done before him that she had a lovely laugh. 'This old horse ain't talking.' She turned to look at him. 'Am I being a nuisance? You would tell me?'

'You're a pleasure to have as a guest, friend Kate. Brother Anselm was only saying this morning that if you're here in the summer he will make a new deckchair.'

'How sweet, but I love this one. It has character, like my other two heroes.'

'Stacie and Craig?'

'Yes, you know they visit every few days. Craig has been accepted at the Academy in Glasgow. Hugh is going to bring my box of memories here when he comes this weekend and I shall find a programme for young Craig. There's bound to be an autographed programme that he would like.' She smiled to herself as she wondered silently if he would also like a rather ghastly mistake of a lamp that neither Hugh nor Kate could remember.

'Don't tell me. Sir John Gielgud?'

Kate closed her eyes and turned her face to the sun. 'I was thinking Bryn Edgar, but I shall give them all to Stacie eventually anyway. I do wish I could see them perform.'

He stood up and so did the dog, backing himself out from under Kate's legs. Ben helped Kate up and stood while she folded the little blanket. 'It could be arranged discreetly, I'm sure. Why don't you talk to them about it?'

'Mainly because it's their night. If they're as good as I think they are then there will be other opportunities.' A flash of the palest blue caught her eye. 'Look, Ben, a butterfly. The first of the season. I hope he hasn't come too early; they're so frail.'

'Deceptive fragility, Kate. They survive through summer winds and storms; they're tougher, I would say, than they look. Many fine things are.'

She looked at him almost coquettishly. 'Are you complimenting me, Ben?'

'If the truth is a compliment.' A bell began to toll from the monastery tower. It was noon. The Angelus.

Kate and her friend Ben, together with Thane, obeyed the

summons of the bell and turned back towards the monastery.
Behind them in the garden the pale blue butterfly flitted silently.

June

The evening smelled of honeysuckle. Kate had worried earlier in the
day that there would be rain; it should not rain in June but it had
tried, grown weary and then given up the attempt. The evening,
therefore, was everything that an early summer evening should be,
light, warm, fragrant. The roses that Kate had planted so ambi-
tiously were justifying her faith in them and the scents of yellow
Arthur Bell roses mingled with the perfume from the peachy pink
climbing rose, Compassion, together with that of the red, aptly
named for this garden, The Bishop. Inside there would be
wonderful scents too, for Maggie had been busy all afternoon and
now it was up to Kate and Hugh to take everything out of the refrigerator and arrange the platters as artistically and sensibly as possible
on the dining room table.

'Don't put that tray there, Katie. The whole point about a buffet
is that the starving hordes can reach the food. There they have to
lean over' – he stopped and read some labels – 'some rather fine
wines and how disastrous if any were to be knocked over.' He examined the contents of the platter carefully as he moved it. 'If this
tastes nearly as good as it looks, the woman is wasted in Friars
Carse.'

'It will do.' Kate was adjusting flowers that were perfectly
arranged. 'They'll be here in a minute, Hugh. Is everything
splendid?'

'*Ça va sans dire.* Goes without saying, Kate. You always gave the
best parties.'

Kate sat down. She was rather pale and the scar on her cheek was
obvious. 'Anticlimax. I feel like a deflated balloon. Do you know,
Hugh, that sometimes I wondered if I would ever return to my beautiful home but the interviews I finally did were a small price to pay
for being left alone.'

'You're yesterday's news, my dear: no longer interesting. Now, would you like a drink or would you prefer just to sit quietly until your guests of honour arrive?'

Thinking about them animated Kate. 'Weren't they splendid? And no one noticed me at all. You were dear to whisk me away.'

'High school productions are not exactly my thing.' He handed her a glass of champagne. 'Stacie is a fetching young thing. I think I shall ask Marcelo to visit, let young Craig see the opposition.' He stood up and put his own glass down on the sideboard. 'A car, Katie, probably the proud parents. We met Craig's father; wonder what his mother is like.'

Kate stood up, nervously smoothed down a new gold caftan, arranged her hair over her face, and breathed deeply with her eyes closed. Then she went to the door and opened it just as someone pressed the bell. Craig's parents stood on the doorstep. Mrs Sinclair was carrying a large bouquet of pure white flowers that she held out to Kate.

'I'm Anthea Sinclair. How do you do,' she said as she handed them over.

'How lovely,' said Kate with real enthusiasm. 'They can't be Boule de Neige, can they?' She was ushering her guests in as she took the roses and buried her face in their fragrance.

'Indeed they are, Miss Buchanan. I planted the bush myself.'

'Kate,' said Kate as she turned to hold out a scarred hand to Craig's father. 'Hello, Spencer, lovely to see you again. I believe you've met my brother, Hugh.'

They had barely greeted one another when they heard the doorbell peal again and this time Maggie and Jim stood on the doorstep. Maggie was wearing a lovely green dress that moved around her as she walked and was probably the most flattering outfit she had ever worn. Jim was buttoned into his best suit. He was perspiring, probably, Kate thought, from the restrictions his starched white collar forced on his neck.

'It's so warm this evening, Jim, why don't you take off your jacket and loosen your tie. Weren't the young ones wonderful.'

The two sets of parents eyed one another as they shook hands and it was obvious that only Jim was ill at ease but he was able to respond to Kate. 'They were fantastic. Maggie and me were just saying we want to see the whole of that play.'

'Preferably with Stacie in it?' asked Anthea Sinclair as she sat down on the sofa where Kate usually sat. There was no sign of the embroidery frame. 'I haven't read the entire play, I'm ashamed to say, and so I don't know how big a part Burgundy has but it would be quite meaningful if it were to become a signature piece. What do you think, Miss . . . Kate?'

'We'll have to leave that to Craig. I mean if we chose our very first part as a signature piece, mine would be the baby bear in *Goldilocks*.'

'I'm sure you were superb,' said Hugh as he handed a glass of champagne to each of the guests. 'To Stacie and Craig.'

'Stacie and Craig.'

'I've given Craig the use of a car this evening and so he'll bring Stacie down when they have finished chatting with all their friends. Very clever of you, Kate, to decide on an opening night party.'

'So kind of you all to allow me to host it. They won't have time for any of us on the last night.' She turned to the Sinclairs. 'I want to admit right up front that, although I thought up the idea of a party, Maggie insisted on providing all the food.'

'It looks absolutely marvellous.'

'I'm very tempted to try to steal Maggie away to London, Jim,' said Hugh.

'She wouldn't go; she's had offers before.' Jim was almost relaxed, even though champagne was not a favourite drink: he just could not manage bubbles. 'Where would she be without the best butcher in Scotland?'

'Ah, then,' said Craig's father, 'the credit rests with me and other producers.'

'I didn't know you were a farming man,' began Hugh with real interest, and Kate got up and moved over to the door.

'Ladies, shall we look at Maggie's marvellous table before the young ones come. Once men get started on farms and shoots and what's the other thing, stretches of water . . . Jim must be very pleased with Stacie, Maggie. Do you think he might change his mind?'

The three women were in the dining room but they made no move to eat although all three glanced appreciatively at the table. Maggie allowed her glass to be refilled. 'I'll let him think for a bit. We're going again on Saturday; actually he'd be there every night if Stacie would let him. She says he's embarrassing her.'

Anthea Sinclair laughed. 'I think Craig feels that way about me. I would have been at every rehearsal if he'd let me. I am just so proud of him.' She touched her eye with a delicate handkerchief and Kate smiled. She could get to like this woman.

'They're both wonderful and have great futures ahead of them. Since Craig has always wanted to be an actor and both you and Spencer are happy with his choice, Anthea, then it's wonderful that he has been accepted by Glasgow, and so easy to get home with dirty washing on the weekends.'

'We're thrilled. We had considered going back down south but not while Craig is in college. We'll discover the delights of a new city.'

That Craig's family would sell their home had been one of Stacie's worries. Kate smiled. 'Wonderful. And Maggie, it won't really hurt Stacie to go to university first and she can join a drama group there. Look at all the exciting people who have come out of the Cambridge Footlights. Wasn't Derek Jacobi one of them?'

No one answered because the men chose that moment to join them and several minutes were taken up with exclamations over the appearance of the party food, and then the taste.

'Seriously, Maggie, could we talk about widening your horizons, as it were,' said Hugh as he reached for his second portion of Maggie's game pie. 'Your talents are wasted in such a small place.'

'No, they're not,' said Anthea. 'Wrong time perhaps to ask but we will be giving a party for Craig before he goes off to drama college. We've been ordering from Edinburgh and London and we won't make that mistake again. Try that asparagus tart, darling. Fabulous.'

Kate sat in a chair near the windows and looked at the colour and the lights and she listened to the sounds of happy people enjoying hospitality in the abbot's house. Was that not why it had been built? She heard Craig's father say that if Stacie were his daughter he would send her straight to the Royal Academy and she heard Jim, emboldened perhaps by his second glass of champagne, forget his feelings of inferiority and accept gracefully the tributes to his wife and daughter. His round rosy face was redder than ever – Kate had been unable to get him to part with his jacket – while he argued that seventeen was too young to decide. 'A good university degree, that's for my girl, and if she still wants to be an actor, then she'll go to the best school there is. Nothing's too good for my Stacie.'

'There's still a year to work on him,' whispered Maggie as she handed Kate a plate.

They did not hear the ringing of the doorbell, so heated was their discussion, but the door opened and Stacie and Craig were there. Stacie carried the biggest bouquet of flowers Kate thought she had ever seen. She put down her plate and stood up. 'How beautiful,' she said as she went over to greet them. 'Are they from Craig?'

'Yes,' said Stacie as she leaned forward to kiss her. 'And from me. Father Benedict sent some down from their hothouses and Craig's mum helped us put them together; she's awfully good with flowers. They're for you, dear Miss Buchanan, the greatest actor of them all.'